Christmas in Pandemonium

Christmas in Pandemonium

Written by: John "Jack" Willems

Edited by: Joseph Mykut & Marie Moldovan

Applications for the rights to perform, reproduce or in any other way use this content must be sent to:

mariemoldovan99@3amigosinkandsplatter.com

Published by I Ain't Your Marionette Press

P.O BOX 184

Larder Lake, ON P0K 1L0

Cover Design by Joseph Mykut

Edited by Marie Dawn Moldovan and Joseph Mykut

Electronic

ISBN: 978-1-998213-49-8

Paperback

ISBN: 978-1-998213-47-4

Hard Cover

ISBN: 978-1-998213-48-1

Jack dedicates this book to Br. James Lindsey, the Benedictine monk who, instead of teaching him and his high school classmates about religion, let them watch old monster movies. A holier gift there never was.

FOREWORD

I am unhappy to provide the Foreword to this pack of lies the "author" calls a novel. I am certainly happy he is calling this a fiction book, as nothing could be further from the truth as to how he portrays yours truly and certain recent events: namely, how I lost my job as Satanic High Priest of the Second Satanic Temple of Pandemonium. Now, if only the publishers would cancel and withdraw this fairy tale from the market, I could be truly satisfied. If things had gone my way, these hardened criminals at I Ain't Your Marionette Press and their ringleader, John Willems, would be bankrupt for publishing this filth. Unfortunately, my attorney tells me this is not an option, but he was able to convince those scoundrels to allow me to write this short rebuttal.

The reader may be prejudiced against me for theological reasons. Yes, I was the Satanic High Priest of that august institution in Pandemonium for several decades, and that may cause some people in this predominantly Christian country to takes sides against me. However, I beg you to look at the facts: we haven't committed human sacrifice in 400 years, no one in our congregation thinks Witchcraft works, and I don't even believe in Satan. We continue to perform the Satanic Rituals in Pandemonium for the sake of tradition. Or we did until my traitorous assistant and those fools on the Board of Trustees kicked me out and replaced the Satanic Rituals with a dog and pony show! That's the real story here: betrayal. Satan betraying God. Judas betraying Christ. Benedict Arnold. Lord Haw Haw and Axis Sally. None of them have anything on Alistair Davis and that Witch mother of his, Delilah.

Not that you would understand that from reading this book. No, from what Mr. Willems would tell you, I was a bad Satanic High Priest, getting drunk at the ritual and shooting my coven in the face with blanks. I dedicated my life to this one-horse town, performing that stupid ritual over and over again, only to be portrayed as some kind of unserious drunk and bad faith dealer. Willems' depiction of the conspiracy against me in a positive light only proves he's in on it, no doubt working hand in hand with the Davis family to wrench control of the Second Satanic Temple from my management.

Yeah, there's a lot of other stuff in this "novel" pertaining mostly to Miles Simon buying the Stranger Church and resurrecting a theocratic vampire to cheat people out of their money. I vaguely remember that happening. What those odd people on the north side of town do is of little concern to me, except for the fact that Mr. Willems uses this story line as yet another opportunity to libel me. The idea that I would agree to curse a man for money. Ridiculous. To do that, I'd have to believe in magic.

My advice to you: go back to whatever bookstore you bought this silly book at and demand your money back. Don't participate in this defamation of me and the wider Pandemonium community. Our ancestors have worked hard over the course of four centuries to give this town a good reputation despite the common, lazy prejudice that worshiping pure evil has some kind of effect on your behavior. Don't swallow propaganda clearly put out by the Davis family to make themselves look good at my expense. Come to think of it, find every copy of this book you can find and burn it. Don't pay for them either. Sure, you get arrested, but that's a small price to pay to prevent these slanders from seeing the light of day.

Insincerely Yours,

Acton Ravenwood

PROLOGUE

The Feast of Christ the King, Charleston, South Carolina, Cathedral of Saint John the Baptist, 11:15 a.m. Gabe Strobel

Fr. Gabe Strobel waited outside the bishop's office. The slim, dark-haired priest had been there since his 8:00 a.m. Mass ended — the one they stick the young priests with. He didn't mind. Gabe had wanted to be a priest since he was 8, and if anyone told him that the bishop would want to speak with him personally someday, well... He passed the time praying the rosary and gazing intently on the Madonna and Child across the hall from his Eminence's office. Gabe loved his vocation, and he was dedicated to helping the Lord in all ways, big and small, as he waited to be appointed the pastor of his own parish. After what seemed like an eternity, the bishop, dressed in the less formal attire of a black suit with Roman collar, arrived.

"Good morning, Father," greeted the bishop.

"Good morning, Your Excellency," replied Gabe. "I heard you wanted to see me."

"Yes, I did. Come in."

His Eminence opened the door and beckoned Gabe in. The young priest took his seat across from his superior's mahogany desk. The bishop slumped into his wooden throne with a sigh. His Excellency must truly have had a burden on his mind since Gabe found those financial records. Indeed, given the signatures on them, which were obviously forged, one could even mistakenly think the bishop was aware of these improprieties. Good thing he caught these discrepancies before it was too late.

"I come with good news," said His Eminence. "Not the Good News, that was earlier this morning, but good news for you, Father."

"That's wonderful," Gabe responded. "What is the good news?"

"Gabe, you know how we, er, appreciate you here and the fine work you have done at the school and the church, but after that investigation you conducted into diocesan finances last week, I believe you are destined for bigger and better things."

"Bigger?" Gabe asked, his voice cracking. "Better things?"

"Have you ever considered the possibility of being the pastor of your own parish?"

"Of course," Gabe said, feeling his voice cracking. "I have friends from the seminary who have that honor already. Is there an opening?"

"There is. St. Michael the Archangel church in Pandemonium. It's an island on the coast, like Hilton Head. The prior pastor, Fr. Timothy O'Scanlain, passed away suddenly."

"Pandemonium," Gabe mused, as his memory began to stir.

Gabe had a pretty sheltered childhood. His parents were strict Catholics who only let him watch the religious station. The word "Pandemonium" seemed vaguely familiar, and the image of Mother Angelica speaking directly to him through the screen began to form.

"As you all know, there is a town," she warned, her voice heavy with disapproval, "a very bad town. A place where people commit unspeakable acts! They worship the Evil One! I will spare you from the details, but suffice it to say, stay away from this very, very bad place! A modern-day Sodom and Gomorrah! Stay away if you value your soul!"

"Father, father," the bishop called, snapping his fingers.

Gabe's mind focused on his superior again. Embarrassed at losing concentration, he turned his eyes back to the bishop, now visibly irritated that he had gone off into his own world.

"I've heard of Pandemonium," Gabe explained.

"Strange town," the bishop said. "I think you should go to town after next Sunday's mass. Get to know the place."

"Oh, thank you, Your Eminence, I treasure this appointment. Even if it's a difficult case," Gabe gushed. "Let us offer praise to God."

The young priest launched into an impromptu prayer, thanking God Almighty for his new position. The bishop closed his eyes and joined, though Gabe could see His Eminence's lips twitch in a way that signaled 'I'm annoyed.' Best to get out of here and not waste his time.

Gabe thanked the bishop again and left the office. He wondered if people actually worshipped the Devil in Pandemonium. He doubted it, but if they did, then they must really need God.

"When I regained enough strength to stand and behold what was now behind; it was then I would find, the treacherous place I had only narrowly just escaped was none other than my own dark and twisted mind."

- Joseph Mykut
  "The Great Escape" a poem
  from the pages of "Cosmic
  Poetry From Darkness Comes
  Light"

TABLE OF CONTENTS

CHAPTER ONE

*The First Sunday of Advent, Pandemonium, South
Carolina, Town Square, 10 am*
Gabe

A quick internet search had confirmed that
Mother Angelica had not lied. Pandemonium did
worship the evil one. Now, granted, Gabe didn't
spend too much time online, what with all of the
pornography and addictive social media. See no evil,
hear no evil, speak no evil. That was the motto of his
parents, and the young priest remained a dutiful son.
Gabe parallel parked his ancient Lumina, given to him
by the diocese, on the left side of the town square in a
metered spot. He exited the car holding a crucifix,
waving it around himself.

Gabe tromped around the town square
holding out the crucifix. It had rained earlier, and the
dark skies still threatened to do so again. Cold water
soaked through his shoes as he marched through the
dark mud. Gabe shivered as the late fall wind
penetrated his inner cassock. After a few minutes of
holding the cross in front of his face and attracting a
few bemused stares, the priest lowered his hand and

looked around at the town he was in. Gabe found it utterly unremarkable upon first glance. He scanned the perimeter of the square: a series of cafes, restaurants, antique shops, and the office of a bus tour company. So…there was tourism here.

At the center of the town square stood a large, brick building with tall wooden doors that indicated the building was important, and sure enough, as he approached the building, Gabe found a historical marker indicating that this was the town hall. The town hall lay in the middle of a large patch of dark, green grass with palmettos scattered about, dissected by concrete sidewalks that shone a bright shade of white. The lawn remained lush even in November, likely a side effect of being near the Gulf Stream. At the eastern end of the lawn, there was a statue of two men. One was a balding man dressed in long robes, and the other wore a rugged jacket and captain's hat. The two men, presumably the town's founders, shook hands.

Gabe then found a line made of bricks emanating from that monument, running east to west. The bricks extended into the road, and given that the town hall was at the center of the city, it effectively cut the town, along with the island it was on, in half. As he approached the line of bricks, he found the line was itself a landmark, labeled 'the Line.'

"The Line to what?" the priest mused.

His eyes followed the Line to the statue, which bore a plaque. It read that *the fallen angel shall have no hold of the island north of the Line and that the Christian God's dominion does not extend south of the Line.* Gabe turned his nose up at the Line. Apparently, these people were so wicked, they thought God could be kept out by a boundary.

His thoughts were interrupted by the sight of a red, double-decker bus with an open top

screeching to a halt in front of the bus tour office.
Maybe he needed to be a tourist today. Gabe walked
over to the bus while looking back at the statue.
Caught up in the scenery, he bumped into a man
wearing jean shorts, a Hawaiian shirt, and a fanny
pack. The man turned around and spat "Excuse you"
in a nasally New York accent. The priest apologized
as a line formed behind him and in front of him.
Plump women with iPhones took selfies, and children
coming up to Gabe's waist ran around the priest like
he was the proverbial Mulberry Bush. They began to
march into the bus. When the priest got to the front
of the line, the bus driver, a short, fat man whose skin
burned red, even in the November chill, asked for his
ticket.

"I'm afraid I don't have one," Gabe
said. "I was rather busy this week. Should have
prepared better."

"That's fine. $20 please."

Gabe pulled out a $20 bill and placed
it in the bus driver's hand and then ascended to the
top deck of the tour bus. Out of the bus company
office came a pale, teenage boy with curly black hair
on his head and chin, who climbed up the stairs to the
second half of the double-decker. He wore a velvet
red vest over a Lynyrd Skynyrd shirt and a trucker hat
with the image of a devil, pissing on a pirate hat.
Apparently, this was their guide, as he reached for the
speaker. Gabe took his seat and looked off in the
direction of the statue as the other tourists settled
down. From this angle, he saw not just the
monument, but also the entrance to the town hall
behind it. Above the front door was an arc that read
'Fieldhand.' The bus started to move around the
square, as the tour guide tried to get his microphone
to work properly, and Gabe's view changed to see the
entrance on the western end labeled 'Stranger.'

"Hello, welcome," the young man's voice finally boomed over the speakers. "My name is Gary Aaronson, and I'll be your tour guide this morning. I was born and raised in Pandemonium, and I'm grateful to all of you for joining me, because otherwise, my parents would make me flip burgers."

A small round of laughter. The bus exited the town square and turned south. Soon, the two men shaking hands were out of view. The tour guide began his canned speech.

"Now, as you all learned in history class, the American colonies were often used as a haven for religious dissenters from the Church of England. Plymouth was founded by the Pilgrims. Pennsylvania was founded by Quakers. Maryland was a haven for Catholics…"

Gary looked at Gabe, dressed in his black cassock and Roman collar, and winked at him.

"…Pandemonium was no different. Fr. Cramner, considered a heretic by the Church of England, wanted to start a colony in America in 1620 so he and his congregation could worship freely. Who here knows what made Fr. Cramner so heretical by the standards of his day?"

This was rather odd, Gabe thought. They were playing this like a colonial history. A little girl in blonde curls, no more than five, sitting in the front row, raised her hand, and Gary pointed at her.

"They were Witches!"

"Yes!" Gary exclaimed. "Fr. Cramner's congregation worshipped Satan!"

And there it was. The truth had been confirmed. Gabe looked around, expecting to see shocked faces, but instead found a host of tourists applauding the bright little girl.

"Needless to say, people in Christian Europe did not appreciate Fr. Cramner's unique religious beliefs, so the Old Heretic, as we Pandemonians are fond of calling him, met Captain John Miller of the *Charon* at a tavern in Amsterdam. Miller, known colloquially in these parts as the Drunkard, agreed to ferry him and his followers to the New World. Captain Miller and his crew were currently wanted for piracy by most Christian kingdoms at that time, so they were not likely to turn down paying work."

The bus turned down a street labeled 'Perdition.' Gabe stared at the sign. These people had no shame.

"Now, Captain Miller knew Fr. Cramner was considered unorthodox, but he was unaware that the Old Heretic worshipped Satan," Gary said. "Miller and his crew soon learned, however, as Cramner and his followers committed an act of human sacrifice during the voyage. The Witches brought the sacrifice, a brigand who had tried to rob them, on board with them bound and gagged. After the *Charon* was no longer in sight of the coast, the Witches tied the poor man to a stake on the top deck, and Cramner disemboweled the man with a ceremonial knife, collecting internal organs into a silver bowl. Part of the flesh was eaten then, while other parts were salted for the sake of preservation."

With this, Gary took out a long, silver knife and showed it to the crowd. The tourists, much to Gabe's disgust, oohed and aaahed.

"This is actually made from plastic," Gary said. "There are more like it in the gift shop. The real knife is in the Second Satanic Temple, which we should be coming up to, given that we are south of the Line. That's local lingo for the Witch part of town. You can use that."

Gabe looked around at the Witch part of town, which appeared to be no different from any other suburban neighborhood in America. White picket fences. Lawn jockeys. Men and women raking up leaves. Kids playing with dogs in their front yards.

"Hey, here we are!" Gary exclaimed.

A large, stone building with several tall spires and stained-glass windows that could very well have been a Presbyterian Church came into view. Only as they drove closer did he see a colorful mosaic which depicted the same robed man he'd seen in the town square, stabbing another man in the stomach. In one stained glass window, the priest could make out the face of the Devil, or rather his popular image, as it appeared to have been copied from a can of deviled ham. Outside the black oak double doors was a sign spelling out 'All are welcome.' Gabe's fellow tourists raised their phones in unison and began to capture the image.

"This is the Second Satanic Temple, now on the National Register of Historic Places, completed in the year 1870," Gary narrated. "The original Satanic Temple was built underground in the mid-1700s to conceal the cult's existence from the largely Christian state of South Carolina. Prior to that, the Witches conducted their ceremonies in the woods by the light of the moon. Sadly, the first temple was lost to history in the year 1857 when the roof collapsed in on itself."

Second Satanic Temple, Gabe mused, like the First Baptist Church. This was too cute. These people clearly didn't understand how dangerous this all was.

"Now, you can clearly see Cramner's sacrifice in the mosaic there," Gary continued. "After that happened, Miller's crew completed the trip ahead of time. One might imagine, they had extra motivation. As anyone who lives here will tell you, the island is typically covered in fog in the fall, which is why the *Charon* ran aground when it attempted to land."

The bus stopped to let the tourists take pictures. Gabe, freezing in the cold, dank, weather, started to shiver. But looking at that temple, he realized it wasn't only the weather that caused him to shake. Gabe dreaded this place. Whatever terrible soul ministered that diabolic church, he or she must truly be a depraved person.

Ravenwood Residence, Noon
Acton Ravenwood

Acton Ravenwood, still dressed in his black robes from that morning's Satanic ritual, tugged the curtains of his front window to sneak another peek at the street in front of his house. Nervous, Ravenwood grasped the golden amulet hanging from his neck to give his hands something to do. He lifted it up to his eyes and looked at the goat's head emblazoned on the profane accessory. The Satanic High Priest rubbed the phylactery in anticipation. Granted, his intended guest wasn't supposed to be here until noon, but patience was a virtue, and a Satanic High Priest can't afford to have too many of those. Makes people think it's all a show, which it was. Ravenwood's last sermon included a pitch for the local bus tour and directions to the gift shop. It didn't matter. It's not like witchcraft was real or anything. Ravenwood's parents started taking him to those services when he was an infant, and he began working in the Temple under High Priest Grimsley in the 70s. He'd never seen so much as a pen float. Nothing happened. Nothing ever happened.

Nothing was happening now. The only thing Ravenwood saw while looking out of his window like a Peeping Tom was his perfectly cut lawn with a flower garden and lawn jockey. Nice as it was, he'd have preferred to see a certain televangelist arrive in his car. Good things come to those who wait. A nondescript sedan with a Lyft tag slowed to a halt right in front of his home. Out came a tall, handsome man with dark, curly hair and a dark navy suit. He had a famous smile that shone bright white. The face that sold a thousand airport books: Miles Simon.

"So, he came," Ravenwood spoke, a grin blossoming on his face.

The Satanic High Priest rushed to the door but tripped over his ottoman. He scrambled to get up. Ravenwood reached for the doorknob and opened it without thinking, right as Simon arrived at the threshold. The televangelist was less spooked than he was mildly surprised and visibly unimpressed. Realizing he'd made an error, Ravenwood took the effort to hide his embarrassment with a smile and offered his hand.

"Mistah Simon!" Ravenwood said, with a thick southern drawl. "Pleasure to meet yah! Come in! Come in!"

As they walked in, Ravenwood felt something squish under his foot, followed by the wheeze of a plastic toy. He looked down to find he had stepped on a plastic toy football with a little Red Devil on it.

"Oh, s'cuse me," Ravenwood said, playing up his accent for effect. "My grandbaby leaves his toys out. I got him this last Winter Solstice. You have to get 'em started young. Go fightin' Red Devils!"

Ravenwood ushered Simon into the living room. Simon scanned the room, nonplussed.

"No skulls, no spell books, no black cats," Simon narrated softly, "not evil, just tacky."

19

Ravenwood, somewhat insulted by the comment, looked around his living room quickly. Sectional couch. Wide-screen television. A cute little breakfast nook. What could be tacky? Okay, maybe the portrait of Robert E. Lee hanging above the fireplace. Simon's eyes had indeed stopped on that picture.

"Mah daughtah is married to a black man," Ravenwood acknowledged, pointing to the portrait. "So, I have to take that down when Cassahndra and Joseph visit."

"Actually, I was looking at the ducks," Simon responded, pointing to Ravenwood's stuffed mallards that sat on the mantle of the fireplace, just below General Lee's portrait.

"Aw, well, I'ma huntah, you see," Ravenwood said.

"Mr. Ravenwood," Simon began.

"Fahthah Ravenwood," Ravenwood corrected him. "That's my tigh-tell."

"I see," Simon said, rolling his eyes. "Do you know why I am here?"

"As I see it," Ravenwood answered, "yah have come to buy the right to be my advahsary."

"Your-?"

"Adversary," Ravenwood said, pushing his accent down. "It's one of the meanings of the word Satan. You want to buy out the Stranger Church so you can use its name and its story to promote your televangelism ministries. Now, for that name to mean anything, you must 'oppose evil' so to speak."

Ravenwood opened his arms wide as if to say, "Here I am."

"Good, you understand," Simon concluded.

"Well, I would ask ye' to be more spahcific," Ravenwood drawled on. "What do ye' want of me?"

"I want you to curse me in public," Simon said. "I want you to cry out to the Devil and ask him to prevent me from becoming pastor."

"Ohh, that would get you the right attention," Ravenwood responded, nodding his head gently, "but I decline."

"You decline? You understand I would be willing to pay you."

"Very well, but my answer is still no," Ravenwood said. "A few decades ago, one of my predecessors, Blaise Jackson, met with Anton LaVey, head of the Satanic Church in San Francisco, and LaVey offered to take over after Jackson passed."

"I know that" Simon spat. "I've read. Jackson told that little pissant that the Satanic Temple was a museum whereas LaVey's church was a sideshow."

"And one does not belong in the other," Ravenwood finished the anecdote in an increasingly formal tone. "You are not dealing with some organization formed to create legal controversies or a coven started by a group of depressed teenagers. Our faith has deep roots in America."

"Look, Ravenwood," Simon said, "you may not be evil incarnate, but let's not pretend you're principled. The number my people gave you over the phone may not have been sufficient, but everyone's got their price. How about this?"

Simon took a napkin off Ravenwood's breakfast table, retrieved a pen from his blazer, and wrote down a number. After the preacher man handed him the napkin, Satan's high priest looked at the number and shook his head. Simon took the number back and added another zero. Upon seeing this updated figure, a supercilious smile grew upon Ravenwood's face. Without saying a word, he gently nodded. Simon would indeed be cursed. The televangelist smiled back. When you are a culture warrior, the most important thing is having the right enemies, and Simon had just obtained that very precious resource. He rose from his chair to leave, but Ravenwood stopped him.

"Ol' Pandemonian tradition," Ravenwood insisted, "let's shake on it."

Ravenwood offered his hand, and Simon took it. Then he let himself out to call another Lyft. Ravenwood waved Simon goodbye and then began to dream of what that extra zero would do for his life.

CHAPTER TWO

The First Sunday of Advent, Pandemonium, South Carolina, Northwestern Sector, 12:30 pm
Gabe

The bus turned north after it made a circle around the Second Satanic Temple. Gary, the tour guide, kept telling them anecdotes concerning the temple. He was just getting to how the Witches 'came out' in the 1950s. A former 'Satanic High Priest' (that's what they were called, apparently) convinced the Witches to announce themselves publicly in 1957.

"An angry crowd gathered outside the Satanic Temple threatening to burn it down," Gary continued. "Fr. Blaise Jackson, Satanic High Priest at the time, cast a curse on them and the mob dispersed."

Gary, being well trained, paused for a crowd reaction, which came in the form of a unanimous "ooooohhh." Well, unanimous save for Gabe, who rolled his eyes.

"I should tell you that the Witch community today disavows any belief in magic," Gary warned. "And here we are crossing into the Stranger side of town!"

Gabe could see the bus crossing over the same brick line bisecting the island at a stoplight. For once, he had a question, so he held up his hand.

"You used the word Stranger?"

"Yes," Gary responded politely. "Stranger was the term used by the Witches to describe Miller's crew, as they were Strangers to Cramner's religious community. The Witches didn't want such Strangers around, so after Cramner paid Miller his fee for ferrying them to South Carolina, Cramner asked them to leave. Miller's ship having been destroyed, he responded that gold was worth as much as lead to them now, but Cramner did not care. He gave the Strangers a month to leave, and to desecrate the island for his dark lord, Cramner announced he would make another sacrifice on All Saints Day."

Gabe looked around as the bus traveled north. The Stranger part of town looked no different than the Witch part of town, save for the fact that the lawns were less well-kept and the houses were more run-down. Gary reached into a compartment in the side of the vehicle and retrieved a portrait that the young priest immediately recognized as an image of the Virgin wearing golden robes as befits the queen of heaven, lacking only the Lord at her breast. "This is a replica of a portrait inside the museum of the Stranger Church, also available at the gift shop," Gary explained. "The image is a very inaccurate portrayal of a one-legged Scottish prostitute named Margaret Boswell the crew carried around with them on their raids, having their way with her as they traveled the seven seas. Today, she's often portrayed as some kind of religious figure, but we have little idea as to what she looked like, as few of the Strangers could read or write, and those that could fixated on the size of her breasts in their journals."

Gabe bit his tongue at the extremely bad taste of the comment. He had half the mind to report this guide to whoever his boss was. Gary continued.

"During the voyage, the Witches performed many other ceremonies, one of which involved desecrating a newly published King James Bible with blood. Boswell picked up the book and carried it back to her cabin, allowing it to dry out. Now, Captain Miller, thinking initially that the Witches were rather pious Christians, had introduced Boswell as his wife, and she appeared to have taken that as a promotion. Boswell took the Bloody Book, as it is called today, and presented it to Miller, saying that a wife should go to her husband if she wants to know of God. Now, the first time she did this, Miller shouted some holy phrases and told her to lie down again."

Gabe bit his tongue a little harder. He began to taste blood.

"Boswell tried a second time, this time the night before the Strangers were to depart for Jamestown to the North, through hundreds of miles of hostile territory controlled by Indians. Miller, along with his crew, found they could not bring all the beer with them, so they had quite a bit to drink that night. When Boswell handed Miller the book, Miller opened it, and his eyes fell upon one particular verse: thou shalt not suffer a Witch to live. Inspired by these words and a lot of beer, Miller began an impromptu sermon, and the first service in the history of the Stranger Church began. Oh, what timing!"

Gary stopped reciting his story and pointed to a church building, not unlike the Second Satanic Temple, with two changes. First, the stained-glass windows had images of classic saints instead of demons and acts of human sacrifice. Second, there was a pale, short man standing out front.

Stranger Church, 2 p.m.
Atticus MacDonald

Pastor Atticus MacDonald waved unenthusiastically at the tourist bus as it passed, standing outside the doors of the church he had preached in for more than 30 years. The old Orangeman, his Celtic features now dulled with age, still carried an Irish tan with him, even after living in America for more than three decades. He wasn't looking forward to this day. Not at all. He loved his ministry. The Stranger Church, having been renovated and modified multiple times over the past four centuries, now looked like an average Protestant church. There were Roman columns in the front, a white steeple atop a slanted roof, and stained glass windows of holy men. MacDonald admitted to himself that this normalcy made him feel uncomfortable, as the Witches had also changed their temple long ago to look very similar. The difference was the inside, where the relics of the church were kept.

A limousine appeared from around the corner, turning into the church's driveway. A limousine, MacDonald thought to himself, my supposed successor has a limousine. When the Elders of the church told him that they were seriously considering Simon's offer, he wanted to check their heads for cracks. Who in God's name just buys a church? Apparently, this kind of man did. The limousine stopped in front of the annoyed pastor, and all the doors opened. A host of black-suited minions exited therefrom, like bats flying out of a bell tower. Simon's sycophants flocked to the front of the church, snapping photographs, taking notes, and examining the flower garden out front. Then, the devil himself emerged from the right rear door, sticking out two thin legs clothed in navy silk and then gripping the sides of the door with his hands to lift himself from the back seat. Simon wore a dark blue jacket to match his eyes and jet-black hair. He was flanked by two assistants who existed to hand him towels. The Orangeman groaned softly as he approached.

MacDonald first became aware of Simon one evening when he heard a noise from the inside of his adopted daughter's room. Worried that Deanna Day might be watching pornography, he came in to find her watching the televangelist's online service. MacDonald sent his daughter to bed and then viewed the program himself. He found it to be a thinly veiled form of entertainment, a laser light show in a sports arena where Simon told his gullible online congregation that if they only gave him money, God would ensure they would get a raise, recover from cancer, and even win the lottery. Later, Deanna would tell her father she only wanted to watch because she had friends at Bible camp who talked about Simon, and quite frankly, she would rather spend her spare time on archery or Lacrosse. If only the Elders had Deanna's common sense, MacDonald thought.

"Pastor MacDonald," Simon said, offering his hand, "what a pleasure to meet you."

The pastor took the hand, as manners required.

"I am here to give you the tour, sir," MacDonald said.

The Orangeman did give Simon a brief tour of the old church, leading him through the stone entranceway into the sanctuary. MacDonald led his heir apparent into the main worship hall: wooden pews in rows before a pulpit, with old stained glass of the older, pre-Reformation saints flanking the sides. Saint Peter seemed to look at Simon with subtle disapproval as the televangelist marched down the nave. The first notable difference from any other church was in the rafters, built from the wood of an old ship, with the words 'Thou shalt not suffer a witch to live' carved into them. The faith's center lay behind the altar: the Bloody Book encased in glass. Simon walked past MacDonald and opened the glass case. The Orangeman tried to stop him, but it was no use. Simon put his hands on the book. Soon, he'd own it.

"Take me to the princess," Simon said.

Northwestern Sector, 2:30 pm
Gabe

"After hearing Miller's inspired preaching, the Strangers formed a mob and proceeded to seek out the Witches' chosen sacrifice, which was being held in a barn built on the south side of the island," Gary continued. "Once the Strangers approached, the Witches' one guard abandoned his post, allowing the Strangers to carry off the woman whom Cramner was to disembowel the next day. Now, the Strangers assumed at the time that the sacrificial victim was herself a Witch, so they logically decided to burn her in an act of divine justice, rather than profane sacrifice."

Gabe exhaled in exasperation at this ludicrous tale, seemingly designed to make people from the past look silly. The rest of the people on the tour, however, just politely nodded their heads. Gary proceeded to the next part of the story.

"The Strangers burned that woman, and many believe that the Stranger church is built on the very spot where she was killed. The next day, Cramner visited Miller and informed him that the woman they burned was not a Witch, but was instead an Indian woman the Witches had kidnapped from the mainland. Unbeknownst to the Witches at the time, she was local royalty, and the Stono chieftain in the area, her father, had arrived with a phalanx of warriors asking where his daughter was. Cramner took Miller to meet the chieftain. After Miller explained what happened and offered an apology, the chief stated he would come back the next day and kill them all."

"Now Cramner and Miller realized that separately, they would both die, but if they put aside their differences and worked together, they could defeat the Stono. Cramner proposed that they make an alliance, and that in exchange for assisting the Witches in the defense of their new village, the Strangers could stay, provided they remained on the North side of the island. Miller agreed to that, but insisted the Witches discontinue any form of human sacrifice, given how it led to certain conflicts with other polities. The Drunkard and the Old Heretic shook on it, as became the tradition in this town, and prepared for war. They crushed the Stono, killing all the men and boys over the age of 10. The women were given to the Strangers as wives, who were carried to their wedding nights bound and gagged."

The crowd gasped, finally shocked by the obscene story this teenage boy was telling. How it took them this long, Gabe couldn't begin to understand. Then, as the bus turned and Gary changed the subject to the beautiful view they had of the Atlantic Ocean, and the crowd once again raised their cameras and let out another chorus of clicks, completely forgetting the rapes they heard about five seconds ago. Gabe groaned.

Stranger Crypt, 3 pm
MacDonald

"So, this is it?" Simon asked, looking at the bones.

The Orangeman nodded. The bones lying before them in the alcove were indeed the bones of the Stono Princess, the church's founding victim. Why Simon would think MacDonald would show him anyone else's bones was beyond him. 400 years later, the bones bore the marks of being immaculately cleaned, untouched by dust, and smooth to the touch. Simon leered over the bones, almost like they were made of gold. He turned to one of his lackeys.

"Hey!" Simon barked. "Get a few pictures!"

"There will be no photographs," MacDonald said, closing the burial shroud.

The preacher man scowled at the Orangeman, but MacDonald stood his ground.

"You don't own the church yet, laddie," he insisted.

The Stranger crypt was a series of alcoves and tombs in a dark, cavernous dungeon, with a curved ceiling hanging above a dirt floor. MacDonald's predecessor had added light fixtures, so they could see what was going on. Simon stopped by the Drunkard's tomb and traced its outline with his hands.

They were getting very close to Theo's chamber, which made MacDonald very nervous. The

Orangeman had told his old friend that Simon would be visiting. Theo moved his things out of the crypt before Simon arrived. Hopefully, he was out and about. The pastor still held out hope that a man like Simon would know nothing about Theo. God knows what such a man would do with that information. They walked into Theo's chamber, and MacDonald was quite relieved to find him gone.

"So, I've seen the crypt," Simon said, moving on. "Show me around my new church, MacDonald. I've heard you've got one hell of a museum."

Town Square, 3:30 pm
Gabe

Gabe shivered while Gary pointed out various landmarks and the other tourists flipped through maps and brochures. Clearly, these people thought devil worship was some kind of joke. The bus approached the town square again, and Gary wrapped up his presentation.

"After the Stono were defeated, Miller and Cramner met again to hammer out the terms of the deal. A city council would be established, with three members from both sides. Each side would have its own mayor. Any tie on the council would result in the measure dying. The Witches would give up human sacrifice, and the Strangers would agree not to turn them into any Christian empire, which wasn't a difficult thing to promise, given that Miller and his crew were also on the run from the law. All of these terms were written down in our town charter: the Bargain. Memorably, they divided the island by the Line."

Gary pointed to the red brick Line on the side of the bus, which Gabe had seen earlier.

"The Line divides the north side of the island, where the Strangers live, and the south side of the island, where the Witches live. The original punishment for being on the wrong side of the Line was death. However, this rule was rarely enforced, and by the 1700s, it wasn't uncommon for housewives to cross the Line to borrow a cup of flour. After the American Revolution, all penalties for crossing the Line were dropped in a new spirit of liberty, but the Line remains an important landmark of our town's founding."

Gabe raised his hand tentatively. Gary indicated he could speak.

"Yes, father."

"I read the placard under that monument," the priest said, pointing at the monument of the Heretic and the Drunkard. "It had a phrase…"

"Oh, yes, that part," Gary said. "Thank you, Father. You see, during the negotiations of the *Bargain*, Miller wanted it written down that not only were the Witches not allowed on the North side of the island, neither was the Devil himself. Cramner was a fallen Anglican priest who had been trained in theology, so he found this idea rather funny. Cramner then made a counterproposal, namely that if the Devil wouldn't be allowed on the North side of the Line, then God shouldn't be allowed on the South side. Miller agreed to this, and that's why those words are in the *Bargain*."

The tour chuckled and applauded the anecdote. Gabe just sat there, stunned that such a place could exist. The town charter presumed to segregate God and the Devil. The bus screeched and scooched to the spot in front of the bus tour office. Gary thanked them all for coming on the trip and mentioned that he was accepting tips. Not wanting to be a cheapskate, Gabe threw five dollars into Gary's open trucker hat and climbed down. Great, he thought, I work in a town founded by Satanists and criminals. How could it get any worse?

He then went back to his car and found a parking ticket. The meter had expired four hours ago.

Stranger Meeting Hall, 7 p.m.
MacDonald

The Elders of the church assembled in the first-floor boardroom of the adjacent meeting hall, sitting in chairs behind a set of tables. Pastor MacDonald, here with the intent to convince the Elders not to sell, sat with his children in the back of the room in the metal foldout chairs. Deanna, a black-haired tomboy with a dark complexion and slim frame, and Gilbert, her tall, lanky brother with a mop-top and a soul patch, tried to provide their father with moral support. Simon arrived with a set of twelve apostles in Armani suits.

"Thank you for helping me with Theo," MacDonald whispered. "How was he today?"

"Fine. We had to convince him to spend time in sunlight," Deanna said. "I didn't even think he could go out in the day. It makes him weak. He couldn't transform into a dog like he normally does when we take him to the park."

"Theo is going to have to push himself a bit," MacDonald asserted.

"Thank you all for coming," Annie Ferguson, head of the council, began. "Today, we are here to entertain what we can only call a rather odd request. Mr. Miles Simon, famed televangelist, is here to offer to buy the assets, physical and intellectual, of the Stranger Church, including its name. Mr. Simon, I suppose we should hear you out."

"Thank you, Mrs. Ferguson," Simon said. "What I want to purchase is the story. The story of a community that stood in the face of evil for four hundred years. That's the story I want to bring to America. I'm willing to pay the price to do that. I believe I have communicated that price to you before this meeting."

"We know of your offer," Ferguson replied. "What can you say about the theology you will bring with you?"

"You know well my theology," Simon answered.

MacDonald snorted. Indeed, all of America knew of Simon's theology. Seed money. Faith healing. Hocking mineral supplements. Simon's 'Prosperity Gospel' put him not in the tradition of the Apostles, but in the tradition of P.T. Barnum.

"Pastor MacDonald," Ferguson said. "We are aware of your opinion of Mr. Simon, but with the money he is willing to pay us, we could start a charitable trust that would provide aid for the poor beyond anything we could previously do."

Yes, yes, MacDonald thought, this perfume could have been sold at a high cost and given to the poor. The old pastor thought about saying that out loud for a moment. Instead of insulting them, he decided it was better to guilt them.

"I assume no one here doubts my commitment to serve the least of us," MacDonald said, looking over his shoulder at his own adopted children.

This did give the Elders pause. They looked at MacDonald's two children, and their dark skin and hair did speak to the Orangeman's commitment.

Gilbert, just finishing seminary, stood up so they got a better look. The Stranger church had set up the mission to benefit the Varnertown Indians, the closest living relatives to the Stono. MacDonald started the mission when the younger members expressed guilt about some of the more unrealistic portraits of the Stranger weddings in the church museum. One drizzly morning in February, Gilbert's mother had dropped him and Deanna, then only an infant, off at the mission with a note that she could not feed or clothe either of them anymore. MacDonald took Gilbert in and fed the boy his lunch, black pudding. After clearing it with the tribe, he adopted both of them.

"No, Pastor MacDonald, we do not doubt it," Ferguson said, "but there could be a mission like Varnertown in every corner of the state with this money. Imagine if the Strangers could give more children like Gilbert and Deanna a home."

"I'm beginning to see where this is going," MacDonald said.

The old pastor heaved a long sigh and hung his head. He couldn't look. Ferguson called for a vote. One by one, the Elders raised their hands, approving the sale of the church to Simon. The charitable institutions set up by the Strangers would be separated from the church and put in a trust along with the purchase price. Simon beamed. MacDonald moaned.

"Title to the Stranger church passes to Miles Simon ministries on Christmas Day," Ferguson concluded.

"May God have mercy on our souls," MacDonald whispered.

CHAPTER THREE

The First Week of Advent, Monday, Pandemonium, Northeastern Sector, 6 p.m.
MacDonald

MacDonald watched the sun go down as he sat on a hill overlooking the Ze'ev part of town and sighed. Behind him, Simon sat on an oriental rug, laid out on the grass. A coterie of sycophants poured him champagne and scooped foie gras onto a thin China plate. This is what he thinks a picnic is, the Orangeman mused.

"When do the monsters show up?" Simon asked again.

"It has to get completely dark first," MacDonald answered, "and they prefer the term, Ze'ev."

The Elders asked MacDonald to take Simon out that night to see the Ze'ev transform. He instead offered to introduce the preacher man to Rabbi Maharam, but the televangelist turned him down. Given his current behavior, that was probably for the best. Simon looked at the suburban neighborhoods below them impatiently. The Ze'ev, for their part, simply went about their business preparing for the transformations by walking into their backyards wearing nothing but blankets. They paid no attention to Simon or any of the other tourists who were camped on the hill above them. When a local news crew discovered them in 1992, the Ze'ev decided to make a business out of their monthly transformations. They set up these events where out-of-towners would watch them transform while enjoying a nice glass of Merlot.

Finally, the transformations began. Involuntarily, all of the Ze'ev hunched over on all fours as fingers thickened into claws. Noses and mouths merged to become snouts. Their faces lengthened into a more animalistic shape. Hair sprouted out of their skin, like grass coming out of the ground on a video set on fast forward. Teeth grew long and sharp, yellowing along with the narrowed eyes, into the color of gold, shining in the night. Nails grew out, and feet and arms cocked into the familiar bent of a dog's legs, but larger and stronger as thighs and arms swelled with newfound muscular power practically bursting out of the skin. The observers from the hill, looking at the Ze'ev through little binoculars, emitted a chorus of oohs and aahhs, if they were able to speak at all. Simon could only tug his assistant's arm to tell him to get a picture. The young man in a suit with slick black hair clicked away on a camera. Simon wanted good pictures and wouldn't tolerate the shaky view from a phone. The Orangeman had seen this a thousand times since he came to Pandemonium in the 1980s, so his attention was instead drawn to the assistant, whom he noticed bore a striking resemblance to Simon. Behind MacDonald, a chorus of howls let out at the sight of the full moon, eliciting another round of gasps and photographs from the tourists.

"Calvin, what did you get?" Simon asked.

"Yes, Mr. Simon," said the associate. "Here is what I have."

The young doppelganger showed his boss the pictures he took. Without a word of thanks, Simon snapped the camera from his hands and cycled through the pictures, mouthing words the Ze'ev would no doubt find offensive. MacDonald ignored the fraudulent pastor and instead approached the associate.

"Atticus MacDonald, lad," he said, offering his hand, "and you are?"

"Calvin Lucas," the associate responded, taking the hand.

"Lucas, you know from your appearance I could swear there was a resemblance to Mr. Simon."

"I'm not allowed to say."

"MacDonald, you're talking the ear off my employee there," Simon interrupted. "Why don't you come over here and talk to me about those furry things below?"

"Mr. Simon, I've told you their preferred term," MacDonald responded. "They are as you see them. The Ze'ev immigrated to this country from the Czech Republic in the 1890s. Once a month, they transform. Most of the time, they are rather docile as they are taken care of by their children, whom they recognize by sight."

"Don't the kids transform?" Simon asked.

"Not until age 18," MacDonald answered. "They typically feed the Ze'ev meat laced with tranquilizers until they go to sleep. The Ze'ev rarely cause any trouble, and they've never been violent as long as I have been here."

"You mean they just sleep? That's boring," Simon complained.

If I could have just stayed in and slept tonight, you and I would be both better for it, MacDonald thought.

Tom's Tavern, 11:55 pm
Theo

"Closing time," yelled Tom, the bartender, "and that means you, my friend."

Tom set his eyes directly on Theo, the thin, dark-haired Irishman in a raggedy coat who was still in the middle of finishing his last whiskey of the night, or rather his last whiskey here. He closed at midnight, which meant Theo would have to evacuate this setting and head to one of the more expensive nightclubs in this tourist town. Even if Theo was Tom's best customer, eventually, even bartenders had to sleep.

"You know, friend," Theo said, "for you, the day is over, for me it may as well be two in the afternoon."

Theo said this while holding his third glass of whisky without a hint of irony in his voice.

"Come on, Theo," Tom said, "you are making a sad Irish cliché of yourself. I want to go home."

"Alright, I'll clear out," Theo said. He threw a twenty at Tom and told him to keep the change.

"Keep the change?" Tom said. "Your tab is 23 bucks. A whole negative three dollars, whoopee?"

"Okay, fine, here's another ten," Theo said, handing over another bill.

Theo shuffled out of the dive bar. As he did, he spied a homeless man across the street holding a sign. It read 'My days are darker than your nights.'

"If you think so, let's trade," Theo muttered.

And then one of the transformed Ze'ev ran in between the two.

"Looks like someone's in for it tonight," Theo whooped. Somewhere in the Northeastern part of town, a preteen Ze'ev boy was going to catch hell from his parents for failing to keep everyone in the yard. Theo became a dog and decided to play along. He had learned that as long as you did not get them too agitated, the Ze'ev could be fun playmates for a dog, and he liked living as a dog better than as a human, or as a falcon for that matter. Theo had only transformed into a bat once. Unlike birds, bats had to constantly flap their wings to fly, and Theo found the experience tiring. But for a dog, life was pretty simple. Eat, crap, play.

Theo took off after the great beast, starting in human form. He decided to be a Husky tonight, a big, beautiful Husky with a black mane. He collapsed onto all fours and let his clothes become dark fur while his feet and hands became paws. The big black animal ahead of him saw something chasing it, so it turned around and batted the Husky playfully. Theo led the Ze'ev back to a public park where they could face off a little without anyone getting in the way. He did not recognize this particular Ze'ev, so it must have been someone who recently started transforming.

Tuesday, St. Michael the Archangel Rectory, 6 am
Gabe

Gabe had spent the last day and a half getting himself situated. He began to unpack and explore the rectory and church building, located right on the south side of the Line, that is the Witch side. The amateur theologian found the library to be extensive. The rectory was quite nice. It had a living room with a color television and cable. There was a full kitchen with a breakfast nook. The bedroom came with a king-sized bed. At least he was well taken care of. He then went into the church and decorated it for Advent, hanging up purple banners and setting up an Advent wreath, both of which he found in a closet. It was a small church with a large crucifix at the head of the nave.

As he visited the church office in the rectory and searched the church register, he found no names. He then searched the book of life and out slipped an envelope with a letter in it, which read thusly:

To my esteemed successor,

It appears you have been appointed as pastor of St. Michael's. You have my sincerest condolences, as this means you have no flock and never will. This church was opened after the Witches came out in the 1960s, and the pope called the Bishop of Charleston and asked what he was doing about it. Your mission is to make it look like the diocese is addressing the issue, so look busy.

See you in hell.

Fr. Tim O'Scannlain

This seemed an odd statement for a dying priest to make, so Gabe called the diocese. He had quite a bit of trouble getting anyone to respond to a single question. Finally, the bishop's secretary deigned to answer his queries. You have no parishioners. When the Witches came out in the 1950s, the Pope made us start this church for the sake of looking like we were doing something about it. No Catholics live in Pandemonium. No, we aren't planning to move you. And Fr. Tim? Yes, he passed away while he was sleeping, in his garage with the car engine running.

"He committed suicide?" Gabe asked, his mouth hanging open in shock.

"Yes, I suppose I should tell you that before someone else does," the secretary said, semi-apologetically. "Having no parishioners must have gotten to him. That's another thing I should tell you: you really don't have a parish."

No parishioners. Not how he would have preferred to start his first…what would you call this? Having resigned himself to the situation, Gabe went to bed with a nice book and fell asleep, waking up only once to the sound of several wolves howling in the distance. It did seem odd for there to be a pack of wolves on such a densely populated island, but they were resourceful creatures.

The young priest got up that morning, made himself a cup of coffee, and walked out the back door to the little brick porch behind the building to watch the sun come up. He was mildly surprised to find a large animal sleeping in the yard behind the church. The beast was quite massive and covered in silver-grey hair. It appeared to have large claws and teeth. Worried it was a bear; Gabe backed into the house and prepared to call animal control. Then the animal began to shrink. Its limbs shriveled. The claws and teeth retracted. The muscles wasted away, and the hair on the animal fell off. All of this occurred the minute sunlight hit the body. The priest mumbled and put down his coffee before he dropped it, unable to form words to describe what he saw. The skin turned squishy pink, like a human, and the remaining hair turned blonde. The massive animal had been reduced to the figure of a teenage girl. Gabe closed his eyes and looked away.

"Kimberly," someone whispered beside Gabe, "Jaysus."

The priest opened his eyes and turned to find a tall, thick, pale man with dark, unkempt hair wearing a very shabby, black jacket and pants. The man came from seemingly nowhere, as he just appeared behind Gabe without warning. Before the priest could get a word in, the man ran over to the girl, lying naked on the grass on a cold December morning, covered in frost. He took off his tattered jacket, threw it on top of the girl, and turned to Gabe.

"This is St. Michael's," the man stated, looking around like he'd seen the place for the first time. His eyes finally fell on Gabe's Roman collar.

"So, you're the new priest?" the man asked. "You're just a lad."

Gabe nodded his head, still unable to form words for what was happening. He had only just noticed that this mystery man's voice seemed to originate from the Emerald Isle. The shabby Irishman walked up to him and slapped him on the left shoulder.

"Father, I'm Theo," the man said. "I know this girl. Do you mind if Kimberly stays here while her parents come to get her?"

"Uh-huh," Gabe mumbled.

The woman on the ground began to stir. She opened her eyes, and saw she was outside for the first time. Then she touched her chest, and upon realizing she was naked, the woman became alert to her situation. She screamed, first softly, then loudly. Gabe and Theo both held their ears as her voice split the air of an otherwise serene morning landscape. She jumped to her feet and pulled at Theo's tattered jacket, desperately trying to comfort herself. Theo raised his hands and then lowered them, trying to calm her down.

"Kimberly, Kimberly," Theo said. "It's me, Theo. You know me. It's going to be alright, lass."

"Theo?" Kimberly moaned, tears streaming down her face as she recognized him. "Why am I here? Why am I naked?"

"You may find this difficult to believe, lass," Theo said, holding his hands up non-threateningly, "but you transformed last night. Like the Ze'ev do."

Kimberly calmed down a bit. Her eyes widened as it appeared the cogs were working in her mind. By contrast, the cogs in Gabe's mind were falling off the hinges as he searched for a wall to lean against lest he collapse.

"A Ze'ev," Kimberly repeated. "I'm adopted."

Now, Theo nodded his head as the light went on. They had an explanation. It was an explanation that made no sense to Gabe, who finally settled on sitting on the ground.

"Did you turn 18 recently?" Theo asked.

"Last week," Kimberly said, nodding. "Oh, God, I had a date! Brody Fenster! Then everything went blank."

"I'm sure he's alright," Theo assured her.

"Well, he was kind of a cheapskate," Kimberly said. "He wouldn't even pay for a Slurpee at the concession stand, though if I killed him, I'd have to pretend we'd make it to a second date when I met his parents at the funeral."

"He's probably fine, lass, most people in these parts know to stay out of the way," Theo said. "Let's get you out of the cold."

Theo put an arm around Kimberly and gently led her into the rectory as Gabe sat on the ground and attempted to process what had just happened. After a few minutes, the young priest was able to get off the ground, and Theo came back out.

"Thanks, Father, we've called Kimberly's parents, they're coming to pick her up," Theo said. "Brody Fenster's okay, though it doesn't look like they're making it to a second date, 'eh?"

"T-that's good, I guess," Gabe stammered. "Glad I could help."

"I guess someone should sit down and explain these things to you," Theo said. "Fr. Tim's wake will be Thursday evening at the Davis house. You should come. The other pastors in town will be there to help you get your sea legs. You aren't the only newcomer these days."

Charleston, South Carolina, Miles Simon Salvation Center, 7 p.m.
Calvin Lucas

Simon's limousine rolled up to the Miles Simon Salvation Center in Charleston. Calvin Lucas drove. The preacher man couldn't give his sermon live this week, so he had to pre-record it. They would be far too busy on Sunday with work. Since he started working for Simon, Calvin had heard a thousand lectures about not wasting the weekend.

The Miles Simon Salvation Center was identical to the main church in Houston, a large series

45

of domes topped with a tower in the middle where the offices of the ministry were located, with three tall white crosses next to the church. The Salvation Centers, soon to be renamed New Stranger Churches all across the country, were built in Texas to be identical, and then transported piece by piece to the site for the next franchise location, where the building was then assembled. The inside of the church contained various kiosks for selling books, clothes, and other knick-knacks emblazoned with Simon's face. There were also coffee shops and fast-food outlets, closed now, but ready to serve biscuits and gravy to Simon's flock on Sunday morning at inflated prices.

They walked into the main arena, and arena was the appropriate word. One of his churches recently replaced the center stage with a basketball court and hosted the Harlem Globetrotters. The preacher man climbed onto that stage and looked out at the sea of seats around him. The church could seat 20,000, but now it was empty save for cameramen and a director. Calvin took his seat in the front row. The cameras pointed at Simon. The men behind those cameras counted down from three. The light went on, and Simon began preaching to a virtual congregation.

"True Christian believers from across America and the world! I thank you for attending today's services," Simon began, failing to note he would not be there himself. "Thank you for coming to protect Christian America. As you know, we at Miles Simon Ministries have decided to purchase the Stranger Church as part of our campaign to take back the country. I want to bring America the story of a group of godly, upright men who founded a church to oppose evil within their midst."

As Simon said this, a black-robed figure with long eyebrows and a red cape came onto the stage carrying a plastic pitchfork.

"With the power of God, they defeated the Devil."

At this moment, Simon blew his breath upon the devil figure, and he collapsed.

"And 400 years later," Simon began again, "that church is still there."

The Jumbotron screen behind Simon showed a picture of the old Stranger church, which was indeed still there. MacDonald had invited Simon to services the following Sunday, but Simon turned him down. Too much work to do. Calvin wished he had gotten to go. He didn't have a religious upbringing, and now the only church he went to was Simon's, and most of the time, he was working.

"I am honored to inherit the role of pastor," Simon continued, "from such a great line of men, starting with Captain John Miller and ending with Atticus MacDonald. I humbly hope I can fill their shoes in warding off the Devil."

"American society is under siege from an alliance of liberals, non-believers, and Muslims. God has been removed from schools, removed from courthouses, and removed from people's lives. Our very way of life is threatened. Well, I am telling you now, I won't stand for it! America is a Christian nation. It has always been a Christian nation. It will always be a Christian nation. This invasion of outsiders will be repulsed. We must fight back. We must take back our country from the usurpers who will destroy us from the inside out. You can't even say Merry Christmas anymore. Think about that! We used to own this country! We used to be this country! And now, it's like you got to apologize for taking off your shoes in your own living room."

Simon transitioned from culture war themes to Prosperity Gospel themes quickly. Calvin caught his services a few times on television when he was a kid, after his mother told him the famous prosperity gospel preacher was his father. He knew the televangelist was an old hand at this.

"No harm shall come to you. Follow the ways of the Lord and you will prosper all the days of your life. The plans you have will succeed. God does right by those who do right by him. All you need to do is have faith. How do you have faith? By planting a seed. A seed of approximately $1,000. Maybe you have just lost your job. Maybe you just had a kid. Or maybe you just want to use that money to visit your old Aunt Millie. I say that the best thing you can do is use that money in the bank as seed money. God will pay you back fivefold."

Simon then segued into his Power of Positive Thinking segment.

"Don't focus on your past mistakes and failures. That's the Devil talking. He wants you to believe that great things aren't in your future. There is no way that you can succeed now. Not you. Not the guy who did that. You can't let him hold you back. Why focus on the negative?"

The televangelist then finished up with his old standby, directed at the youth group: drugs, sex, and alcohol.

"God has a great plan for you, young people, but so many throw it away with drugs, sex, and alcohol. You see it everywhere in our culture. Television, the internet, the streets, it's all there. Jesus weeps. Young people are throwing away their potential for a reckless and dissolute life. These problems are tearing our country apart. You can't get stuck in this trap."

And now for the main event: faith healing. The guitars blared. The lights flashed. The fog machine let loose. A host of the "sick and injured" lined up and down the aisles. Some in wheelchairs, others in walkers, a few more with heads shaved. Attendants lifted the first man in a walker on stage. Simon approached. He struck a defiant pose. He placed his hands on the elderly man's forehead.

"Shattered lumbar spine, BE GONE!!!!"

The man stood straight up, the walker tossed aside. He walked from the stage under his own power, strutting down the aisle. Calvin had seen the same man in the gym earlier that day. A woman in a wheelchair rolled onto the stage via a ramp. Simon cocked back his hand again. "Muscular dystrophy, BE GONE!!!" Simon lightly struck the woman. The woman rose from her wheelchair, which security quickly removed, and ran off stage, praising God. Calvin got her this gig after seeing her teach a Brazilian Jiu-Jitsu class. He'd also recruited the next guy, a man with a shaved head who ambled towards Simon. Simon grasped the man's baldness and held it to his breast. "Lung cancer, BE GONE!!!" The man grasped his chest and looked relieved. After the check he got from Simon, he'd be able to pay his rent. The televangelist worked his way through the fake infirm until he got to the little boy with brain cancer. He put his hands around the boy's head and proclaimed.

"Holy Spirit, banish this demon of brain cancer!" Simon yelled.

The boy rose and then collapsed. Simon looked down on the boy, who struggled to get up. Simon's face contorted in anger as he came to a grim realization.

"Wait, is this a real sick kid?" Simon asked. "How did this happen?"

One of the attendants raised his hand.

It's my nephew, Mr. Simon. I thought you might be able to help.

"Who are you?" Simon asked.

"The name is Jim. I'm new here."

"You were new here. You're fired," Simon said. "Damn it, can we get that in post?"

Wednesday, Pandemonium, Shooting Range, 11 a.m. Deanna

Deanna aimed the AR-15 down the range and pulled the trigger, hitting the center. Her father applauded. The machine retrieved the bullseye. MacDonald replaced it with a fresh target.

"Excellent," MacDonald enthused, "you're really on point today. Third bullseye since we started. Would you like to try the crossbow next?"

"Sure," Deanna answered, picking up the crossbow from the table and aiming it down the firing range. She let loose her first bolt, once again hitting the target dead center. Deanna was a sharpshooter, having attended firing ranges since she was eight. Chalk it up to the advantages of homeschooling.

MacDonald parted with the Witch school system when Gilbert attended his first sex education course in the seventh grade. Ironically, the Witches, who once held massive orgies on their side of the island, now promoted abstinence, as sex among teenagers is somewhat inimical to careerism, the Witches' true faith. MacDonald agreed on the end of such education, just not the means. The school taught abstinence by showing a series of images of diseased genitals leaking infected bodily fluids and covered in unhealthy pustules. When her father asked why they could not teach chastity by giving the example of the saints and apostles, the Witch principal rolled his eyes and said this was more effective. MacDonald took Gilbert and Deanna out of the public school and homeschooled both of them, which often took them to odd places, like the firing range.

Deanna rearmed the crossbow. She didn't know when she would ever use these skills or what for. The question never occurred to her. She learned European History, Calculus, and Greek without asking what those were for either. She just liked Greek, and this satisfied the state board of education as much as anything else did. Deanna released another arrow. It hit dead center.

"Break for lunch?" her father asked.

"Definitely," Deanna responded, "I made chicken salad."

Deanna and her father ate in the car and talked about Theo's recent travail in sunlight. MacDonald told her that as long as he had known Theo, he could be out in the sun, but it made him weak.

"Are you positive he isn't just hungover?" Deanna said.

"No, Theo cannot get drunk, or get the downside the next morning. His body metabolism is different from ours. He mostly drinks alcohol because it is liquid bread: the one thing he can consume other than blood."

"When I was twelve, I saw him passed out on the floor. I had to drag him back to the crypt."

MacDonald laughed.

"Yes, you did. And I won five dollars. Because you see, Theo didn't think you would do that just because he played dead."

Deanna was livid, stunned really. Her right eyebrow tremored with rage.

"You realize I put AA pamphlets in his coat pocket?" Deanna asked.

MacDonald started cracking up and hit the steering wheel with his palm. Deanna's eyes glared at him until he calmed down. Once Deanna had forgiven him a bit, MacDonald explained that Theo might not age, but his body does change over time.

"For instance," MacDonald began, "you know how he has to sleep in a desecrated church? How that crypt was built over the spot where they murdered that woman?"

"Yes, they tainted that place forever."

"Not really. When that poor girl was killed, the church had not been erected yet. As a matter of fact, I don't even think it's the same spot. Theo's been sleeping in a regular church for nearly forty years without incident."

"Seriously? So, nothing stops Theo from entering a regular church?"

"Only his mind. Someday, I'll tell him that."

"You know, one day the rest of us are going to keep something from you."

"Impossible. I'm omniscient."

They exited the car and returned to the firing range to find Gilbert waiting for them. He had gotten his work for the day done by lunch and taken the afternoon off. He wanted to see if Deanna could measure up to him.

"I've been practicing," Gilbert said, taking out his assault rifle. "Let's compare."

"Let's," Deanna answered.

The two of them fired five shots each down the shooting lane. Gilbert got two bullseyes, one close miss right off-center, and two shots in the outer rim. Deanna got three bullseyes and two close misses.

"I told you," MacDonald crowed. "She's a better shot than I am, even."

"Guess I'm a bit rusty," Gilbert admitted. "You'll have to school me."

"As I understand it, you will school the rest of us tonight at Bible study," Deanna said, "your first one."

"Don't remind me," Gilbert said. "I'm choking up. I came out here to relax."

"You'll do fine, boy," MacDonald assured him.

CHAPTER FOUR

The First Week of Advent, Wednesday, Stranger Meeting Hall, 7 p.m.
MacDonald

"Thou shalt not suffer a Witch to live," Gilbert recited the verse.

He decided to just go ahead and start with the big one. The verse was scratched on the arch above the entrance to the church. The words may have never been carried out literally, but they remained in faded red paint. Members of the church, some of whom may have grown up as Witches and married into the Stranger church, passed under those words every Sunday without thought. The other members of the Bible study looked at him with a little stunned disbelief. Most people wouldn't broach the topic. Namely, how could the church synthesize belief in the Witches' pure evil with tolerance of them? Deanna and MacDonald tried to warn Gilbert away from this subject, but he was determined to take it head-on.

"Does anyone have any questions or thoughts before I begin?" Gilbert asked.

No. No one had any thoughts. The Stranger crowd, arranged in a semi-circle of steel chairs in a nondescript conference room, looked at the floor or the ceiling and cleared their throats as the young buck attempted to untie the Gordian knot of Stranger theology. They were all content to watch him fail and then pretend it had not occurred.

"Here is what I think that it means," Gilbert began. "First, at the time it was written, Moses had to make some very harsh laws to keep the people of Israel together in the desert. We read elsewhere that a man was stoned for gathering wood on the Sabbath, so we have to understand it in context. This particular legal code cannot be applied strictly throughout the ages to all people, as it is part of the Mosaic law, applied at that time. St. Paul makes clear in his epistles that the old Jewish law does not apply to the whole church."

"Does that mean the Ze'ev should kill the Witches?" asked Kimberly Smith, still recovering from recent revelations about her original parentage.

"No, that's not what I'm saying," Gilbert admitted. "That would be insane."

"So, the passage has no application."

"Well, it has some application," Gilbert answered. "Nothing in scripture has no application. I don't think it means that we should kill the Witches, or that the Ze'ev should."

"So, what does it mean?"

"We shouldn't kill the Witches," Gilbert responded, "but we shouldn't just be okay with them practicing witchcraft either."

"The Witches haven't really performed witchcraft in years," Deanna said.

"I guess my point is that none of us would kill the Witches, but we don't seem to care about the fact that they worship Satan," Gilbert explained, "and we should."

"It's kind of difficult to bring that up in polite society," Deanna pointed out.

Pastor MacDonald could see a controversy brewing between his children and decided to head it off. Gilbert had fallen into a rookie mistake. He decided to address one of the hard scripture passages first, which is something theologians love to discuss in the wee hours of the night, but those discussions are rarely suitable for public consumption. He decided to take over.

"I think what Gilbert is trying to say here is that religious tolerance is a cornerstone of our society, but that this has to be balanced out with a recognition that not all religious faiths are equal," Pastor MacDonald preached. "We should be wary of the Witch's philosophy that puts so much emphasis on worldly success to the exclusion of all other considerations. It will not end in happiness, and it won't serve the greater good of the community. Therefore, we should not be afraid to speak openly of our faith in front of them. Always be prepared to give a reason for the hope you have, as St. Peter tells us."

"Right, a religion based on worldly success won't make you happy. So, what does that say about Miles Simon?" asked Kimberly

"Let's break for the evening," Pastor MacDonald said, realizing that now he had made a wrong turn.

Thursday, Davis Family Plantation House, 5 pm MacDonald

MacDonald drove down the dirt road leading to the Davis house, flanked on both sides by dead oak trees. Hecate tried to keep them alive and even grow a garden, but something about the soil here wouldn't allow it. The land was barren, which is probably why the Davis family donated land to the city for a graveyard. The Orangeman passed by generations of dead Satanists as he headed to Fr. Tim's wake. Witch graves today were more or less the same as everyone else's. They even had pictures of winged babies and roses on them. The closer you got to the Davis Plantation House, the more you started seeing the cairns that used to mark the Witches' graves: piles of smooth rocks stacked on top of each other. He parked in front of the ancient plantation house, a classic piece of antebellum architecture, with white Roman columns stratifying two stories, a slanted roof, and two sets of circular stairs flowing from the balcony to the front porch. The exterior also showed the age of the house, as the paint peeled and faded.

As he made his way to the front door, the ancient porch begged for mercy under his weight. The Orangeman reached the dark oak door and knocked twice. A minute later, the door opened to reveal Hecate Davis, a slender, blonde woman in her late 40s, a former homecoming queen.

"Pastor MacDonald," she said, "always good to see you. Fr. Tim is in the parlor."

He walked into the old plantation house. The inside was very modern. Clean, red carpet flowed up and down the hallways. The kitchen had a look of sleek steel from its faucets and pans. The walls were painted bright white. Hecate and her sister, Delilah, had to keep up appearances as they were running a business out of this house. They maintain the outside as well, but something about the land seemed to want to age everything on it. Hecate led MacDonald to the parlor where the priest was on display. The diocese, which sought to keep up appearances in a way not unlike the Davis sisters, insisted on having a wake in town for all of his 'parishioners.' The Catholic Church never could admit that it hadn't converted anyone in this town for 60 years. The errant whore could be stubborn, as his mother used to tell him.

The parlor was about the size of a typical living room, though shaped like a nave with a head where the decedent was. Sure enough, Pastor Overstreet from the Church of the Tobacco Fields and Rabbi Barry, the younger rabbi studying under Maharam, were already sitting in the front row of the pews set up for mourners. MacDonald greeted them with handshakes and then turned to the body. The diocese hired Hecate and Delilah to prepare the corpse before it was buried in Charleston because they were the best in town. They lived up to their reputation, as the deceased had been excellently prepared to face the afterlife. The subtle makeup and hair coloring made Fr. Tim's face look so lifelike.

"Hecate," MacDonald said, "you did a wonderful job."

"Would you believe Alistair did this?" Hecate said, referring to Delilah's 24-year-old son with Down Syndrome.

"He's a good boy," MacDonald said, taking his place among his colleagues.

Ravenwood was late, as he usually was among meetings of the pastors. Twenty minutes in, he entered the parlor and made his way to the body. By that time, the wake was practically over, as there were no other attendees. The four of them moved into the living room for the reception that the Davis sisters had prepared. Delilah, a plump blonde woman, greeted the visitors and cracked open a bottle of cabernet.

"Thank you, Delilah," MacDonald said. "I know that the two of you are technically on the clock, but we would be delighted if you sat down and had a drink with us tonight."

"We would love to, Pastor," Delilah said. "Let me just go talk to Alistair and make sure he is good to maintain the buffet."

The mourners made their plates, took their drinks, and sat down. Hecate told them there was bourbon available if they wanted something stronger. MacDonald countered that he could do with a glass of scotch, and Hecate obliged him.

"Right there, stop," MacDonald requested, as Hecate poured him a snifter. "My children worry about my health."

"You are getting up there in age," Hecate said. "As I understand it, you retire later this month."

"That I do to my great regret," MacDonald moaned.

"What are you worried about?" Ravenwood asked. "Aren't you being given a retirement package?"

"The sorcerer wants to know what I am worried about," MacDonald mused. "My church is being handed over to a confidence man."

At that moment, there was another knock on the door. Hecate rose to answer it. She returned a minute later with a young man wearing a Roman collar.

"You must be the new priest," Overstreet guessed. "My condolences."

"I didn't know him," the man admitted.

"I know," Overstreet answered. "My condolences for being appointed here."

The priest hung his head. He had heard that he had no flock.

"What's your name?" Overstreet asked.

"Fr. Gabe Strobel," the priest replied, offering his hand.

Overstreet took that hand.

"Darrell Overstreet. I'm the Field Servant, meaning I'm the chief pastor of the Church of the Tobacco Fields, which is the historically black church in town, though we have several white members."

"Yes, he's often attempted to poach Hecate and Delilah from me," Ravenwood interrupted, taking another sip from his bourbon.

Hecate and Delilah blushed politely. MacDonald knew from the way they talked about him in private, they didn't have the best opinions of Ravenwood, whose "Satanic Rituals" varied between banal and silly.

"I would never dream of it," Overstreet responded, his lip rising with a hint of contempt. "Hecate and Delilah have told me exactly how much they value your enthusiastic sermons."

"I suppose I should ask for your name next," Gabe said, offering his hand to Ravenwood. Ravenwood took the hand and gave it a lazy shake.

"Acton Ravenwood," he responded. "Satanic High Priest."

Gabe's face betrayed a small moment of shock, but he recovered.

"So, you're the person who runs that Temple?" Gabe asked.

"Don't give the Devil too much credit," MacDonald interjected. "He runs a tourist trap where he pretends to worship Satan. He has no real faith in the fallen angel. I'm more of a Witch than he is in the sense that I believe the Devil is real. I assume the same is true of you."

"And you are?" the young priest asked.

"Pastor Atticus MacDonald," the Orangeman introduced himself. "Head pastor of the Stranger Church, or at least I am until Christmas Day. This man beside me is Rabbi Barry Flom, associate rabbi of the Temple Ze'ev."

"The Rabbi Maharam could not come tonight," Barry explained. "As he gets older, his mobility is an issue."

"Ze'ev," Gabe repeated.

"I hear you saw Kimberly Smith transform on Tuesday," the rabbi said, winking at MacDonald. "That must have been disturbing for an outsider. If you have any questions, I will answer them."

Gabe visibly struggled to find the words. Overstreet took pity on him.

"Maybe you should explain how these transformations are possible," Overstreet suggested.

The priest nodded.

"The complete story has been lost to history," Barry began, "but the myth is that at some point in the old country, the community suffered a pogrom. When the oppression was too much to bear, the chief rabbi pleaded with the Lord for aid, and the Lord provided aid in the form of the transformations. The Emperor's minions then attempted to round up the community on a full moon, and were torn to shreds for their troubles."

"The same thing happened to an angry mob of Strangers when the Ze'ev immigrated here in the 1890s," MacDonald interjected. "Twenty-five men bearing pitchforks and torches went to drive them out of town. Six came back."

"The Lord has his way of protecting his chosen people," Rabbi Barry said, taking back the reins. "We went public like the Witches in 1992 after some college students caught a Ze'ev transforming on a camcorder. Ken Burns made a documentary about us. I'm a little surprised you hadn't heard."

"I am not a great consumer of media," the priest responded.

Gabe then turned to Overstreet.

"What about you?" he asked.

"Me?" Overstreet replied. "You mean: is there anything weird about the black people in this town? No, we're pretty boring."

"Well," Ravenwood began, "if you believe the old wives' tales—"

"Which you shouldn't because they are old wives' tales," Overstreet interrupted, rolling his eyes.

"Father, while you may not have any parishioners, the people in this town are nothing if not polite," Delilah interjected, sensing an argument coming. "My sister and I would like to hold a reception for you next Friday, if you are amenable to that."

"Of course, it would be an honor," Gabe responded.

"In the meantime," Hecate said, "if you would like to pay your respects to Fr. Tim, he's in the parlor."

"I suppose I should."

"Young man," MacDonald said, "I had my differences with him, but we all considered Tim a friend."

"I see," Gabe replied. "My condolences."

With that, Gabe went to pay his respects, and MacDonald took his leave.

"Dear colleagues, Sorcerer. I have other things to attend to."

Stranger Rectory, 10 p.m.
MacDonald

"That was a dirty, rotten trick that you played on me," Theo groused.

"Yes," MacDonald replied, "but after what happened in Ulster, I needed to get you out of your head."

They were in MacDonald's study, a small room with a large bookcase containing every theological treatise imaginable and the odd collection of old myths. A large steamer trunk sat at the foot of the pastor's oaken desk. The Orangeman had just told Theo that the desecrated church he had been living in since 1982, wasn't. The vampiric Irishman had lived for nearly 400 years, but the immortal never showed an interest in the finer points of theology. He hadn't even learned to read until he was more than 150. When MacDonald told Theo the church was desecrated, he believed the old Orangeman. Now, he had learned that his best friend had been lying to him for almost 40 years.

"I could have burst into flames!" Theo yelled. "I mean, I didn't, but you didn't know that back then."

"I did know it," MacDonald asserted, his voice marked by a subtle confidence. "You were never going to burst into flames, Theophilus. It is all in your head."

"How did you know that? You just had faith?" Theo asked.

MacDonald got up from the table, walked over to his desk, picked up the old, bent silver cross that had been framed, and threw it at Theo. "Here, catch."

Theo instinctively did as commanded, catching the cross in his right hand.

"This is in a frame," Theo explained.

"It wasn't in '79, back when we put the nails in ole' Scratch. Fr. Eric threw this at you, and you pressed it up against his head."

"And it burned me, too."

"Without leaving a mark on you, Theo!" MacDonald interjected. "Don't you know what this means? You can live in a normal flat."

"So, I'm just crazy, is that it?"

"No, you're human, and getting more human by the day by the look of things. Sit down and have a beer with me."

"I'm not having a beer with you."

"Theo, the Elders sold the church, you just can't stay. "

"The Elders told me I could stay."

This was indeed true. When the Elders of the church hired MacDonald, they were a little wary of his request to allow a male friend of his to sleep in the crypt, but Theo introduced himself and offered to pay rent, claiming to be independently wealthy. The Elders remained skeptical, as Theo dressed like a vagrant, not a millionaire. However, the check for the rent cleared.

"As long as I am pastor, that was the deal," MacDonald responded. "The deal has changed. It's not like I'm happy about it either."

"Oh, so that's the issue, you're not happy," Theo spat. "I'm going to my crypt. If you need to speak with me, shove off."

Theo took his leave, storming out the front door past Gilbert and Deanna, who were listening to the aforementioned conversation. After Theo slammed the door behind him, MacDonald followed up behind.

"Alright, I just admitted that I lied," he said. "Now one of you has to convince him to move."

Gilbert and Deanna looked at each other.

"Rock, paper, scissors, shoot!" Gilbert called quickly.

Deanna instinctively went for rock, and Gilbert knew to go for paper. Deanna covered her eyes, and MacDonald smiled. Somehow, she always fell for it.

Friday, Stranger Crypt, 8 am
Deanna

Deanna knew that Theo generally didn't go to bed until 9 am, so she got up early to try to convince him to move out. The crypt was indeed old, but it had electric lighting, and Deanna had visited Theo there since she was six, so she could probably find her way to his lodgings in the dark. She carefully walked down the old stairs. When Deanna reached the bottom, she could feel her foot compound the ancient dirt. Her nose scrunched at the stale smell of the old bones, but she pressed forward. The dead stopped scaring her when she was seven.

Deanna found Theo where he normally was, sitting in an old armchair next to his coffin in the middle of a bare chamber, watching a television. Today, the Irishman had turned on the idiot lantern he had set up in the crypt to watch the English Premier League. Arsenal v. Liverpool. His Northern Irish team, Donegal Celtic F.C., was difficult to follow in the States, though Deanna had introduced him to the internet, making it somewhat easier. Theo had not decorated his living quarters so much as he settled into them. Ancient pictures and mementos from his long time on Earth collected dust among the bones of the residents. The old Celtic himself had not aged a day since MacDonald introduced him to the elders, though occasionally he would dye his hair slightly gray, to add distinction. As soon as Deanna approached, Theo looked up and cried, "Hullo, Arun."

Arun was a pet name Theo had for Deanna, which meant something in Irish, though she forgot. Deanna smiled and waved. She walked around the various clothes and overturned furniture that Theo had left on the ground. How he lived like this, she never knew. The women of the Stranger church often said that Theo's problem was that he needed a wife. MacDonald told Deanna in private that Theo had been married before, and it didn't work out. Deanna had problems believing that any woman on Earth could civilize Theo. She decided to tolerate Theo's habitual messiness to convince him that he needed to get an apartment.

"You seem like you're in a better mood," Deanna ventured. "Did Donegal win?"

"Last time they played, yes," Theo answered. "That was last week. I just don't hold onto things for long. Holding grudges makes life unbearable when you live to be eighty. It's impossible at four hundred. Do you have a cross on you by the way? I'd like to try something."

Deanna looked down at the necklace with a golden cross she wore around her neck. She took it off and held it out. Theo grabbed it.

"It doesn't sting," he said. "It doesn't sting."

"Why would you think it would?" Deanna asked.

"Being among the undead, you get used to the almighty being your enemy."

"Why do you think God's your enemy?"

"It might be the fact that holy objects like that used to burn. You know, I went into a consecrated church in the 1680s, and I burst into flame. It's not just a manner of speaking."

"Yeah, but your body changes over time," Deanna pressed. "I mean, you know I'm a Christian, like my brother and my Dad. I don't like hearing you talk that way."

"Well, why shouldn't I think of God as my enemy?" Theo asked. "You'd like to convert me? Like your father? Is that it?"

"All things being equal, sure."

"Well, why should I be converted, m'lady? I need not worry about hell as I am immortal. Well, I'm immortal provided I don't meet the wrong end of a stake some time."

Theo was probably the most infamous unbeliever in a town founded by Satanists, and Deanna knew this. Her Dad was his friend and had tried to convert him since before either of them came here, with no results. Now, she was being put on the spot.

"Here goes. Dad says you are getting more human, so you could die," Deanna began, "and I am your friend, and I would like to see you go to Heaven. So would Gilbert, and all those kids you play Santa with at Christmas."

"Hmmm…." Theo mused, leading Deanna around the crypt. "Well, the Lord's Prayer, you say, does it not say 'on Earth as it is in Heaven'"

"Well, yes, it does."

"So, it is not only about going to Heaven, but also about what Earth is going to look like, right?"

"Sure."

"And your holy book says something about how every knee should bow."

"Yep."

"So, you, assuming you believe all of this, you would not want to just convert me, you would want to convert everyone," Theo said, stopping at a particular alcove in the crypt covered by a shroud, "the Witches, the Ze'ev, the whole state of South Carolina, the whole world basically."

"Ideally, that would be the case."

"So, we would not just be Christians, we would be Christians together," Theo continued, "and form some kind of Christian society."

"Yes, we would."

"The last time we were a Christian society," Theo finished, heaving a sigh, "this is what we did."

With a twitch of his hand, Theo pulled back the shroud over the adjacent alcove to reveal the bones of the Stono princess. Theo had led Deanna to the final resting place of the church's founding victim. Deanna sniffed the stale air a bit, realizing she had been led right into that one.

"I had a family once," Theo said, "before I met you or your father. This is what happened to them. A man believed God wanted them to die, and he made it so."

"I'll go," Deanna responded.

Theo stopped her by raising his hand.

"Deanna, I'll find an apartment," Theo said, "provided you help me. Your father has tried to make me sing God's praises for years, and I assumed you and Gilbert would take over after he died. I wanted you to know where the battle lines were."

Then suddenly, they heard the sound of a picture being taken. Theo looked to his side to find a young man in a suit, holding a camera.

"Wow, so those are the princess's bones," the man said. "Sorry, before the sale, we weren't allowed to take pictures, but Mr. Simon wants all this documented now that the purchase sales agreement has been executed."

"Sir, who are you?" Theo asked.

"My name is Calvin Lucas," he introduced himself. "I work for Mr. Simon. You must be Deanna. I believe I met your father. And you are?"

"Theo. I'm afraid I have to take those pictures. I don't like being photographed without my permission."

"Oh, sorry, I didn't see you," Calvin apologized. "Let me just delete these. There we are. I do need to take pictures of the crypt."

Calvin walked around taking pictures of all the relevant relics, and Theo took his leave.

EconoSuites Lodge, 8 p.m.
Calvin

"Son, what are these?" Simon asked, holding the photographs Calvin took.

Calvin's arms trembled with fear. He couldn't fathom what he had done wrong, but apparently, it was something.

"These are pictures of the relics you asked me to take," Calvin explained.

"Now you see, Calvin. That's why you're here," Simon said. "Even though that bitch in Florida gave birth to you, I am your father."

Calvin winced at Simon's derogation of his dead mother. Lying back in the tattered bed,

Simon could see the look of pain in his bastard son's face: a sign of weakness. It noticeably disgusted him.

"That means it's my responsibility to help you make it through the world," Simon continued. "First lesson, learn to read between the fucking lines. What I needed you to do was obtain 'dirt' on that MacDonald fella."

"Dirt," Calvin repeated, unsure as to what that meant.

"Yes, Calvin, that man MacDonald does not like me," Simon said. "Can't imagine why, but we need to ensure that this sale goes through without a hitch. If some great voice in the desert were to call out, say a voice with an Ulster accent, we need to silence that voice immediately, Calvin. Understood?"

"So, I should have been looking for evidence of what?" Calvin asked.

"I don't know, son," Simon said, looking at the water-stained ceiling with exasperation. "Embezzlement, drug use, child molestation. Hadn't this guy got two adopted kids?"

"Dad---"

"Don't call me that," Simon barked. "You can call me that when you've earned it. Find dirt."

Simon got up without another word and walked to the door. Calvin flipped through the photographs he had taken, searching desperately for 'dirt' that wasn't merely dust. No, he merely attempted to do as he was told. Stupid, he thought. Then the viewer shifted to one photograph he recognized as being of the pastor's daughter. Darn, Calvin thought, forgot to delete that one. Then he realized that the photo should have had that Theo guy she was speaking to, but there was only the girl, speaking to seemingly nothing. Someone else was supposed to be there, as the pastor's daughter, clearly in deep conversation with nobody. Just Deanna and the bones.

"Wait, what is this!?" Calvin asked.

CHAPTER FIVE

The First Week of Advent, Saturday, Pandemonium,
Miller Memorial Stadium, 11 a.m.
Calvin

       Calvin grew up in north Florida. His mother's boyfriend once took him to a Seminole game. He knew how the South was with football. Namely, that for six days a week, the Old Confederacy may be divided by race and creed, but on Saturday, there is only one church the South attends, and it is truly universal. There is no White, no Black, no Jew, and no Witch when kickoff starts. Pandemonium was no different, which is why Calvin and the father, who didn't recognize him, had to attend the annual Blood Bowl: the football game between the Strangers' Winthrop University and the Witches' Cramner University.

       Calvin had done his homework. He knew the customs. As members of both the Stranger and Witch communities drove up to Miller Memorial Stadium that morning and began the pregame tailgate rituals, the two groups became not unlike two friends who had known each other long enough to insult each other confidently. Simon, however, had not done his homework, and he now strode among the Strangers' sacred tailgate with little to no idea of any significance of the handshakes, or the ancient game scores being recounted, or even the mascots. At least he knew to wear blue and yellow, the Winthrop Buccaneers' colors, because Calvin had told him to.

"I am a huge Winthrop Bucs fan!" Simon yelled loudly while making faux antlers with his fingers.

"Mr. Simon," Calvin explained, "Bucs stands for Buccaneers, not the deer. Because Miller and his crew were pirates."

"Oh, right," Simon said. "Roll Tide!"

"Wrong team, Mr. Simon. The proper cheer is Full Mast."

"Oh, Full Mast!"

Three Strangers grilling a hog over a fire pit looked at Simon like he was wearing a tutu and waving a wand. They all just shook their heads at him in pity.

"What the hell is this thing called again?" Simon asked Calvin.

"The Blood Bowl, sir," Calvin answered, "it's the annual football game between the Witches' school, Cramner University, and the Strangers' school, Winthrop University."

"They have a school?" Simon asked while smiling. "What else do those Devil worshippers have in this town?"

"Libraries, restaurants, movie theaters," Calvin recounted. "It's a regular town, sir."

"Where the hell is MacDonald? He was supposed to meet me here," Simon demanded.

Calvin spotted a squat, Northern Irish gentleman waving his arms under a tailgater tent. Calvin pointed out MacDonald to Simon, and Simon headed towards the rotund Celt. MacDonald's children, Gilbert and Deanna, sat under the tent, along with that Theo person Calvin saw the day before, and then didn't see in the photograph. The Irishman seemed to be trying to intentionally stay out of the light. For a second, Calvin set his eyes on Theo, but the minute Theo's eyes met his, Calvin shifted his gaze.

"Pastor MacDonald, I hear you are about to receive a great honor today," Simon greeted.

"I'm being made an honorary football captain," MacDonald responded. "I have to call a coin flip. That is about all I am qualified to do. Gilbert, explain this game to me again."

Gilbert tried to explain the rules of football to his father for what had to be the one-thousandth time. Simon interjected every so often in a way that showed he knew as little as MacDonald did. Theo poked the food on his plate and then passed it to Deanna.

"Theo, it's pulled pork," Deanna insisted. "It's good. You should try to eat real food."

Wonder what that means, thought Calvin.

"Look, I'll just stay with what I know I can stomach," Theo said, tipping a can of beer into his mouth.

Theo leaned back into his chair. Back, back, until he fell to the ground.

"Theo!" Deanna called.

Gilbert ran to Theo and helped him off the ground.

"Theo, you okay?" Gilbert asked. "Taken in a little too much sunlight?"

"I've been in the sun longer than this," Theo replied.

Calvin listened to all of this intently while Simon started chatting with the nearest master griller, bragging about his grandmother's non-existent sauce.

Too much sunlight. Trying to eat real food. What the hell was this? Theo seemed to be trying to make sense of it himself, and then his eyes fell on the beer can.

"Atticus! It's the sunlight *and the beer*! I can get drunk during the day!" he yelled.

"And apparently, you're a lightweight," MacDonald responded while taking the beer out of Theo's hands.

MacDonald then turned to Calvin.

"You must forgive my eccentric friend," the Orangeman pleaded. "He picked up a few odd habits in Ulster. Had a bad run-in with the Provos. Affected his head."

A man in a grey suit tapped MacDonald on the shoulder.

"Time to go, Pastor MacDonald."

"Certainly, man," he answered.

The Orangeman was led away, still holding Theo's half-finished beer. Theo started trying to find another one, with only Deanna there to keep him away from it.

"Och, give my head peace, Arun," Theo pleaded. "I haven't gotten drunk in 400 years, let me live a little."

Deanna laughed politely while subtly pointing to Calvin. Theo paid her no attention but instead spotted yet another beer sticking out of one of the open coolers.

"I have to find out what these people are hiding," Calvin muttered under his breath.

Deanna

Deanna and Beth became friends when they met in Kindergarten before MacDonald had decided to homeschool. Beth attracted a large number of bullies, as kids with unusual tics tend to do, and Beth had all of them. She would stare off into space for long periods and talk to herself or some imaginary friend you could not see. One day at recess, a group of second graders decided to have a go at Beth, and she found herself cornered between the monkey bars and the outer fence. Deanna intervened and got a black eye for her trouble. Both of them ended up in the nurse's office that day ("You should have seen how the other girls looked," Deanna insisted when her father showed up).

And that's how the MacDonald family got box seats. Beth's family was big Cramner boosters, and they knew how to get the primo tickets. Knowing that her friend and a stocked buffet were waiting for her, Deanna suggested about thirty minutes before kickoff that they head in. They finally tempted Theo into the stadium after promising him that there would be beer in the luxury box. Gilbert led them up the stairs of the stadium while Deanna dragged Theo around by his left hand, quite drunk. Deanna would have told him to go to AA, but Theo hadn't had a drinking problem until this afternoon.

Gilbert found the luxury box and knocked on the door twice. The door opened to reveal Hecate Davis, dressed in the red and black colors of the Cramner Red Devils, standing there with a glass of white wine in her hand.

"Gilbert! Come in! When is your Dad coming up?" Hecate greeted.

"He told me that the officials should get him here by the second quarter," Gilbert responded, walking in with Deanna and Theo in tow. "Though he seemed doubtful about that."

"Good grief!" Delilah Davis exclaimed, sipping red wine in a recliner. "You would think it would take less time to flip a coin."

Deanna looked for Beth. Her twin brother, Bryce, sat in the corner with his Ze'ev friend, Gary, with an iPad open to a sports gambling website. Delilah's son, Alistair, loaded up his plate with chili dogs at the hot buffet. Theo slumped into a chair next to Delilah, who looked surprised to see him intoxicated. Deanna wasn't the only person in town who knew of Theo's tolerances.

Finally, the bathroom door opened, and Beth came out. She had a thin, mousey face, with blonde hair draping her slim body. She dressed in the same red and black colors her aunts wore. The colors clashed with Deanna's blue and yellow when they hugged. After exchanging the requisite pleasantries, they got some popcorn from the buffet and took their seat on the balcony of the luxury box. Beth took out her own iPad and brought up one of their favorite movies: *Grease 2*. They often bonded over their affinity for terrible movies, which brought them together far more than any dispute between God and the Devil could ever divide them. At some point, the game began, though neither of them noticed. And then her father arrived.

"Deanna," the Orangeman said, walking out on the balcony, "it appears the Red Devils have taken the lead."

"Uh-huh."

"Now, Gilbert would have to explain to me how this happened, as it's a bunch of nonsense to me."

"Uh-huh."

"You know, I volunteered to coach a rugby team for Winthrop one year. That's a real sport."

"Why is Winthrop called Winthrop and not Miller?" Beth asked. "I mean, our college is named after Cramner."

"I don't know," Deanna answered, hoping her father would shut up.

"Deanna, how can you not know?" MacDonald asked, in feigned surprise. "Beth, the Drunkard may have founded the church, but he wasn't the best theologian. Robert Winthrop was the second pastor of the church, and he invented most Stranger doctrines."

"Yes, that," Deanna muttered, reaching for a piece of popcorn.

"I mean, he borrowed a lot from other churches he visited," MacDonald said. "He went to Catholic Masses, Anglican services, Quaker Meetings, and got chased out of Boston by some very angry Puritans. You might say he took a buffet approach, and there's some question as to how much of it he actually believed."

"Go, Winthrop," Deanna offered, having completely lost track.

"But as my congregation has told me over the years, he did us proud," MacDonald finished. "I would say he did rather well in life for the son of an illiterate buccaneer and a 14-year-old Stono woman who didn't speak English."

"Thank you, Pastor MacDonald," Beth responded politely. "Can I get you something as I get up? How about you, Theo?"

Theo turned to Beth and started to spew out some measure of nonsense before Deanna cut him off.

"No, Beth," Deanna said. "Theo is fine."

"I could use a scotch, if you don't mind," MacDonald answered. "By the way, everyone appears to be walking off the field."

"That's called halftime, Dad," Gilbert explained, being patient with his father.

"Oh, so we're halfway through this," MacDonald sighed. "Good."

"You aren't concerned that the Buccaneers are behind, Atticus?" Hecate asked, sipping her Chardonnay.

"No, unlike Theo, I've never gotten into competitive sports," MacDonald said. "I've always been disturbed by how it causes some people to act."

Acton Ravenwood

"INTERCEPTION!!!! Marcus Brady has the ball!"

"And there is nothing but green grass in front of him!"

"The Forty, the Thirty, the Twenty, Ten, TOUCHDOWN!!!!!!"

Acton Ravenwood threw a beer can against the wall and let loose a sidewinder of cursing not seen from a Satanic High Priest since Blaise Jackson famously dispersed the crowd in front of the Second Satanic Temple. The other Cramner fans in the luxury box, many of them members of Ravenwood's congregation, turned their heads as Ravenwood threw another one of the adult tantrums. Granted, a Cramner fan could be forgiven for having a fit right now. Marcus Brady of the Winthrop Buccaneers had picked off David Wojkowski, quarterback of Ravenwood's Red Devils, and taken it the distance to put the underdog Buccaneers up 10 points with half a minute left to go in the Blood Bowl. Ravenwood had thirty dollars riding on this game, which he had given 3-to-1 odds on. Cramner was undefeated with the fifth-rated defense in the country, and Winthrop had a true freshman quarterback that year. How could it happen? Somehow that freshman quarterback, who shit a brick against Georgia, had thrown three touchdowns and Wojkowski had the worst game of his career.

The clock ran out, and it became official. The Blood Bowl, a replica of the ceremonial urn Cranmer and his followers used to gather the blood and organs on the *Charon*, was carried out onto the field and handed over to the Winthrop head coach, who looked directly into the camera, and with a wink of his eye, credited his victory to Jesus Christ. No national championship this year, no trip to Baton Rouge or Pasadena even, and ninety dollars down the tubes.

"Damn it!" Ravenwood cursed. "When does that fan bus get here?"

In frustration, Ravenwood cracked open a bottle of Demon Rum (a local distillery) and proceeded to forgive his team in the only way he could.

CHAPTER SIX

The Second Sunday of Advent, Second Satanic Temple, 10 a.m.
Ravenwood

When you make a deal with the Devil, you're gonna get burned. That is true even when the Devil is a cartoon on the side of a bottle of rum. Ravenwood discovered this as he woke up at his house earlier that morning, with a throbbing headache and scorched throat. Getting too old to be doing this, Ravenwood said to himself. What hurt more, of course, was remembering why he did it. The dark priest took one look at the clay Red Devil figurine on his dresser and threw a shot glass right at it, which shattered on impact. It was Sunday, and he had a job to do.

Ravenwood managed to pull himself into his Toyota Camry XL and drive to the Second Satanic Temple. The temple had 20 rows of pews laid out in a circular shape around the altar, practically identical to what you would find in any church. The only noticeable difference lay in the altar, which was a stake protruding out of the ground where the sacrificial victim was to be tied up in the old days. A podium on the front of the altar, draped in a ceremonial cloth bearing the number 666, stood in front of it, which was used for readings. Ravenwood entered his closet in the back of the temple to change into his ceremonial vestments. Alistair Davis, Delilah Davis's illegitimate son, was already there and changed into his robes. Alistair had the shortened neck, flattened face, and small features of a 24-year-old man with Down Syndrome.

"Hi, father," Alistair said. "How are you this glorious morning?"

Ravenwood reached for the sink and vomited. He then pulled on his traditional black robe, fastened a gold sash around his waist, and dropped a silver chain around his neck, weighed down by an ornate amulet emblazoned with a goat's head. Ravenwood looked in the mirror and doused his grey hairs with water, trying to tame them. Those grey hairs had multiplied over the years and gotten more unruly as they grew in numbers, almost as if they were planning a revolt against his skull.

The opening hymn "My Sweet Lord" by George Harrison, started to play, indicating to Ravenwood that he had better get his ass out there and start walking down the aisle. When Alistair began his term as Ravenwood's assistant, he tried to prevail on Ravenwood to change the music. Black Sabbath, Metallica, and even Depeche Mode. Something dark and horrible. Ravenwood was a child of the 70s, however, and he liked what he liked.

As Ravenwood and Alistair made their way to the altar, the high priest surveyed today's crowd. Most of the temple was filled with tourists who wanted to see a Satanic service. In the first three rows were his actual congregants, a smattering of older Witches who still bothered to go to services, and the Davis family.

Hecate and Delilah Davis sat in the front row, and Bryce and Beth, fraternal twins, sat next to their aunts. Beth, who waved at her cousin, wore a nice Sunday flower dress. Bryce, outfitted in mandatory slacks and a polo shirt, hid his face behind a *Scientific American* magazine in full view of everyone. Hecate could never quite get Bryce to pretend to care about services or do much of anything he did not want to, for that matter, but she elbowed Bryce, nonetheless.

"Could you please try to support your cousin?" she asked sternly.

Bryce flashed a peace sign at Alistair, who smiled and returned the sign. They arrived at the altar. The dark ceremony had begun. The tourist cameras flashed. Ravenwood widened his arms to welcome the congregation to this unholy celebration, and in doing so, split his head open in pain.

"We welcome you to today's services. Please, no flash photography."

Next came the creed, which traditionally stressed the values of Pleasure and Wealth over Virtue, Power over Truth, and Pride over Love. Over the years, passages denying the equality of man and mandating the separation of the races were added by a series of Satanic priests after the Civil War and removed by Grimsley in the 70s. Ravenwood had made his own version.

"Recite we, the Diabolic Creed. There are many Paths to the Ultimate Reality, No One Better than Another. We Reject No One, But Instead Embrace Ourselves. Pleasure and Wealth can Best be Accomplished through Hard Work. Power and Truth are Relative Terms. We Take Pride in Just How Much We Love."

Ravenwood then sent Alistair to do the readings. Originally, the sacrifice called for three

readings from the Greater Book of Solomon the
King, a book of spells by which the Witches would
wish misfortune and misery upon their enemies. By
the 19th Century, curses were reserved purely for the
Yankees and the Freedmen, replaced with a series of
spells for the protection of loved ones. When
Ravenwood started in this job, the curses were
stricken from the Book entirely, and Grimsley
introduced using outside materials. In the present day,
the Book has been completely dispensed with. Alistair
went to the podium with three articles he had
downloaded from the internet: one how-to guide by a
Wiccan in Minnesota instructing the reader how to
make an amulet which warded off evil spirits (Beth
got out a journal and took notes), an interview in the
London Times with Ozzy Osbourne, and, most
importantly, the front page of the *Pandemonium Lament*
detailing last night's game. Ravenwood gritted his
teeth. Time for the sermon.

"Did anyone here catch the game last
night?" he asked. "I mean, not to use a play on words,
but what the hell was that? Would it kill Coach
Phillips to throw the ball on first down? And now the
season's shot. Don't tell me that we're still bowl
eligible. Those bowls are meaningless. Yes, they're
meaningless to the kids, too. Where are we going?
The Tangerine Bowl? The Domino Bowl? Most
important game of his career, and Wojkowski throws
a pick-six with 34 seconds left on the clock. Say
goodbye to the first round of the draft, kid."

Hecate audibly groaned. She had once
told Ravenwood his sermons were more like tangents.
He thought she should be thankful. In previous
sermons, he lectured the crowd about using the trash
receptacles and complained about people not mowing
their lawns. Now he just bitched and moaned about
his football team. He'd grown a lot as a cleric. No one

was paying attention, of course. The tourists used Ravenwood's sermon as an opportunity to walk around the church and take pictures of the stained glass smiling Satans and the votive candles. Bryce flipped through his magazine. Beth pleasantly whistled the Andy Griffith theme song. Delilah beamed at her son, who was always a little embarrassed when she did this in public.

"...I'm writing the athletic department. This is ridiculous. Another season with Coach Phillips and I'm nevah, and I mean nevah, buyin' a ticket again. Damn him. Damn that man. I know I'm in public. Why can't I damn a man during my sermon? Who do you think we worship here?"

And with that, the sermon came to an end. Now came the time for petitions, which Alistair had prepared. The traditional petitions asked for gold, revenge against enemies, and the embrace of beautiful women. The more modern petitions were a little different.

"For marginally increased incomes, we make this exchange."

"For gradual improvements in technology, we make this exchange."

"For top SAT scores and admission to better universities, we make this exchange."

"For hard work and intelligence to be rewarded, we make this exchange."

"For help in our romantic and social life, we make this exchange."

"For the making of a better world without poverty or suffering, we make this exchange."

"That was very nice, dear," Delilah called out. "Your mother loves you."

"Mom!" Alistair yelled. "Not in front of everyone!"

The crowd was awed. Alistair turned a bright shade of red. Another hymn blared out from the speakers: "God Only Knows" by the Beach Boys. As the song came to an end, Ravenwood rose to lead the congregation in prayer.

"Father Below, or Mother, Protect our Loved Ones and Give Us Success in All Our Endeavors, May Our Children only Know Success, and May all who Call us Enemies Come to a Reasonable Settlement and Realize We are Not So Bad to Do Business With, We Give You Thanks for all in the World that is Good that you are Responsible for, Without Taking Anything Away from Other Deities which may Exist."

Ravenwood made up his own version of the Common Prayer. Traditionally, the prayer asked for earthly power and deliverance from virtue, but Ravenwood's predecessor had gotten rid of that dreadful nonsense in the 70s. He was thinking of putting another revision into the Satanic Sacrificial Rites that would move the time to 11 a.m. This would attract more tourism dollars and allow him to sleep in. What tourist would want to visit anywhere at 10 a.m.? And to think Cramner did his rituals at 3 a.m. What were they thinking?

The congregation then started to greet each other while Alistair went behind the altar to fetch the sacrifice. The high priest retrieved the ritual knife from a box underneath the podium. The sacrificial knife had not been needed since 1963, really because bugs, unlike bunny rabbits, can be killed without a knife. Ravenwood still used the knife, the blunt end, to crush the bug, just for the sake of using it. The bug in question was a black palmetto whom Alistair had caught the day before in a Nike shoebox, which he had punched holes in. The stake in the middle of the Altar now only served "as a reminder of how far we have come," as Ravenwood liked to put it. Traditionally, the sacrifice would also make use of the silver urn Cramner used on the *Charon* to make his original sacrifice, desecrating the voyage. However, Ravenwood lost it the year beforehand, and so far, Alistair had not been able to find it either at the Temple or at Ravenwood's house.

And then he lost the bug. Alistair placed it right before him on the podium, but Ravenwood, never too quick with his hands, lost track of it, and the insect scurried away. Alistair ended up crushing it with his foot. Ravenwood cursed under his breath and told his assistant to tie it down to the microphone next time. The aforesaid microphone picked the high priest up, leading to an embarrassing moment where he smiled shyly at the crowd. Delilah was not amused.

"Without my son," she said, standing up and pointing at Ravenwood, "he wouldn't be able to find his car keys!"

"Why does everyone in this family," Hecate asked, "have to make announcements in the middle of services?"

"The Ceremony is finished," Ravenwood intoned. "Flash photography is now allowed. The High Priest and his Assistant will be available afterward for questions. Please visit our gift shop in the adjacent building."

Fr. Ravenwood read the final line of text and called for another hymn. "White Rabbit" by Jefferson Airplane came on, and Fr. Ravenwood and Alistair walked down the aisle as tourists took pictures. As they came to a stop, both of them turned around and greeted the tourists. This was their job, and it paid fairly well. The out-of-towners began asking the typical series of questions.

"Don't you worry about actually going to hell?"

"Not really, never having been there before, I can't say it's that unpleasant, and neither can you," Ravenwood answered.

"What happened to the silver urn? I visited here four years ago. I thought you had a silver urn."

"For all I know," Ravenwood replied, "Wojkowski gave it away last night when he threw that pick."

"Do you feel your traditions have been watered down over time?"

"Of course," Ravenwood responded, "would you have preferred they not be?"

At this point, the congregation, the actual one, kind of, was making its way out, and the crowd turned to them. Hecate led the Davis family out of the chamber. She made sure all of them were smiling, and they would answer questions. *"And that means you, Bryce."*

"Do you worry that your traditions have been degraded?"

"Oh, God no," answered Delilah. "Those poor bunny rabbits. What were we thinking?"

"Do your children enjoy being at the ceremonies?"

All eyes turned to Bryce and Beth, including Hecate, who could give a look that would stop a rhino in its tracks. She had it aimed right at Bryce.

"I don't really believe it," Bryce responded, "but this is what my family does, and I can go along, at least until I graduate. Besides, nothing happens."

"I like being here," Beth replied. "Nothing happens."

While the crowd had swamped the Davis family, Ravenwood and Alistair had made their escape to the backroom to undress. Ravenwood quickly took off his robes and hung them up, as did Alistair. After he was done, Ravenwood thanked Alistair for his time and hoped he had a good Sunday. Alistair stood there.

"How can I help you?" Ravenwood asked innocently.

Alistair just nodded.

"Yes?"

A few moments of bare silence hung over them, and then Ravenwood finally relented. He took out his wallet, removed the ninety dollars he had lost the night before, and handed the cash to Alistair in agreement with the bet they had made on Thursday.

Stranger Meeting Hall, 1 p.m.
Gilbert

When Simon bought the Church, he agreed to hire Gilbert on as the local youth pastor. It wasn't the ideal situation to begin his career in ministry, but he wanted to serve his community. So, after church, he arrived at Room 206 in the Stranger Meeting Hall, ready to begin his calling. Gilbert set up the entertainment center in the room and opened up the packet of prepared materials the ministries sent him. He could admit to being a bit nervous at the beginning of his first day as a youth pastor. This nervousness did not abate when Simon's lower management handed him a series of lesson plans to follow based on arcane statistics he did not understand as he had not been a math major in college. The Strangers Church did not even have a youth group before Simon got there. The Church had

Sunday school, but it ended in the Ninth Grade. Simon's church had a youth ministry backed up by analytics so sophisticated, the Braves could very well have been using them. Gilbert, however, wanted to be a minister to follow in his father's footsteps. Gilbert wanted to do for others as his father had done for him. And now was his chance. As teenagers filed into Room 206, which Gilbert had furnished with bean bag chairs and Christian life posters, he passed out lesson materials from the ministries.

"Hello, guys," Gilbert began, his voice cracking at first. "You all may know me as Deanna's older brother."

Gilbert nodded at Deanna, who had taken the front bean bag right in the center in support of her brother on his first day. Deanna nodded back and gave a smile.

"Today, I begin my life as your youth pastor, which is a great honor. It is always a great honor to be able to serve the Lord. How about you all, do you feel great today?"

The crowd gave a muted sound of vague approval. This is what they were doing today instead of watching football.

"We have a great program, beginning with some media," Gilbert said, popping in the DVD with the ministry approved lesson plan.

Bright blue and yellow colors illuminated the big screen as the audio blared out worship songs so modern sounding that they passed right by guitars and went straight to synthesizers. What came next was a segment of clips from Miles Simon's 'Hour of Power' directed at young people. These clips centered on the 'demonic' dangers of drugs, sex and alcohol, and how God would shield them if they only had faith. Then came on a series of sketches involving various unconvincing actors in their twenties pretending to be teenagers being offered drugs, alcohol, and sex, all of which ended in someone dying after having tried one of these three things. There was one particularly painful sketch (it made Deanna wince) that compared a girl who had sex before marriage to used toilet paper. The video ended with a claymation cartoon portraying a 17-year-old burning in hell for having tried marijuana at a party.

"Well," Gilbert began, as he removed the DVD, "that was…something."

The lesson plan called for a discussion about the DVD.

"Does anyone here have any questions?" Gilbert asked.

"My aunt uses medical marijuana because she has stomach cancer."

"Yeah, and comparing someone to used toilet paper is kind of shitty."

"Okay," responded Gilbert, "those aren't so much questions as they are objections, but well taken."

"Hey, did Moses really kill 3,000 people?"

"Well, that is what it says in the Bible, but that doesn't relate to the DVD," Gilbert answered.

"Moses killed 3,000 people? To hell with the DVD!"

Gilbert could see this sentiment spread throughout the group, so he decided to step out in front of the parade and lead it. As the youth group began to mutiny, Gilbert held up his hand and then gathered up the Lesson Plan material, depositing it into the wastebasket.

"To answer the question, yes, the Bible says that Moses killed 3,000 people after the Golden Calf. Back in the Bronze Age people used violence to solve a lot more problems than we do today. This doesn't mean God approves of mass murder. It means God meets people where they are, like a kindergarten teacher who holds up her left hand to teach five-year-olds what their right hand is. Also, keep in mind that in ancient mythic literature, numbers tend to get exaggerated, so he may have only killed like 50 people in reality," Gilbert explained.

"No, I don't think that women who have sex before marriage are like used toilet paper, but sex does inevitably lead to emotional connection even with protection, so I would advise waiting until marriage just as a way of protecting yourself emotionally. Medical marijuana is a complicated issue. The Bible condemns drunkenness but does not require you to abstain from all alcohol. I don't think your aunt's doing anything wrong, but no one in this room thinks that people smoking weed in their basement all day are living productive, meaningful lives."

Someone else raised their hand. Gilbert nodded his head.

"Why did the Elders sell the Church?"

"Miles Simon offered a lot of money to the Elders that can be used to help the community," Gilbert explained, "and it has been. The money has been put in a trust. My father didn't agree with them, and I don't like the decision too much either, but it was theirs to make."

"Is it true that if you give money to the church God will reward you?"

"Not necessarily, and not necessarily in this lifetime," Gilbert responded.

"Then why does our new pastor keep saying that on television?"

"I don't know," Gilbert replied. "He will be explaining his beliefs to us and everyone watching the broadcast every Sunday."

Gilbert had started saying things that could get him fired on his first day if the people at headquarters found out, and he was aware of this, so he looked up at the clock and saw that 2 p.m. was upon them. Noting that the lesson was over, he asked if anyone had any other questions. The entire youth group headed for the door, and Gilbert breathed a sigh of relief that his first lesson was over. Two people remained behind: Deanna and a single boy with brown hair and soft features.

"Well, that was my first day and I may be fired if those comments get out," Gilbert said. "But other than that, how did I do?"

"Honestly, I would have ditched the video," Deanna answered, pointing to the boy, "but you might want to talk to this guy."

"Yeah, my name's Aaron," the boy introduced himself. "I'd like to speak with you privately."

"That's fine," Gilbert responded. "Deanna, could you excuse us?"

Deanna left the room, and Aaron watched her leave. Once she was gone, Aaron spoke.

"You know Theo, right?" Aaron asked.

"Yes, what about him?" Gilbert asked.

"I hear that he can hypnotize people," Aaron whispered. Gilbert could tell he was probing for something in particular.

"Yes, he can affect people, though he does not like to do this today," Gilbert explained. "He did it in the past when he and my father were in a jam, and before that for all we know."

"So, I have heard he can change certain things about you," Aaron said.

Gilbert hated engaging in this kind of talk, which ran around and around without actually getting at anything, so he decided to cut it short.

"Okay, I think I get where this is going. You are asking if Theo can make you straight," Gilbert guessed, lowering his voice. "You're having homosexual feelings and you want to know if Theo can make you straight because there are rumors that he can."

Aaron looked around to make sure no one was listening to them. Once he was sure they were alone, the boy nodded his head.

"No, Theo can't make you straight," Gilbert answered. "He can make you feel straight temporarily, but it always wears off over time. He did it once for someone in the congregation. It didn't last."

"But it will work for a while?" Aaron asked.

"For a very short time. My father asked him not to do it again, because the last guy he did it for started coming back to him for a 'boost' every week. That was back in the 1990s."

"Well, what am I supposed to do?"

"I can't answer that question for you. Traditionally, the faith hasn't had many kind things to say about homosexuality. Attitudes are changing. I have heard some people say sexuality fluctuates over time, but I wouldn't presume that any 'cure' will ever exist. I can say that God did not create you to be miserable and that He is allowing you to feel this way to bring about some greater good. Pray about it. This just may be a cross you have to bear. All of us have a cross we have to bear."

"You're positive this won't work?"

"Theo won't do it anymore. He regrets that he did it the last time."

Aaron hung his head. He gave a small cry underneath his breath. Aaron stood up and left the room, with Gilbert close behind.

Econosuites, 7 pm
Calvin

"Theo won't do it anymore. He regrets that he did it the last time."

Calvin turned off the recording and absorbed what he had just heard. Per his instruction to find 'dirt' on MacDonald, he decided to put a recording device in the youth group classroom earlier that morning while the good Christians were at church. Sure enough, the Orangeman's son, in imitation of his father, wasn't a team player, and they now had a sufficient excuse to fire his ass. But the recording delivered so much more. So, this Theo character could hypnotize people? Very interesting. Almost like an old movie character. Calvin jotted down some notes and underlined the last bit: 'Vampire?'

CHAPTER SEVEN

The Second Week of Advent, Monday, Dave's Chop Shop, Noon
Calvin

"Of course, Theo's a vampire! Were you born yesterday?"

The trucker laughed at Calvin's seemingly ludicrous question, and so for that matter did the rest of the people in the restaurant. The waitress put her fingers in her mouth to make mock teeth. Calvin would have thought this was some kind of secret.

"Yeah, technically it's a secret," said the black man sitting next to the trucker. "I mean, the rule is that you don't find out until you've lived here for five years unless Theo tells you early."

"Well, Theo hasn't told me," Calvin said.

"Have you bothered to ask him? Because I bet he would!"

"Hell, half the time he poses for tourists!"

The waitress took out a picture and gave it to Calvin. It showed a little girl elevating above a chair in mid-air.

"Theo plays Santa Claus every year at the Stranger church. This is my granddaughter sitting on his lap last year. You can keep that one. I've got a hundred copies."

"So, Theo doesn't appear in photographs?" Calvin asked.

"Doesn't appear in photographs or on camera," the trucker repeated. "Gosh, that would have helped the Ze'ev back in '92."

"Doesn't eat food," yelled the cook from the back. "God knows I've tried."

"He turns into a reindeer for Christmas every year," the waitress said. "I've seen him become a dog too."

The locals, a weird mashup of Halloween clichés and redneck, continued to chime in. Truckers sporting hats with demon heads overlaid on Confederate flags talked about how Theo could mud with the best of them. The cook, a Jewish man, said if you had to spend a night as a wolf, best do it with Theo. The waitresses moaned about how he never seemed available for a date.

"I've seen him become a bird."

"Yep, he walks up walls too."

Calvin furiously took notes while everyone just shouted out facts about Theo, who was a real man about town.

"He's got deep pockets, too. Donates thousands of dollars to those missions the Strangers run."

"There's a real vampire in the world," Calvin said. "How do people outside of this town not know about it if there's no real attempt to keep it secret?"

"Well, no one's trying to expose him, really. Why would they?"

Rental Office, 5 p.m.
Calvin

"A vampire? Son, you've got to be fucking with me," Simon spat.

Calvin called his father to tell him that he might have some dirt on MacDonald. The preacher man sounded skeptical over the phone, and he wasn't less skeptical in person.

"You don't have to take my word for it," Calvin insisted. "Let me take you back to the Bar-B-Que joint to have dinner. I'll pay. You can go there and ask those same people, and they'll tell you. Let me show you the picture."

Calvin took out the picture of a levitating girl.

"That's Photoshop," Simon said. "We could create something like that with the right technical people. We probably already have them."

"Then check this picture," Calvin begged, taking out the picture of Theo he had taken in the crypt.

"Look for what, nothing? Calvin, you're grasping at straws here."

"Mr. Simon, does this building have a receptionist?"

"Yeah, she's out in front."

"Come with me, please."

Calvin led Simon out of the office and to the receptionist desk, wondering why he took this job. He then remembered that his father offered to eventually give him a share if he didn't go blabbing to the media about the world-famous televangelist having an affair with a Florida stripper. Not the same share his legitimate children would get, but worth a lot of money regardless. The receptionist, a thin woman with black hair, wore a tight black dress and pale makeup like she was hosting some horror show later that night.

"Ma'am, can I ask if you know Theo?" Calvin asked.

"You mean the vampire guy?"

"You put her up to that, Calvin," Simon said.

"You mean like a bribe?" the receptionist asked. "No, I need this job. If I screwed with customers, I could be fired. My boss already makes me wear this ridiculous get-up to satisfy out-of-towners."

"Okay, Calvin," Simon relented, "so, what if he is a vampire? You make it sound like no one cares. That's the opposite of dirt, Calvin. Dirt is defamatory, and it's supposed to be hidden."

"Mr. Simon, *he can influence people*," Calvin pleaded. "I overheard MacDonald's son say he can turn gay people straight temporarily. He could do other things."

"Like what?"

"Like, convince people to give you money. Donations would skyrocket. People would buy mineral supplements. Power crystals. We might even move that modern mineral cure that's basically bleach."

"Huh," Simon grunted. He sat down on a couch in the lobby and rubbed his chin. After five minutes, he made a decision.

"Approach him and tell him I want to speak with him," Simon proposed, "when you can find him."

"Shouldn't be a problem," Calvin said, "he doesn't exactly keep a low profile."

Tuesday, Pandemonium Lofts, 4 p.m.
Deanna

Beth came with Deanna to the north side of town after school to help Theo shop for apartments, as the two would always find an excuse to waste an afternoon together. Beth tried to convince the Irishman to give the South side of the Line of town a look. Homes are a little nicer there. The crime rate is lower. Internet service is much better. But Theo insisted on being on the Stranger side of the Line near Deanna and MacDonald, who was getting older. They found an apartment building on the far western side of town called Pandemonium Lofts, the choice of the hipster millennial, close enough to the rectory in case he needed to be there. They were offering a two-bedroom open floor space with a high ceiling. Theo had problems understanding the necessity for all of these amenities. He had been living in church basements for about four centuries.

"Washer, dryer, what do people do with their time with all of these automatic devices?" Theo asked. "And this box."

"Microwave, Theo," Deanna said. "It's called a microwave."

"Well, what would I use it for?"

"You might want to heat the cow's blood before you have some," Beth suggested. "Or cool it down in the fridge."

"The other box," Theo said. "I just want the cheapest place available."

"Oh no, you aren't living that way anymore," Deanna insisted.

Deanna turned to the landlord, who was showing them around and asked what the utilities cost for units like this. He gave her an answer of about $200 altogether. The rent would be around $1,000 monthly.

"I don't know how it got so expensive," Theo sighed. "In the 1640s, all our landlord asked of us was some bushels of wheat and a young calf every harvest season."

"I didn't think Theo was hard up for money," Beth said.

"He's not," Deanna replied, a little peeved. "We'll take it."

Deanna forced Theo to sign the lease, utility agreement, and a series of other papers. Even after 250 years of literacy, his handwriting was still chicken scratch. He tried to get by with an X on the signature line, but Deanna made him do it again the right way. Theo was officially a lessee.

"Theo, doesn't it feel good to be away from that dark, drab crypt?" Beth asked.

"Maybe," Theo replied. "Give me some time. I only now realized that my body has changed enough to allow me to sleep anywhere I want."

"And go into a church," Deanna interjected. "Dad's last service is Christmas Eve."

"You would like me to attend?" Theo asked.

"He'd like to see you there," Deanna answered. "I haven't asked, but I'm sure of it."

They walked out to the car to find a young man in a dark suit waiting for them. Theo and Deanna both recognized this man.

"Hey, don't you work for Simon?" Theo asked.

"Yes, my name is Calvin Lucas," the young man answered. "Mr. Simon has a proposition for you, Theo."

"I think I've heard this proposition before from a thousand others," Theo replied. "I've rejected them, but I'll always hear a man out. Tell Simon I do my business at night, so I'll meet him tomorrow night."

"Very well, I will tell him that," Calvin said. "He'll be very pleased."

"I'm sure."

Calvin left them having delivered the message. They all got into the car, and then Beth had a suggestion.

"It's still early. We could stop by *Eye of Newt* and pick up some supplies."

Deanna rolled her eyes. Another magic shop. Beth would buy all kinds of junk to ward off

'evil spirits.' She hated watching con artists take Beth's money.

"Actually, Beth, I'm broke and Theo would probably like to get home," Deanna said.

"Oh, you're not broke," Theo said, handing Deanna a bill. "I owe you $50 for looking after me when I got drunk on Saturday. Come to think of it, I see Tom's Tavern across the street. Good location for an apartment, Beth. And there's still thirty minutes of daylight left. Why don't you girls go enjoy yourselves and I'll go enjoy myself."

With that, Theo exited the car and walked over to the Tavern to repeat last Saturday's sins. Deanna was left with no excuse.

"Let's go shopping!" Beth exclaimed.

Eye of Newt, 5 p.m.
Deanna

Some Christians would be afraid of the skulls and dark candles which decorated this place. Growing up in Pandemonium, Deanna was really more annoyed by them. This was the cheesiest stuff she could imagine, yet her best friend constantly bought it. Beth, for some reason, had this fear of evil spirits. Half of her room in the guest house was, in some cultural tradition, used to ward away demons, ghosts, and poltergeists: votive candles, holy water, a dream catcher hanging above her bed, wind chimes, burning sage, and a Pentagram made in salt posted to the door.

"Hello," the cashier greeted, "welcome to *Eye of Newt*. Please let me know if I can help you find anything."

"Do you have anything to ward off evil spirits?" Beth asked.

Deanna groaned.

"Our specialty," said the cashier, who beckoned them to the back.

"I'm sure it is," Deanna muttered under her breath.

And, indeed, the store did have a wide variety of amulets, salts, rings, enchanted rugs, and other icons to ward off ghouls of every variety. The cashier offered to show her some Japanese wind bells. There were also ocular paints to deflect the evil eye. The cashier took a Roman amulet out of the drawer (one of the top-line items), but she put it away when Beth blushed at its phallic shape. Deanna tried to pull Beth away.

"And would you like to buy anything?" the cashier asked Deanna.

"No, thank you. I'm a Christian. I don't believe in this stuff," Deanna responded, rolling her eyes.

"In that event, let me introduce you to our mini-gargoyle," the cashier pushed on, taking out a small figurine of an ugly, bat-like creature. "Contrary to popular belief, gargoyles are not representations of demons. During the Middle Ages, Christians would decorate churches with these ugly figures, thinking they would scare demons away."

"And it fits in your purse," Beth said. "I'll take it."

The mini gargoyle was $50. Beth forked the money over. The cashier placed the mini gargoyle into a brown paper bag, which Beth tucked away in her purse. As they left the store, Deanna felt the need to say something.

"Beth," she whispered into Beth's ear, "that woman was just trying to take your money."

"Yes, it's a shop," Beth replied, rolling her eyes. "That's how that works."

"Yeah, but most shops sell something of value."

"This has value to me!"

"Beth, there are no evil spirits!"

"You sound like my brother," Beth groused.

"A broken clock is right twice a day," Deanna shot back. "I don't know why you buy this stuff."

"I know, you don't, and you can't understand," Beth said. "And maybe I don't want to be around you right now."

Beth walked out of the store without looking at Deanna and hurried away before Deanna could say anything.

Wednesday, Davis Plantation House, 5 p.m.
Bryce Davis

"A mini gargoyle," Bryce chortled.

Gary, his Ze'ev friend with brown hair and freckles, snickered along with him. Bryce's sister had bought yet another stupid piece of garbage. The two of them fell to the ground with merriment. They had to get off the floor quickly as there were too many wires on the concrete blocks below them to sit comfortably. They were standing in Bryce's bedroom/laboratory wearing dirty lab coats, and before Bryce made the above wisecrack, they had been creating a potato launcher/rail gun using bits and pieces he had picked up from the junkyard and the dumpster behind the electronics store. Bryce's room was a mishmash of the various projects he had started (and occasionally finished). Beakers, burners, antennas, wires, keyboards, and monitors lay strewn about the room, making it difficult to walk. Bryce slept on an old operating table in the center of the long, dimly lit basement. Hecate and Delilah had given up trying to get Bryce to clean his room, just so long as no important visitors saw it, they didn't care.

"Ohhh…." Bryce moaned. "Well, that was fun. Let's get back to work."

Working was a relative term. Gary had a real job with the bus tour company, and Bryce worked in his aunts' funeral home business, but this was their life's work: making absurd devices for pure entertainment. Bryce did most of the work building the rail guns, while Gary supervised him. Supervising was not a relative term. Bryce had a great scientific and technical mind, but the things he put it to were a little bizarre. For instance, Bryce built a remote-controlled drone at the age of 14. Gary used it to spy on the neighbor girl getting undressed. Bryce created a mini-EMP when he was 15. Gary would knock out the vice principal's computer to erase his permanent record. Last year, Bryce, after obtaining fissionable material from a Syrian man online, built a primitive atomic bomb in his lab/room. Gary made him take the thing apart, because good God, "why the hell would you build such a thing in the first place?" Gary yelled this at the top of his lungs when he saw the bomb, and Bryce's aunts overheard. This was when Bryce's aunts told Gary he had to supervise. It was to make sure Bryce didn't make another atomic bomb.

Today, Bryce was making a railgun. Or rather, he was perfecting a railgun. The first few times they tried it; the gun wouldn't fire. Now, Bryce was sure he had worked the kinks out.

"Time to test it," Bryce said.

Bryce handed one of the railguns to Gary, and they both walked up the stairs out of Bryce's lab/room and out the front door of the plantation house. Bryce and Gary strolled to the back of the house, facing the woods. Those woods were the last forest in Pandemonium, largely due to their position on the south side of the island. The Strangers had long ago felled the trees on the northern side of the island as part of their shipbuilding industry in the colonial era, and the forests never come back after you pave over them. Bryce led Gary to a big cypress behind the house. It looked like it could collapse with a good knock.

Bryce raised the gun and looked down the sights. He aimed squarely at the trunk of the cypress, fully expecting to strip the bark off. Bryce squeezed the trigger and fired the potato at the tree. For a split second, the potato flew towards the tree in mid-air, leaving an orange streak across the boys' eyes. Then, the projectile impacted with the trunk. It not only stripped the bark but then proceeded to shatter the entire tree into a million splinters, which flew out every which way including into Gary and Bryce's faces. The tree's remains fell towards the house in their direction. Gary and Bryce dove out of the way at the last minute as the burning branches from above fell on Hecate's rose bushes, setting her newly planted garden on fire.

"Oh, shit," Bryce said.

CHAPTER EIGHT

The Second Week of Advent, Wednesday, Charleston, South Carolina, New Stranger Church Offices, 8 p.m. Theo

Theo was real impressed by Simon's office. He'd never seen any preacher with an office like this. Nice leather sofas in the lobby. Widescreen televisions. Dark wood and glass on the walls. Theo had not been in business in forever, but he remembered what those businesses used to look like. Nothing like this. Now granted, he found it odd that an office for a church didn't have any crosses or bibles or things like that. I could have entered this building back in the old days, Theo mused to himself. Simon had framed pictures of himself on the cover of magazines. Huge desk, Theo could have slept on it. A large selection of managerial liquor. Remembering the turn of the nineteenth century when protestant preachers talked about demon rum, Theo couldn't help but smile. And there was the man himself. Theo knew the type. If one of his employees came in here, he would be on the phone for 30 minutes just to prove how important he was. But the minute Theo came in, it was all lovey dovey.

"You must be Theophilus," Simon greeted. "Come in, come in."

"Yes, that is me," Theo introduced himself. "You wanted very badly to speak with me."

"I did. I have a business proposition for you."

"Let me guess. Three shows a day. I walk on walls. Turn into a dog. Lift massive heavy objects with a single hand. And then I pose for pictures afterward."

"You sound like you've heard these before. I wouldn't waste your time with something like that."

"So, what are you wasting my time with?"

"From what I hear, you can exert certain influences over other people. Make them believe things they normally wouldn't believe. Make them do things they normally wouldn't do."

"And what do you plan to do with that power?"

Simon laid out his plan. Theo would appear on his television show and use his unique powers of persuasion to convince the crowd and the viewers at home to increase their contributions. Rather than using paid actors for faith healing, who constantly threatened to write tell-all books, Theo would simply hypnotize the crowd into believing that faith healings had occurred. Theo would also convince Simon's audience to buy tapes, books, trinkets, and herbal supplements. Finally, if he was amenable to it, he would use his powers on zoning boards, the IRS, and state attorneys general to grease the legal process for Simon's business.

"And for this," Simon concluded, "I would make you a 50% partner."

"So, you think that using my powers to convince people to hand over money has never occurred to me in over 400 years?" Theo asked.

"But you don't have the television network I do."

"That's the flaw in your plan, Simon. I don't appear on camera."

"At the very least, it will work in person though, and you should see how many people I can pack inside that church."

"This is where I will have to cease being polite," Theo answered, firmly. "Usually when someone proposes something like this, I stick to telling them it won't work. Here, maybe that would work, but I won't do it. I think your proposal is a scam, which I will not be part of. Simply put, I would not use my powers to persuade people to buy false herbal supplements, or give you the extra $1,000 they have stashed in their pillow."

"Okay, so the carrot doesn't work," Simon said. "I'll bring out the stick. If you don't agree to do this, I'll fire Gilbert MacDonald."

"This is between me and you, Simon. You leave Gilbert out of this."

"Not the way it works my friend. Play ball or Gilbert's job is gone."

"I'm afraid Gilbert will have to find another job. I'm not doing it, Simon."

Theo then walked out on the balcony of the office, turned into a bird, and flew away.

Thursday, New Stranger Church Offices, 10 am
Gilbert

Theo explained Simon's proposal to Gilbert that night. It didn't take long for Gilbert to decide the appropriate course of action. Using the old computer in the Stranger Church office, he typed up a resignation letter in the middle of the night, signed it, and then drove to Simon's office to deliver it. Hopefully, this resignation will go smoothly, and both sides could part ways amicably. Hope is a virtue, not a guarantee.

"You can't quit I'm firing you!" Simon screamed.

"Mr. Simon, I don't think it works that way," Gilbert said. "I think if I quit, you can't fire me."

"I'll make sure you never work in this town again!"

"I don't think your bad reference would matter that much to people in this town. Would probably be a mark in my favor."

"Go fuck yourself you fucking shit stain!"

"Mr. Simon, trying to use Theo to hypnotize people into giving you money is not just immoral and illegal, it's also a really bad idea," Gilbert said. "You don't understand how the vampire gaze works. I don't understand it either. Theo comes the closest, but sometimes even he's been surprised by what he can force people to do. It's also addictive. Once someone's been exposed to the gaze, they want more and more of it. Like heroin. That's why Theo doesn't like using it. That's one of many reasons."

"I don't have to listen to this. Security! Security! Escort this man from the building!"

Gilbert left the office, throwing his hands in the air. He didn't wait for security but instead walked out of the office under his own power. There was no point in reasoning with Simon. His father had taught Gilbert that sin rots the mind, and Simon's mind had rotted through.

Pandemonium, Ravenwood Residence, Noon
Ravenwood

Ravenwood straightened the hat. He meticulously buttoned the coat. He dusted the musket and fitted the ancient firearm gently inside the hand of the dummy. He then tightened the belt and saluted the mannequin.

"Col. Davis," Ravenwood said, "reportin' for duty."

Ravenwood had assembled the uniform of one Col. Robert Davis of the C.S.A. It was among his most treasured possessions, right alongside the Confederate money in his safe, the picture of Pope Pius IX that Robert E. Lee kept on his desk, and an autographed picture of James Baskett in costume and character on the set of *Song of the South*. This was how he enjoyed his free time, amongst his tokens of nostalgia. Ravenwood looked forward to spending a full day engaged in his latest fantasy.

And then the phone rang. Ravenwood groaned and picked it up.

"Ravenwood, where is my fucking curse?!" Simon yelled. "You promised me a curse!"

"The curse is comin'," Ravenwood promised. "I couldn't do it last week. Too hungovah. I'm staying sober this week par-tick-que-lar-lee for the occasion."

As he said this, Ravenwood lifted a glass of bourbon to his lips and sipped. He only woke up an hour ago, so he would call this an eye-opener.

"This better be worth the wait," Simon threatened.

"It'll be worth it, Simon," Ravenwood assured him, taking a rabbit cage out from under his bed. "I'm pullin' out all of the stops."

Simon hung up on the other end. Ravenwood leered at the rabbit inside the cage and showed off his buck teeth. They'd be bringing back the 1960s this week.

Friday, Davis Guest House, 5 p.m.
Deanna

Deanna drove to the Davis residence to beg for forgiveness. She automatically turned from the main path to the guest house Beth lived in. For some reason, Beth ran from the main building when she was six and refused to go back. Her aunts just let her live in the guest house, which was an American Foursquare, cozier than the big plantation house. It even seemed to smile at Deanna as she approached it.

Deanna did not bother to knock on Beth's door as she entered. It was her best friend who lived here, and Deanna was accustomed to coming and going. Beth was watching a pre-recorded episode of *Mr. Rogers' Neighborhood* in the first-floor bedroom, which is odd for a girl of 18, but Beth consumed an episode practically every day. She said it calmed the nerves. Deanna knocked on the frame of the bedroom door.

"Hi, Beth, can we talk?" Deanna asked.

"Oh, hi Deanna," Beth responded. "Yeah, we can talk."

"I need to apologize for what I said on Tuesday. I didn't respect your beliefs, and that was wrong."

"It's okay, we all make mistakes. If you don't feel like shopping for that stuff with me, I can just go alone. Then we can shop for clothes and music."

"I don't know Beth. I feel like we actually need to talk about this stuff. I mean, look at this room."

Deanna pointed to the Pentagram made from holy salts on the door, the dream catcher above her bed, the roman candles, and even the mini gargoyle on her desk.

"I have Christian stuff as well," Beth pleaded. "I bought this rosary once that the girl behind the counter said was blessed by the pope."

"I'm not worried about black magic," Deanna continued. "I'm worried about people using your beliefs to take advantage of you. I mean, if you're concerned about evil spirits, maybe you should tell your aunts you don't want to go to the Satanic rites anymore. If you don't find that too forthright for me to say so."

"I don't, but I also don't think the Satanic Rites are the problem," Beth mused, absentmindedly looking off into the distance. "I've never seen any evil spirits there."

"Well, no, I would expect not," Deanna replied, raising an eyebrow.

"I accept your apology, Deanna," Beth said, her face suddenly turning a bright shade of red. "Now we can move on to having fun here while everyone else is having that reception for the new priest."

"I remember that. Is that tonight?"

"Yeah, my aunts are hosting in the plantation house."

Davis Plantation House
Gabe

Gabe approached the front door of the plantation house and knocked. He remembered that the Davis sisters were Witches, so he was a little surprised to find Christmas lights hung up on the top of the house. Delilah Davis answered the door, wearing a pair of soft felt antlers and a Christmas sweater.

"Happy Holidays, father," she greeted. "Your reception will double as the community's Christmas party."

"Oh, do you celebrate Christmas?" Gabe asked as he took off his coat.

"Traditionally, we celebrated the winter solstice," Delilah explained, taking the coat, "but this is America and the pressure to assimilate is strong."

Yes, yes, it is, Gabe thought, as he walked into the living room. Hecate and Delilah had decorated the room with silver tinsel and branches of holly. They even put a tree in the center with an unironic angel on top. Hecate stood near the tree on a ladder hanging stockings and ceramic balls. Gabe noted that Pastor MacDonald was already present, so the priest took his seat next to him.

"Good to see you again," Gabe greeted.

"Good to see you as well," Pastor MacDonald replied. "Fr. Tim was buried in Charleston by his family last Sunday."

"May His eternal light shine upon him."

Delilah and Hecate both lowered their heads in a moment of silence.

"Oh, I assume you would like a drink, father," Delilah said. "BRYCCEEE!!!!"

A male teenager with blonde hair wearing a waiter's uniform came into the room.

"Could you see if Fr. Gabe here would like a glass of wine?" Delilah asked.

"Why do you make me wear this?" Bryce muttered under his breath.

"I'll take a glass of the red," Gabe ordered like a customer at a restaurant.

"Pour him a merlot, Bryce," Delilah commanded, like a field sergeant talking to a private.

Bryce poured Gabe a glass of dark red wine.

"Father, this is my nephew," Delilah said.

"Are you a Witch as well?" Gabe asked.

"No, I'm a rationalist, though some prefer the term Bright," Bryce replied. Delilah elbowed him in the ribs. Next, the thick, dark-haired man Gabe met in his backyard walked into the room. Theo offered Gabe his hand.

"Miss Smith and her parents appreciate the use of the Rectory, Father. They've spoken with the Ze'ev about Kimberly spending full moons with their community, as they generally know how to deal with it."

"Glad I could help."

"Theophilus is the only baptized Roman Catholic in Pandemonium," MacDonald said. "Though I have tried to drag him away from the Church of Rome."

"I haven't been to Mass in years," Theo sighed, shaking his head.

"Well, there is always time to start again," Gabe offered.

Theo appeared to think about this for a minute.

"Well, I used to say I would burst into flames, but recently I learned I haven't got that excuse. I'll take some time to think about that."

***

"Fr. Gabe, Rabbi Maharam."

Rabbi Barry lowered the ancient teacher onto the couch next to the priest. He was a small man who used to be much larger, now weighed down by age, though it could be his extremely long, white hair that caused his back to curve, given how much of it there was. Maharam weakly grasped the arm of the chair. Gabe could see that his joints were filled with arthritis, as they were inflamed.

"Father, thank you for providing shelter to Ms. Smith," the old rabbi said. "We met with her and her parents on the last Shabbat. She was a very shy girl who must have been truly embarrassed to wake up in a strange place naked."

Gabe had to lower his head toward Maharam's mouth to hear him. The room had filled up quickly since the young priest arrived, and now the plantation house buzzed with energy.

"I'm happy I could help," Gabe replied. "Admittedly, I was so shocked I really couldn't refuse. I had not heard of the Ze'ev before I came here. It must be difficult living with your...condition."

"I was told as a boy it was a gift from the Lord," Maharam reminisced, fiddling with his beard. "What gift from the Lord is not also a burden? And what burden is not also a gift?"

Maharam then closed his eyes and dozed off for a second. Rabbi Barry reached over in concern, but Maharam came back to.

"Forgive me, father," the ancient teacher requested, smiling at the ironic phrase. "I may not be able to stay long."

"Of course," Gabe replied. "Is it tiring? Transforming?"

"Not at all," Maharam assured, winking at the priest. "I usually get my best sleep as a wolf. Of course, now, I'm allowed to sleep in the living room and not the yard. As the years piled on, I became an inside dog. Barry, please take me home. All this talk of sleep is tiring."

Barry took Maharam by the hand and lifted him from the couch. Gabe watched as the young rabbi led the old rabbi out the front door. His eyes then turned to Ravenwood, the man MacDonald referred to as the Sorcerer, stumbling around the crowded room, drunk as a skunk, and wearing a confederate uniform. Gabe grimaced at the sight of the man, who had no compunction about making a fool of himself.

"Disgusting, isn't it?"

Gabe turned around and found Pastor Overstreet standing behind him, sipping a glass of merlot. Overstreet had a look of contempt aimed at Ravenwood. His contempt was less angry and more tired.

"Yes, I've tried to get Hecate and Delilah to come to my church for years," Overstreet continued. "Ravenwood treats his shrinking congregation like dirt. Why they put up with it is a mystery to me."

"They don't genuinely believe it?" Gabe asked.

"They believe in tradition," Overstreet answered, "good and bad. I have dealings with them. You see, the Davis family was the largest slaveholders on the island. There are some attendant guilty feelings for that, so they manage a trust where they donate to the Fieldhand community through my church. Why they don't just go to the church they give to, I'll never know. Yes, I do. Hecate likes to keep up appearances. The Davis family always does. They didn't make their aid to the church public until the 70s. Southern society wouldn't like them giving all that money to a black church, and they wanted to fit in. Always trying to serve two masters."

A moment of silence passed between them. Ravenwood found a corner and then fell into it. The sight of him reminded Gabe of something he said at the wake.

"What are the old wives' tales?" Gabe asked.

Overstreet closed his eyes and breathed deeply. Sore subject. Gabe was just about to take back the question when Overstreet answered it.

"Old tales about my people being able to speak with the dead, move objects with their minds, see the past in dreams," Overstreet began. "I've never seen any evidence of it."

The sound of a clinking glass interrupted their conversation. Hecate had decided it was time to call the room to attention. They all turned towards the Christmas tree where she stood, tapping her champagne flute.

"Attention! Attention! Thank all of you for coming," Hecate said. "As you know, we held this reception for the sake of Fr. Gabe, who is the new priest in town. As such, it is only appropriate for us to give him a chance to speak and introduce himself to all of you."

Hecate beckoned to Gabe with a finger. The priest, unable to refuse such a request, walked in front of the tree. The crowd before him clapped.

"Hello, my name is Father Gabriel Strobel. I have been assigned to St. Michael's parish," Gabe began, trying to come up with words to say in this moment. "Thank you for the welcome you've given me. I know I have no parishioners, and that you might be satisfied with your own faith homes, but I invite you to come to mass anyway. The Catholic faith is meant for all members of the human family."

The arrangement of Strangers, Witches, Ze'ev, and Fieldhands that stood before him in the party applauded politely. Gabe saw Ravenwood vomit into the corner, forcing Delilah to go fetch a washcloth. Something about the scene lit a fire in the young priest's mind.

"For the Witch community in particular, I would implore you to stop going to any Satanic services," Gabe continued. "The threat of the diabolic is real and by continuing these ceremonies you could be endangering your own souls and lives, to say nothing of the threat to the community at large."

The room then let out a chorus of chuckles. Gabe turned bright red.

"This is not a laughing matter," he insisted.

The room then burst out into open laughter. Gabe tried to shout over them, but to no avail. The room got ever louder. Finally, the Irishman from the other day spoke up.

"Father, they're laughing at you because Fr. Tim stood where you are standing twenty years ago and said the exact same thing," Theo explained.

"Well, he was right then!" Gabe shouted back.

"Boy," MacDonald began, shaking his head, "you might want to start by asking questions rather than making demands."

"Like what?"

"Like maybe, how likely is this diabolic activity?" MacDonald asked. "All these people have lived in this town their entire life and have never seen that man (pointing to Ravenwood, now completely passed out) do so much as pull a rabbit out of a hat."

"I saw a massive wolf turn into a teenage girl a week and a half ago!"

"That's the Ze'ev," Theo said. "They don't count."

"They don't count?"

Theo just shrugged his shoulders.

"Different thing. They don't count. You were talking about worshiping Satan. They're Jewish. Doesn't count."

"I can't believe you can just compartmentalize like that!"

"Look, father, would you really like to see something supernatural?" Theo asked, a rather wicked smile growing on his face.

"Actually, yes, I would," Gabe replied. "Enough games."

Theo walked towards the wall. He turned his head back to Gabe.

"Father, I think you'll find the games have only begun," Theo cracked.

The Irishman put one foot on the wall. Then he put the other foot on the wall. Then another and another. Theo was halfway up the side of the parlor when Gabe realized he was standing horizontally, in defiance of gravity. The Irishman reached the ceiling and then turned upside-down, walking towards the center of the ceiling, right above the young priest, who cowered below. Then, Theo transformed into a bat in the blink of an eye, and flew down to the floor, right in front of Gabe. Then he turned right back into a man again and said "boo!" Gabe hit the deck.

***

Gabe lay on the floor. His head hurt a little. The young priest began to realize he had passed out. He saw someone offering him a hand and he took it. The hand pulled him up and toward an adjacent room. Only when it laid him in a seat did Gabe realize that MacDonald had been the one leading him.

"It appears you met my friend, Theo," MacDonald said, "and he introduced himself to you in a fairly visceral way."

"That, that man," Gabe stammered. "He changed into a bat."

"Yes, he does things like that, I often apologize for him. Not the politest way to usher you into your tenure in Pandemonium, but it surely gets the job done."

"Impossible. Just impossible."

"I've learned not to use that word. It serves you well outside this city but inside it will do nothing but lead you astray. Now, I knew Theo before I came here. He came with me, but still."

"How did he do that?"

"Theo is, for lack of a better term, a vampire. I met him back in Eire in the 1970s when I was a Presbyterian minister in Ulster. We helped each other out of a tight spot. He came with me when I secured the position here. Don't worry he does not bite, though I can't make the same guarantee for every vampire I've met. And as you can see, his manners could use some improvement."

"Impossible," Gabe repeated.

"Deanna, could you come drive the priest home?" MacDonald called. "He's not feeling well."

CHAPTER NINE

The Second Week of Advent, Saturday, St. Michael's Church, 3 pm
Gabe

MacDonald's very gracious daughter took Gabe home last night. When she asked about protection against evil spirits, he thought at first she was making fun of him, along with everyone else. Eventually, Deanna prevailed upon him that she was serious, or at least trying to make him feel better, so he gave her a St. Benedict Medal.

The following day, Gabe stayed at home and licked his wounds. His first attempt at evangelization in Pandemonium ended in such utter failure, Gabe understood what drove Fr. Tim to kill himself for the first time. A vampire. Right after the Witches with southern twangs and Jewish werewolves, there was an Irish vampire in town. Gabe read the town's Wikipedia page again. Before he came to town, he only skimmed the first half. While Gabe missed the Ze'ev the first time, there was nothing online about an Irish vampire.

Or he would have forgotten it if Theo had not come that afternoon. Gabe heard the church door open, and he came to see who had come to find the great undead man standing in the threshold of the church. Not wanting to speak to the man, or vampire, who just humiliated him in public, the young priest tried to exit the chapel before the Irishman saw him, but unfortunately, Theo spotted him creeping behind the podium.

"Father, I'm here to apologize and ask for forgiveness," Theo began. "Mostly because Atticus made me, but also because I am sorry. Please forgive me. I mean, you have to. You are a priest."

"You are right about that," Gabe answered, coming out from behind a corner. "So, you are a vampire. Does this town have aliens I need to know about?"

"Not yet," Theo replied, with a wry smile. "If you've spent the evening trying to look me up, don't bother. Unlike the Witches and the Ze'ev, I'm a real Pandemonium secret. People who live here for five years get to know my special condition unless I tell them beforehand. Any other questions?"

"I am sure I will have several," Gabe responded, "but I guess I have to ask: Do I have no parishioners?"

"Maybe, you have one," Theo answered, offering Gabe his hand. "But I warn you, I am the greatest sinner the world has ever known."

"So, you need confession."

"Not right now. Maybe later. I don't know."

"Why wait?" Gabe asked. "God will forgive."

"Will I forgive God?" Theo asked. "Haven't been in a Roman church in a while, Father. I just recently learned I can attend without exploding."

"Why don't we work on what I can do first and see if we can get the other part later?"

Gabe motioned toward the confessional. Theo looked at it with a skeptical eye, but then he nodded. Theo walked in, and the priest followed him, closing the door. The Irishman sat in the chair opposite Gabe. This was an open confessional room. A screen would be pointless here.

"Bless me, Father, for I have sinned. It has been 375 years since my last confession."

"Okay," Gabe said. "I'm ready when you are."

"Hmmm..." Theo started. "Well, I think usury is still a sin, and I have this savings account. I think I get 0.4%."

"That's terrible. I get 0.55%, and I have a CD. Is that really it?"

"I can be fairly accused of overindulging in the drink. It's difficult to say you've had too much when you can't get drunk. At night, at least."

"Anything more serious than that?"

"You mean consuming human blood?"

"Well, with you being a vampire...not that I would assume."

"Of course not. Yeah, I used to do that. Last time was 1747. I only ever sucked Redcoats during the occupation. Haven't had a drop since then."

"But you did kill British soldiers. Tell me about that."

"Not much to tell. Tommy pushed us around a lot back then. It's really how this happened to me."

Theo motioned his arms in a way to indicate that 'this' meant his vampirism. Perhaps it was curiosity inappropriate for the confessional, but Gabe pushed a little further.

"You became a vampire to fight the British Empire?"

"In a manner of speaking," Theo said. "Yeah, now that I remember it, that's a pretty big sin, so I should get it off my chest."

"What's a pretty big sin?"

"Selling my soul to the Devil."

"Well…yeah, I would say so."

"Okay, so it's the mid-seventeenth century. I'm an Irish peasant who can't read, and I'm married to a teenager. We have a kid. That's Moira and Sean. Then, the devil himself, that's Oliver Cromwell, Old Ironsides, the git, shows up and says it's Connaught or Hell for us. That New Model Army is there to move us away where we're going to starve to death, and then some bloke named Jack shows up and offers to give me the power to kill them all in exchange for my soul. Turns out he works for the big guy below."

"That's a terrible situation. I'm sorry. You took that deal?"

"Yeah, and I killed those Tans."

"And your village?"

"Died anyway. That's a whole different story."

"Oh, okay, so is that it?"

Theo sighed heavily

"No, I should tell you about Scratch."

"Scratch?"

"The other vampire. Okay, so when those Roundheads showed up, they had a commanding officer. A guy named Abner Shepherd. That's Scratch. I mean, he wasn't Scratch yet, but he's getting there. After I killed his entire company, I threw little Ironsides off a cliff. Didn't drink his blood. Wouldn't have it if he gave it to me. I think that's the end of it, but that guy Jack wants me to kill the Scots the Roundheads were going to settle there on our land. I can't do it. Redcoats, sure, but I've never hurt lasses or wee ones. Not my nature. One day, I walk back to my village and find everyone dead, and that bastard Abner Shepherd is back, only now he's got long teeth and claws, a lot like myself."

"You have claws?"

"Used to. My body changes over time. That's not important. Scratch kills my entire village, including Moira and Sean."

"That's terrible. I'm sorry to hear that."

"Yeah, but I guess the sin is that I go on this quest for revenge. I mean, I do kill Scratch, but it takes me more than 150 years."

"Well, that's wrath, though I'm guessing Scratch was a danger to others."

"Oh, Father, you don't know. This guy would wipe out whole Catholic towns from the history books in old Eire. If you saw how much he hated priests. Jaysus."

"So, you killed this Scratch person, who was another vampire."

"Three times."

"Three times? How do you…"

"You can resurrect a vampire with a particular spell and an act of human sacrifice."

"You didn't…"

"No, father, I didn't kill two people so I could bring Scratch back and kill him three times over. Once was more than enough, thank you."

"Who would…"

"Father, there are some screwed-up people in the world. Last I checked, this was a confession, not a tell-all…"

"But he is dead now?"

"Yeah, I killed him back in Ulster with my friend Atticus and this priest from Rome's vampire-hunting division. If Gilbert and Deanna knew the stuff we were up to back then...."

"The Vatican has a vampire-hunting division?"

"Wow, they don't tell you priests a lot."

"Scratch is gone now? I mean, for good?"

"He could come back, but that would require someone to have his remains in their possession, and I keep those buried under my ottoman at the Stranger Church. I mean, the first time, I didn't think he could come back, so I just left his bones lying around."

There was an awkward silence. Gabe realized that he had crossed a line and showed a little too much interest in Theo's sins.

"Is there anything else?"

"Yes, oh, I guess I should confess to the fornication."

"You had sex outside of marriage?"

"Yes, with my second wife, and this other woman I never married. I think I employed a few prostitutes between them. Then I had a one-night stand in Ulster before I met Atticus. I think that's it."

"What about masturbation?"

"Earlier I confessed to drinking human blood and now you want to talk about wanking?"

"You were confessing your interest rate!"

"Yes, I wank, Father," Theo confessed. "Vampires do that, and I assume so do priests."

"Point taken."

Silence passed between them for a moment.

"Do you have anything else to confess?"

"No, that's it."

"You have to say an Act of Contrition," Gabe said. "It's on a little card."

Gabe handed Theo the aforementioned card, and Theo took the card and read the little prayer. Gabe didn't know how to react. How do you assign a penance for murder, blasphemy, desecration, fornication, and bargaining your eternal soul? He could theoretically tell Theo to go on a pilgrimage to the holy sepulcher or join a monastic order. Then, again, that might frustrate Theo and drive him away from the church. But if the penance was too little, then he might just drift away. Gabe knew that studies showed that religious faiths that required little of their adherents tended to suffer from high turnover. Then, again….

"Alright, father, what's the damage?" Theo asked.

"Two Hail Marys and one Our Father," Gabe answered.

Theo blushed and chuckled a little.

"Alright, father, let me go say them."

Theo left the confessional and knelt in one of the pews. Gabe heard words that were nothing like Latin, so he assumed they must be ancient Gaelic. After a few minutes, the Irishman stopped praying.

"I guess I should offer to say mass now that you have made your confession. It is after five, so we are on the eve of the Sabbath," Gabe offered. "You are cleared for communion."

"Mass sounds good, but I'll hold off on communion, Father," Theo responded. "I'm afraid of what it would do to me."

So, Gabe did say mass. Theo last attended the ceremony before Vatican II, so he couldn't follow it very well. He didn't know when to kneel or when to stand. Gabe hadn't bothered to write a homily, and after that, he couldn't possibly think of one. When it came time for communion, he offered it to Theo again, but Theo only shook his head. When the mass was finished, Theo took Gabe's hand.

"Thank you, Father. I'll be seeing you."

Third Sunday of Advent, Pandemonium, Second Satanic Temple, 10 a.m.
Ravenwood

When Ravenwood explained to Alistair that he would be changing the ritual that Sunday, his assistant seemed nervous. When the high priest described his 'curse' ceremony, Alistair tried to convince him not to do it. It would disturb the older congregants. It would alienate his mother and Aunt Hecate. You would look goofy. Ravenwood decided to persevere.

Admittedly, he expected his 'congregation' to be shocked, as they were set in their ways. They expected the normal greeting (inane), the normal readings (irrelevant), the normal sermon (a waste of time), normal petitions (dull), and a normal sacrifice (insectoid). These expectations were broken when Ravenwood started his procession down the nave of the Temple, wearing a full-length black shawl over his head while carrying a scythe. One of the older congregants took a look at his reaper-like appearance and grabbed his heart in shock. Ravenwood had bought the costume at a Halloween Express. Alistair, following behind him, smiled sheepishly at his mother, who looked at Ravenwood, appalled at the sight. Tubular Bells played over the sound system.

"Welcome to the Black Mass," Ravenwood intoned, attempting to imitate Christopher Lee. "We come together to worship our Dark Lord in an act of profane sacrifice."

Ravenwood raised his hands and began the Satanic Rituals in their original rendition.

Recite we Diabolic Creed. We reject the One God, Creator of the Imperfect Physical World. We Embrace the Spiritual Master, Satan, who Defeated the One God's Fallen Son. We Deny the Physical Resurrection. We deny the Power of the False Spirit. We Place Our Trust in the Lord of Might. We deny the Lord of the Weak. Pleasure and Wealth over Virtue. Power over Truth. Pride over Love.

"Rather old-fashioned," Hecate remarked, "but difficult to complain given what's typically on hand."

"It's obscene!" Delilah screamed.

Ravenwood turned around and approached the Greater Book of Solomon the King, a scene which brought gasps from the audience. He blew dust off the ancient tome and then opened it. The book fell apart in his hands. He then recited a few phrases in Latin. Or he thought it was Latin. Ravenwood never bothered to learn what 'hocus pocus' and 'alakazam' were. After trying to piece the rotted tome back together, Ravenwood then gave his sermon.

"Fellow acolytes of the Dark Lord Below, we now face the greatest threat to our coven of ill repute that we have faced in centuries," Ravenwood began. "I am referring, of course, to the reinvigoration of the Stranger Church by the greatest Christian missionary of the age: Miles Simon."

The only sound in the Temple was Bryce Davis laughing. Hecate slapped him on the thigh to shut him up.

"Under Miles Simon's leadership, the Stranger Church will restore America's Christian heritage, which we have worked so hard over the past few decades to undermine. The drugs, the sex, the lack of faith. It all began here at the Second Satanic Temple (Bryce laughed harder)," Ravenwood said. "Simon has taken the fight right to us. We must strike back with a horrifying curse, which my assistant will provide now."

Alistair approached the podium.

"For Miles Simon to falter in his faith, Deliver to Us Dark Lord."

"For Miles Simon to fail in his business ventures, Deliver to Us Dark Lord."

"For Miles Simon's family to leave him, Deliver to Us Dark Lord."

"For Miles Simon's congregation to abandon him, Deliver to Us Dark Lord."

"For Miles Simon to take ill and die, Deliver to Us Dark Lord."

"My God, what if any of it were to happen," Delilah gasped, "think of the lawsuits!"

"Father Below, damn Miles Simon, damn him to hell!" Ravenwood petitioned Satan.

"And teaching children to curse!" Delilah screamed.

"Aunt Delilah, we're 18," Bryce snorted.

"Oh, damn it, Bryce! Shut up!" Delilah yelled.

The sound system belted out the audio from the rape scene in *Rosemary's Baby*. Alistair cursed under his breath. He'd tried to convince Ravenwood to play this new music. Someone named "Marilyn Manson," but this was not the time to play the music of some bimbo pop star.

"And now, the sacrifice," Ravenwood announced.

Ravenwood reached underneath his chair and retrieved a cage containing a white bunny rabbit. He laid the bunny rabbit on the podium. The bunny tried to jump away, but Ravenwood caught it.

"Lord Satan, We Offer this Sacrifice of One of Your Enemy's Creatures Unto You. Grant us our Wishes and Deliver Us Into Lust!!!"

Ravenwood took a deep breath and then ran the knife against the bunny's throat. Delilah let out a brief scream and looked away. Hecate stared in disbelief at Ravenwood. Beth collapsed. Bryce turned around to find his sister on the floor, having passed out at the sight of the blood pouring out of the bunny rabbit's throat at this moment. Alistair ran down from the altar to make sure his cousin was okay.

"Our Grim Sacrifice is
Completed," Ravenwood finished. "All of you
have made Your Choices. The Dark Lord
Knows His Own. And He Will Collect Those
Who Pledge Loyalty to Him. The Kingdom of
Hell Awaits."

Fifteen minutes later,
paramedics came and took Beth away on a
stretcher. Ravenwood watched as the
ambulance rolled down the street, and then he
felt a hand clamp down on his shoulder. He
turned his head to find Delilah Davis boring a
hole through his head with a glare.

"You'd like to see some witchcraft?"
Delilah asked. "Why don't you see what this
old Witch cooks up?"

Stranger Rectory, 5 p.m.
Deanna

"You just passed out?"
Deanna asked.

"Yeah, it was bad," Beth
moaned. "All that blood."

Beth looked weak, like she had
eaten something that disagreed with her. She
had just gotten out of the hospital earlier that
afternoon. Her aunts sent Beth over to try to
take her mind off it. Deanna sat Beth down
on the couch and reached into her pocket.

"Hey, Beth, I got this for
you," Deanna offered, taking out a thin piece
of silver. "Merry Christmas."

"Oh, what is it?" Beth asked.

"It's a St. Benedict medal,"
Deanna answered. "The new priest told me it
wards off evil spirits."

"Wow! Thanks, Deanna," Beth said, putting the medal around her neck.

They would have started one of their favorite awful movies they had seen a million times, were it not for the fifteen or so men in dark suits busting through the door. Deanna jumped to her feet and tried to stop them.

"What are you doing? What is this?" Deanna asked.

At this moment, Calvin appeared in the doorway.

"Due diligence," Calvin answered. "The church had to turn over all relevant files pertaining to the management of the church within a week of the sale."

"All of those files are in the church office," Deanna said. "You're just trying to find more information on Theo."

"And for the past forty years, Theo has lived in the church," Calvin asserted. "You can call an attorney, but right now, we're taking those files."

The black-suited men ransacked MacDonald's home office. They broke open locked drawers and cabinets, grabbing whatever papers they could find. Beth started recording the scene with her phone. Deanna argued with Calvin.

"You nasty little troll! What do you think this will accomplish? Theo already told you no, and Gilbert has quit!" Deanna yelled.

"Theo told us no when we knew nothing about him," Calvin said. "Let's see how he feels after we do an exposé on him."

CHAPTER TEN

The Third Week of Advent, Monday, New Stranger Church Rental Offices, 3 a.m.
Calvin

Some people might say it was sinful for a minister to force his employees to work until the wee hours of the morning on the Sabbath. One relatively new secretary said just that when they got to midnight, and she was fired when Simon overheard her. Everyone else kept their nose to the grindstone and pushed forward, sifting through all of MacDonald's papers and notes. Calvin, nearing exhaustion, flipped through another ancient folder of church bulletins and sermon notes, trying to find something, anything he could on Theo. After burning through that end, he tossed that folder aside and turned to a notebook. Nothing but notes on the Institutes of the Christian Religion.

"Come on, someone has to find something about Theo," Simon demanded. "I won't take no for an answer. Has anyone checked this guy's personal diary?"

"Wasn't in the take, sir!"

"Why the hell not?!" Simon yelled.

This process of searching MacDonald's voluminous records over and over failed to produce any evidence of Theo other than his name being associated with the annual Stranger Christmas celebration. Calvin opened another box of files and took out one packet and binder after another until a very old folder caught his eye. The ancient file smelled of dust, and its edges cracked at Calvin's touch. The tab at the very top bore the words "Scratch Evidence." A cassette tape fell out of it, labeled "Holy Trinity Church, Clifton Street, Belfast 1979." Calvin grabbed the tape and opened the folder. Inside, he found some notes concerning Theo, along with another, less benevolent bloodsucker.

"Mr. Simon," Calvin announced. "I found something about Theo."

"Great! Let me see it!" Simon demanded.

"There's more, though," Calvin said, handing Simon the case file.

Simon flipped through the file, first quickly, then slowly. When he came to the end, a broad smile grew on his face.

"Very good, my son," Simon said. "In you, I am well pleased."

Stranger Rectory, 9 a.m.
MacDonald

MacDonald rummaged through his office, in the vain hope that Simon had not gotten his hands on *that file*. The case file he maintained on Scratch, however, was nowhere to be found. A flood of despair welled up within him.

"Have you found anything?" MacDonald asked, seemingly to thin air.

Mist seeped out of all the drawers and cabinets in the room, from between books on the shelf, and from the large chest on MacDonald's floor. The mist gathered in the middle of the room and then formed into the shape of a man. Theo emerged from the mist and shook his head.

"Nope, they've got it," Theo said. "If they don't already, Miles Simon Ministries will know the existence of Scratch fairly soon."

"Good Lord," MacDonald sighed, "I should have burned it when the church was sold."

"Why bother keeping it?"

"I wanted there to be a record of our ordeal in the event Scratch was resurrected. Same reason I kept my war chest."

MacDonald nodded toward an old chest against the wall that Theo knew to contain spare ammunition, guns, and explosives leftover from their encounter with Scratch in Belfast during the Troubles. Thankfully, Simon's minions had not seen fit to bring a lock pick with them, and the chest was too heavy to lug away.

"There's nothing for it now, we have to move the remains," MacDonald said. "We can't risk Simon resurrecting Scratch."

"Why would Simon resurrect Scratch? The first thing the old Devil would do is cut Simon's head off," Theo said. "If Simon has your old notes, surely he knows that."

"That's how a rational man would think, but greed makes people stupid. Simon's already tried to convince you to scam his congregants, so he's got the idea that he can make money from the vampire's gaze."

"Yeah, I suppose that underestimating Simon's greed is not a safe bet. Meet me in the crypt at midnight, and we'll move the bones."

"Where to? No one in this town knows about Scratch but us."

"Okay, you know how I went in on Saturday to apologize to that priest?" Theo asked. "Well, this is a long story...."

Tuesday, St. Michael's Church, 1 a.m.
Gabe

Theo had called Gabe the day before to ask if they could bury someone at the church. Gabe told him it would be allowed if that person were a Catholic or married to a Catholic.

"Oh, he's neither," Theo replied. "He might even suck you dry if you suggested as much, but we think you should make an exception here, Father. Call it a favor for an acquaintance of mine. I told you all about him last Saturday."

Gabe didn't protest after that. He was fairly certain the bishop would forgive him if the bishop cared about what happened in this town at all. He had no parish, but at least he could serve some purpose. Theo told Gabe they were planning to do this at night, to avoid suspicion. The priest stood at the entrance to the church, shivering in the pouring rain in December. Pastor MacDonald drove up to the church in a long, ancient station wagon, with the back seats folded down. There appeared to be an old wooden coffin in the back. Theo was nowhere to be found until a bird landed on the top of the station wagon and transformed into a man.

"There's a spot that was intended for a graveyard around back," Gabe said, cold rain dripping off his nose. "There were never any parishioners, so there's plenty of space."

"I think we need to bury the screw in the church," MacDonald answered, getting out of the car in a raincoat. "I'd prefer to have a locked door between those bones and the general public. Also, I've always felt a little safer with Scratch buried under consecrated ground."

Gabe, not one to argue, opened the twin doors that marked the entrance to the church. On the inside, there was a very standard Catholic church decorated in Advent colors.

"Do you need help carrying it?" Gabe asked after turning around.

Just as he spoke, Theo grabbed the dark, wooden coffin with both hands and picked it up by himself, carrying it on his back into the church.

"Strength of ten men," Theo said. "It comes in handy occasionally."

"Which way to the basement?" MacDonald asked.

Gabe walked to the hatch leading down to the basement of the church. The basement contained the breaker and a water heater for the church and the rectory. Gabe had never been down here before. Fr. Tim left a map of the church and the rectory in his shirt pocket when he died, and the police laid it on the rectory couch. Only part of the basement was paved. The rest opened onto a dirt floor.

"So, we don't have to break concrete today," MacDonald said. "That's fortunate. We can put back the jackhammer."

"You were serious?" Gabe asked.

"Dead serious," Theo answered for him. "Father, if Simon finds this, half the people in this town could be dead by Easter time."

"Do not call anyone on Earth your father; for One is your Father, He who is in heaven,"

140

MacDonald said, winking at Gabe. "Sorry, call it the prejudices of an old Orangeman. Let's get to work."

Gabe swallowed hard. Theo put the coffin down. He and MacDonald took out shovels and started to dig a grave. MacDonald had to stop and rest a third of the way through, so Gabe took over. When they finally reached six feet down, MacDonald told them to stop.

"I believe that's more than the standard in this country," MacDonald said.

Theo picked up the coffin again and set it down next to Gabe.

"Would you like to take a look at the old bastard?" Theo asked.

Would I like to see the bones of a vampire? Gabe asked himself. He had no compelling desire, but he also didn't *NOT* want to. Maybe I should just in case I'm ever curious. Gabe nodded. Theo flipped open the coffin. Gabe looked inside and saw a set of very clean bones, stunningly normal, save for two slightly enlarged incisors in the mouth.

"He looks so human," Gabe said.

"He was, once," Theo said.

Theo closed the coffin and put a padlock on it. He then raised the coffin above his head, jumped into the grave, and then turned to mist which seeped over the coffin as it lowered itself into its (hopefully) final resting place. The mist came to the surface and then reformed as a man. Gabe and Theo then began refilling the grave.

"Hey, father," Theo said, shoveling more dirt on the coffin. "Don't mind the Orangeman. It's just the way he is. You should have seen the fights he got into with Fr. Eric."

"I'll try to take it as a compliment," Gabe replied.

They finished the grave and exited the basement. Theo took off into the night, toward the crypt, leaving Gabe alone with MacDonald.

"Goodnight, Pastor MacDonald," Gabe said politely.

"Now see here, priest," MacDonald began, "I saw what you did giving that medal to Deanna, plying my daughter with Roman superstitions. To say nothing of the designs you have on Theo. I know well the machinations of the pontiff and his blasphemous claims to infallibility. You have your flock. Keep them well."

The Orangeman then got in the station wagon and drove away.

"This town is strange," Gabe remarked, dully.

Tuesday, Bothwell School, 11 a.m.
Bryce

"Solomon Bryce Davis! To the principal's office now!" screeched the intercom at Bothwell School.

Bryce sighed. Unfortunately, despite being a brilliant student, Bryce taking a trip to the principal's office was not an irregular occurrence.

Bryce appeared at Steve Jorek's office, five minutes after he had been called. Jorek's haggard secretary was visibly having problems staying awake, no doubt after having rewritten the same letter for her boss for the 24th time last night. Jorek would fire her, hire someone else, and then fire the next person. The last secretary made it two weeks.

As Bryce entered the principal's office, a familiar stench filled his nostrils. Jorek often did not bathe for days at a time, and he rarely brushed his teeth. Bryce gagged as the principal's musk filled the room through the fat, pale tyrant's pores. While the students wore blue blazers, khakis, and ties, Jorek would normally wear a stained t-shirt and a pair of jean shorts.

"Bryce," Jorek began, "please have a seat."

Bryce did as he was told.

"Do you know why you're here?" Jorek asked.

"No," Bryce answered, truthfully.

"Yes, you do."

"But I don't."

"Don't contradict me. Confess now."

"Okay, sure, I confess," Bryce lied, thinking whatever the punishment was for whatever he did would be easier than sitting here and having to listen to this.

"How can you confess when you don't even know what you did?"

"You just said that I did know."

"Don't talk back to me!!!!!"

Of course, this was just the beginning. Jorek would ask Bryce to explain himself. Seeing how Bryce had no idea what he was talking about, this was impossible. It was also irrelevant because before Bryce could get a word out, Jorek barked, "Shut Up." Conversations with Steve Jorek were often like this. He would ask you a question, and he would tell you to shut up before you could answer. Then he would lecture you about "taking things seriously" without bothering to explain what those things were. Jorek would then tell you how everything was your fault, without explaining what "it" was. He would ask you if you had any questions and then wave you off if you were foolish enough to ask any. Finally, the two-ton tyrant finished off all his speeches like this.

"Do I make myself clear?!"

"No," responded Bryce.

"Don't talk back to me!!!!"

Bryce still did not know what he had done other than exist. Alas, as his many past co-workers, employees, and business associates could attest, existence was all Steve Jorek needed to go off on someone. After the first few beatdowns, Bryce had done his homework and looked Jorek up. Before becoming the headmaster of Bothwell school, Jorek ran his law firm…into the ground. He had been an attorney who was disbarred for threatening opposing counsel with physical violence. Because of his behavior, the Supreme Court of South Carolina changed the ethical rules to remove the requirement that attorneys be "zealous advocates" for their clients, finding it encouraged poor behavior in court. Through his uncivil antics, Jorek made national news, where he caught the attention of the Bothwell school.

Why was this psychotic and potentially dangerous individual hired to run a school? Bryce had been a student in Pandemonium schools long enough to know the answer: namely, that while the desire to assimilate in America is strong, the Witches still had values slightly out of tune with society. Whereas most Americans really want to see their kids succeed, the Witches, whose religion revolved around Earthly power, *really, really, really* wanted to see their kids succeed, particularly in the workplace. Thus, in response to parental demand, Bothwell had set out to give its students the skills needed to excel in their chosen careers by simulating something in the schoolhouse that most kids in America wouldn't get until the workhouse: an unhinged, immature, and emotionally unstable boss. If you could tolerate Principal Steve Jorek, you could work for Steve Jobs. Jorek was pretty good at his job: being a complete ass.

"Let's take a look at your locker."

Bryce got up and led the stinky tyrant to his locker. They had to stop once as Jorek insisted on telling a sophomore boy that his hair was too long, using a gay slur against him. The sophomore shrugged and went back to class. Jorek once began an assembly by calling the entire student body a grumble of maggots for what he considered insufficient cheering during the last pep rally. Finally, they reached the locker, which Bryce began to open.

"Did I ask you to open your locker?" Jorek asked.

"Well, no," Bryce admitted, ceasing.

"I didn't say stop!!!"

Bryce finished opening his locker. He had nothing in there that was against school rules, which in the wider scheme of things was irrelevant. Jorek started tossing the contents of Bryce's locker onto the floor. Bryce gathered his books as he would be expected to put them back in after Jorek was done.

"Aha!" Jorek exclaimed. He had found the offending contraband: Bryce's yearbook from last May. Jorek sat on the floor, crossed-legged like a five-year-old, and flipped through the yearbook, scanning each page for the suspected insult. At last, he came to the offending image: Jorek's picture in the back of the book, with a thin mustache drawn in ink along with an eyepatch and a blackened tooth.

"I thought I saw you draw that," Jorek exclaimed. "The cameras never lie."

Jorek pointed to the camera hanging from the ceiling above him. In an attempt to simulate the actual environment of corporate workplaces, the school had put cameras in every hallway to monitor the students at all times. Cameras, however, are not impeccable, as Bryce had not created the caricature. Gary had, last June. What Jorek had seen was Bryce writing a note to himself concerning new materials for his rail gun, which were supposed to be coming into the local hardware store that Saturday.

"You ungrateful children have never appreciated what I have done for you!" Jorek yelled at the top of his voice. "Detention for everyone and you have Bryce Davis to thank for it!!!"

Bryce sighed. This would be the fifth universal detention this semester.

Wednesday, Bothwell School, 4:55 p.m.
Beth

Beth looked at the clock. It was nearing 5 p.m. The end of yet another universal detention. Above the entrance of the hall, there was a banner announcing, 'YOU ARE HERE BECAUSE OF BRYCE DAVIS.' No one hated Bryce because they knew Jorek would pick on someone else if it were not for him. Being Jorek's punching bag was largely considered a public service.

The bell rang. Beth got up and hurried to the door. Beth then slowed her pace to avoid attracting attention, but steadily made her way to the front of the school. Jorek stood in front of the double door entrance of the school, bellowing out insults and orders in equal measure to the exiting students. Beth didn't notice him, even though he covered half the doorway with his girth. Once outside, Beth started in a full-on sprint, making a beeline for the boundary of campus. She was almost there when-

"Hey bitch," said the voice, "are you late for a Virgins Anonymous meeting?"

Nope. Not today. She hadn't gotten away today. Waiting right by the flagpole was Hannah White, lead cheerleader, smoking a cigarette with the rest of her posse. Hannah was a gorgeous redhead with huge breasts and a size-four stomach. And yes, she had a thing for picking on Beth.

"You look like someone redecorated your face with buckshot," Hannah continued, laying into Beth. "Where's your little violin case?"

Beth looked down and realized she had forgotten her violin in the detention hall, and thus had to retrieve it. Beth turned around and began to head back into the building. Hannah and her girls decided to follow her.

"Forgot it again?" Hannah yelled. "Jesus, Beth you're a spaz. I swear you'd forget your breasts if you had any."

Beth and the squad passed by multiple teachers on the way back to her last class, all of whom paid no attention to them as Hannah continued piling on Beth. Just keep your head down and keep going, Beth said, it will all be over soon. Beth made it back to the detention hall, retrieved her violin case, and then turned around. Hannah was right there waiting to flick the drag she was working on right in Beth's face. Beth kept walking right past her and back out of the school. Hannah lit another cigarette and followed her out.

"Hey Beth, me and the other girls are having a bet about when you're going to kill yourself," Hannah shouted. "I said, put me down for next week!"

Beth made it past Jorek at the double doors a second time, violin in tow. The foul tyrant was busy giving another girl detention for looking at him the wrong way. Just as Beth was about to take off again, Hannah hurled one last aspersion her way.

"If I were your mother and I saw that face in the emergency room, I'd want to kill myself too!"

147

Beth decided she had had enough. She reached into her purse, grabbed the St. Benedict medal, pulled it out, and showed it to Hannah.

"Get back, foul spirit!" Beth yelled.

Beth held the medal in front of Hannah's face. She and the rest of the cheerleading squad began to giggle and then break down into laughter. Not the effect Beth was looking for. Beth scanned the room around to find everyone else in the area looking at Beth like she was nuts. Finally, her brother approached her.

"Beth," Bryce said quietly, "who are you talking to?"

Beth had done it again. She had let Hannah get to her and embarrassed herself in public.

"No one," Beth said, calming down. "Rough day."

Bryce nodded. Beth closed her eyes and started to cry a little. Beth worried her family sometimes with her behavior, but no one ever believed her when she tried to explain these things, so it was just easier to pretend nothing happened and move on.

Bryce walked his sister to his car, past the flagpole, which had a plaque on its base with nine names on it, one of which was Hannah White. Underneath the names, the plaque read, 'Dedicated to the memory of the 1994 Bothwell Cheerleading Squad. They will always be forever young.'

CHAPTER ELEVEN

The Third Week of Advent, Wednesday, Davis Guest House, 7pm
Beth

"She's so mean!" Beth whined.

Beth leaned her face into Deanna's shoulder and sobbed. Beth was still recovering from her latest encounter with Hannah White and her squad. Of all the dead people Beth saw on a daily basis, Hannah and her girls were the meanest. Her own ancestors in the plantation house were scary, but at least left her alone. Deanna patted Beth on the head and held her. If only Deanna could do something about these bullies like those girls in Kindergarten. Unfortunately, Deanna couldn't fight the undead like second graders, if for no other reason than that, unlike Beth, she couldn't see them.

"Have you tried going to the principal—oh, wait, no, I forgot, Jorek, that won't work," Deanna said, interrupting herself.

"The last time a person went to Principal Jorek because of a bully," Beth replied. "He gave the bully a special award for service to the school."

"Well, you have to stand up to her then," Deanna suggested. "Beth, you let people walk all over you. You have to stop letting it happen."

"I know, but I don't know how to start," Beth responded.

"How to start being confrontational? Let me show you."

Bryce appeared in front of the door of Beth's room.

"Shoot," Deanna exclaimed. She then started eyeing the window.

"No, no, no, I've trapped you," Bryce insisted. "You must debate religion with me!"

He had done it. He had cornered the pastor's daughter again. Bryce, the most annoying atheist on Pandemonium Island, had dragooned another unfortunate soul into a debate about religion. Bryce declared himself an Atheist when he was twelve…in the middle of a Satanic ritual while Ravenwood was trying to give a sermon. He tried to convince Rabbi Maharam that God didn't exist during Gary's Bar Mitzvah party. Bryce told Fr. Ravenwood to his face he didn't believe in the fallen angel, and Ravenwood responded that he agreed with Bryce, which Bryce didn't quite expect. Now he had his sights set on Deanna, and she was trapped.

"You know, a very good historical case could be made that the 'historical' character of Jesus never existed," Bryce asserted, completely ignoring Deanna's plea.

"Why would the apostles die for him if he didn't exist?" Deanna asked.

"A very good case can be made that the apostles, as you call them, did not exist either," Bryce replied.

While Bryce and Deanna were arguing, or rather, while Deanna was attempting to escape, Beth looked at the teapot she boiled earlier and mentally grabbed it with her telekinesis. She then lifted the teapot and poured herself a cup of tea. Beth floated the teacup up to her hands while Bryce and Deanna were preoccupied. She never did this when others were watching. It raised too many questions.

"Why don't you try the ontological argument?" Bryce asked.

"The what?" Deanna asked.

"Well, if you don't have any arguments, then your belief in God is like the belief of a teapot orbiting the sun," Bryce declared.

"Not really, I don't claim to have a personal relationship with a teapot," Deanna answered.

"Your claim to a personal relationship has been explained by science," Bryce explained. "Tests have been done showing that when religious believers pray, a particular part of the brain lights up. This does not happen with atheists."

"So, atheists have deficient brains?" Deanna spat. "That would explain a lot."

"An ad hominem attack! I knew it," Bryce declared. "Well, I think I have won this battle of the wits."

Bryce, satisfied with his 'victory,' left the room with his head held high. Deanna, relieved to have 'lost,' turned back to Beth.

"Well, do you have a plan to deal with Hannah?" Deanna asked. "Tomorrow is the last day of the semester."

Beth ruminated on the decision, and as she did so, her eyes fell upon the mini gargoyle on her desk. Deanna's little medal hadn't been enough to repel Hannah, but maybe this would be. If it worked in the Middle Ages....

Thursday, Bothwell School, 2pm
Beth

Hannah White and the rest of the 1994 Cheerleading Squad chased Beth around the locker room, screaming curses at her while their eyeballs hung from their sockets. Beth should have known better than to let them corner her in a locker room alone, but sometimes it took a while to get dressed after gym. Sometimes, they would appear as they normally did on Earth, but other times they would appear the way they died, covered in bullet holes. A punk kid had gunned them down after cracking under the pressure in 1994. The squad didn't have to insult Beth when they appeared like this for her to be scared. That was a given. All Hannah White and her coterie of dead hangers on had to do was scream bloody murder. Beth dodged behind lockers. They passed through them. She would run. Hannah would appear in front of Beth with blood squirting out of her head. Beth would scream "Go Away." The cheerleading squad would describe how they would gouge her eyes out.

Finally, they cornered her. Hannah and her girls backed Beth into a corner of the locker room. Beth then took out her purse, rummaged around in it, and retrieved the mini gargoyle. Triumphantly shoving it in Hannah's bloody face, Beth screamed "Get back!"

"Is that your twin?" Hannah responded.

The cheerleading squad rushed Beth, and she backed into the trashcan behind her. Just when she thought there was no escape, it all came to a stop. The cheerleaders were gone, and Beth was left stuffed in the trash. Then she heard wheels. Beth could see a different spirit, pushing a transparent yellow mop bucket, enter the room.

"Anyone in here?" the new ghost called, though Beth knew he could see through the wall.

"Thanks, Jarvis," Beth said.

"Miss Beth," said Jarvis, a translucent Fieldhand Janitor who shone with a golden light. "What are you doing in such a mean place?"

"Same thing as always Jarvis," Beth said, "Hannah White."

Beth crawled out of the trashcan and took a seat on a bench in the locker room. Jarvis took a pack of cigarettes out of the pocket of the grey uniform he was wearing, removing a single cigarette therein and lighting it before taking a long drag.

"These things are going to kill me some day," Jarvis chuckled, "and that day was April 7, 1975. I would offer you a hand if I could."

"You already helped me today," Beth said.

"You mean by chasing Hannah and her girls away?" Jarvis asked. "Yes, I did. And now what is this?"

Jarvis was looking directly at the mini gargoyle. When Hannah and the squad had backed her into the trash, Beth had dropped it on the floor.

"Oh, this," Beth sighed. "This is my attempt to stop her. I bought this at a store thinking it might ward her off."

Beth closed her eyes and concentrated on the gargoyle. It stirred and then levitated. she deposited the statue into the garbage.

"Well, that's fifty dollars down the drain," Beth said. "You know people never offer refunds for stuff like that when it doesn't work."

"The stuff that works is free," Jarvis replied, sitting down next to her. "You need to know how to use your powers better. Talk to your kin in the plantation house sometime."

Beth shuddered. Now that she *really* didn't want to do. Beth first ran from the house when she started seeing spirits in Kindergarten. One day she was playing in her room, and she saw a figure pass by. Beth walked into the hallway to see who it was. The figure was a woman wearing a wedding dress, drenched in blood, which poured from a gap in her head. Beth fled from the house into the guest quarters. After a week of crying whenever her aunts tried to carry her back into the plantation house, they relented and let her stay out there. Beth had only been in the main building a few times since then. She could recognize a few spirits. The Bloody Bride. An old man in a uniform covered with bullet holes. An elderly biracial woman dressed in Victorian clothes. Beth would leave whenever she saw one, and she never talked to them.

"But that place is scary," Beth moaned. "I used to live there, but the first time I saw that Bloody Bride, I ran."

"Of course, you did, you were five," Jarvis said. "When I was a child, I spake as a child, I understood as a child, I thought as a child: but when I became a man, I put away childish things. You've already started."

He pointed gently to the mini gargoyle in the trash.

"They aren't your enemies. They want to help you. It's normal for kin," Jarvis insisted, floating out of the room. "Speaking of, I've got to look out for my kin, so there's a city council meeting I need to be at."

Town Meeting Hall, 7p.m.
MacDonald

Pastor MacDonald made a point to attend city council meetings since 1997, when Ravenwood convinced the council to allow 'a traditional Witch Christmas.' This meant an orgy on the front lawn of the Town Meeting Hall, though the city council didn't know that. After seeing Ravenwood strip naked in front of the Stranger's holiday creche and have sexual relations with a woman he met on Craigslist, the Orangeman learned not to put his trust in princes, so it was best to keep an eye on them. The old pastor waddled to the main chamber of the town meeting hall, down the stairs of the chamber and toward the main stage, raised on a dais. On the stage were four desks with two seats each: two for Strangers, Fieldhands, Ze'ev, and Witches. Just like the entrances to the building, just like the seats in the audience, carefully divided in four with the Fieldhands on the far left and the Witches on the far right and the Strangers and Ze'ev in the middle. After the Jim Crow years, it was considered better to keep the Fieldhands and Witches on opposite sides of the room, particularly when debate got heated. MacDonald took his seat in the Stranger section and took out his notebook.

First in was the Mayor, Cory Mayfield, a thin, tale black man in a dark suit. He was the first Fieldhand to hold the position. MacDonald remembered the night Mayfield was elected with a kind of smug satisfaction. The Witch candidate was ahead by five points a week before the polls opened.

And then Ravenwood endorsed him and his campaign went to pot.

The town council began to take their seats. The Strangers and Witches, despite being historical enemies, now both voted Republican, and the Fieldhands and the Ze'ev voted Democratic, so the respective partisan groups often met in private to discuss matters before the meeting. Overstreet took out his pen to take notes in detail. This wasn't a regular meeting.

A town council was called to a special meeting to approve a special request: Miles Simon wanted a variance to the town zoning laws, and building codes for that matter, to construct his "New Stranger Church" in downtown Pandemonium. Simon had constructed such portable churches all across America, and architects and engineers had, in light of the nature of the buildings and their size and proportions, called them "dangerous," "likely to fail," and "also kind of ugly when you look at them from a distance." Local building codes didn't have a category for a portable and assembled megachurch, so the town council would have to approve a variance. The building inspector did not approve.

"I would have to hang up my codebook if I were to do such a thing," said the building inspector. "If we allow Mr. Simon to build this monstrosity, we're asking for a collapse."

"Thank you, sir, for your testimony," Mayor Mayfield said. "Next up, we have an attorney from Miles Simon Ministries: Mr. James Warrenton."

An elderly gentleman with a lionesque face and a white halo of curly hair approached the podium. He was exactly the kind of slick barrister MacDonald had learned to both trust and distrust. Trust: if you could afford them. Distrust: if they're lips were moving. Warrenton began.

"I am shocked that this body would consider such a severe restriction of religious liberty," Warrenton began.

"What do you mean?" Mayfield asked. "You mean the building codes? I don't think you can call the building codes an infringement on religious liberty. You can have your church. You just have to make sure that it doesn't fall down on people's heads."

"And what if Mr. Simon believes that using shoddy workmanship in his buildings is a sign of his faith in God's providence?" Warrenton asked. "Some faiths don't allow medical care or forbid buying insurance. How is building churches using cut-rate labor and materials any different?"

"Well, I never thought of it that way," Mayfield said.

"Of course not," Warrenton continued, "I would never imply this was intentional. That is why we are asking for a variance. I can't imagine this body would want to interfere with sacred first amendment rights, would they?"

MacDonald looked up, expecting, well not expecting, but hoping, that the council could see themselves being fooled. As usual, the princes disappointed the pastor. The council members all looked at each other and shook their heads. They all voted to approve the variance, with no further debate. MacDonald just shook his head in despair.

Friday, Charleston, South Carolina, Trinity United Methodist Church, 10a.m.
Gilbert

Gilbert arrived for an interview for the job of youth pastor at the Trinity United Methodist Church dressed in a nice grey suit Theo bought him as an early Christmas gift. Theo figured he owed Gilbert, as he was the reason Gilbert didn't have a job anymore. The pastor of the church welcomed Gilbert and told him to sit down.

"Wow, a real Stranger, huh? You guys are famous in these latitudes."

"Yeah, but it's not about our story," Gilbert replied, "which can apparently be bought and sold. It's about His story."

Gilbert pointed to the cross hanging above the pastor's head.

"Very to the point."

"It is the point," Gilbert continued. "The story of the Strangers is the story of someone getting Christianity exactly wrong, which is I guess what you would expect from a bunch of unchurched, illiterate pirates."

"Exactly wrong?"

"The point of the church is self-sacrifice," Gilbert explained. "What the original Strangers did was sacrifice someone else, trying to win God's favor that way. That's the oldest story in the world. Humans try to get closer to God, and we do it by sacrificing others. Christ tried to show us the way, but we don't do that because it's difficult. The Strangers told themselves they were punishing that woman for witchcraft, but what they were really doing was trying to make up for their own sins by burning someone else. We've killed the Witch, and thus earned God's favor. It's not that different than what the Witches did, killing that brigand to gain the favor of their god. What God wants is self-sacrifice."

"Well, hey, that's a unique take on the Stranger story. I hadn't heard it before."

"It's the same story of the church as a whole," Gilbert said. "The wars of religion, the inquisition,

Cromwell. It's the same thing. Burn the heretic to appease God. It's human sacrifice. Falling away from the path Jesus taught us and doing our own thing again. The point of the cross is that if you have to sacrifice someone, it had better be you."

Miles Simon Ministry Offices, 9 p.m.
Calvin

"So, we're getting the bones tonight," Calvin said.

"That's the plan," Simon responded.

"How do we plan to resurrect him without a human sacrifice?"

"What the hell are you talking about?"

"A human sacrifice. It says it's required right here."

Suddenly, a mad look appeared on Simon's face, like he could have killed Calvin for bringing it up. The look told Calvin, reading between the lines, "shut up."

"You're real funny, son," Simon spoke through a very fine slit in his mouth.

Simon left Calvin's office and slammed the door behind him. Calvin sighed and flipped through the Scratch file again. His eyes fell on the audiotape. They had never played it. Calvin walked around the office, still buzzing at 9 p.m., and asked if someone had a cassette player. The receptionist led him back to the supply closet and gave him the oldest piece of equipment he'd ever seen. Calvin took it back to his office, popped the tape in. Out of the tape player came a cold voice with a clear English accent.

"My congregation, dear brothers and sisters in Christ, a tragedy has occurred in our age.

Not the tragedy of death, but the tragedy of life. Not grinding poverty, but wealth and prosperity. Not a tragedy of pain, but a tragedy of pleasure. 400 years ago, Christendom was at a crossroads between the kingdom of God and the kingdom of the papist Anti-Christ. The battle of Armageddon had been set. But then, Man decided that he was tired of war. He did not ask if God was tired of war, Man merely decided he was. Man wanted to starve no more. He did not ask if God wanted him to starve. That thought did not occur to Man. So, the battle had been set, but Man walked away, concerned as he was not with the Kingdom of God, but with mere peace and prosperity."

The voice seemed to be addressing a congregation, but Calvin couldn't hear one. He read the label on the cassette. The voice continued.

"Then, a greater tragedy occurred. It was not that Man failed, but that he succeeded. He succeeded without God. He multiplied the loaves, and now the poor eat and Christ hath nothing to do with it. It would be better for them to starve. Man healed the sick using vaccines and antibiotics. He did not speak of the Lord. Better that the sick die than to be healed in such a way. Great wonders Man brought about Earth, all after he abandoned the Almighty. Why did the Almighty allow it? I will never understand. The Kingdom of God abandoned while the Kingdom of Man flourishes."

"I will not allow this ultimate blasphemy. The Lord may forgive Man for failing, but He cannot forgive Man for succeeding. The Kingdom of God may not be abandoned. It may not be ignored. The human race approaches the final prophecy. The lions and the lambs will lay down with each other within a century. The Kingdom comes without the King. The Lord does not tolerate this disrespect. He will not allow Himself to be forgotten, and I will be His vengeance. Man's victories are an abomination, and they must be turned to ashes by His righteous wrath. God cannot die, so Man must."

The audio stopped. Calvin felt like a ghost had passed through his chest. That was him. That was his voice, Scratch. They were about to do it. They were going to resurrect him. They were going to bring *that* back to the mortal world.

"Spooky," Calvin uttered.

"Good, I always like to have an effect on my audience."

It was the voice. The same cold, English voice. It came out of the cassette tape.

"Who was that?" Calvin asked.

"Do I have a cold? I thought you would have recognized me, Calvin. I wanted to thank you for listening to my sermon. It's so disappointing to have no congregation to preach to. You should ask that nasty little papist in town what it's like."

"This isn't real," Calvin said.

"Oh, Calvin, if only you knew my love for you, even if a mother should forget her child, I will not forget you. I will follow you to the ends of the Earth."

Calvin reached for the cassette tape and turned it off. He breathed heavily for a while. That wasn't real, he thought. It couldn't be.

CHAPTER TWELVE

The Third Week of Advent, Saturday, Pandemonium,
Stranger Crypt, 1 a.m.
Calvin

Calvin shined a flashlight into the dark crypt. He didn't see anyone down there. They chose this time in hopes that Theo would not be present when they came to get the remains. Calvin learned how to kill a vampire from MacDonald's research, but he figured it was easier said than done. He wanted to make sure that he avoided running into Theo as he did this.

"Alright, let's go," Calvin whispered.

Calvin let the men Simon hired run past him. They were members of a criminal syndicate in Charleston. Everything they were doing tonight was legal, but not exactly above board. They were allowed in the church as part of the due diligence process, and they could inspect any kind of relic within the church. The ministry's attorney stated his legal opinion, which was that if Scratch's bones were in the crypt, then they were relics under the purchase sales contract. Why Simon didn't just wait until the closing, Calvin couldn't begin to fathom, but Simon figured that MacDonald might try to "screw him" by taking the bones out of the church beforehand.

Calvin walked slowly down to the crypt, behind the hired men. He found the men had already started digging in the spot MacDonald's notes said the bones were laid, right under the Ottoman. They were supposed to be six feet down. What the old pastor called the "American Standard." He kept rather meticulous notes. Calvin watched them as they dug, deeper and deeper. He stood in the dark among the bones of Strangers long since passed. He cast a glance at the alcove where the princess' bones lie. The men stopped digging. Calvin stepped forward. The hole was deep, twice as deep as it should have been. There was nothing there.

"Grave robbing can often be disappointing."

Calvin heard the voice from the ceiling, he looked up and found Theo, hanging over him. The hired men pointed guns at Theo and fired. He turned to mist immediately and then drifted to the ground, reforming as a man with two feet in the dust. Dropping their guns and scrambling in every direction, the hired men ran out of the crypt, leaving Calvin alone with the immortal Nosferatu. Terrified, Calvin couldn't move.

"You came here to resurrect a vampire? Unnecessary, I am here," Theo announced.

Theo grabbed Calvin by the throat and lifted him in the air, slamming him against the stone walls of the crypt. Theo opened his mouth and his canine teeth elongated. A demoniac glare appeared in his eyes. Calvin felt a warm trickle down his leg. He had pissed himself.

Then Theo dropped Calvin, who fell into the dust on his ass. Pain traveled up his tailbone, but he could barely feel it. Theo's teeth retracted and he looked down on Calvin with a kind of pity.

"Lad, how old are you?" he asked.

"Twenty-one," Calvin answered.

"I'm guessing this is Simon's idea."

"Yes."

"You go back to your master and tell him that if he had succeeded at bringing Scratch back, Scratch wouldn't take the deal either. That little show I gave you. Scratch wouldn't even give you the courtesy. He'd have killed your men from the ceilings, one by one, before any of them knew what was happening. Then, because you displeased him, he'd keep you around for a while. Stick a pear of anguish up your arse and make you taste from the heretic's fork. Use the Google to look those up. Finally, he'd drain you of blood, slowly. Why would Simon think Scratch was interested in a deal?"

"H-h-h-e says everyone has a price," Calvin blubbered, "and there was a plan in the file for a machine to capture him."

"The bottle machine, of course," Theo mused. "Well, I fell for it. The Brits captured me once after the Rising. Word to the wise, it's an excellent prison, but a poor threat. Tommy caught me off guard. You won't be so lucky. Now go."

Calvin struggled to move his legs he was so frightened, but Theo wouldn't take that excuse.

"I have extended you mercy! Go before I change my mind!" Theo growled, with his canines growing in length again.

Calvin's legs relearned how to move properly. He ran out of the crypt, up towards the exit of the church. His father wouldn't be happy about this.

Temple Ze'ev, 10 a.m.
Calvin

"You got to be fucking with me," Simon whispered under his breath. "I'm going to ruin that blood-sucking mick."

Calvin looked around the room uncomfortably. Just how ethnic slurs would play in a synagogue, he could only guess, but he guessed not well. He handed a skull cap to Simon who put it on before they sat through Simon's appointment at the synagogue. He was doing a tour of Pandemonium's churches in an attempt to prove his respect for local institutions. A reporter for the *Daily Lament* caught some of his comments concerning the 'monsters' and thus he had a little catch up to do. The rabbi seemed very good-humored about it, as did the Ze'ev in general. The community had families of all ages, but the elderly were the largest contingent. They seemed to appreciate a young man like Calvin in attendance. Simon, however, appeared uncomfortable in a *shul*.

"I grew up in an evangelical culture," Simon explained, "so, this is very formalistic to me."

Formalistic it was. Jews normally divided themselves into Orthodox, Conservative, and Reform, but the Ze'ev were, as the Rabbi Maharam said, stuck with each other, so they took turns alternating between traditional and modern worship. Today, they were Orthodox, and a divider separated the men and women. Chanting in Hebrew filled the room from both sides as the great teacher led his community in worship. Calvin tried to keep up with the English translation, though he easily got lost as everything went backward in his mind. "Glorified and Sanctified be God's Great Name." "Holy are You and holy is Your name. Holy are they who praise you daily."

The synagogue had intricate mosaics lining the walls and ceilings and a bright chandelier above the altar. The windows let in a good deal of light, giving the building a high gothic look, held together by the large window above the altar with the Star of David. The stained-glass windows showed an image of a wolf lying down with a lamb. An obvious choice, Calvin thought. One of the Ze'ev, dressed in a long robe, opened the grand Ark and took out a large Torah scroll, decorated by a silver capper at the end, which he took to the rabbi, elevated above the community in the center. The elderly rabbi recited the Torah in a cadence that felt ancient in Calvin's ears. When the chant ended, Rabbi Maharam spoke in English.

"Today we read in Exodus that we should not allow a witch to live," he said. "This town has proven that often the worst way to misinterpret a text is to take it literally. That passage is in the Tanakh as much as it is in the rafters of the Stranger Church. You won't find either of us walking down to the south side of the island with torches and pitchforks. That happened once, and we learned from experience that there is a better way."

"But," the rabbi continued, "we should ask why our ancestors thought it wise to kill a Witch? Is it because they feared the power of witchcraft? No, they did not. The modern conceit that people in the Bronze Age were somehow dim witted or superstitious is a prime example of temporal snobbery. Moses knew the Pharoah's magicians had no real power, because he knew what real power was having experienced it firsthand through the burning bush."

"Yet he still commanded such figures to be put to death," Maharam said, "not in spite of the fact that he knew them to be frauds, but because he knew them to be frauds. People would go to witches seeking some magical solution to problems, and willing to pay for them. Imagine that, paying someone for a love spell, or for a healing miracle…."

Maharam then quickly turned his head to Simon, who didn't notice as he was checking his phone. Calvin, however, could see the old wolf's piercing eyes aimed straight at faith healer.

"…or a curse."

Now, the entire synagogue turned their eyes at Simon. Perhaps word had gotten out about him paying off Ravenwood, or maybe the Satanic High Priest was just a little too obvious what with killing the rabbit and all. Calvin felt the need to alert his boss to the attention directed at them by tapping him lightly on the shoulder, but the televangelist just swatted his finger away.

"Of course, it didn't work," the old teacher continued. "It may have appeared to at first, but whenever your wounds healed or your enemy met a cruel fate, it was but a coincidence. A coincidence that the beneficiary would no doubt chalk up to magical intervention, but a coincidence, nonetheless. The Witches we know have long since stopped believing in magic, instead putting their faith in meritocracy. A more effective form of idolatry, though a less fantastic one."

"You may ask about our own transformations: aren't they the product of magic?" the rabbi asked, raising a pointer finger in the air. "Yes, real magic, real power because they come from a real God. Not false idols made of wood and stone, and certainly not CGI."

"In the end, the conjurer is a con artist. He promises that which he can only appear to deliver, and his fee is fraud. Moses did not tolerate such people, and neither should we. However, as we do live in a different time, I would not suggest stoning such men. Shunning them from polite society is more than sufficient."

The service ended. As the Ze'ev gradually moved out of the building in a haphazard manner, sporadically stopping in the aisles to talk with each other, Simon made his way to Rabbi Maharam to personally apologize for the "monster" comment, though the old teacher left the room before the televangelist could reach him. Having failed to offer his shallow apologies, Simon rounded on Calvin.

"Okay, how do we find the bones now?" Simon said. "They're included as relics in the contract. I own them. If they remove the bones that's theft."

"Are you sure?" Calvin asked. "Mr. Simon, I have to tell you, I played that cassette…"

"I don't care what you did. I have a problem. *Find a way to solve it*!! I've still got another ass to kiss in this town."

The Fourth Sunday of Advent, Pandemonium, Church of the Tobacco Fields, 10 a.m.
Calvin

Tell old Pharaoh, Let my People Go!
The Fieldhand congregation sang out the refrain of the ancient spiritual. Calvin and Simon clapped awkwardly as they sat in the back pew of the Church of the Tobacco Fields, Simon's last stop on his tour of Pandemonium's religious institutions. The Church of the Tobacco Fields was a classic, brick building with a white steeple. On the inside, they had velvet backed pews, a $5,000 organ, an immersion level baptism font, and cedarwood paneling. Impressive. However, Calvin found it difficult to

believe, as the placard outside claimed, that this building was founded in the exact spot in the exact tobacco field where Jacob Freeman, an itinerant free black man who served as the church's first pastor, held his first sermon. Seemed like a detail born from legend rather than fact. It was not likely Calvin would express such skepticism here though. When the legend becomes fact, print the legend.

Up in front, Pastor Darrell Overstreet led the congregation through another verse while the man on the organ ran his fingers up and down the ivory keys. *So Moses Went to Egypt's Land.* Overstreet bobbed his head up and down while pacing across the stage. His flock hopped on their feet, from the tiniest toddler to the old ladies whose bones poked out of their skin.

If Not I'll Smite Your Firstborns Dead!

The pastor could hold a crowd, better than any Calvin had seen, though admittedly, he hadn't seen much. Really only Simon's preaching, which tended to be a performance. This wasn't a performance. It was a show.

Tell ole Pharoah, Let my People Go!

The man on the organ pushed out a final gust of sound indicating the hymn had ended. The hands in the air shook wildly, releasing one last blast of energy from the congregation. As Overstreet approached the podium, Calvin took his seat. He'd heard that black pastors gave good sermons. Supposedly they didn't need cue cards.

"Thank you, thank you," Pastor Overstreet began, grabbing the microphone, "thank you all for being here today. Particularly you, Mr. Simon."

Simon, who had been checking his phone again, suddenly came to attention at the mention of his name. All the eyes once again turned to Simon. Calvin nervously eyed the floor. They'd been called out twice in one weekend.

"Thank you for being here, Mistah Simon!" Overstreet continued. "You like that. How I ex-agg-er-rate my diction? I bet Ravenwood did that for you when you visited."

"Oh," Simon responded, his cheeks burning bright with embarrassment. "I've never met with that devil worshipper. I wouldn't be in the company of such a man."

"Well, if you're going to be Pastor of the Stranger Church, you should probably get used to him," Overstreet warned. "Me and MacDonald have had to put up with him for nearly 40 years. Hell, his daughter's right over there!"

Overstreet pointed to a white woman with bright red hair and freckles standing next to a black man and a biracial toddler in the front row. The woman covered her mouth to hide the fact that she was chuckling.

"Thanks for being a good sport, Cassandra," Overstreet said. "But Ravenwood's an okay sort. The Witches generally are these days. They didn't used to be. You know what they used to do? What the Witches did that was oh so evil? You know what they did that was so goldurn bad?"

A moment of silence passed before Simon realized he was supposed to answer. Then, he ventured his best guess.

"They worshipped Sat—"

"They owned slaves," Overstreet corrected him.

Another moment of silence. This one a great deal more awkward.

"Yeah, the Witches owned slaves. They wanted to get into growing tobacco when they got to America. Later, some of them tried cotton," Overstreet said. "The Strangers were shipbuilders, fishermen, and smugglers. They might have had a few house servants, the wealthier ones, but most of the Strangers didn't own slaves. That's why when the Confederates tried to draft them, they rioted. Not that the Strangers were angels of light. Black people don't live on the north side of the Line for a reason."

"They don't tell you that on the bus tour," Overstreet continued, now turning away from Simon and pacing up and down the stage again. "The slavey, I mean. They don't tell you the Witches owned slaves or that the Temple supported Jim Crow until the 1970s. You don't hear about how Cramner University didn't allow black students until the 1965."

"Sorry for the impromptu history lesson, Mr. Simon," Overstreet said, reminding Simon that this sermon began with him. "It's just that people forget that we are in South Carolina, in the old Confederacy. They just tell you the nice little story on the bus tour. And in schools. And in the museum. But that's not the full story."

"For instance," Overstreet continued, turning on his right heel. "They tell you the First Satanic Temple was lost when the roof caved in, but they don't tell you why the roof caved in. They don't tell you about Imhotep."

A chorus of "ooooos" erupted from the room at the mention of the name "Imhotep." Simon smiled nervously, clearly ignorant of the reference.

"Imhotep was a Satanic High Priest back in the days of slavery," Overstreet explained. "The name was given to him by my predecessor, a freeman who preached to an enslaved congregation, many of whom were enslaved by Imhotep."

"Those Witches were reeeallll afraid that they were going to lose their slaves," Overstreet explained. "Then they'd have to pick their own cotton."

A small round of laughter emanated from the pews. Simon laughed after the moment had passed in an attempt to fit in.

"Imhotep, he told them he'd come up with a spell to preserve the peculiar institution in perpetuity," Overstreet continued the story. "All those rich Witches had to do was show up to services that Sunday at the First Satanic Temple. Why of course they showed up! In record numbers! Plantation owners and their wives and little children filled the pews of Imhotep's temple. They prayed to the fallen angel to let them keep their slaves!"

Overstreet stopped pacing. He turned to the congregation and bowed his legs while holding his right hand out. Calvin felt tension building in the room.

"And when all those Witches were in their seats and the pews were full, Imhotep signaled for his overseers to set off the charges," Overstreet whispered into the mic. "And that's when the roof came down. 500 people died."

Calvin heard some soft chuckling within the congregation. Overstreet headed it off.

"Now as good Christians, and not-so good Christians, we should pray for our enemies," Overstreet warned. "Sorry again, Cassandra, for bringing up sensitive subjects."

The redhead shot the people around her a dirty look.

"But those old slavers made a mistake," Overstreet said. "They got into business with the wrong man. That's how the rich are in this world. They think they got the tiger by the tail, until the tiger turns around and they realize, no, it's got them. Poor folks wouldn't have trusted Imhotep. They'd have seen that bad deal."

"So, Mr. Simon, consider the deals you make, and the company you keep," Overstreet said, now winding up the sermon. "And may your congregation do the same."

The man on the organ ran his fingers across the keys again, alerting the crowd to the start of another hymn. As the Fieldhands got back on their feet, Calvin helped Simon do the same, but with a different purpose: leaving. Calvin quickly identified the nearest exit and pointed to it. Simon nodded and let his illegitimate son guide him out of the building. After they got out, Simon cursed Ravenwood.

"You'd have thought that prick could have given me a heads up about that," Simon spat. "Roof caved in my ass."

Second Satanic Temple, Noon
Gabe

After saying mass at 9 a.m., which disappointingly, Theo did not attend, Gabe decided that if he was here to contest evil, then he may as well do it. Taking a poster board and a stick, Gabe created a sign ('Shut down Satanic worship') and proceeded to the Second Satanic Temple to let people know as they left that their souls were in mortal jeopardy. When he arrived, Gabe saw, even without entering in, that Ravenwood's service was not what he was expecting. From within he heard pop music, the Beatles from what he could tell. Through the window, he could see Ravenwood at the pulpit, still wearing his pajamas. When services ended, Gabe lifted his sign and shouted "Stop holding these ceremonies. Your soul is in mortal danger." Tourists lined up and took photos of him.

"Are you part of the show?" One man wearing a fanny pack asked.

"No," Gabe answered. "You need to stop going here. This is a real protest."

More people took photographs. Gabe sighed. A familiar blonde woman came up behind him.

"Father, have you come to protest this week?" Delilah asked.

"Yes, I have," Gabe replied. "You should stop attending these rituals."

"I would were it not for my son, Alistair," Delilah responded. "Trust me, whatever you think you are doing to destroy this temple, Ravenwood already beat you to it twenty years ago."

"Oh, a protest, Fr. Tim used to do that," Hecate remarked, who had followed behind Delilah. "This is always good for the tourists. I wonder why he stopped?"

"Don't you worry about your immortal souls?" Gabe asked.

"They already answered that question," yelled one of the tourists.

"Father," Hecate began, "maybe you should speak to Fr. Ravenwood. Usually, he and Fr. Tim had worked out some kind of agreement."

Maybe she was right, Gabe thought, the way to kill the snake was to cut off its head. Gabe headed inside to speak with the Satanic High Priest and demand a stop to these unholy rituals. Ravenwood demanded a free lunch out of this.

"Meet me and my assistant at Grill on the Square at Noon tomorrow."

CHAPTER THIRTEEN

The Fourth Week of Advent, Monday, Grill on the Square 12:30 p.m.
Gabe

"Yes, this cheese and sausage board is to die for," Ravenwood gushed. "Please have some, Father."

"I must admit it is very good," Gabe admitted, taking a bit of sausage. "That is not what I wanted to talk to you about though."

The priest and the sorcerer were seated with Alistair Davis, halfway through an appetizer.

"What did you want to talk about?" Ravenwood asked.

"I want you to end the Satanic rituals," Gabe repeated, as he had been saying this for weeks. "For the sake of your own congregation and the sake of everyone else in this town."

"Oh, good God, no," Ravenwood answered. "Do you know how many tourism dollars it brings in? The Chamber of Commerce would have my hide, to say nothing of the trustees."

"At any moment, demons could be summoned by those rituals, which present a real spiritual threat to the people of this city," Gabe insisted.

"Father, I assure you that demons are no more likely to be summoned by my services than yours. I have never seen an act of magic performed successfully. Not unless you include a Penn and Teller show."

"Even if no demonic influence appears, your congregation is still putting themselves in jeopardy of spending eternity in hell."

"You mean that awfully convenient place where 'bad' people go after they die? If I didn't know better, I would say the concept is invented purely for the sake of getting people to behave themselves."

"Okay, taking it on that level. If your own congregation started taking your church's philosophy seriously, imagine how people would act. Imagine people being encouraged to act selfishly."

"Doesn't take much imagination."

Their orders came and they ate. Ravenwood finished his Reuben quickly and then headed for the door.

"Sorry to leave so soon," Ravenwood said, "but I've heard this conversation before, I find you boring, and I've gotten my free meal out of this."

"Gee, thanks," Fr. Gabe responded, sarcastically.

"Father," Alistair said. "Stay and have a beer with me."

Gabe looked at Alistair, who winked at him. Ravenwood had already exited the restaurant. Gabe nodded his head. They ordered beers. Alistair had this local brew. A stout called Original Sin. Fitting for the Satanic High Priest's assistant. Gabe ordered an IPA, as he was in a bitter mood after that encounter. After a few sips, Alistair spoke.

"If you want to see the Satanic philosophy in action," he began, "go to Bothwell school and hang around the principal sometimes. He'll give you quite an awakening."

"What do you mean?" Gabe asked.

"Principal Steve Jorek torments my cousin Bryce for no good reason. He does that to a lot of kids there, not just Bryce. That's what he's hired to do. The school board wants the principal to be an abusive asshole."

"Why would anyone want to abuse their own children like that?"

"Best preparation they could have for the 'real world.' He is a perfect simulation of an actual abusive boss. A lot of people can't succeed in the professional world because they cannot work for someone like that. Those Witch kids, they'll be used to it. When all you value in the world is success, weird stuff like that happens.

"I didn't go to Bothwell because of my condition. I nearly didn't go anywhere. Grandma and Grandpa wanted Mom to get rid of me. They wanted Aunt Desdemona to get rid of Beth and Bryce. They were pretty mad when she didn't. I think that's what got to her eventually. Suicide is pretty common among young people in Pandemonium, particularly on the Witch side of town. If success is the only thing that makes life worth living, most people don't have lives worth living. It's pretty logical when you think about it. That's what scares you when killing yourself makes sense. If I believed any of this garbage, I would have done it a long time ago."

"So, convert, change your life philosophy," Gabe suggested.

"I have a better plan," Alistair answered. "You don't ever try to change people's minds about anything all at once. My mother and I have something planned. I am setting up a presentation for both the spiritual leaders of the community and the trustees for a reform of the Satanic ritual. It will be after Christmas. Fr. Ravenwood doesn't know about it yet. I would appreciate you being there, as I'm hoping to get the support of all the other spiritual leaders in the community."

"I don't know how helpful I will be in evaluating a reform for a Satanic ritual," Gabe said. "I mean, I just tried to shut you down."

"Come. You might be surprised."

Pandemonium Lofts, 2 pm
Theo

Theo singlehandedly carried his coffin up the stairwell of the apartment. The complex had a loading dock, so Gilbert was basically able to back the moving car right up to the entrance so Theo could unload without interference of sunlight. Despite needing no additional help, Hecate apparently volunteered Bryce to come over, as he was arguing with Deanna in the doorway of Theo's new flat.

"Wow, you came all the way across town to annoy me," Deanna said.

"No, I came to help Theo move when I could be building a flame thrower," Bryce complained. "Where is he anyway?"

"Behind you," Theo called out. Bryce moved out of the way as Theo carried in the large coffin, setting it down in the bedroom.

Theo surveyed his new digs. He had already moved in the couch, a chest of drawers, a television, a few chairs, and now his sleeping arrangement.

"What is there for me to do?" Bryce asked.

"We haven't decorated yet," Beth offered, carrying a box of pictures of Deanna and Gilbert when they were younger.

Bryce found a refrigerator magnet and stuck it on the fridge.

"If my Aunt Hecate asks, I helped decorate," Bryce said.

"Hey, Deanna, is this that little fly who's always bugging you?" Theo asked.

"Yes," Deanna answered, dreading what came next.

Theo turned into a dog right in front of Bryce's eyes. Then he became a falcon, a cloud of mist, and then back into a man.

"There's a scientific explanation for all of this," Bryce insisted, rather confidently.

"What is it then?" Theo asked.

"I don't know. There's a scientific explanation for this. I just don't know what it is yet," Bryce explained. "Science may not know what it is yet either. But in the future, it will. Science has a pretty good track record explaining the physical world."

"That's a leap of faith," Deanna pointed out.

"Yes, it is," Bryce affirmed. "Science has earned my faith. Religion and magic have not."

"Let's change the subject," Beth interjected, hanging up a photograph. "Theo, I wonder if the internet works."

"Only one way to find out," Theo said, turning on his SmarTV.

Theo turned it to YouTube, which displayed a series of videos from Miles Simon Ministries.

"When did you become a fan of Simon's channel?" Deanna asked.

"Since I needed to keep an eye on the sneaky bastard," Theo replied. "Case in point."

Theo spotted a video entitled 'The Mysterious Theophilus.' He selected it. The video started.

"Miles Simon bought the Stranger Church to bring their story to America and reinvigorate our Christian heritage. As pastor, he has made a shocking discovery: namely that Pandemonium contains not only diabolical witches and the now-famous Ze'ev but also a real vampire."

Deanna and Gilbert audibly gasped. Theo just whistled. Cat's out of the bag now. The screen showed an image of a dark figure with large fangs.

"Most citizens of Pandemonium have met the mysterious figure known as Theophilus. They know of his arcane and diabolic powers, but most consider him a benign figure. How much do we know about him though? Theophilus is rumored to be nearly 400 years old. What has he been doing with his time? Miles Simon Ministries has investigated his background. Let's dive deep into his past."

Deep into my past, Theo thought. Let's see what they actually got right, what they thought they got right, and what they're lying about. The screen turned to a picture of Ireland. A skull and cross-bone markers appeared on the map.

"First, while historical records of vampiric activity are difficult to come by, oral history and written reports from Ireland in the 17th and 18th centuries reveal several incidents of humans being sucked dry of blood. Some of these reports come from occupying British soldiers, but other reports come from peasant farmers, both Catholic and Protestant. These stories tell of a blood-thirsty vampire who killed without reason or mercy, at times even killing and consuming *women and children*. Furthermore, these stories, while springing up all over Ireland, come disproportionately from Ulster, the region Theophilus was originally native to. Does this mean that Theophilus's reputation for only drinking animal blood is a fraud? While we cannot confirm or deny this, it certainly causes one to ask questions does it not?"

Theo looked on Deanna and Gilbert's faces, which were already turned toward him. Yes, he could see some questions coming up in their heads. Most of those deaths came from Scratch, but he never pretended to be an angel. The voice over continued.

"There have been five murders in Pandemonium since Theophilus moved here in 1982. Do we know for a fact that he was involved in none of them? Miriam Greenblatt died from loss of blood due to bodily wounds. Can we really be sure she was stabbed? We ask the residents of Pandemonium to think about these facts and consider whether Theophilus is really all that he seems."

The video ended. Deanna collapsed into the couch behind her. Gilbert looked Theo directly in the eyes. Bryce just rubbed his chin. Beth spoke first.

"Theo, Simon just revealed your existence to the whole world," Beth said. "You don't seem upset."

"It was going to happen eventually," Theo responded, shrugging. "I figured someone would blab. I'm a little shocked it wasn't Ravenwood. The tourist revenue he passed up."

"What do you plan to do?" Bryce asked.

"Face the music when it comes," Theo answered. "Maybe Ken Burns will do a documentary about me."

Beth pulled Bryce away, indicating that perhaps they needed to leave. Deanna didn't speak until she was alone with Theo.

"Is any of it true?" she asked.

"Is any of what true?" Theo responded. "He really didn't accuse me of much of anything, now, did he? He just put up a bunch of smoke and expected you to assume there was some fire."

"Is there any?"

"An ember, let's get you home."

Tuesday, Stranger Rectory, 10 a.m.
Theo

It wasn't long before the media started calling. The major outlets wanted to speak with the great Nosferatu, and Theo couldn't blame them. MacDonald helped him arrange a press conference to present himself to the world. Deanna bought Theo a new suit and helped him get dressed.

"You look pretty dashing when someone forces you to," Deanna said.

Theo admitted to himself she had a point. Theo was reminded of the old feudal lords, the kind that treated his family like animals. In years past he would dress up like this to fit in with those people. Helped make business connections, among other things.

The media arrived. An array of cameras appeared in front of the church. Theo walked out in broad daylight, and he made sure not to squint or look tired. It made the right impression. As soon as he appeared, a symphony of clicks emitted from the cameras. Theo imagined the front page of the paper showing an empty podium as he still didn't appear in photographs. Those front pages would likely become historical artifacts that needed to be explained to you.

"Hello," he began, stumbling over the first words with nerves. "My name is Cormac O'Duinn, though most people know me as Theophilus, or Theo for short."

"I am here today to answer the allegations leveled against me. Of course, Miles Simon would point out that he has not leveled any allegations against me, only asked questions. I will provide a few answers that I hope will assuage fears. However, I do not need to remind you that I have lived among you for nearly four decades without incident before Simon's 'expose' of me, which, once again, made no solid accusations. Nor could it, given how weak the evidence was."

Theo read the note cards in a nervous monotone. Public speaking had not been his strong suit.

"First, I must address the insinuation that I drank human blood in Ulster. I have tasted human blood in the distant past during my first century as a vampire. However, I only targeted members of the British military in uniform during an occupation of my home country. I did not target any civilians, and I have never tasted the blood of a woman or a child. That was a different time, I was a different man, and my country suffered heavily under British rule. Even so, I ceased this practice because I realized it was morally wrong, and I have made my amends with the British government. The last time I tasted human blood was October 22, 1747. If anyone in this room has reason to hold a grudge against me, it is Atticus MacDonald, who is Northern Irish in ethnicity. Atticus has forgiven me and we have been friends for decades."

Okay, Theo thought, there's the answer, now the explanation. He nearly jumped as the cameras shot another round of photos. He moved on to the next notecard and continued.

"How then to explain the civilians drained of blood across four centuries if they were not killed by me? The answer is that I am not the only vampire who has ever existed. While it may appear suspicious that death appears to follow me wherever I go, in reality, I followed death. Feeling a responsibility towards the general public, I have taken it upon myself at times to hunt down and kill other vampires which were active in a given area. Another vampire was responsible for the deaths in Belfast in the 20th century. Atticus and I, along with a priest named Fr. Eric Burton, killed him in the 1970s, and he cannot harm anyone anymore. The Vatican maintains a division of priests to hunt vampires, but that division currently only has one priest, the same who assisted Atticus and me in 1978, and it is only maintained on the rare chance that I turn bad. That is not a real possibility, a fact acknowledged by the Holy See."

Other vampires. Atticus told Theo it was preferable to keep the name Scratch out of his response. There were enough nuts in the world looking for a cult leader that Scratch's identity was worth hiding as long as Simon didn't reveal it. Time for questions.

"How many British soldiers did you kill?"

"Over the course of approximately a century? I would say maybe 100. I generally only did so if I felt the occupation was being particularly oppressive to certain villages. I regret those actions, but ask that they be viewed in the context of British occupation."

"Is the British Government aware of these acts?"

"Yes, and I have been given amnesty for them in a deal with the government. Suffice to say, I paid a price for that."

Yes, the bottle device. The Brits caught up with Theo after the Easter Rising and captured him using this little device that sucked mist into a bottle and kept it there. Nearly thirty years waiting in a bottle until someone let him out. Yeah, he'd done hard time.

"What did you do for the British Government at the end of World War II?"

"That's classified information I am not at liberty to speak on."

That was true.

"Can we call the Vatican and verify all that you have told us concerning these other vampires?"

"Fr. Eric Burton has assured me that you may call him personally and he will verify everything I have told you. I have his phone number, which I have given to Mayor Mayfield. I ask only that you take into account the time difference between here and Rome."

The questions stopped. The media seemed satisfied. Unfortunately, a large mob behind them was not satisfied. Marching behind the media was a group of Simon supporters. Church ladies riding in motorized scooter. Men in bow ties and suspenders who carried old Bibles with them. Those kids at church who aren't allowed to read Harry Potter. You know, *those people*. They all came armed with red roses.

"Roses," Theo mused. "Hadn't seen that one in a while."

The angry mob was coming towards him. Theo ran for the rectory. Jesus, sunlight made him weak. By the time he got through the door, he was huffing and puffing. MacDonald closed the door behind him. The angry mob started pelting the building with rocks and trash.

"The ministries own the building," Gilbert said. "Simon's followers are damaging his property."

"It's nothing to him," MacDonald replied. "Just like those men out there, Theo. They're not from around here. They don't know you like the rest of us do."

"I've had people call from all over town," Gilbert assured him. "They're still expecting you to be Santa on Christmas Eve."

The only person not talking was Deanna.

"Arun, I'm not proud of what I did to those British soldiers," Theo replied.

"This might take me a while to get used to," Deanna said.

"Theo and I might need to speak privately," MacDonald interjected.

MacDonald led Theo into his office. In the other room, they heard a rock crash through a window.

"Deanna and Gilbert will no doubt take care of that," MacDonald said. "Theo, this might be for the best."

"Yeah, the Ze'ev made a lot of money off that documentary," Theo thought aloud.

"What I meant was that eventually, Deanna and Gilbert have to know about Scratch."

"Why?"

"Who is going to help you keep guard over Scratch's remains when I die. I'm not a young man."

"I hadn't thought about that. I still don't feel like dragging them into this."

"Be careful, if Scratch is resurrected, he may drag them in himself."

Miles Simon Ministry Offices, 7 p.m.
Calvin

"AHHHHH!!!!!!" Simon screamed.

Calvin dove behind a desk as Simon threw a shot glass against the wall. His clandestine father exploded into such rage Calvin wondered if he'd breathe fire next. He'd had enough bourbon, that it might just happen if someone clicked a lighter.

Theo hadn't relented, even after the expose, and it appeared Simon's dream of hypnotizing people into giving him money directly wasn't going to come true. Hence the current temper tantrum. Simon couldn't get Theo to bend, he couldn't find Scratch's body, and Ravenwood's curse hadn't created any kind of bump in his online viewership...and he knew who to blame.

"You incompetent fuck," Simon growled, eyeing Calvin. "Get the hell out of my goddamn office. If you don't have a solution to this problem by 10 a.m. next morning, you're dead to me. Understood?"

"But---" Calvin started.

"Get to fucking work and fix this or you're fired!" Simon yelled.

Calvin got up from this chair and left the office. He could hear Simon sobbing behind him as he left. Pathetic, and yet so powerful. This man has the maturity of a toddler, and yet he commanded thousands of people. In any sane world, he wouldn't be in charge of a burnt-out match. Yet he held Calvin's fate in his hands. Life's a bitch.

Calvin sat down in his office. Simon expected to be able to just hypnotize people into giving him money, and he was angry to be let down. A month ago, he didn't know this power existed. It was magic he was asking for, and it would take magic to fix this. Where would he find magic?

Calvin's hand fell on the desk, and on the cassette tape with Scratch's voice on it. He picked it up and looked at it. No other choice. If he wanted to keep his job, this was the only possible way out. Calvin looked at the cassette, sighed, put the cassette in the player, and pressed play.

"Welcome back, Calvin," the voice said, immediately. "Has the Lord's providence led you to me?"

"In a manner of speaking," Calvin answered. "Mr. Simon expects me to find a way for his dream to come true."

"Mr. Simon? Isn't this man your father?"

"He is…how did you know that?"

"The Lord, as a sign of his favor, has granted me knowledge of all things in the present in my disembodied state. I know Simon is your father. I know how he speaks of your mother and the way he speaks to you. It truly is a travesty, my son."

Calvin felt a little something in his chest as the voice called him "son." He didn't recognize it.

"He wants me to find your remains. If you know all things, do you know where they are?"

"Of course, and I can even tell you the spell necessary to resurrect me. I would rather speak with your father personally, though. After all, he is trying to make me a business partner in his enterprise. Do you think you could play my tape for him?"

"Sure. You would be willing to speak with him?"

"Of course, your father seems like a very hard man, but business is business. I do want to tell you that your father is far too harsh with you. You're quite diligent in your service to him. How terrible he doesn't appreciate it."

"That's kind of you to say."

"One last thing, Calvin. I would prefer that you be in charge of the mission to resurrect me. You seem like such a bright boy. I am looking forward to meeting you, face-to-face."

"I look forward to it, as well. You're nothing like MacDonald says."

"Oh, you mustn't listen to the Apostate. He's lost the true faith. No doubt under the influence of my vampiric rival. Good-bye for now."

"Good-bye," Calvin said, turning off the tape.

Calvin did not feel frightened by Scratch. He felt a kind of warmth. Finally, someone who would listen to him.

CHAPTER FOURTEEN

Fourth Week of Advent, Wednesday, Pandemonium,
Miles Simon Ministry Offices, 10 am
Calvin

Calvin told Simon that he had found a way to locate Scratch's remains that morning.

"Alright, boy, whatcha got?" Simon asked.

Calvin took out a cassette player and laid it on the table. He then started the cassette inside. Scratch's original sermon against modernity replayed, and Simon did not appear moved by it. He shot a rather peeved look at Calvin for wasting his time. Calvin wondered if he was about to be fired, but his new savior intervened.

"Mr. Simon, patience is a virtue," Scratch interrupted. "Generally, I let people listen to my sermon first before I speak to them personally, but it appears I'll have to break that rule for you."

"What was that?" Simon asked, looking in disbelief at the cassette.

"Allow me to introduce myself, Mr. Simon. My name is Abner Shepherd, though you may know me as Scratch. I believe you are attempting to resurrect me."

"Is this some kind of sick joke? Calvin, how the hell are you doing this?"

"I wouldn't start tearing into your son again, Mr. Simon. I find it rather unbecoming of a future business partner. Suffice to say, Calvin here is not playing a trick on you. I am Scratch, and I would like to take you up on your offer to go in with you 50-50 in your business endeavor. If you wish to confirm this, you can test me."

"Test you? Calvin, clearly someone is just broadcasting a radio signal. Tell me who it is and clean out your desk."

"Very well, Mr. Simon, it appears I must commit a miracle despite your lack of faith. I will tell you something Calvin would have no way of knowing. When his mother revealed to you that she was pregnant, you initially thought about leaving your wife and marrying her. You even bought an engagement ring. Yellow gold with a 1-Carat diamond. You decided against it, but you still keep the ring in your pocket."

Simon's face grew long. His mouth hung open as if some weight were on his tongue. Simon reached into his pocket and retrieved a yellow gold ring with a 1-Carat diamond.

"How did you know that?" Simon asked.

"In this spiritual form I have taken, the Lord has rewarded his good servant with knowledge of all things in the physical world as they are presently arranged," Scratch explained. "I know that, and I know where my remains are and I can tell you the resurrection spell. The question is, are you willing to do business?"

"Well, of course. You're interested?"

"Mr. Simon, the Lord sent me as an angel to bring back the Kingdom of God abandoned by modern man. I see your ministries as an invaluable tool in ushering in the new Kingdom. I am particularly interested in the power of television and the internet, which you have used to such great effect. As for the money, well, a teacher is entitled to his payment, as St. Paul might have said. Suffice to say, money is a secondary concern for me. My main concern is to get in front of a camera and spread the Word."

"Theo says you can't appear on camera."

"With most normal cameras, that is true. However, I can tell you how to construct a device that will allow me to broadcast my image, along with my vampiric gaze, to the masses. Get me in touch with an engineer, and we can produce this device."

"Seems too good to be true. What's the catch?"

"The catch, as you put it, is that resurrecting me requires killing another human being. Are you willing to do that? To prove your commitment to our partnership, I would insist on you performing the ritual personally."

Simon looked around the room, evidently concerned that there be no additional witnesses.

"I am ready to do what is necessary to make this transaction work," he promised.

"Well then, fetch me an engineer, and we will begin our work," Scratch commanded. "Thank you for introducing us, Calvin. We'll be seeing each other in the flesh very soon."

The tape stopped.

"Boy, that was something," Simon said. "Go get that engineer."

Stranger Meeting Hall, 6 pm
Theo

MacDonald did not formally retire until midnight Christmas Day. This left time for one last Stranger ritual to take place in the Meeting Hall. A Stranger ritual of MacDonald's own making. Children from the Stranger part of the island arrived by car for this annual gathering, followed by a series of church vans carrying underprivileged children from the Varnertown mission. Thankfully, the protestors from around the church had moved on. Rich, poor, and in-between, the children of Pastor MacDonald's flock assembled in the main chamber of the meeting hall for what could be the last reenactment of a relatively young Christmas tradition, sitting cross-legged before a throne surrounded by artificial snow made from cotton.

And then he appeared. Theo, dressed in full Santa Claus gear and carrying a large bag of presents, walked through the front doorway of the meeting hall and bellowed "Ho, Ho, Ho!" in a flawless German accent. Santa Claus always seemed to be a German tradition to Theo, and having spent some time in Deutschland before the Great War, he could turn it off and on whenever he wanted. The children cheered as he came into the room and sat in his appointed place. Theo was on his throne and all was right with the world.

Gilbert and Deanna followed him in, dressed in green elf costumes. They had to carry in cloth bags containing presents, which had been paid for either by the parents or the church depending on the parents' income level. Pastor MacDonald sat in the back of the meeting hall and chuckled joyously, as the children began to form a line in front of Santa. Theo welcomed the first child onto his lap: a six-year-old named Brian Davies.

"Brian, what would you like for Christmas this year?" Theo asked.

Brian asked for the latest transforming robot that the good people at Mattel had come up with. Theo remembered giving that same toy to Gilbert when he was about that age, though, at that time, it was a different franchise. Same idea though, as toy sellers always find a new version of the tin soldier. Brian was one of the children from the Varnertown mission, and he had given his Christmas wishes to the people at the mission the week beforehand. Theo always wondered what would happen if a kid changed his mind the following week, but it hadn't been a problem. Gilbert looked through the charity bag, colored green, and found the toy robot which had been labeled for Brian. Gilbert handed it to Theo who handed it to Brian. Brian's eyes lit up, he hugged Theo, and he had his picture taken. This would result in a photograph where a child would appear to be levitating in mid-air, a unique memento. Some of the parents in the audience were young enough to have such photos of themselves.

Next came Suzy Wilson, a middle-class Stranger seven-year-old who lived in town. She got up on Theo's lap and asked for a bicycle. Deanna left the hall momentarily to retrieve the pink bicycle, which Suzy's parents had bought just for this occasion. Theo remembered getting Deanna a bike like that when she was five. Theo tried to convince her to take a doll, but she wanted the bike. Deanna wheeled the bicycle into the hall. Suzy ran to the bicycle. Deanna herded Suzy back to Theo for a picture, and then Suzy went back to her parents.

One by one, the children sat on Theo's lap and asked for dolls, race cars, the latest video game, etc. Theo never understood the attraction of video games, until he played one with Deanna the year before. So, this is how boys these days replace hunting and war? Other than that, the toys changed, but rarely in any way that indicated children did. Boys always wanted to be the latest version of the warrior: the cowboy, the soldier, the space marine. Girls always wanted to be the latest version of the princess: from Cinderella to CEO Barbie.

Eventually, the line dwindled. The presents were handed out. Theo rose from his seat and led the children outside, explaining he had to get back to the North Pole. He then transformed into a reindeer before them in the blink of an eye. A chorus of amazed "wows" erupted from the children. He then galloped off into the woods as the children chased behind him.

Christmas Eve, Friday, Pandemonium, Stranger Church, 7 p.m.
MacDonald

The rain let up for MacDonald's last sermon on Christmas Eve. He arrived two hours early, as he always had, to prepare the pulpit. MacDonald then practiced his sermon, finally retiring to the private quarters in the Church to put on his robes. They were purple which matched the season. MacDonald would always find a little time for quiet reflection before services. Put him in the right mood. He could hear the prelude as people entered in. He sat down and prayed. The response he received was always the same. He would try to convey it this morning. MacDonald moved out of the private quarters to the front of the church. The leaders of the procession stood before him. The front led with a golden cross, and the next man behind holding the Bloody Book, which had been taken out of its case for just this occasion. The Choir started 'O Come All Ye Faithful.' And the procession started.

As he moved down the main nave of the church, MacDonald looked over the crowd, the largest he had ever seen. Every seat in every pew was filled. Slowly moving down the aisle, he could see the City Council and Mayor Mayfield, who rose to greet him. MacDonald acknowledged them. The Davis family sat in attendance. Hecate had confiscated Bryce's *Scientific American* for the occasion. Pastor Overstreet sat with his family, having decided to allow for a substitute preacher at his own church just to be present. In the pew in front of him, Rabbi Barry helped the ancient Maharam sit down next to Fr. Ravenwood. And in the front row sat MacDonald's children next to Theo, now wearing his newly purchased Sunday best. So, I finally got him out of the crypt, MacDonald said, or at least someone did. He smiled at Deanna.

The service proceeded as it would have any Christmas Eve. MacDonald led the Church through their statements of faith. *I believe in the One God, the Father Almighty. Creator of Heaven and Earth.* MacDonald had picked out the scriptures to be read with a specific aim in mind. First, the Book of Esther, with particular emphasis on the end of the story. Then First Corinthians would be read (And now abide faith, hope, love, these three; but the greatest of these is love.). When the children were called up, MacDonald nearly shed a tear. And finally, John's

Gospel on the resurrection. After this was done, it was time for the sermon.

"Today I end my time as the Pastor of this Church. Technically, I cease being the Pastor tomorrow, when Mr. Simon begins services at the new church building downtown. However, celebrating this service is the heart of my job, and it is the heart of my life. Being Pastor of this church has been the greatest honor of my life. Truly, I have had the great blessing to call you all friends."

St. Michael's Church, 7:30 p.m.
Calvin

Calvin waited in the van with Simon's two hired criminals and Scratch. Scratch told Calvin Gabe would be going to MacDonald's final service, and sure enough, the priest had left an hour ago. The ministries sent out invitations to each of the religious leaders in the city, and as Gabe had no parish really, he didn't need to celebrate mass on Christmas Eve.

"Looks like you were right," Calvin said, watching the car disappear into the distance.

"Not much of an accomplishment for someone with omniscience," Scratch confessed, speaking from the cassette. "Now let's move in. My bones are in the basement."

Calvin gave the signal. The professional criminals came from Charleston, and they had burgled their way through a few houses. It was already dark, and few people were in this part of town on Christmas Eve. Perfect time to break into a church. The things you do in Christian ministry, Calvin thought. That wasn't even getting into the murder they were supposed to be committing tonight. One of the professional criminals quickly picked the locks on the church and entered therein. As he entered the church and the hired hands made their way to the basement, Calvin's eyes fell on the cross over the altar.

"I shall be resurrected in imitation of my Lord," Scratch said.

Stranger Church, 7:45 p.m.
MacDonald

"For my final sermon, I would like to talk about the virtue of Hope. Yes, Hope is a virtue, or obviously, St. Paul would have not placed it along with faith and love. This may sound strange to modern ears. We think Hope is good to have. We would not want to give up Hope, but to lack it does not strike us as a failing, merely a reason to be cheered up. This is because we do not understand the word."

"Hope does not mean mere optimism, the belief that we will be successful in all of our endeavors. If that were all that it meant, it would not be a virtue. It would be a delusion. The optimism of our time tells us that if we only work so hard, or follow such rules, or just keep our heads down that we shall not suffer. This belief shall not survive the first contradictory piece of evidence. Who can maintain when they look upon our world and its many injustices that the just shall always be rewarded and the unjust always punished? What of all the tyrants who die in their beds? What of all their victims whose only crime was to uphold the natural law established by nature's God? Look upon the unfortunate in our midst. Do they look so unworthy? Now let us examine ourselves. Do we really deserve the blessings we have? I can only answer for myself.

Being the Pastor of this Church for the last 38 years has been a blessing I can never deserve and can only attribute to God's grace and providence."

St. Michael's Church, 7:45 p.m.
Calvin

Calvin kept looking at the crucified savior above the altar while the professionals found the hatch to the basement and picked the lock. This was a harder nut to crack, but the lockpicker said he'd seen worse.

"I wouldn't stare too much if I were you," Scratch said. "Remember the danger of idolatry. It sickens me to be surrounded by these Roman superstitions."

"You really believe that God wants this?" Calvin asked. "I never had much training in religion. I think my Mom had a Bible she got from a hotel."

"I will be your spiritual mentor. And yes, Calvin, I do believe that this is what God wants. Do you know that Moses killed 3,000 people once to keep the Israelites from falling into idolatry?"

"I heard that. I think someone explained that God speaks to people on the level they are on."

"Yes, and the ancient Israelites were on a far higher level of union with the almighty than our decadent society. It is that holiness I will restore once I have ascended."

Stranger Church, 7:50 p.m.
MacDonald

"Hope is not the belief that we shall not suffer if we do all the right things. Hope is the belief that when we do suffer, that we shall not suffer alone and that God will have the Last Word. Hope is the belief that suffering is not for nothing, that instead it serves a higher purpose of redeeming us and the world at large. Hope is not swayed by the illusion of evil triumphing. It knows that there is a higher reality where the Devil has already been defeated."

"I warn of the danger of optimism because of what hides behind it: Hope's true enemy, Despair. Take for instance the man who claims that God will bless the righteous with wealth and leisure. The minute such optimism is defeated, and if we take Christ's words seriously, it will be defeated rather quickly, this man is revealed to be someone who has little if any self-worth not utterly dependent upon worldly success. A man who cares that much about success is that man who needs it so badly because outside of it he has no reason to go on living. A better description of Despair is difficult to imagine."

"Despair appears when we suffer. Not because we suffer, mind you, but in the way we look at suffering. Despair whispers to us that we suffer needlessly, that we suffer alone, and that we suffer because God is negligent, or worse, malevolent. Despair proclaims that what we have done is too great and cannot be forgiven and that this world, so clothed in sin, may never be redeemed. Despair lays out the arduous work God asks of us and tells us that like the Pharisee He will not lift a finger to help us bear the load. Despair tells us that God will not have the Last Word. That the only justice that exists is that which we can create on Earth, and by that, I mean, very little if any."

St. Michael's Church, 7:55 p.m.
Calvin

Calvin walked down to the basement where the hired hands were waiting for him. Scratch directed Calvin to his grave.

"Forward, forward, there," Scratch instructed. "You're standing over me. Don't worry, I won't be giving you bad luck."

"Dig here," Calvin commanded, pointing to the spot beneath his feet.

The hired hands went to work with the shovels they brought. They didn't concern themselves with the client taking orders from a cassette tape or the command to rob a grave.

"Why not use the priest as the sacrifice?" Calvin asked.

"I have my reasons for the selection I have made," Scratch answered. "When the time comes, all will be apparent."

Stranger Church 7: 55 p.m.
MacDonald

. "What I do not understand is how Despair has infiltrated the Church. Do not pretend to not know what I mean. We see the statistics. We hear the scandals. The pews are empty. The name is sold off. Young people don't want faith anymore, and when we hear of a Bishop or a Pastor getting his hand stuck in the money till, or worse, we understand why. Increasingly, the Church has become a sterile museum of what Western Civilization used to be about. The optimist looks at the situation and says, rather understandably, that the Church has failed, and that by extension God has failed."

"I, however, am not an optimist. When my parents signed me up for this journey on the day of my baptism, they weren't expecting my life to be a walk in a rose garden, and any expectation I had that it would be did not survive long. It is my role as a father and a pastor to disabuse my children and my congregation of any such notion."

"I respond with Hope. God only asks us to be faithful. He does not ask us to be successful. Hope means we have to look at our current adversity not merely as a technocratic problem to be solved. Our suffering has meaning, one that the Lord is trying to convey to us. And more importantly, he allows us to suffer to redeem us. The Church has committed sins too. We Strangers could have warned the rest of the Church about that before the sex abuse scandals, and the embezzlement, and the rest. The victim of our sins lies in the crypt beneath our feet, and in the heavens above us."

"Finally, Hope tells us that the present suffering should not sway our faith that God will have the Last Word. The pews are empty. On the Last Day, they shall be full. The clerics are corrupt. The weeds will be separated from the wheat. God appears to lose. He always loses on Friday. On Easter, he always wins. Oh, and by the way, Merry Christmas."

And with that the Orangeman ended his final sermon.

St. Michael's Church, 8:30 p.m.
Calvin

The hired hands cracked the coffin open, revealing the bones within. Calvin surveyed Scratch's remains. It looked like a normal set of bones, save for the two large fangs hanging from the mouth.

"I think those are the right ones, yes," Calvin guessed.

"You've found them," Scratch confirmed. "Now, tell the men to extract the remains in the coffin and then cover the grave. It may be inevitable that the priest or the Irishman discovers that I am missing, but we can delay that a little by covering our tracks. Put the bones into the black bag. No need to be gentle, as they are my remains, I don't mind."

Calvin repeated Scratch's orders to the men, but they already started. They accepted that the tape player was giving the orders. Calvin walked out to the van as the men loaded up the bones. After filling in the grave and locking up the church, they took off. Calvin hung his head.

"Please tell me the cops did not see us," Calvin pleaded.

"The only witness to what we have done so far was an 84-year-old Witch who plans to write a letter to the paper about hoodlums running around in black outfits," Scratch responded. "Keep your mind on the plan. Do you remember the next phase?"

"It would be difficult to forget. How do we get to MacDonald alone?"

"From my position in the great beyond, I know the Apostate's thoughts. He plans to visit the church one last time after his final service. He is the nostalgic sort."

Stranger Church, 8:30 p.m.
MacDonald

Of course, the service went on for another fifteen minutes or so. The Strangers do have a formal structure to their services, after all, requiring affirmation of doctrine. They normally celebrate the Lord's Supper only once a month, but they made a special exception for Pastor MacDonald's final service. After communion, the choir started up the final hymn 'Joy to The World.' MacDonald gave his benediction. "Go forth to love and to serve the Lord. Now and always." He added the last part. The congregation noticed as he was not typically one to ad-lib.

The entire church stood and cheered. MacDonald started to cry in earnest now, walking down from the pulpit one last time. In his last act, he took the Bloody Book and put it back in the case where it would remain. He instinctively moved to his children. Gilbert and Deanna rose from their seats and walked with him down the aisle as his final service ended.

CHAPTER FIFTEEN

Christmas Eve, Friday, Stranger Meeting Hall, 11:45 p.m.
MacDonald

MacDonald clinked his glasses with his flock one last time, then lifted the champagne glass to his lips. The church meeting hall had been done up with pictures of MacDonald and his achievements during his four decades as Pastor. His initial appointment. The Varnertown mission. His speech to the National Conference of Churches.

"If you want to see my greatest accomplishment," MacDonald said, "go take a picture of Theo wearing a suit, if for no other reason that it may not occur for another 50 years."

"Atticus, you know I don't appear in photographs," Theo answered.

"Like you can't sleep in apartments?" MacDonald asked. "Someone, give it a shot."

Someone did indeed take a picture of Theo with MacDonald with Gilbert and Deanna in the background. After the picture was taken, MacDonald got up and insisted on touring the church by himself one last time. He walked to the entrance where Annie Ferguson waited for him.

"Atticus," she said, "I wanted to speak with you in private."

"Well, you've got me," MacDonald said.

"I wanted to admit we were wrong," Ferguson confessed. "We shouldn't have sold the church. After that 'expose' Simon did, we realize that. Whatever good we do with the money now isn't worth it."

"What matters is what we do from here," MacDonald replied. "We still have the missions. Take care of the needy. We can at least do that."

MacDonald and Ferguson shook hands and parted ways. The former pastor walked into the church. As he crossed the threshold, the bells of the church began to toll. They played the tune to 'God Rest Ye Merry Gentleman.' Christmas Day. The Orangeman smiled as he walked back into the main chamber. He visited the pulpit once more. His hands traced the glass case for the Bloody Book. MacDonald walked up and down the aisles of the church, stopping where his children sat. Finally, he turned to the crypt. He turned on the lights. Walking past where Theo lived nearly four decades, MacDonald made his way to the bones of the Indian Princess. He pulled aside the burial shroud and viewed the cleaned bones.

"I wish I could show you how they've changed," MacDonald said. "Those illiterate barbarians who killed you have become something so different. They're good people, the Strangers, they really are. Not perfect. No one is. It takes time. That's what people don't understand. I'm sorry this happened to you, but out of this sin came something wonderful. It doesn't change how wrong it was, but I want you to know that you didn't die in vain."

"Neither will you."

There was a cold, English voice behind MacDonald. A familiar voice from the past. One he'd wished he'd never heard. It froze him for a moment. Slowly, he turned to see Calvin alongside several other men, pointing guns at him. Calvin held a tape recorder, and it was playing a familiar recording.

"We meet again, Apostate," greeted the voice of Scratch. "You will be coming with us."

"Hello, adversary," MacDonald replied, dully. "What if I refuse?"

"Then, we need someone else to serve as the sacrifice," Scratch pointed out. "Maybe it will be someone you don't know, or maybe it will be Gilbert or Deanna. In any event, my ascension approaches."

MacDonald rose his eyes to heaven. Was there any chance this cup could pass from him? Any way out of this? Or was this the time Lord? Would Theo be able to handle Scratch without him? What would happen to his children? To his congregation?

The butt of a gun pressing up against his temple gave him the answer. The Lord speaks in not so mysterious ways. The men took his cell phone and handcuffed him. Calvin and the other men led him out of the crypt at gunpoint into a van waiting for them behind the church. MacDonald went in first, followed by Calvin and his men. The Orangeman felt the car move. Calvin's hand shook. He could barely hold the gun. MacDonald could see Calvin was scared.

"You don't have to do this," MacDonald said. "Simon may fire you, but you have other options. We can go to the police."

"Yes, Mr. Simon will fire you, Calvin, but that isn't the reason you should be doing this," Scratch answered. "The reason you should be doing this is that as long as your decadent society allows it, men like Simon will rule over you forever. I have a plan for your father, believe me."

"Is that what this is about? Revenge?" MacDonald asked. "You want revenge on Simon for treating you as a burden?"

"I mean nothing of vengeance," Scratch insisted. "I hope to redeem Simon. Your father will learn to appreciate you in a whole new way, Calvin."

"He's your father?" MacDonald asked.

"Illegitimate," Calvin responded, "that's why I'm a Lucas, not a Simon. He's got a real family back in Houston. Look, I'm nobody. The ministries are my only chance to make something of myself."

"Calvin, when I bring the Kingdom back in glory, you will sit at my right hand," Scratch promised.

MacDonald's eyes fell upon the cassette tape. He remembered making that in '79 before he, Theo, and Fr. Eric took Scratch out. The bloody puritan had infested an old presbyterian church on Clifton Street, bombed by the IRA. He decorated the pews with the blood drained bodies of his victims. Before they cornered him, MacDonald recorded Scratch giving a sermon to his "congregation" that was essentially concentrated despair. MacDonald made the recording as evidence that Scratch existed in case the Royal Constabulary ever had questions, a situation that never occurred. Supposedly they were busy with other things. In hindsight, it was rather foolish to just leave it lying around.

The van stopped outside the new church Simon had put together on the fly. Three huge crosses towered over the white building filled with large windows.

"Here!" Scratch announced. "Simon's new church will be the place of my resurrection. Take me to the stage."

Calvin and the other men led MacDonald into the new church: a temple built to Mammon. The entranceway was filled with restaurants and coffee shops so worshippers could eat while Simon begged them for money. A book shop stocked with all of Simon's bestsellers carried his smiling visage. Television screens inside rotated advertisements with various herbal supplements and crank panaceas Simon hocked to his online flock.

"Disgusting!" Scratch proclaimed. "I assure you that once I have returned, I will be chasing the money changers out of this temple!"

MacDonald hated to agree with the demon about anything, but Simon's obscene commercialism so offended him that he couldn't help it. As they walked into the main worship hall that was more like an arena large enough for a professional sporting event, MacDonald spoke.

"I understand you don't find Simon to be the best father figure," MacDonald pleaded. "You haven't found a better one. Scratch may not kill you, but he will always lead you to ruin."

"Ruin is exactly where the world is now," Scratch countered, as they walked down the aisle to the stage. "The faith is dead."

"Yes," MacDonald answered, "and we have killed it."

As they entered the arena, MacDonald spotted Simon on the main stage sitting down next to a make-shift altar. As they approached the televangelist, the Orangeman noticed him tapping his feet nervously on the floor of the stage while staring at a long sharp knife. The demon wanted to see how committed his new business partner was.

They climbed on stage and MacDonald got a view of the altar, which was a set of steps leaning over a bathtub filled with Scratch's remains. Calvin surrounded the altar with black candles in the shape of a Pentagram as his father began to hyperventilate. The hired men forced MacDonald to kneel before the altar, gagged him, and began to light the candles. Simon then dismissed them. MacDonald looked down on Scratch's large canines and sighed. So, this is how it would end. The prosperity gospel preacher started chanting in Latin, incorrectly, MacDonald noticed. The Orangeman wondered if there was some way to contact Theo. Running would do no good with armed men behind him and his sexagenarian legs beneath him. No, his time had come.

The clock in the town square struck midnight, as the bells began to tome. Merry Christmas, MacDonald mused with melancholy. He thought about his last sermon. Given current circumstances, he was glad to have hope, as there wasn't much room for optimism right now. Simon stopped chanting. So, the spell was over. The candles all went out at once. The Orangeman could feel something present, but he couldn't describe what it was. It was almost like there was an absence present, a black hole which entered the room, from which no light could escape. MacDonald felt the blade press against his throat. Last chance to turn back. He clearly wanted to. His hand was shaking. Simon, however, surprised the Orangeman and ran that knife across his throat.

Pain, yes, pain was present. It definitely hurt. It was really more the cold that stuck out to him. People don't talk about the cold feeling in death. They talk about ghosts passing through you like it was a shiver, but never you passing from yourself. It was like his own ghost left his body along with the blood, which was considerable. His vision faded. It is finished.

Calvin

The blood filled the bathtub with Scratch's remains. Calvin's father held the knife in his hand as it dropped crimson rain. There was nothing at first. Just Simon holding a bloody knife in the darkness. Then, the blood in the bathtub boiled and stirred. It took form. Red muscles and arteries appeared and wrapped themselves around the bones as vines. A heart emerged from the blood, and then eyes and a brain, all of which lifted themselves into place. Nerves branched out from the brain-like roots. Skin grew onto the figure like moss on an old stone. Once complete, the pale skin stretched over the angular frame like a death shroud, concealing filth within. Then came the hair, which sprouted out of the top of Scratch's head like wheat springing from the summer ground. Calvin looked down to find a thin, pale man with matted brown hair, a mole on his left cheek, and two very large canine teeth. A dark shadow settled over the figure, that solidified into a plain, dark tunic. Finally, the eyes opened with a start that made Calvin jump. The shape smiled, and his body levitated itself upright until Scratch floated before them vertically.

Scratch turned his head to Simon, now visibly shaking from top to bottom. The thin man's eyes lit up with an unnatural red glow, and Simon's body went slack. The televangelist, now calm, wiped the blood off of the knife and calmly handed it to the hired men.

"Yes, Mr. Simon, good," Scratch intoned, his voice echoing in the dark arena. "Good and faithful servant."

Simon walked to the front row and calmly took his seat. Calvin looked at his father and found a faraway look in his eyes, which were directed at the back wall just slightly above where Calvin was standing. Calvin then turned his head back to Scratch.

"Calvin, I'm glad to meet you in the flesh," Scratch said, holding his hand out.

Calvin took the hand tentatively.

"Yes, you will see that the pearl of great price you have sought is worth the cost," Scratch said.

Scratch snapped his fingers and a blaze of white light shone from his body. Calvin closed his eyes, and after a moment, the light died down. He opened his eyes and saw none other than Atticus MacDonald standing right in front of him.

"How---?" Calvin began to ask.

"As he was the sacrifice, I can impersonate the Apostate," Scratch answered before Calvin could finish. "That is why he was the sacrifice. There are tradeoffs, however, as I have lost my omniscience now that I have a body. Now, I only know what MacDonald knew before he died, along with my memories from my last incarnations."

"Okay, so now what do we do?"

"First, we neutralize the Irishman."

Christmas Day, Stranger Rectory, 4 am
Deanna

Deanna woke up, hearing a scratching at the door. It was loud. Like something or someone wanted to get in. It was coming from downstairs. She walked down the stairs to the first floor of the rectory. The scratching was coming from the front door. Deanna opened the door to find a large dog on the other side.

"Theo?" Deanna asked.

It didn't look like Theo's normal dog form. This was more like a wolf, complete with sharp teeth and a white mane. The wolfdog whimpered.

"Theo, why don't you just come in?" Deanna asked.

The wolfdog liked that instruction. It jumped across the threshold at the invitation, licking Deanna in the face. The wolfdog pranced around the living room playfully.

"Theo, knock it off," Deanna pleaded. "Transform and tell me what the problem is."

The dog didn't comply. Instead, it bolted out the door as quickly as it came. Deanna was left mystified.

"I'll talk to him tomorrow," Deanna said.

Theo

"No, Deanna, I didn't come to visit as a dog at four in the morning," Theo said. "At four, I was in my apartment, ringing in Christmas with an egg nog."

Theo came to visit on Christmas morning so they could unwrap presents. Deanna asked him a strange question about showing up as a dog earlier that morning, about which Theo didn't have the foggiest idea.

"So, some random dog came up to the house and started scratching the front door?" Deanna asked.

"What was it that Sherlock Holmes said? When you eliminate the impossible what remains, however, improbable, must be true," Theo quoted.

"Pretty sure that was Spock, actually," Deanna responded.

Up above them on the second floor of the rectory, Gilbert appeared and leaned over the railing.

"Guys, Dad's feeling a little under the weather," Gilbert explained. "He'd like us to celebrate Christmas in his room, so he can stay in bed."

Theo and Deanna went upstairs to find MacDonald bedridden in a dark room. The curtains were drawn tight. Theo found the whole scene a little odd, but if the Orangeman was feeling ill, it was no big deal.

"Deanna, Gilbert," MacDonald greeted. "I apologize, but we must have our holiday festivities here this year. Gilbert, could you bring up the gifts?"

Gilbert did indeed bring up the gifts from under the Christmas Tree. Deanna got a new crossbow from her father and the newest iPad from Theo, which she had picked out for him the week before. MacDonald gifted Gilbert a collector's set of C.S. Lewis's greatest apologetic works. MacDonald's children had the text of his final sermon framed, along with a picture of his retirement party. Deanna pointed to the translucent figure of Theo's outline in the photograph. Theo's body was becoming more human over time. Gilbert also got his father a new pipe and a bottle of scotch.

"Thank you, Gilbert, I am sure I will enjoy this scotch once I am in better shape," MacDonald said. "You know, I would like to check on Mr. Simon this morning."

"Why?" Gilbert asked, somewhat annoyed.

"Oh, I'm just so full of Christmas spirit that I'd like to show a little charity, even to those least deserving."

They all chuckled at MacDonald's bon mot. MacDonald grabbed the remote and turned on the SmarTV, bringing up Simon's YouTube channel to his latest sermon. Gilbert noted mentally that it was unusually well watched, with nearly 100,000 views despite being on for only an hour. The video started.

Simon appeared on screen, but not on stage. Instead, he stood in front of a generic background, generated by a green screen, in his signature suit, but crying. Real tears fell down his cheeks, reddened with sorrow. His eyes were upturned, possibly to the almighty?

"My Lord, I am heartily sorry for having offended thee," Simon sobbed. "Have mercy on me a sinner."

Gilbert and Deanna fell silent. Theo, normally unfazed by much of life after four centuries, blinked twice, stunned by the sight of a genuinely repentant Miles Simon.

"Brothers and sisters in Christ," Simon continued. "I must confess that I have sinned against my wife and against my Lord. There's no hiding from it now: I have had an affair with a woman named Gloria Lucas. She even gave birth to a child, which I have shamefully hidden from the public. I loved the darkness rather than the light because my deeds were evil."

"Wow, he quoted the Bible," Gilbert said. "I mean, it's a paraphrase, but I didn't think he could do that."

"I must do penance, and that begins with stepping back from my ministry," Simon announced. "This is a time for prayerful discernment. Starting today, I will step down from active ministry. Good-bye, America, and pray for me."

The segment ended. The room remained silent. Finally, Deanna spoke.

"So, I guess…that's good?"

The phone next to MacDonald's bed rang. The Orangeman picked it up.

"Hello, this is Atticus MacDonald. Yes, yes. Oh."

"Dad, what is it?" Gilbert asked.

"It's the Ms. Whittington down at the Varnertown Mission," MacDonald replied. "Miles Simon Ministries has sent a group of their executives with a buffet line of food. Simon's treating the homeless to Christmas dinner."

"No," Theo said, softly. "No, he did not."

MacDonald handed Theo the phone. For a split second, MacDonald's hand grazed Theo's finger, and a chill went down Theo's spine. The moment passed, and Theo held the phone to his ear.

"Sarah, this is Theo. Really? They say they're from Simon. And they plan to spend Christmas serving the poor? Text me a photograph."

Theo hung up the phone, and after a second it buzzed again. Theo's eyes lit up. He then showed the phone to Gilbert and Deanna, and the text clearly displayed a photograph of Calvin holding a tin of roasted turkey in front of the mission.

"I have to see this in person to believe it," Gilbert said. "Dad, do you mind if me and Deanna go and check this out?"

"Please do," MacDonald answered. "I'm far too under the weather to join you, so send me more pictures. Simon might actually be in the midst of a real conversion experience."

"That would be a Christmas miracle," Deanna cracked.

Varnertown, South Carolina, Varnertown Mission, 2 p.m.
Gilbert

Gilbert half assumed this to be a joke. He fully expected to arrive at the mission to find nobody there, except maybe a man holding a note explaining how he'd been fooled. No, it was legit, at least on the surface. When he and Deanna parked their car across the street from the mission, they found several of Simon's associates lined up behind a buffet, serving turkey and mashed potatoes to the local homeless. At the very end, a woman Gilbert recognized as Simon's secretary handed out little baguettes to people. The local media lined up in front of the bread line and photographed the 'salvation directors' as Simon commonly called them. Calvin raised his hand and hailed them down.

"Now, I can apologize," Calvin offered, jogging over to them. "I'm sorry we broke into your father's study and took his notes. I'd give the 'I was following orders' excuse, but that never works. Suffice to say, the orders are different now."

"You're Simon's son," Gilbert said.

"Yes, I am. Needless to say, it's been a very strange 24 hours for me."

"For a lot of us. What happened?"

217

"I spoke with a friend of my mother's a month ago, and she didn't like the way I was being treated. She had an old photograph of my mother and Simon together. Two days ago, she put it online. You can google it. There was no point in denying it."

"So, repentance is a last resort?"

"No," Calvin answered. "I know this is difficult to believe, but he wants to use the name Stranger to serve the poor and spread the faith with humility. My father knows he needs the Strangers' help to do that, that's why he is offering to give Gilbert his youth pastor job back. He knows that his past actions have been a scandal, but he's willing to make it up."

"Now he is," Deanna growled.

"What my sister is trying to say," Gilbert said, giving Deanna a stern look, "is that conversion is a lifelong experience. My Dad has taught me that anyone saved over a weekend will be lost over a holiday."

"Oh, my father's conversion is genuine," Calvin said. "He's speaking with your father about spiritual guidance now."

New Stranger Church, 7 p.m.
Scratch

Simon drooled down his neck as Scratch gazed deeper and deeper into his eyes. Behind him, a host of salvation directors, a term that made Scratch wretch, absorbed the same hypnotic power. The Bloody Puritan surveyed Simon's office, a gaudy display of indulgence unfit for a Christian and obscene for a man of the cloth. Wide-screen televisions. Leather furniture. Endless photographs of

Simon. A wall of expensive managerial liquor. Nary a cross in sight.

"Simon," Scratch began, counting the bottles of whiskey on the wall, "teetotalism is not in my personal theology, but it might do you some good."

"No more booze," Simon agreed groggily.

"That's the beginning," Scratch ordered. "Remove these awards and placards you have collected. Sell the furniture and the televisions. You need only a desk and a straight wooden chair. This is supposed to be the office of a parson, not the drawing room of Ceasar."

The salvation directors under Scratch's power started moving the furniture out of the office, collecting the liquor bottles and mementos, and unplugged the widescreens. Simon kneeled on the floor in prostration before his new idol. Scratch looked out the window. The night was young.

"You sent Calvin to serve those vagrants?" he asked. "Is he still there?"

"Yes," Simon droned.

"That means the vagrants are still there," Scratch concluded, opening the window. "Good, they aren't the only ones that need to feed."

The pale man turned into a falcon and flew out the window, in the direction of his prey.

CHAPTER SIXTEEN

Second Day of Christmas, Saturday, Pandemonium,
Davis Guest House, 8 am
Beth

Beth woke up that morning with the St.
Benedict Medal she got from Deanna around her
neck. Even if it didn't keep Hannah away, it did make
her feel a little safer. Almost as much as the dream
catcher and the Japanese bells. Beth weeded the
garden on Tuesday and didn't see one spirit come
from the Plantation House. Not the Madam, not the
Colonel, and especially not the Bloody Bride. Maybe,
someday, she'd go back into the plantation house and
have breakfast. With that confident thought, Beth
went into the parlor of the guest house to find Pastor
MacDonald sitting on the couch.

"Oh, Pastor MacDonald," Beth said,
somewhat surprised, "I didn't hear you come in. Is
Deanna here?"

"No, Deanna's not here," MacDonald
answered, "though it's her I'd like to speak to you
about. Beth, you must excuse me. I would normally
knock and wait for you to let me in, but I'm just now
getting used to not having a body."

"Not having a body?"

MacDonald then levitated off the couch and shone with a powerful golden light she'd seen before from Jarvis. Beth squinted her eyes. The light dimmed somewhat so that Beth could see MacDonald as a spirit now.

"I'm dead, Beth," MacDonald explained. "I know you can see dead people. I need your help. Technically, I'm not supposed to be doing this, but Deanna and Gilbert are in a lot of trouble."

Beth screamed and ran into her bedroom, slamming the door behind her. MacDonald sighed and spoke up.

"Beth! If I wanted to, I could float through the walls into your room and speak to you there," MacDonald insisted. "I was always taught not to go into a lady's room without permission."

"No, no, no!" Beth shouted. "No spirits here! This is my safe space! Go away!"

MacDonald shook his head.

"Beth! Deanna is in real danger," MacDonald pleaded. "She could die."

Beth slowly opened the door.

"Die?" she asked.

"Yes, Beth, she could die, or worse," MacDonald said, now floating above the electric stove. "You know Theo?"

Beth nodded her head. She first met Theo when she was eight. Her aunts let her celebrate Christmas with the Strangers, and Theo presented her with a new set of watercolors. Since then, Theo had been over to the plantation house a couple of times for parties and Beth invited him in once when she and Deanna were having a sleepover. Deanna forgot her iPad and Theo delivered it to them as a falcon. Apparently, his clothes and anything in his pockets would transform with him, allowing him to carry a cellphone he never answered.

"There is someone like Theo, but he's not a nice man," MacDonald explained. "He killed me the night before last, and now he looks like me. You'll see when we go over there."

"Will this other vampire want to kill me?" Beth asked.

"Hmmm…Maybe, but right now he's pretending to be me to cause maximum damage later. But if you don't warn her, Deanna might fall under his control, and we definitely wouldn't want that, would we?"

"I guess not," Beth gave in, quivering with fear. "Where is Deanna now?"

"With the beast."

Pandemonium, Stranger Rectory, 1 p.m.
Beth

Beth and MacDonald made their way to the rectory. MacDonald warned Beth not to be alone with Scratch.

"How will I know Scratch when I see him?" Beth asked.

"People will be talking about him as if he were me," MacDonald answered, "and given your special abilities, he won't be difficult to spot."

Beth knocked on the door of the rectory and Deanna answered.

"Beth, come in," she greeted. "How are you doing?"

"Oh, I'm fine," Beth responded. "I just wanted to check in on you given how weird things were getting with Simon undergoing this sudden change in behavior."

"Yeah, I could use someone to talk to about that. He's not the only person acting strange. Gilbert and Theo think Simon's just playing, but my father spoke with him earlier today, and apparently, he believes Simon is genuine. Then again, he's a little under the weather."

"Ahh, is that Beth?" called a voice from the second floor. "Deanna, you should bring her up here and let me tell you what's going on."

The voice from the upper room had an English accent, quite distinct from MacDonald's familiar Northern Irish brogue. Deanna didn't appear to notice, as she reacted to her father much as she would have.

"Dad, I don't think Beth should disturb you when you need rest," Deanna protested.

"Oh, I am feeling much better now," the voice insisted. "Come to think of it, let me come down."

A thin, pale man with skin wrapped tightly around his bony features and matted brown hair walked down the stairs. Only when Beth got a good look at the man did she see two large canine teeth poking out from his upper lip. His eyes contained a kind of burning malice, and it was aimed directly at Beth. Those eyes were not directed at MacDonald, who, thankfully, he seemingly could not see.

"Act natural," MacDonald suggested. "He's supposed to be me."

"Oh, hello, Pastor MacDonald," Beth greeted, trying her best to be polite, "I hear you've had some momentous things happen in the past few days."

"Miles Simon has spoken with me and has expressed interest in true religious conversion," the shape said. "This could mean big things for the

223

church. Using Simon's network, the Stranger Church could become a major Christian denomination in the United States."

"If you think Simon is sincere," Deanna spoke to the monster.

"Oh, I believe he is," the shape answered. "I think you'll find that in the coming days; remarkable conversions will be more common than you could ever expect. Beth, have you considered your final destination after death?"

Beth blushed as the shape asked what her aunts had trained her to think of as a very personal and private question. Deanna simply seemed annoyed. Beth, ever the junior cotillion and perfect lady her Aunt Hecate trained her to be, gave a standard answer.

"Most people want to go where their ancestors are when they die," Beth repeated. "I want to be where my family is."

"Yes, but didn't your father run when he found out your mother was pregnant?" the shape asked. "To say nothing of your mother's suicide."

"Dad!" Deanna yelled. "That's enough. Beth, I'm sorry. Something has gotten into my Dad."

"It's perfectly fine," Beth interjected. "I was thinking you and I could have a sleepover tonight. I am sure this has been a lot of excitement."

"That sounds great," Deanna said, sounding relieved. "Let me get my stuff."

Deanna then turned and left the room, leaving Beth alone with the shape, much to MacDonald's frustration. As soon as Deanna left Beth's sight, the shape's eyes lit up crimson red.

"He's attempting to hypnotize you," MacDonald explained. "It doesn't appear to work. It might have something to do with your unusual mental abilities. Just play along for now."

"Beth, you will have a conversion experience, and real encounter with the living God," the shape commanded. "You will then help me convince Deanna to trust Simon and the ministries."

Beth simply stared ahead blankly and pretended to be under Scratch's power. After a few moments, the eyes stopped. Deanna came back into the room with a bag and pulled Beth out of the door. Once they were out of the rectory and back in the car, Deanna spoke.

"I'm so sorry, I can't imagine why my father did that," Deanna apologized again. "It must have been humiliating."

"Alright, Beth, now tell Deanna the truth," MacDonald ordered.

"Yes, I agree that something is wrong with your father," Beth responded. "I believe he may be very ill, and that both you and Gilbert should probably stay away from him for a while. It could be contagious."

"Don't you think you should tell Deanna about the extraordinarily dangerous theocratic vampire in her house? Or at least tell Gilbert, who I should note is still there?" MacDonald asked.

Beth ignored MacDonald, who continued complaining all the way to the guest house.

Davis Guest House, 2 p.m.
Beth

Beth and Deanna finally arrived at Beth's house with MacDonald flying above them trying to shout at Beth to just tell Deanna about Scratch.

During the drive, Beth had turned up the radio and then got Deanna to start singing along with her. Once inside the house, Beth told Deanna she was using the restroom and then closed the door behind her.

"Beth! Why aren't you telling Deanna and Gilbert that the person they think is their father is an immortal demonic creature trying to kill them!?" MacDonald demanded.

"Pastor MacDonald, how long have you been dead?" Beth asked.

"Since early Christmas morning. Why?"

"I've been seeing dead people since I was six. I saw a woman in a wedding dress walking by my room with blood coming out of a hole in her forehead. I ran out of the house and wouldn't come back. When I told my Aunt Hecate what I saw, I spent the summer in a psychiatric facility. I only got out by lying to people and saying I was 'better.' When you see dead people, you don't advertise the fact."

"But Beth, don't you think this is a different situation?!"

"Pastor MacDonald, if I told Deanna that this thing pretending to be you, Scratch you called it, is a bloodthirsty vampire, how do you think she would respond? She wouldn't believe me. Deanna would think I'd gone crazy!"

"Hmmm...you're right, but what if you told Theo? He knows about Scratch. You need to get to Theo. Suggest a visit."

"I will tonight."

"Tonight?"

"We just got here, it will look suspicious, and I would ideally find a way to tell them without revealing I can speak to the dead. I couldn't do that over a phone call. I'll suggest stopping by tonight when Theo will be awake to talk about her father's bizarre behavior. I'll look very concerned, and suggest Gilbert come with us. That's assuming Theo can meet with us."

St. Michael's Church, 5 p.m.
Theo

"Yes, Deanna, I agree with you that we need to talk about your father," Theo calmly assured her. "I think he might be ill. Severely ill, but we can't talk tonight. I have something to look into. You and Gilbert just stay away from the house for now. Stay at Beth's house tonight. I'll get back with you tomorrow."

Theo hung up the phone and looked into the empty grave he and Gabe had just uncovered in the church basement. After seeing Simon's complete and total change in behavior, almost like lead turning into gold, Theo decided that the only power on Earth capable of such a change would be Scratch. He asked Gabe to help him dig up the bones again, but they were nowhere to be found.

"How could this be? I told no one. I rarely leave the rectory," Gabe wondered. "I swear Theo I didn't tell anyone."

"I don't think you did. When you've fought Scratch as long as I have, you learn a few things about him. One of those things is that he wants to be brought back. When I investigated the people who resurrected Scratch before, their notes seemed to indicate that somehow Scratch had given them the spell himself."

"What do we do?"

"You stay here and do nothing, maybe prepare some holy water if it makes you feel better. I will investigate at the New Stranger Church and see if they have resurrected Scratch. Tell Gilbert if you have no other choice. I would rather not get him or Deanna involved, but if Scratch is active, he needs to know."

Theo exited the basement and then the church. He looked at the three large white crosses of Simon's artificially manufactured greed temple, lit up in the early evening by green Christmas lights. He turned into a falcon and aimed for them.

New Stranger Church, 7 p.m.
Theo

Theo landed on the middle of the three large crosses in front of the church. He spied an air vent. The Irishman never had to be invited into a desecrated church. The desecration was the invitation. He wondered if that worked for all churches now. Theo transformed to mist, evaporating and spreading out with the droplets of the haze. He wafted through the air ducts around the building. Mist was one of his more useful forms: impervious to attack and easy to hide. He could see from every droplet of his being and feel every side of the metal duct as he drifted against it. Unfortunately, it made attack impossible from his position as well. He found his way to the offices. A familiar voice stood out.

"You can build this, right?" Calvin asked.

"I can build it, I'm just not sure what it is. I mean this thing you want to build channels dark energy humans typically don't work with. With the specifications I've been provided, I can't say I can't make it. I can build this and then apply for five patents. What are you using it for?"

"That's not your business," Calvin answered. "Suffice to say, we need this to promote our evangelical efforts."

"Okay, I'll build it, but it will cost you."

"Money is not an object," Calvin promised.

Theo tried to get a closer look. He seeped out of the vent and, over Calvin's shoulder, caught a glimpse of a blueprint. It was for a large camera, the kind used to record a television show or a movie. Calvin stirred a bit. Theo backed off into the vent.

He then felt himself being pulled down the duct. A vacuum-like sound filled the small metal tube. He tried to resist, but he was being sucked involuntarily. The freedom he had as gas had been turned into a straitjacket. A nagging dread filled his mind as Theo realized he had experienced this only once before, and he didn't like what came next. His gaseous body quickly flew down through the labyrinthine ventilation system into the basement. The Irishman found himself collecting at the bottom of a very large bottle, connected to a machine. Theo cursed himself as he realized that he was trapped in the very same device the Brits kept him in for more than 20 years. He'd fallen for it again.

Well, he thought, they had him. How the Hell he hadn't managed to get any smarter than this over 400 years of life, well, who knows. Best see who my captors are. Theo took the form of a man and stood up in the bottle. He looked around and saw through the clear glass cage that Calvin was waving at him while leaning back in a chair. Theo punched the wall of the bottle and succeeded at doing nothing but scuffing his knuckles. He held his hand in pain and let out a cry of frustration at his own stupidity. Theo then tried using his eyes. The light just reflected off the glass. It was no use. He had been trapped again. Theo checked his cellphone: no coverage. Calvin walked up to the speaker system and activated it.

"We've blocked all signals out of this room," Calvin explained. "You can't get out and you can't hypnotize me."

"Clever," Theo replied. "Did Scratch teach you to make this?"

"No, actually Simon made this as a countermeasure against you or Scratch, whoever he needed to use it against. It worked. I'll have to tell him that."

"Sure, tell the brainwashed dummy that his idea worked. I bet he'll be so elated that he'll stop drooling for a minute."

"My Dad seems happy. Scratch has taken away all of his ambition and greed."

"It's not real, Calvin. He doesn't really love you."

"Oh, it's very real. The Kingdom's coming back. It's for real this time."

"The Kingdom? So now you're talking like this? He's got his claws into you, boyo."

"He might get his claws into Deanna later."

"Careful, lad, I might have to pull that tongue out of your mouth."

"Night, night," Calvin taunted.

Calvin turned out the lights and left the room.

CHAPTER SEVENTEEN

Third Day of Christmas, Sunday, New Stranger Church,
10 a.m.
  Gilbert

Gilbert wondered if he should have stayed the night at Theo's place, as his father was acting stranger and stranger. MacDonald would hover over him, make offhand comments about theology that seemed rather…unorthodox to say the least, and he seemed to appear and disappear at will. Gilbert tried to find some excuse not to spend the night with him, but much to his surprise, his father left on his own at sundown.

"I am feeling better. Furthermore, Miles asked me to do a special service and I have to practice my sermon," MacDonald explained. "It will take a while so don't wait up for me."

The sound of his father referring to Simon as 'Miles' clanged in his ears like a bronze pan bouncing on a tile floor. Since when were they on first name basis? The Orangeman hadn't lied about having another sermon, as Gilbert checked his Gmail account to find a message from his father inviting everyone on the old church's email list to a special service at the New Stranger Church downtown. He then found a response from Deanna asking why he was having a service there and not the old church.

So, Gilbert slept in his own bed that night. He woke up once at 2 am to the sound of a wolf howling and went back to sleep. Gilbert drove to the New Stranger Church the next day, mulling over Deanna's question. Why was he having a service here? Why not the church in his front yard he preached in for nearly 40 years? MacDonald was obliged to answer that question.

"We need Simon's organization," MacDonald announced.

MacDonald invited the Strangers to worship with him in one of the more intimate conference rooms of Simon's new church. The arena Simon preached in wouldn't do for this meeting where MacDonald spoke with the flock he tended to for four decades. Deanna brought Beth along, which was the first time she'd bothered to bring Beth to any church event. Gilbert looked at Beth and saw a faced weighed down with concern, perhaps even fear. Children sat on their parents' laps and old men and women held hands as MacDonald laid out his plan to convert America.

"We have a real community of faith here, we do," MacDonald began. "More importantly, we have a powerful story. A story that America needs to hear. Using the resources of Simon's organization, we can deliver that story to the rest of the country and the rest of the world."

"Simon was a self-centered and avaricious man, but he could see the problem. America's Christian heritage is slipping away. Homosexuality and licentiousness are celebrated. Church attendance plummets, revealing a deep spiritual sloth. I know how all of you feel after the last election. The people who built this country are denigrated as backward yokels. With these resources, we could put a stop to it and reverse the tide. I know Simon's conversion is sudden, but I believe he had a real experience with the one true God."

"Annie, I know you and the other elders approved the sale because of the good the money could do for the poor. Imagine how much good it will do to have a mission like Varnertown in every mid-sized city in America. Consider the good the money Simon has pledged will do. We have to start seeing Simon's church as our church. Our story is his story. I know you had regrets about selling, and at the time, it may have been the wrong decision, but now God has turned it for the good."

"I know this seems, well, overly optimistic, but I truly believe that the recovery of Christian America begins here. The Lord has delivered this bounty unto us. We should use it."

Gilbert raised his hand. MacDonald pointed at it.

"How does this square with your last sermon?" Gilbert asked. "You know? Not putting faith in worldly power and technocratic means?"

"Gilbert, you must understand," MacDonald answered, raising his hands in a gesture of soft defense, "I made that speech expecting it to be my last. Practical considerations of monetary resources and international reach were the furthest thing from my mind."

Right, thought Gilbert, he doesn't sound like the man who fed me black pudding on that cold day in Varnertown.

MacDonald ended the meeting with a prayer.

"Lord, grant us power and glory in our crusade for righteousness."

Gilbert spoke a very soft amen as if he wasn't sure what he was agreeing to. It was time for youth group, and Simon had rehired Gilbert as part of his penance. Gilbert led his charges to one of the other conference rooms intended for youth group meetings. The room was so large, it made the relatively small Stranger crowd seem tiny by comparison. Multimedia display, a big collection of board games, and even a kitchenette in the back. Deanna sat in the front with Beth, who still looked rather frightened.

"Hello, everyone," Gilbert greeted, "I assume you all have a lot of questions. Yes, my Dad has been acting a little strange lately. And Mr. Simon, well, he seems like an entirely different person. You aren't the only person surprised by these changes."

"But I'm not going to talk about that," Gilbert continued. "I'm going to talk about a passage of the Gospels that's been sticking in my mind since this all started, going all the way back to when the church was sold. Does anyone here know about the Temptation of Christ?"

Deanna's hand went up, which Gilbert pointed to.

"He was tempted by the Devil in the desert," Deanna said.

"Yes, he was," Gilbert replied. "What was the first temptation?"

"Satan told him to turn stones into bread to feed himself," Deanna answered.

"Right. Satan asked Jesus why don't you turn stones into bread. Christ answered that Man shall not live on bread alone. What Christ was saying is that he could go around feeding the poor and clothing the naked all day–after all, he certainly did that–but that's not the primary reason God became Man. The primary reason God became Man was to

234

save Man from his own Sin. Christ taught us to take care of the less fortunate not primarily for the less fortunate but for our own souls. Christ didn't come here to save us from poverty. He came so that sins may be forgiven. What's next?"

Kimberly Smith raised her hand.

"Satan offered Christ all the kingdoms in the world if Christ would bow down and worship him."

"Yes, thank you, Kimberly," Gilbert answered. "And Christ rejected him. First, because as the Lord says, you can't do evil so that good may come of it. You can't take money that comes from swindling people and use it to do good, even if it's something very good. Don't quite know where I came up with that example, but there you go. More importantly, that's not the kind of Savior Jesus is. People didn't expect a messiah like Jesus, they expected a warrior who would overthrow the Roman occupation, so when the real messiah came, they didn't recognize him. Today, we expect a messiah to restore the church's lost cultural dominance, but that's not why God became man. Jesus didn't come to win some culture war, then or now. He came to redeem us."

Another hand. This time it was Aaron Parker.

"Satan took Jesus to the top of the temple and told him to throw himself off, so angels could rescue him."

"Yes, Aaron, and Christ told Satan not to put the Lord your God to the test. You definitely shouldn't go around expecting miracles. If you see one, it's a blessing, but don't put your faith in that expectation. More importantly, we have to ask why God doesn't just perform miracles every day if he wants people to believe in him. Why doesn't He appear on Richard Dawkins' front lawn and make the trees dance for him? Why not have the Virgin Mary appear and do an interview with Anderson Cooper every day? The answer is that this would be the equivalent of forcing people to believe in Him. God won't do that and thankfully, no human can."

Calvin

"OOOHHHHH."

Scratch looked into Simon's bright blue eyes and gave him another blast of vampiric gaze. The televangelist wrapped his arms around himself and rolled on the floor in ecstasy. Calvin watched in envy. Scratch gave him a blast earlier when he began to express doubt. Under the gaze, Calvin imagined Simon and his mother standing together, welcoming him into the choirs of heaven. What his father saw under the gaze, he could only guess.

"Have I satisfied you?" Scratch asked.

"Oh, yes," Simon responded. "Yes, I feel it. I love you."

"Of course, you do. I am your salvation. Are you willing to do what is necessary?"

"I stand at the ready to serve you, Father. Tell me the almighty's will."

"First, sign the will."

And Simon obeyed. He turned to the updated Last Will and Testament the legal department prepared earlier, leaving the ministry to Calvin, along with Simon's entire fortune. Soon, Calvin would be a millionaire. He wanted to have a real relationship with his father, but Scratch told him that necessary sacrifices had to be made. Two hypnotized witnesses

put their imprimatur on the Will, and Simon was now
ready for other orders.

"What more do you require?"

"I know from the Apostate's
memories that there were three members of the
conspiracy to keep me deceased. One, the Apostate, is
dead. The Irishman we have trapped. Now, I need
you to dispatch the final member of that conspiracy:
the Roman priest. He is no doubt alone, as he has no
flock to tend to. Go to the church and kill him."

Scratch handed his puppet a knife.
Simon looked into his reflection in the blade and then
nodded at Scratch.

"Thy will be done."

Gilbert

The youth group left. Gilbert paced
the room. Deanna and Beth sat waiting for him to
speak.

"Well, Beth, that was your first
Christian sermon. Sorry if you felt left out," Gilbert
said. "Overall, what did you think?"

"I think you let out a lot of strong feelings,"
Beth replied. "That's good."

"Yeah, a lot of strong feelings,"
Gilbert mused. "Has anyone heard from Theo lately?"

"No, I've checked my phone, have
you checked yours?" Deanna asked.

Gilbert did check his phone. There
was a missed call and a message. He played it.

"Hello, is this Gilbert? This is Fr.
Gabe at St. Michael's. Theo told me to call you if he
went missing, and he hasn't checked in since
yesterday. Maybe we should talk."

"Theo went on some kind of mission without telling us," Gilbert surmised, "though he apparently told the new priest."

"Why would he tell Fr. Gabe, but not us?" Deanna asked.

"I don't know, but he says it's something he can't say over the phone, so we should go down there. Let's drop Beth off at the plantation house first," Gilbert said, turning to Beth. "Your aunts will kill us if we keep you out too late."

St. Michael's Church, 7 p.m.
Gabe

Gabe finished another game of solitaire. He read through half the library already. What does a priest without a parish do with his time? Gabe would do anything to get a visitor. When Theo visited, Gabe got excited he had something to do. He didn't know if this was enough time for Theo to be gone to call Gilbert, but he did it anyway. Then he got Gilbert's voicemail, saying they would swing by. Gabe prayed for something to happen.

A knock on the door. His prayer was answered. Gabe opened the door to find none other than Miles Simon. He stood there in the darkness with a butcher knife in his hands and a far-away look in his big bright eyes, the light of the moon reflecting off of both his eyes and the knife. The televangelist seemed to sway, though there was no wind. Just the dead silence of the night.

"Mr. Simon," Gabe stammered, "w-what are you doing here? W-what's with the knife?"

"My father tells me you must die," Simon intoned, turning the point of the knife at

Gabe's throat. "The father commands and the son obeys."

The mesmerized televangelist lunged at Gabe, who dodged to one side. The knife grazed the young priest's neck. Gabe tried to grab Simon's hand, but the preacher man pulled away with an unnatural strength. Simon the slashed at Gabe, cutting into his cassock as the priest jumped back.

Seeing no way to disarm Simon, Gabe ran into the rectory motivated by instinct and panic in equal parts. Simon gave chase, running the young priest down with the bloody knife in his right hand. Gabe threw a side table behind him, which tripped up his attacker momentarily. He ducked into the kitchen as Simon got back on his feet. As Scratch's servant recovered, he found another butcher knife, which he threw at Gabe's head. The knife landed, point first, into the bulletin board, just above Gabe's right ear. Near delirious after the close call, the priest ducked into the library, only to realize he had trapped himself as there was only one exit. Gabe felt his stomach drop a good two inches as he turned back to find his assailant coming right at him with the knife cocked back. Simon brought the knife forward. Gabe jumped sideways, as the knife slammed into the concrete wall to his left, where his head had been a split second earlier.

Gabe ran around Simon. He was beginning to collect his thoughts, which had been scattered about his mind in a frantic jumble since a mad televangelist began to assault him with a deadly weapon. Now thinking semi-rationally, Gabe figured he had only one shot: head for the front door. The young priest ran for the entrance, only to have Simon dive and grab his right foot. Gabe crashed to the floor. He felt Simon crawl on top of him, until the preacher man was above Gabe's head, holding the knife. The young priest could see his own face on the surface of the blade. He decided to use his last minutes on Earth to pray to God for mercy for the time when he stole a 50-cent candy when he was four. Just as he was about to make peace with his maker, Gabe heard a familiar voice.

"Drop it."

Gabe looked up to find a familiar, swarthy young man with long black hair pointing a handgun at Simon's head. Gilbert stood in the door warning Simon to get off of Gabe. He sounded uneasy, and the pistol in his hand shook with fear. The assailant's eyes narrowed on the young man, and a demoniac smile grew on his face. Simon got off his knees and lunged at Gilbert with an enraged snarl.

Two shots rang out, one immediately after the other. Gabe threw up his hands to shield his face from the blood and flesh that sprayed from the back of Simon's head. The preacher man stopped and dropped the knife. The force of the slugs knocked his limp body backward. The corpse keeled over until the cracked skull fell to the floor, right next to Gabe's nose.

"Aieeeaaaahhhh!!!!!" Gabe screamed like a six-year-old girl.

Slowly, he stopped screaming, and gradually, his breathing slowed down. He looked up at Gilbert, who was now crouched above Simon's lifeless body, running his hands down his throat, evidently searching for a pulse.

"Good God, Deanna, he's dead," Gilbert gasped.

Deanna appeared behind Gilbert, carrying a crossbow. She looked down at the body with grim satisfaction.

"Couldn't have happened to a more deserving guy."

"Deanna, I just killed a man," her brother stammered, his eyes still glued to the head wounds. "That's your reaction?"

"Deanna," Gabe repeated. "Gilbert. I need to speak with you."

"Well, that's what we came here for," Gilbert said, getting up from the corpse. "What happened here?"

"That man---"

"Was serving dressing to the poor yesterday," Gilbert mused. "Now, he's threatening a priest with a knife. Miles Simon became St. Francis of Assisi, right before he decided to commit attempted murder. My father has suddenly become very enthusiastic about televangelism, when I've always known him to find that branch of Christianity cheesy and profane. Theo is out of communication. And I just killed a man."

"I think you're saying you would like an explanation," Gabe guessed. "You have to keep in mind that Theo told me this in confession. I can't tell what his sins are, but I can tell you other facts I learned in confession given that the need seems to have arisen."

"Please," Deanna demanded.

***

"And that's what I know."

Gabe finished his story as Gilbert and Deanna lifted Simon's body into the back of the priest's car. As he explained who Scratch was and what Theo thought had happened, they decided they needed to report this to the police quickly. Gilbert argued that perhaps they should wait until the morning if there really was a bloodsucker out there that could lift a car above his head at night, but Gabe insisted, partially to get the body out of his rectory and partially because he was afraid of the cops thinking they were guilty of something.

"Thanks, father, but lots of cops know my Dad," Gilbert said. "I go to church with a few of them."

"Still, I don't want you to go to prison on my account," Gabe stammered, still effected but what he had just witnessed. "I mean, he is a famous televangelist. This may be difficult to believe."

"It's not even the strangest thing to happen since Christmas," Deanna cracked, crawling into the passenger seat. "Let's get in."

"Why don't we call the cops and tell them to come here?" Gabe asked.

Gilbert shook his head.

"No, we don't force those people to go out at night with that thing out there," Gilbert said. "The cops and coroner have no idea that Scratch exists. We could be setting them up to get sucked dry. If someone is taking the risk here, it should be us."

Should be us. Those words struck Gabe with a certain moral authority to which he relented. Gabe got into the driver's seat and started the car. Gilbert took shotgun while Deanna climbed into the back seat. As they rolled out of the driveway, it occurred to Gabe they were all taking this rather well.

"You don't seem surprised by Scratch," Gabe remarked.

"We grew up with a vampire," Gilbert replied, as Gabe turned the car down Main Street. "Theo is my father's best friend. He's like an uncle, really. If there can be one vampire, there can be two. If there can be two vampires, one of them can be a sociopath. Not all the humans I know are that nice either."

"One in particular," Deanna spat, looking out the window. She pointed to the New Stranger Church, which they were just passing. Inside the glass front, a series of televisions screens showed Calvin's face with the caption 'Simon's newly acknowledged son named heir apparent.' Outside, a host of Simons fanatical congregants pressed their hands up against the glass in apparent devotion to their new leader.

"This isn't the town I grew up in," Gilbert sighed, as he pressed the gas, speeding past the church. "Something's changed. My Dad has changed. The people I grew up with have changed."

CHAPTER EIGHTEEN

The Fourth Day of Christmas, Monday, Pandemonium
Police Department, 9 a.m.
Gabe

"I swear that's what happened," Gabe pleaded.

The two officers, one white, one black, with identical crew cuts, raised their eyebrows at him in unison. Gabe wiped his forehead. He sweat like an ice cube in hell. Gabe didn't ever think his vocation would require him to explain a dead body to anyone, especially the law. They had arrived at the police department last night without any issues. Then, the cops spent the next six hours interrogating Gilbert and Deanna while the coroner checked the body. Gabe had only been in for thirty minutes, and he felt like he was about to collapse. And this came from telling the truth. Imagine if he had to lie.

"What do you think, Jackson?" the white cop asked.

The black cop bit his lip and tilted his head, giving it a second of thought.

"Well, Taylor, I think the priest is fucking us like an altar boy."

Gabe pissed his pants. The liquid poured down his leg and soaked into his socks. He didn't even know he had a full bladder. Officer Taylor apparently noticed as he looked down to see Gabe's urine pooling on the floor. He and his partner then looked up and smiled.

"Shit man," Jackson cursed, "we were just playing around."

"Playing around," Gabe repeated.

"Yeah, man," Taylor said, "I grew up in the Stranger Church. My daughter and Deanna do 4-H together."

"Ohh, thank God!" Gabe prayed. "Has word gotten out about Simon?"

"No, we were going to tell the papers and television stations later today," Jackson explained. "Gilbert told us he had to get something from the office."

New Stranger Church, 10 a.m.
Gilbert

Gilbert walked through the front door of the church. He waved at security so as not to look suspicious. Simon's ID was burning a hole in his pocket. Hopefully, word of Simon's death would not spread so quickly as to alert the ministries from keeping him out of the building. Gilbert headed for the elevator, used the ID to access the top floor, and then waited to arrive at the office level. Gilbert decided that he would just act naturally. Or as naturally as he could after killing a man. Once in the elevator, Gilbert turned his head to see Simon's bleeding head in the elevator door. Shocked, he rubbed his eyes, and the image disappeared. Gilbert blinked twice, as his heart fell back into his chest. Looking at the steel door, he realized it was only his own reflection.

When the elevator stopped, he exited and walked down the hall, past the receptionist. No one cared to stop him, though after what he heard about Scratch, he felt a little apprehensive walking around here. He half expected to see some physical demon pop his head out from the doorway or a claw to come and stab the backside of his head. Once or twice, he would jump when an office worker appeared in the hallway. Gilbert worried he was attracting attention, but the people on this floor were unusually calm and pleasant. A few even waved and smiled at him as he passed them by, despite the fact that Gilbert had never seen these people before. Simon's secretary stopped Gilbert in the hall to ask how the youth group was adjusting, and volunteered to arrange a meeting between the youth group and Simon.

"It must be so confusing for all of them. We just want to show them that this is a good thing and they should be proud their church will now be a model for the rest of America."

When Gilbert turned in his resignation to Simon earlier, this same woman refused to tell him where the bathroom was on his way out. His father's wisdom rang in his ears: people who are suddenly nice to you for seemingly no reason only seem to have no reason. Gilbert looked deeply into the secretary's eyes, and they betrayed a faraway look. She was already under Scratch's spell.

"Actually, I was looking to speak to him," Gilbert said. "I had some ideas for the youth group."

Gilbert was an awful liar. It came from being out of practice. Theo or his father would have chuckled at that and rolled their eyes, but the secretary nodded her head. Maybe hypnotized persons are more agreeable with everyone. He'd have to ask Theo. She led Gilbert directly into Simon's office.

Simon's office was a shadow of the office in Charleston. It had no furniture save for a single wooden chair next to his desktop. Gone was the expensive alcohol, the magazine covers with the televangelist's face on them, and even the Persian rugs. This was the office of a puritan, not an indulgent television star.

Gilbert reached for the desktop, which Simon, or Scratch, had apparently forgotten to log out of. Maybe a vampire from the 1640s didn't understand how modern machines worked. Gilbert found an application on the desktop labeled "church security." He opened the application and a series of video feeds apparently coming from security cameras appeared on screen. There were more than a few odd sights. The basketball court had been converted into some kind of pit, with security guards dumping buckets of what appeared to be blood, hopefully from animals, into the center court. In the lower depths beneath the main stage of the church, Annie Ferguson's husband, Harold, was building some strange device. His body moved in a kind of robotic way and he hammered and sawed away at some kind of wooden thing. That gave Gilbert pause. He hadn't thought that Scratch could be going after Strangers, only Simon's people.

Finally, his eyes fell on a video feed with a strange device with a very large bottle attached to it. The screen bore the name 'Prison Room' with the designation 'B5' indicating the room was in the basement. Theo was nowhere to be seen, but then again, he wouldn't be. Now, would he? This was video. Gilbert opened the desk drawer and looked inside to find an old file with the words 'Scratch

Evidence' in his father's handwriting. He opened it to find a series of articles from the 1970s concerning deaths in Belfast where the victims were drained of blood, testimonies from people long since dead attesting to the existence of a vampire with brown, matted hair and long claws, and an ancient schematic for a device with a large bottle connected to it. The notes on the side of the schematic indicated it was intended to capture the subject *in the form of mist.*

"Bingo," Gilbert whispered, comparing the device on the video feed to the device on the schematic. Gilbert took the ancient file from the desk and put it in his jacket. Before he left, Gilbert noticed a much larger binder labeled 'Scratch project.' Seeing as he wouldn't be needing it, Gilbert stole the ministry's 'intellectual property' and then headed towards the elevators. Gilbert thanked the secretary awkwardly, found the elevator, and took it down to the bottom floor.

As the elevator reached the basement, the doors parted to reveal Annie Ferguson, now looking to be under the same spell that affected everyone else here. Gilbert forced a smile and waved as she passed by him. The halls in the basement were narrow, windowless, and overtopped by long steel pipes. Gilbert remembered that Theo's powers worked in artificial light, so if Scratch wanted to jump him here at 11 in the morning, there would be no stopping him. Hopefully, Scratch kept the same hours Theo did and spent high noon sleeping in a coffin. Gilbert located the door to Room B5 and peeked inside to find Theo asleep in the bottle.

Gilbert walked into the room and tapped on the jar. Theo woke with a start. The Irishman pointed to a valve on the device's control panel. Gilbert understood and turned the valve. The jar decompressed, and Theo turned to mist, wafting into the room. He then reformed and spoke to Gilbert.

"Where's Deanna and your father?" he asked, grabbing Gilbert by the shoulders.

"Deanna is at Beth's house, or she should be by now," Gilbert answered. "I don't know where Dad is. I assume he's at the rectory. He could be under Scratch's influence given how weird he's acting."

"You know about Scratch? Of course, you do. Gabe probably sent you here. Gilbert, I didn't want you to find this out from some random priest. What do you know?"

"I know Scratch is another vampire and that he's dangerous. That's about it. Deanna knows the same thing. It's the reason I waited until daylight."

"Good on you. I'll tell you the full story later, but right now, we have to get everyone safe. You go find your father. I'm useless in sunlight, so I'll go speak with Deanna."

"Sounds like a plan. Theo, I had to kill Simon yesterday."

Theo winced when he heard that. He then put an arm around Gilbert and gave him a bear hug.

"It's always hardest the first time. If Scratch is active, he may not be the last person you have to put down. I'm warning you, Gilbert, the powers he has bring out the worst in people. Protect yourself. If your father is under Scratch's influence, some holy water will knock him out of it."

Gilbert took out a vial of holy water. His father would have told him not to put his faith in such idolatry, but it couldn't hurt to take just one.

"Gabe bottled it for me," Gilbert explained. "Theo, we're underground, Scratch could be in the room now as mist."

"If that were true, you'd be dead," Theo answered. "We've had enough scraps that he knows not to allow someone to spring me. Let's keep our escape quiet. Here's a thing your father and I used to do in Belfast. Open your jacket."

Before he could ask why, Theo transformed to mist and then wafted his way to Gilbert's direction. Gilbert then realized what he was doing and opened his jacket. The mist seeped into Gilbert's jacket. Theo would hide himself from sunlight using Gilbert's clothes. Once the mist was completely concealed, Gilbert turned around, and looking as naturally as possible, walked slowly down the hallway toward the elevator. He passed by an open door where he saw Harold Ferguson, thankfully with his back turned, working on that same strange device Gilbert had seen on the video feed. Gilbert took the elevator to the ground floor and then walked out the front door with Theo still in his jacket, shielded from the neutralizing rays of the sun. Gilbert waved at the guards and said he was headed out for lunch. To make it convincing, he actually walked into Grill on the Square and then headed to the bathroom where he opened his coat. Theo seeped out of Gilbert's clothes and took the form of a man again.

"Nifty trick," Gilbert remarked. "Theo, what is that thing that Harold Ferguson was building?"

"It's called a rack," Theo replied. "Any church Scratch is pastor of will have plenty of them. Believe me."

Davis Guest House, Noon
Beth

"Gilbert killed a man!!!" Beth yelled.

"Quiet! I don't want to make a big fuss," Deanna whispered. "The cops say it won't be a problem since our stories all line up."

The image of a bleeding corpse filled Beth's head. The corpse turned into the Bloody Bride, passing by the window of the plantation house. Beth could feel that same familiar panic come up her spine and turn her brain to mush.

"Good God! Deanna! Why would you tell me such a thing?!" Beth breathed.

Deanna shrugged.

"We're friends, we tell each other everything," Deanna answered.

Deanna collapsed on the couch while Beth blushed bright red.

"Well, Beth, how does that make you feel?" MacDonald asked, floating above the coach.

Beth thought it was rather unfair for MacDonald to shame her when she couldn't defend herself. Before she could respond, Theo burst through the door.

"Theo," Deanna gasped. "Thank God! You're alright!"

"I'm practically immortal," Theo said. "You worry about yourself. Are you feeling okay?"

"I've been better," Deanna responded. "Do you think this Scratch person has been brought back?"

"Wait, wait, wait," Beth interrupted. "You know about Scratch?!"

"Yeah, Gabe told me last night," Deanna answered. "How do you know?"

"Alright, Beth, time to spill the beans," MacDonald said.

Beth took a large breath.

"I cannot tell you how I know," Beth pleaded. "Because if I tell you, you will call me crazy, but here is what I know. I know about Scratch. I know that your father...."

Beth looked into Deanna's face one last time before she did it.

"Your father is dead. Scratch used him as the sacrifice. As a result, he can now disguise himself as your father. Gilbert isn't going to check on your father. He's stepping into a trap!"

Deanna and Theo looked at each other.

"Could he..." Deanna began.

"I've never seen him pull that trick, but he always finds a way to surprise me," Theo answered.

"Beth, why can't you tell me how you know this?" Deanna asked, sounding a little mad.

"Because I can talk to dead people!" Beth yelled. "Your father came back to me because I can see dead people and he asked me to tell you that Scratch is disguised as him. He's actually right over there!"

Beth pointed at the wall, which was nothing but blank space to anyone but her. Deanna looked at her like...she was crazy. I knew it, thought Beth.

"Please just check it out," Beth begged, defeated.

Stranger Rectory, 1 p.m.
Gilbert

Gilbert knocked on his father's office door.

"Come in."

Gilbert walked into the room. He found his father sitting behind his desk. The bent cross he typically kept on the desk had been removed. Odd, Gilbert thought. He also found it odd that all the windows in the room had been covered up. Normally, his father enjoyed having some sunlight infiltrate his study.

"Dad, I think you may not be safe," Gilbert began. "Theo thinks Scratch has been resurrected. Yes, I know who Scratch is. I think he may have gotten to you, and that's why you're acting so strangely."

"Is that so, Gilbert? It's my fault you should think so," MacDonald answered. "This must all seem so sudden to you. I have not yet revealed how Simon came to his sudden change of heart."

MacDonald rose from his seat. He literally rose, as he was now levitating above the desk. Gilbert unplugged the holy water behind his back.

"The Lord has blessed me. I am his anointed one," MacDonald announced. "Gilbert, with this gift, I can restore what God has lost over the centuries. The universities, the papers, the state! Christendom reborn!"

Gilbert took out the holy water and splashed it on his father's face. He expected MacDonald to snap out of it. Instead, his face melted off. Like a wax figure in an oven, the Orangeman's features oozed down his skull to reveal the visage of a thin man with large incisors. Gilbert felt his entire body go numb. A frantic panic raced through his mind, but his body wouldn't cooperate. Gilbert's entire being just stopped functioning as he realized the truth. His father had not come under the influence of Scratch. His father was Scratch.

"Gilbert," the shape croaked, "you know the truth. I don't want to make a puppet of you. I want a true believer. I can tell you are. You will sit at my right hand when I usher in the Kingdom of God."

Gilbert finally got his hands to move, and as soon as he did, he realized they were shaking. He felt around his pockets with his hysterical fingers, but unfortunately, he had only one vial of holy water. He hadn't expected to need a second one.

"Your answer?" it asked.

"No, just no," Gilbert answered. "I'd rather you kill me."

"That would be a waste of a puppet," Scratch said.

His eyes began to shine, and then a bullet shattered the window behind him, sprinkling Gilbert with shards of glass. Sunlight flooded into the room, and Scratch's body exploded into auburn flame. While the Bloody Puritan screamed in agony, Gilbert turned and ran out of the office, down the stairs, and out of the rectory. He spotted Deanna aiming an assault rifle out of the back of their car. Beth sat behind the wheel. Gilbert dove into the passenger seat as the car took off.

"How did you know?" Gilbert asked.

"Call it intuition," Beth replied.

Davis Plantation House, 4 p.m.
Bryce

"Why it's absolutely deplorable!" Delilah cried through the phone. "You must do something!"

Bryce snorted while reading his Scientific American on the couch opposite to his Aunt Hecate. Delilah was complaining to the temple trustees about Ravenwood's latest service, which she had attended the day before. Gone was the ancient ceremony and the scythe, and in was Ravenwood in a confederate uniform. Ravenwood spent his sermon reenacting the First Battle of Pandemonium, where he played the role of Col. Robert Davis and put the Davis family in the position of the revolting Stranger militia. At one point, he took out a replica musket and fired at them with a blank. Bryce found the service amusing, but his Aunt Delilah apparently didn't think so.

"I want justice!" Delilah thundered. "Our family has been attending that Satanic Temple since it was built *with our family's money!"*

Delilah slammed the phone down. Bryce shook his head while lying down on the couch. When he was younger, he would make a big deal about not believing in El Diablo, but he soon picked up that neither of his aunts did either. They were just more polite about it. Too polite for his taste, and too tied down to tradition. Yeah, the Davis family had deep roots in that temple. That's called a sunk cost.

"Why do we bother to go?" Bryce asked. "I don't believe that Satan exists and neither do you or Aunt Hecate. No one believes that stuff."

"Col. Robert Davis donated the money to build that Second Satanic Temple," Delilah protested, "and for someone to mock his descendants in that building in such a way! It just burns me up."

Delilah turned to Hecate, also sitting on the couch.

"Why did you sell that uniform to Ravenwood?" Delilah asked, exasperated.

"He was willing to give me $50 for it," Hecate answered.

New Stranger Church, 7 p.m.
Scratch

The police contacted the ministry concerning Simon's death earlier that day. Scratch would have preferred for Simon to kill the priest before committing suicide. The plan was to make them look like star crossed sodomites, but God laughs when we make plans, as the Apostate would say. Now, they had to inform Simon's foolish congregants of his death and explain that Calvin was the new head of the ministry, with some guidance from his new spiritual mentor: Atticus MacDonald.

The ministry contacted the media and informed them of Simon's untimely passing, claiming he was shot down by a deranged lunatic. The press wouldn't buy that, but the online congregation would, so they said that very thing in a video with Gilbert's mugshot in it. They asked the ministry's fanatics in the area to come to Simon's temple to Mammon for a special message from newly appointed pastor, Calvin Lucas, and his new spiritual mentor. Scratch prepared Calvin to introduce the flock to their new shepherd.

"Brothers and sisters in Christ, thank you for coming," Calvin proclaimed, his voice booming with a confidence that only comes from being filled with the Lord's divine power. "This is a new day for Miles Simon Ministries. Today, we turn away from the false god my father presented to you. The true God cometh behind me, and I am unworthy to untie his sandal."

Scratch, again in the guise of Pastor MacDonald, walked on stage. He looked into the crowd. Scratch hoped the Strangers would come, but it seemed only a few came. The Parker family, the Ze'ev girl with her adopted parents, the basketball coach, two of the trustees. Not enough to fulfill his mission on Earth. As soon as he got to the podium, he transformed into his true form, and the eyes blared red. The crowd all gaped in unison as the vampiric gaze put them under Scratch's spell. The Bloody Puritan gave his general orders.

"The Irishman is the Anti-Christ. Find him and kill him. And his associates."

CHAPTER NINETEEN

The Fifth Day of Christmas, Tuesday, Southwest Sector, 2 a.m.
Scratch

Scratch looked down on the two vagrants on the street below him. Even from far above, he could smell them. He recognized them as Moors, likely of the kind brought to this continent by the colonists. They seemed to predominate in this sector of town. Scratch considered coming to America when he was a young man. He ran into a good Puritan on his way to Massachusetts, who told him that England was lost. The man didn't know how right he was.

Scratch's body yearned for sustenance. He tried to drink cow's blood once. It wouldn't stay in his stomach. If you are lukewarm, I shall spit you out. Better to be hot or cold. He crawled down the building, taking a position above one of the lost souls beneath him. During his time in the Great Beyond, the Lord informed Scratch that few of the elect remained on Earth, so he had no fear of striking down the righteous. Simon, his unwilling and unwitting servant, now faced judgment. He may have served Scratch well, but who could question the perfect designs of the Almighty? Scratch remembered when he was first allowed to see the face of God, his body broken and bleeding to death on the rocks. The Irishman had thrown him off the cliff, clearly having been empowered by the Devil. Then, the Divine appeared as an angel of light, shining with power. The Lord told Scratch He had appointed him to a special task. He would be brought back to wreak the Lord's vengeance on a world that completely had fallen away from God, and no man deserved to be spared. Only the Strangers could be saved, provided they submitted to Scratch's authority, and through him, the world could be redeemed again.

  The other vagrant turned his head to check something in that filthy cart he pushed around. Quick as Spring-Heeled Jack, Scratch dropped to the ground, stuck his claws into the first vagrant's stomach, and then slit his throat with one fatal swipe. The second turned around. Scratch visited his gaze upon him and the forsaken fell slack. Scratch disemboweled the man quickly, like gutting a deer or a wild pig.

  He picked up one of the bodies and poured the blood directly into his mouth. Sweet crimson. Sustenance. He could feel power returning to his limbs. Scratch needed to feed more and more often in these latter days. The Lord was hastening the apocalypse, and Scratch needed to work more diligently as His final horseman. After he was done, Scratch looked at the bodies. Better to have servants than evidence. Scratch held out his right pointer finger and concentrated on it. The nail on that finger grew into a long, thin claw, which he used to cut into his left vein. His blood poured on the bodies, and they stirred. Scratch could feel his control over them as they came to life. He made the deceased vagrants lift themselves from the ground. The two familiars, each having the gaunt face of a lifeless slave, struggled to their feet. Their dead eyes turned to Scratch, as if to him for instruction.

"Go to my new stronghold and wait," Scratch commanded. "There will be more of you. I must feed, and the night is young."

Pandemonium Lofts, 9 a.m.
Theo

"They're just disappearing," Pastor Overstreet explained. "No, I haven't seen any bodies, but we keep track of the people on the street, and they're just gone."

Pastor Overstreet contacted Theo to report that a few of the homeless on his side of town had gone missing. The Church of the Tobacco Fields ran an outreach program to people living on the streets in their part of town, and they kept tabs on the people they served. Over the past few days, several church volunteers told Overstreet that men and women living rough were disappearing all across the island, and on the mainland. He had tried to convey this to the police, but they were skeptical. Then, after receiving an email from Gilbert warning him to stay away from Pastor MacDonald, Overstreet thought to call Theo

"How many are we talking about?" Theo asked.

"I think ten of them from my count," Overstreet estimated. "That's just from the southwest side of the town. I've contacted the Varnertown mission and they're missing a few over there. Do you think–?"

"No," Theo answered, firmly. "I know. I saw them last night. I'm sorry."

Pastor Overstreet swore under his breath, and then after a moment, raised his eyes above in prayer. Asking for help from both God and the Devil, Theo thought. Atticus used to do that too. Maybe, soon, they all would.

***

"I think he's creating familiars."

Gilbert and Deanna loaded up ammunition and holy water into their tactical vests. They were about to begin their first night of hunting Scratch. Theo spent the night before surveying the New Stranger Church downtown for signs of the Bloody Puritan. What he found were a lot of homeless people entering the church through the service entrance in the back.

"How can you tell?" Gilbert asked.

"Well, for one, I assume they ain't going there for soup and crackers," Theo answered, "and familiars have a certain gait, and homeless people have another. I've run into plenty of both in four centuries of life."

"Did it look like they were coming from any particular sector of town?" Deanna asked.

"From the look of them, it seemed that they were coming from the Fieldhand section of town," Theo replied, "which means he'll probably be somewhere else tonight. The old Devil is smart enough to rotate."

"Do we have some way to track him that doesn't involve listening to the police radio and waiting for someone to report a murder?" Gilbert asked.

"No, but we know where he won't be tonight," Theo responded. "The New Stranger Church because Scratch knows not to feed on his own minions. That's where the two of you will be tonight, doing reconnaissance."

"You want us to see if he's making this army of familiars?" Deanna asked.

"I think he's collecting the familiars in the basketball court. I saw them creating some kind of blood pit on the security feed in Calvin's office," Gilbert interjected. "We also need to see if there are any Strangers under Scratch's spell in there and free them if possible. Yesterday, I saw Harold Ferguson building a torture chamber. If that's actually used on someone, he'll never forgive himself."

"If you get into a situation with those things, remember, they aren't full vampires," Theo reminded them. "A bullet or knife to the chest will turn them to dust, right quick, and they dissolve in sunlight."

"Knife or bullet to the chest, got it," Deanna repeated. "Theo, do you have an idea where Scratch will be tonight?"

"I've got a hunch," Theo said. "Tonight's a full moon. The old boy always liked a good challenge."

Aaronson Residence, 5 p.m.
Bryce

Bryce arrived at Gary's house just before the transformations began. As a Ze'ev between the ages of 12 and 18, Gary had the responsibility of making sure his parents didn't get out of his backyard after they turned into massive beasts. Bryce typically kept him company on nights like this. Gary's parents, Alter and Dobah, allowed this provided they didn't trash the place.

Bryce sat on the back deck and watched the Aaronsons make their monthly preparations. Gary's father, Alter, a bearded man with light brown hair, inspected the fence in the back yard, making sure it would not be knocked down haphazardly. He found a semi-loose board and then asked Gary to help him stabilize it, which Gary did, re-nailing the board in place until it was firm. This was to keep anyone from getting out too easily. The Ze'ev were large animals on a full moon, and if they really wanted out, nothing would stop them. That is why Gary was there to keep them from getting too excited. Gary's mother, Dobah, a petite woman who had dyed her hair blonde, was in the kitchen preparing the ground beef from Mark Gottlieb's kosher butcher in the old market district. The Ze'ev would not likely keep to themselves if they were left to starve, and hopefully with the sedatives mixed into the meat they would sleep through the night. Dobah had also baked a brisket for Gary and the other children who would be staying over. Once inside, Bryce and Gary sat down and turned on the Atlanta Hawks game and waited for the other members of the party.

The Gottliebs arrived. Mark Gottlieb, the father, was a local butcher. Dobah thanked them for the donation of the beef, and of course, they never thought of it as a donation, given they would partake of it later. The Gottliebs had two young daughters, Batya and Tzivah, aged 12 and 10, They all had curly black hair and pale skin on thin frames. The two girls stole Bryce and Gary's spots on the couch after they made the mistake of getting up to the get pizza. Then the rabbis arrived. Barry helped Maharam along into the living room. The ancient teacher would not sleep in the yard with the rest of the transformed Ze'ev. Even in wolf form, he was too old to endure the winter cold, and would instead sleep on the couch like an elderly dog.

"Gershom," the ancient rabbi greeted, with Gary helping him take off his socks, "how good to see you again."

"Good evening, Rabbi Maharam," Gary replied. "I hope the walk over here was not too cold."

"Not at all," the old teacher said. "Brisk perhaps."

Gary's parents and the adult Gottliebs stripped down, covered themselves in blankets and walked down the stairs of Gary's back porch as the full moon came into view. The transformation began. Involuntarily, all of the Ze'ev hunched over on all fours as fingers became claws and noses and mouths merged to become snouts. Hair sprouted out of their skin. Teeth sharpened. Nails grew out. Thighs and arms swelled with newfound muscular power. All across the northeastern part of the island, the same transformation occurred among the Ze'ev. Transformation night had begun. Inside, Bryce watched the rabbi transform with great interest.

"I wonder how it occurs," Bryce mused, as he watched the rabbi turn into a beast.

"The rabbi says that there's no explanation for it," Gary answered. "Back in the 1990s, geneticists tried to isolate some kind of gene. They couldn't find anything. Not everything can be analyzed that way."

"I can't accept that," Bryce protested. "There has to be some solution the human mind can understand."

"Batya," Gary called, ignoring Bryce's riposte. The Gottlieb's elder daughter answered. She would help Gary feed the party from the ground beef Dobah had prepared. Soon, Gary would be going through his own transformation, so Batya would have to take over Gary's responsibilities when he turned 18 in March. Gary showed Batya how to roll the beef up into little balls for consumption, keeping one eye on the lawn in the event anyone got rowdy. The portions had to be small enough to keep anyone from choking, but large enough that it did not take all night to feed them.

Once the meat balls were prepared, Gary and Batya stepped onto the lawn. The beasts barked happily at the sight of their own young. Gary took a single ball and fed it to his father, who was the largest animal in the herd.

"Be careful and keep your fingers clear," Gary said. "My uncle Mendel lost half his hand when he was 14."

"Why not just throw the balls?" Batya asked.

"Throwing the balls could turn it into a free for all," Gary explained. "You might throw a ball intended for my Dad that my Mom might jump out in front of. Then you've got a fight on your hands."

"Why not just use steaks?" Batya asked.

"Too expensive, they eat a lot," Gary said, feeding a ball to Rabbi Barry. "Now you try."

Batya did as Gary instructed, and she did just fine for the first time. Once, Alter made a go at one of the balls meant for Mark Gottlieb, but Gary broke them up quickly. That will happen every once in a while, he explained. Gary told Batya and Tzivah to stay outside and watch the Ze'ev to make sure they fell asleep. Gary and Bryce went inside to sit down. The Rabbi Maharam scrambled onto the couch and then fell asleep with his head on Bryce's lap.

"I can't move," Bryce said.

"Yep, he's a biggun'," Gary said, getting another slice of pizza.

A loud shriek emanated from the porch. Bryce and Gary turned and saw Batya, turned a shade of ghostly white, run through the kitchen, shaking. Gary caught her as the rabbi stirred, awaken by the disturbance. Batya shook and babbled until Gary finally got her to speak sense.

"Tzivah," she finally managed to say. "A man came out of a tree and…"

Bryce ran to the porch. He threw open the door and found Tzivah, lying in the cradled hands of a tall, pale man with long claws and teeth, dripping with drops of dark, crimson blood. Tzivah's body lay limp, with blood gushing out of her neck and her skin having turned white, identical to the full moon hanging above them. The monster feasting on her licked his lips, lapping up another quart of her blood. Bryce, frozen in fear for a moment, made a step towards the monster, only to find himself frozen again, as the monster's eyes turned bright red, stopping Bryce in his tracks. The pale man then dropped Tzivah's body on the deck and then approached Bryce with hungry eyes.

"Grrrrr……"

Scratch turned his head to see Maharam approach him and growl. The ancient beast coiled its hind legs. Scratch attempted using his eyes on the animal, to no effect. The Ze'ev pounced, colliding with Scratch and knocking him over the railing of the deck. Scratch fell to the ground with the 500-pound beast on top of him. The weight would have killed a normal man, but Scratch ceased being human long ago. His ribs stretched under the weight, and then he recovered. The Bloody Puritan extended his claws and dug them into the side of the old animal's gut. The beast howled in pain and fell over.

Bryce started to come to, just as Gary's hand emerged from the house and pulled him inside. Gary's parents stirred from their slumber, awakened by Rabbi Maharam's howl. Before Scratch could fully recover, two more Ze'ev, these ones in their prime, were upon him. Scratch took a claw to the face, and a tooth right through his hand. Alter opened his massive maw and fit it snuggly around the vampire's throat. Canine teeth penetrated Scratch's throat, but he pried the jaw open and clawed back, breaking Alter's right tooth and slicing open Dobah's eyelid.

Inside, Batya pounded at the window as her little sister continued to bleed out. Gary, seeing Tzivah and Rabbi Maharam were fading fast, reached for the medical supplies from the kitchen and then ran out to the back deck.

"Dude!" Bryce shouted. "What the hell are you doing?"

"I can't let them just die!" Gary answered. "My parents will kill me!"

"Metaphorically!" Bryce answered. "There's someone out there who will kill you literally!"

Gary paid no heed but went outside and fell upon Tzivah. He hastily wrapped her neck still bleeding profusely, with bandages. The bleeding didn't stop, but Batya came up behind him, taking her sister. Gary then descended from the deck to Maharam, who was whimpering in pain from his wounds. He covered the wound, applying pressure to staunch the bleeding. Maharam tried to nuzzle him in the direction of the door, but Gary wouldn't take the hint.

"See, he even agrees with me," Bryce said, looking at him from the deck.

Scratch

Scratch took to the trees, deducing that the beasts had him on strength, but they couldn't match him on agility. The Bloody Puritan looked to move on, but before he could, a falcon came out of the sky and pecked at his eyes. Scratch turned to mist and then wafted out of the yard. When he reformed, the bird became the Irishman, and all of the Ze'ev behind him in the neighborhood started jumping their respective fences.

"Looks like someone bit off more than they could chew," the Irishman taunted.

Scratch smiled. His eyes lit up bright red. Behind him came a congregation of alligators. Snakes came out of holes in the ground. Birds of prey filled the sky, enough to block out the full moon. Theo transformed into a wolf, and the Ze'ev fell in line behind him. Time for a fight.

New Stranger Church, 9 p.m.
Gilbert

Deanna and Gilbert looked at the church, now protected by heavy security. Men in security uniforms carrying assault rifles guarded the doors and walked the roofs of the church. It would figure that Scratch would put them on high alert.

"How would Theo break in?" Deanna asked.

"He'd turn into a bird and land on the balcony," Gilbert answered. "We don't have that option."

"I see one option that's open to us," Deanna replied.

Deanna pointed to a haggard looking man dragging his feet down the driveway towards the church. Gilbert, who had served the homeless at the mission before, could see what Theo had been talking about. The homeless and the dead did not walk alike. Given that they were vampiric familiars, his initial instinct was to keep his distance, but Deanna then pointed to an open garage door the familiar walked towards. The guards flanking the door stood aside when the familiar approached. Apparently, they had been told to let them pass.

"That entrance goes straight to the basketball court," Gilbert explained. "Not sure that's the place we want to end up."

"Unless it's the only way in," Deanna pointed out.

Deanna made a move toward the entrance of the church, and Gilbert stopped her with a hand on her shoulder.

"Knives only, don't go loud," Gilbert suggested, "and we should play the part."

Gilbert looked at the man approaching the door, who appeared to have slept rough for a while. Not the way he was typically taught to dress for church, but they didn't have much of a choice. Deanna didn't seem to like the prospect more than Gilbert, but she nodded her head in assent. Gilbert then spotted two more figures dragging their feet towards the entrance. He pointed at them.

"Best to approach directly," Gilbert whispered, "we don't want to be wrong and hurt someone alive."

They walked up to the unfortunate souls headed towards Scratch's new domain with hunter knives out as if this was a mugging. It was a woman and a man, both of whom wore clothes that stunk with sweat and urine. Gilbert held up his hand as if to ask them to stop. Both figures opened their mouths to reveal long, pointed canines, dripping with saliva. Their eyes were pools of unending black, and their skin shone pale in the light of the full moon, not unlike their wicked incisors. The male figure lunged at Gilbert, who drove the hunter's knife to the left side of the chest. The familiar's face turned stiff as the blade pierced his heart, and for a second, Gilbert thought of Simon again. Then, the face cracked like dried mud at the bottom of a dead lake, and burst into dust as the entire body crumbled to a pile of dirt, leaving only the tainted clothing behind. Gilbert stood there, holding the knife and shaking.

Deanna, on the other hand, took the offensive and shived the female familiar as if she were Ravenwood putting that rabbit to rest. As the second familiar fell apart, she sifted through the clothes.

"Ewww," she remarked, shaking her head. "The things I do for this town."

Gilbert snapped out of his momentary shock and regained his focus. Right, getting dressed. After taking the clothes back to the van, Gilbert put on the tattered jacket, stained shirt, and soiled pants of Scratch's down and out victim as Deanna put on the attire of the female familiar, torn jeans and a muddy, white coat.

"How do I look?" Gilbert asked.

Deanna gave him a go over.

"A little like Theo," Deanna answered. "Close enough."

They got out of the van and began to drag their feet toward the open door where the guards stood by another familiar stumbling in. Gilbert worried they would recognize him as he worked there as recently as yesterday. Approaching the door, the guards paid neither of them any attention. Apparently, they didn't notice me, Gilbert thought, as they crossed the threshold of the door. Then, as they moved deep within the corridor leading to basketball court, the door slammed behind them.

"Stupid kid! Thought we'd fall for that! Be a nice dinner!" a guard yelled.

Be a nice dinner, Gilbert thought, wonder what that meant. It didn't take them long to find out, as they moved into the basketball court and found center court filled to the brim with familiars. It would appear at a distance to be a homeless encampment with people packed in like sardines. However, Deanna and Gilbert were seeing it up close and could see these poor souls were hungry for more than bread and soup. As they stood at the entrance of the court, the dozen or so familiars closest to them bared their teeth like the couple outside and started dragging themselves toward Gilbert and Deanna. As they stepped back into the corridor, Gilbert looked above and saw security guards pouring blood into the pit from the bleachers above. Just like the video feed, except the pit was full. Deanna grabbed Gilbert's arm, telling him to turn and run, so he did.

They turned down the corridor, trying to find some way out of this place. The main door was obviously closed, but there had to be a side entrance or something, so Gilbert scanned the cinderblock walls for an exit. Gilbert spotted a door and ran to it, only to find it closed by a Master Lock. Just as he was about to run again, Deanna stopped him.

"Only a Master Lock? I learned how to pick those at Bible Camp in the Sixth Grade," she said, taking a bobby pin out of her boot.

"Is that what they teach at Bible Camp?" Gilbert asked.

271

"That's what you learn when you put a bunch of pastor's daughters together," Deanna cracked. "Cover me."

Gilbert turned and found the familiars slowly approaching. He thought about taking out his gun, but he didn't know if the guards outside had bothered to alert anyone to their presence here. If their positions were reversed, Gilbert would have been pretty sure he was dead too. He took out the hunting knife and targeted the lead familiar, stabbing it right in the heart. Dust exploded from the mobile corpse. He then moved onto the next, and the next. Each time, it got easier, but the horde grew larger. The entire corridor filled with vampiric zombies and the smell of death, walking toward them in sweat-tainted clothes. Then he heard a click behind him.

"I've got it!" called Deanna. "Let's go!"

Gilbert dove through the portal and Deanna slammed it behind them, locking the door from the other side now.

Gilbert collapsed onto the floor gasping for air. As the fire in his lungs burned down, he recognized his surroundings. They were in the tunnels under the main stage of the church, where he had found Theo the day before, near to where he saw Harold Ferguson. Now, the tunnel was darker, lit up the red, neon glow of emergency lights.

"Not that I'm complaining, but could we have found a creepier place to escape to?" Deanna asked.

Deanna was seventeen, going on eighteen, and she hadn't yet learned not to tempt fate. As soon as she completed her wise crack, the dark halls before them echoed with the sound of a mirthless, uncharitable chant. Gilbert couldn't make out who was speaking, but it didn't sound good, not that anything would in a place like this. Deanna panted on the floor. After a moment's rest, Gilbert helped her up. He held a finger up to his lips to indicate quiet, and Deanna mouthed silently "I know."

Slowly and softly, they walked toward the sounds of the chants, down the darkened hallways, lit only by the occasional red emergency light. In any other building, this would be a perfectly innocuous scene in the lower depths of a church at night. Far more frightening would be a walk through Theo's crypt; a trip Gilbert had made thousands of times since he was eight. Here, cinderblock walls and pipes, bland as they were, scared him in a way the Drunkard's and the Princess's bones never could. Theo told them Scratch wouldn't be here, but Gilbert could see his face around every corner they passed.

As they approached the chants, Gilbert finally made out what they were saying. "The world has abandoned Him." "We will avenge Him." "The world has forgotten." "They will remember." "The world does not hear His voice." "We will make them listen." Gilbert could see light coming out of an open doorway, casting shadows of cultists on the ground. He recognized this room as the place Mr. Ferguson was building his rack the day before. Then he heard Mr. Ferguson's voice. Were their Strangers here?

Slowly, Gilbert and Deanna stepped in front of the doorway. Inside the room, they found Mr. Ferguson, along with several other members of their father's old congregation. The basketball coach. The church secretary. That woman who made cinnamon buns every Christmas. They all sat in a semi-circle, repeating their petitions to their new lord, facing his altar at the head of the nave: a rack where Aaron Parker lay, stretched to his breaking point and bleeding from his chest. Gilbert recognized Mr. Parker, his father, standing by the crank, and Mrs. Parker, holding a bloody knife with a faraway look. Suddenly, the chant stopped. Gilbert and Deanna backed out, thinking they had been spotted, but no, the time for prayers was over. Time for the creed.

I BELIEVE IN ONE GOD, THE FATHER ALMIGHTY,
CREATOR OF HEAVEN AND EARTH
SPURNED BY MAN IN THIS SINFUL WORLD
HE SHALL SOON HAVE HIS REVENGE

I BELIEVE IN JESUS CHRIST, HIS ONLY SON
BETRAYED BY MAN IN THIS GODLESS AGE AS HE WAS ON THE CROSS
I BELIEVE IN HIS TRUE PROPHET WHO WILL AVENGE THE FALLEN SON

I BELIEVE IN THE HOLY SPIRIT
THE RESURRECTION OF THE TRUE PROPHET
THE PUNISHMENT OF SINS
THE REBUILDING OF THE DEFEATED CHRISTENDOM
AND DIVINE JUSTICE, AMEN

And with that, it came time for the offering. Mr. Parker moved towards his son and pulled down the boxers he was wearing to expose his genitals. Mrs. Parker grabbed hold of the tip of her son's penis and stretched it out with one hand, while raising the knife up high. A demonic gleam shone in her eye, and on the metal. As Aaron hysterically begged his mother

274

for mercy, Gilbert pushed himself forward, his hand reaching into his tactical vest to retrieve the holy water he'd packed earlier that day. He ran down the center aisle, past Scratch's dark congregation, unplugged the cork on the bottle, and splashed the holy water on Mrs. Parker's face, just as the knife began to come down.

In mid-swing, Mrs. Parker's face went from resolute, to confused, to horrified, as she slowed her arm and dropped the knife at the foot of the rack. Gilbert, only partially realizing that it worked, then proceeded to douse Mr. Parker, who was already reaching for the knife. Gilbert reached Aaron and made a move to loosen the straps, until he turned around and realized that Scratch's disciples were beginning to recognize his presence. In the back of the room, Deanna was already doing her best to spritz the rest of the congregation, but they could have used an aspergillum as it wasn't reaching the front row, quickly closing in on Gilbert. Gilbert took out another bottle and sprayed the oncoming rush, which slowed a few of them but then the basketball coach laid him out.

Slammed to the ground, Gilbert had the air knocked out of him as Coach fit his sausage fingers around Gilbert's thin neck. Gilbert might have been a wizard with a gun, but he couldn't match this old guy for strength. He thought of just letting Deanna save him, but then Coach made a move for the knife, forcing Gilbert to think fast. He reached past his tactical vest to his chest to find the cross his father gave him on his twelfth birthday, and then shoved it into coach's face. As he did, the man loosened his grip and keeled over.

Gilbert struggled to his feet and looked up to find the rest of the room now standing around in various states of disorientation, save for

Deanna who was finishing up by splashing holy water on a few toddlers. Gilbert breathed easy until he heard Aaron moaning above him. He then reached for the straps and undid them. Aaron, exhausted and still bleeding, held his hands up as if to ask, "Get me up." Gilbert and Mr. Parker obliged him, lifting Aaron off the rack. Mrs. Parker looked again at the knife and began to shake uncontrollably while Mr. Parker apologized profusely to his son, putting him back on his feet. Surveying the room, Gilbert decided he needed to give directions.

"Everyone, I understand you may not know what you were doing five minutes ago, but we can sort that out when we get you to the hospital," Gilbert said. "I know the way out of here, but there may be guards. Deanna, get your gun ready."

The room all of a sudden turned serious at the sight of Deanna taking out a Glock. Deanna threw Gilbert an inquisitive look.

"Ready, to shoot your way out of here, Sundance?"

"In a manner of speaking," Gilbert answered. "Let's get moving."

Gilbert led them out of Scratch's obscene chapel, with his own gun unholstered. Mr. Parker and Mr. Ferguson carried Aaron in their arms. Whatever fear he had left him earlier as he now needed to get the people he grew up with out of the bowels of hell. Gilbert remembered the exits from the day before. He knew the fire exits were too far away, but the front door was just upstairs, which is where they all started heading. The group began to ascend. As his feet pounded up the steps, Gilbert remembered that the front of the church was made of glass. Safety glass, but not bulletproof glass. He had no desire to take a life, but he might have to fire a few shots to get out of here.

They reached the ground floor, and Gilbert threw open the emergency exit to come upon the front of the church, where a contingent of guards waited for them. Gilbert pointed this gun at the guards and then nodded in the direction of the glass front of the church in such a way that Deanna would get the idea. Deanna then turned her gun towards the glass and fired, once, twice, three times, and the glass began to crack. One more shot and the wall collapsed into a cascade of shards. The guards, in evident shock, stumbled over themselves.

"Make a move, and I'll kill you!" Gilbert shouted, not quite convincing himself. "I've killed before!"

The guards backed off as Deanna waved the Strangers through the now open hole in the front of the church. One of the guards made a sudden move and Gilbert fired into the air above, aiming for a suspended light. He kept his gun pointed toward the guards, daring them to blink, while he heard Deanna herding the group outside. After that endless moment, Gilbert felt Deanna tap on his shoulder, telling him it was time to go. Gilbert turned and ran out the front with his sister, towards the van still parked across the street. The Parkers were already loaded up in the back. Gilbert could hear gunshots behind them, but most of them were half-hearted. Climbing into the driver's seat, Gilbert looked to his right to find Deanna saddling up in shotgun, while taking out an actual shotgun and pointing it in the direction of Scratch's terror tower. Gilbert looked in the back and confirmed Aaron and his parents were in place. He then started the van, shifted into drive, and gunned it.

The Sixth Day of Christmas, Wednesday, Northeast Sector, 2 a.m.
Theo

The alligator flew through the air and crashed against the wall of the two-story condo. It had been tossed by an enraged Ze'ev after trying to take a bite out of the superior beast's arm. One by one, the Ze'ev mauled enough of the critters to make an entire line of luggage. They then crushed the snakes Scratch summoned underfoot. The serpents could get in a bite or two before being smushed by a giant Ze'ev paw, but all it did was slow the great beasts down. One of Scratch's furrier minions, a coyote from the mainland, tried to stare down a Ze'ev and soon regretted it, as the poor predator soon found its head enclosed in the larger animal's massive jaw, pressed under foot until its neck snapped.

In the air, Theo took the form of a great eagle and conducted a dog fight against the murder of crows and an unkindness of ravens. Theo had his own air force, calling in a few favors from falcons in the area. Scratching, biting, and pecking, Theo stayed in the air until the weight of the battle was against Scratch.

Then, he saw Scratch riding down the street on a black bear. Theo did a dive-bomb on the pale man, who turned into mist. Theo passed through him and hit the ground, reverting to human form. Scratch turned into a falcon and flew off. Some habits never change, Theo thought. The black bear turned on him. Theo cracked his knuckles. So, the King has retreated, time to take out the Queen. The bear stood on its hind legs and swiped at Theo. The Irishman dodged and hit the bear square in the jaw, dislocating its mandible. The bear, moaning in pain, fell over. The advancing Ze'ev surrounded it, tearing it to shreds.

Then, one of the Ze'ev attacked Theo out of nowhere. Huge claws scratched across his face, tearing at his nose and cheeks, while the jaws fit around the top of his skull. Oh well, he was never a looker, but why the attack from his supposed ally? Theo punched the Ze'ev in the stomach, knocking the air out of it, then throwing the beast against a tree. The other Ze'ev circled the rogue wolf cautiously, growling at the stunned animal. Then, upon closer inspection, Theo recognized this particular creature as a playmate he'd had recently: Kimberly Smith. He never forgot the face of a Ze'ev on a full moon. Kimberly, clearly under Scratch's influence, recovered and approached Theo with an intent to kill in its eyes. The other Ze'ev circled the two of them in defense of Theo, but the Irishman waved them off.

"Back off, back off," Theo warned. "She's not herself."

The other Ze'ev obeyed, but Kimberly lunged forward, snapping her snout at Theo. Theo saw the opening and grabbed the snout. He turned Kimberly's head and wrestled her to the ground. Then his own eyes lit up, bright blue, as he looked into the creature's large yellow eyes. Kimberly thrashed scratching away at Theo's muscular shoulders. Theo ignored the pain, and just whispered as he focused his eyes on the beast.

"Remember me, remember me, we're friends."

The beast stopped swatting at Theo's figure with its claws. Its breath slowed into a normal, calm rhythm. The animal sat up, and as she did, the other Ze'ev backed away further.

"That's a good lass," Theo cooed.

CHAPTER TWENTY

The Sixth Day of Christmas, Wednesday, Northeast Sector, 7 a.m.
Theo

The Ze'ev woke up the next morning naked, but not naked in their back yards like usual. They woke up naked in the middle of the street, which normally meant their children had some explaining to do. However, they looked around and saw their neighbors in the same state of undress, and the gradually realized something was off. Kimberly Smith found herself waking up naked in public for the second month in a row, understandably quite embarrassing for the captain of the cheerleading team.

Given that the Davises were looking after Gilbert and Deanna, Theo figured he owed Hecate and Delilah the same, so he walked over to the Aaronson house to check up on Bryce. He arrived to find an EMT loading the Rabbi Maharam into an ambulance. Waking up, the old teacher rubbed his abdomen, now covered in bandages. Theo peered into the house to find Bryce and Gary, both looking shellshocked, huddled behind the couch along with a girl who was bawling her eyes out. The Irishman waved at Bryce from the door.

"Theo!" Bryce shouted. "We need help!"

"Invite me in," Theo requested.

"What? Why?"

"You have to invite me in, remember?"

"Theo," Gary said. "Come in."

Now having the proper permission, Theo ran inside and stopped by Gary and Bryce. He looked down to see a girl, no older than eight, covered in blood and pale as the night fog. Theo had seen this before: she'd been drained and quite forgone by now.

"Wee, lass," Theo whispered, running his hand down her cold, dead face.

A single tear escaped his eye. Even after having seen children starve to death in the streets and crushed under a soldier's boot for 400 years, something about seeing a dead child still got to him. It took him out of the present, back to that deal Nick offered him in the old country: kill the Scots, lasses and wee ones included. Theo couldn't imagine taking the old devil up on that offer, and even though he'd gone from man to monster and back over four centuries, in some ways, the Irishman never really changed.

Theo's memory was interrupted by the feeling of two adults running past him. He looked down again to find the girl's father cradling her body in his arms. The older girl threw her arms around her mother.

"Why? Why would this happen?!" the father moaned into the sky, pressing the girl's dead body against his chest. "Who did this?!"

Theo raised his hand. He brought Scratch here. He was responsible.

"If you all want to kill me, any other day, I'd lend you a stake," Theo said, "but I need everyone's help to prevent this from happening again."

Town Meeting Hall, 11 a.m.
Theo

"There's another vampire?" Mayor Mayfield asked.

Theo dolefully nodded his head and yawned. He hadn't gotten much sleep over the last week or so, but he had to push on. Theo had brought Scratch's remains here, thinking he'd never be resurrected. Now, Mayfield had to run a city dealing with the equivalent of the ten plagues of Egypt. Theo mused that even after being a common playmate on transformation nights, he probably wasn't too popular with the Ze'ev right now.

"Jesus, Theo, if we knew that you were capable of doing all of this…"

"You probably wouldn't have had me for the last 40 years regardless of how much money I donated and to who," Theo finished the sentence. "Control over animals is another power I don't use often. Doesn't seem fair once you get to know them."

"How do we kill this thing?"

"I am working on that. I've called in the big guns, too. Fr. Eric Burton should arrive in Charleston tomorrow afternoon from Rome."

"Why don't we just send the SWAT team into that new church?"

"You could do that if you wanted to get the SWAT team killed. Scratch's powers work indoors day or night. Only sunlight hurts him. Lightbulbs don't do a thing."

At this point, there was a knock on the door.

"Come in," Mayfield responded.

An aide walked through the door and whispered into his ear.

"Simon's followers?" Mayfield repeated. "Outside?"

Mayfield opened the curtains to his window and was greeted by a tomato smashing into the pane in front of him. Theo peeked out the window and found that Simon's fanatics from out of town were tearing the town square to pieces. They were clearly under Scratch's influence. As he moved over to the window, Theo could see a man taking an ax to the park benches, while a group of old ladies tried to tear down the statue of the Heretic and the Drunkard shaking hands. Watching men in bow ties setting garbage cans on fire on the front lawn of the town square brought a new level of guilt to his mind. Then he found Annie Ferguson and her husband among the mob, along with a few other Strangers.

"They say they want Theo," the assistant explained. "They say Pastor MacDonald told them he was evil incarnate."

"That's not Atticus," Theo said. "Atticus is dead. I need to make a call."

Downstairs, the sound of a battering ram hitting the two front doors of the building on the north side echoed throughout the halls. The mob was coming in.

Pandemonium Central Hospital, 1 p.m.
Gilbert

The television showed the angry mob surrounding the town hall. Gilbert watched the scene from the back of the room while Deanna tried to talk Mrs. Parker through what happened the night before. They had spent the morning talking to the Strangers in the hospital who were recovering from being in Scratch's flock. Gilbert tried to get a fuller story out of Aaron, who could remember a bit about his ordeal in the Devil's hands.

"He kept saying he didn't want to brainwash us, but he would if we wouldn't follow him," Aaron recounted, lying in a hospital bed with a bandage on his chest. "He asked for true believers."

"He said something like that to me as well," Gilbert said. "He wanted a willing servant, not a puppet. Anything else?"

Aaron looked sick for a minute, then he spoke.

"He made us drink his blood," Aaron moaned.

Gilbert felt a little sick himself for a moment, wondering how many Strangers Scratch still had under his control.

"Why weren't you hypnotized?" Gilbert asked.

"He did use his eyes on me for a while," Aaron said. "Then he let me go, said I deserved to die rather than serve the Lord."

Aaron closed his eyes for a while.

"Called me a Sodomite," he whispered, looking at his parents. "I haven't told them."

"How did he know?"

"When he uses those eyes on you, it's like he can see inside your mind. Scratch probably knows the Strangers pretty well."

"Almost like he owns us or something," Gilbert muttered, turning to Deanna. "What's the news?"

"Well, the police called and told me that the ministries reported us breaking in last night," Deanna reported, "and they told the ministries to jump in a lake. Might have something to do with that."

Deanna pointed to the television screen where the mob was trashing downtown. The rioters were demanding that Theo and "his associates" ("Us," guessed Deanna.) be turned over. The city refused to give in to those demands. The scene then shifted to a familiar red brick apartment building.

"Theo's new digs," Deanna said, "and to think, we just got him to move out of that crypt."

The mob knocked down the front door of the apartment building and rushed in. Terrified tenants started climbing out of their windows.

"Aaron, did you ever seek out Theo after our conversation?" Gilbert asked.

"I found his apartment," Aaron admitted. "He told me he couldn't help me. Is this my fault?"

"No, this is Simon's fault," Gilbert answered. "Deanna, we need a new home base."

"I'll call Beth," she responded.

Davis Guest House, 3 p.m.
Beth

"Beth, when do you plan to speak with your dead relatives?" MacDonald asked.

Beth was preparing beds for Gilbert and Deanna, who called an hour ago saying they needed a place to hide from Scratch. Beth telekinetically spread out the sheets and fluffed the pillows, making it look like the guest room was putting itself together. She'd been using her mental abilities to do small chores for years, provided the objects were light. Levitating dusters floated amongst the lights, followed by an air freshener that glided in mid-air. MacDonald's spirit continued to bug Beth about this or that thing, and Beth continued to be polite and put up with it. Then MacDonald asked that question, and Beth was done being polite. All the objects in the room dropped at once.

"When I am good and ready! You don't know what it's like! Nobody ever believes me! Not my aunts! Not Alistair! Not even my own twin brother! Oh boy, did Bryce make fun of me when I said I could see dead people! Those people in the plantation house are scary! Have you seen the Bloody Bride?!" Beth yelled.

"Yes, yes, I did," MacDonald responded, motioning Beth to calm down with his hands. "I went into the plantation house earlier today and I spoke with all of your dead relatives. Your grandparents. Your Aunt Isabella. Col. Davis, who I found to be a man possessed of a great deal of wit and humility. And your Aunt Hepzibah who is a much gentler spirit than you might expect from the head wound she is forced to sport."

"You spoke with the Bloody Bride!" Beth screamed, turning white.

"I spoke with your Aunt Hepzibah. Technically, she's your great-great-great-great Aunt Hepzibah, and I may be forgetting a few greats there, but she's actually quite proud of you and Bryce. And by the way, now who's being rude?"

"I can't talk about this right now. I have to prepare things for Gilbert and Deanna who could be arriving any minute."

At this moment, Deanna came into the house without knocking, followed by Gilbert.

"Beth, have you heard from Theo?" Deanna asked.

"Not yet," Beth answered. "I saw what was going on downtown. He might be having some problems getting away. The mob got into the town meeting hall."

There was another knock on the door. Beth answered to find her aunts, Alistair, and Bryce on the other side. Bryce looked a little worse for the wear given the night he had.

"Beth," Aunt Hecate said. "We couldn't help but notice you had visitors. Do you mind if we ask your guest why the city has gone mad all of a sudden?"

"Ms. Davis," Gilbert began. "I'm sorry for this imposition, but I'll explain what I can."

Gilbert recounted everything that happened since Christmas morning. When he came to the part where his father died, Hecate stopped him.

"I'm sorry to hear that," Hecate interrupted. "It must be very difficult to lose a parent in the middle of this, though you haven't had much time to mourn."

Gilbert, realizing he hadn't had much time to mourn, took a deep breath and fought off a choking sob. He then finished his story.

"I understand," Hecate said. "Where is Theo now?"

"Theo said he'd meet us here," Gilbert responded. "Sorry to use your property as a headquarters."

"You are quite welcome given the circumstances," Hecate said. "Alistair, would Fr. Ravenwood be at the Temple tonight?"

"It's Wednesday," Alistair answered. "On Wednesday, Ravenwood rents the Temple out to tourists, normally teenagers, who perform these silly rituals. The kids look stupid, nothing happens, and Ravenwood pockets the money."

Delilah sniffed the air curtly.

"The Colonel paid for that building," she spat.

"Why are we concerned about the Satanic Temple?" Gilbert asked.

"If Scratch believes that he fights for God," Hecate suggested, "it stands to reason that the Second Satanic Temple would be a target, and given that he hasn't attacked it yet, I would assume it's his next one."

"I hadn't thought of that," Gilbert admitted.

"Scratch did," Deanna said. "Look."

Deanna pointed to the television. The local news was showing by helicopter that a horde of zombified homeless had emerged from the New Stranger Temple and was moving in a Southeastern direction.

"I'll call Ravenwood," Delilah said. "Bad as he is, I don't want him dead."

Delilah took out her phone to call Ravenwood. Apparently, he picked up because she started talking.

"Acton," Delilah began, "I am calling to warn you that you might be attacked tonight. Tell those annoying voyeurs to go away and give them their money back. What? No, I am not lying to you! Turn on the television, or just look at your phone! It's on the news!"

Delilah cocked her head back in disgust. Beth could hear the dial tone. Ravenwood had hung up on Delilah.

"His funeral," Delilah remarked.

"No, we can't just let them die," Gilbert said. "Deanna and I will meet Theo at the Temple. You all stay here."

Town Square, 7 p.m.
Theo

Theo turned into mist and hid in the Town Meeting Hall's air system. Once the crowd saw he wasn't there, they left the building, but they wouldn't leave the town square. He thought about hypnotizing them, but there were so many that he'd likely be overwhelmed. After the sun went down, Theo wafted up to the top of the building and turned to human form. He checked his phone and found a message from Gilbert. Theo called back.

"Theo, you okay?" Gilbert asked.

"Yeah, I got out," Theo responded. "You guys at Beth's house?"

"No, we were there, we're driving to the Second Satanic Temple now, there's a host of familiars headed towards us. Scratch is targeting the Second Temple. Alistair says there will be people there."

"Maybe, but that seems a little obvious to me. This may sound odd, but I don't think Scratch would be too offended by Ravenwood's little tourist trap."

As he said this, Theo scanned the dark skyline of the city, and he spotted a falcon, headed in the direction of St. Michael's Church.

"I think he's headed for Fr. Gabe," Theo said. "I'd bet he'd take a real priest over a fake Witch any day of the week."

"You sure? The familiars are already halfway to the Temple."

"I don't doubt that, but it's a distraction. Gilbert, you and Deanna can handle those things. Hold them off until morning. Keep that idiot Ravenwood alive."

"So, you're not coming?"

"You've got this. I've got to protect the priest. I'm the reason he's involved in this."

Theo hung up the phone and then called Fr. Gabe.

"Theo? There's an angry mob looking for you and an army of zombies on the loose."

"The more pressing issue is that Scratch is looking for you, right now. Get inside the church and have some consecrated Eucharist at the ready. No, I'm not taking communion tonight."

Theo turned into a falcon and took off in the direction of St. Michael's Church. He caught sight of the other bird, now encircling the church. Theo aimed at the other falcon and attacked. Just as he was about to sink his claws into his nemesis's back, Scratch dodged, apparently having caught Theo's approach in out of the corner of his eye. Instead, Scratch now pounced on top of Theo's back, digging his claws in deep. Theo did a barrel roll and got a claw around to Scratch's face. Theo caught the Bloody Puritan's left eye, and Scratch let go. The Irishman then snapped his beak at his enemy's back side, but Theo got a slash across the face for his trouble. Eye for an eye.

Theo released his adversary. He circled, still feeling the claw he'd received in his eye. As he came around for another pass, the Irishman found himself flying towards Scratch head on at break neck speed. The two birds reared up, baring their talons, and locked claws. Scratch's momentum was apparently stronger as both of them headed in that direction as they moved together, entangled. Around and around, Theo rolled with Scratch in the air, scratching and pecking at each other. He'd fought the Bloody Puritan like this before. A part of him actually found it familiar. Deanna and Gilbert had less experience dealing with Scratch. Hopefully, they'd be able to adapt quickly.

Second Satanic Temple, 8 p.m.
Gilbert

Gilbert and Deanna walked up the stairs of the Second Satanic Temple. It occurred to Gilbert that he'd never actually been in this building. While the catholic priest in town always bothered to protest, Gilbert's father never cared to. The Orangeman had merely rolled his eyes whenever they drove past the temple. Gilbert pushed open the heavy black oak front door and found Ravenwood sitting in the back pew, watching a group of teenagers in Gothic attire posing in front of a mirror, covered in blood.

"Bloody Bones! Bloody Bones!"

The teenage 'vampire' wearing fake fangs and a cape straight from a dime store catalogue led his pimply and hormonal congregation through this occult ceremony on the main stage of the temple. The hormonal high priest inverted a crucifix in a mirror covered in fake blood. The gullible high schoolers held their breathes in anticipation as their leader chanted another set of scary words taken straight from an online horror forum.

"Devil's Deal! Devil's Deal!" they chanted.

The Dark Lord did not appear.

Gilbert approached the real Satanic High Priest, who appeared quite smug in his confidence that the supernatural was a scam he personally ran.

"Fr. Ravenwood, there's a horde of vampiric familiars heading in this direction," Gilbert said. "You have to get these people out of here and help us barricade the doors."

The 'coven' turned to see Deanna and Gilbert, interrupting their profane ritual. They all waved politely and the MacDonald children waved back.

"You all need to leave," Deanna warned. "There is a horde of zombies coming."

The coven laughed.

"Hey, is this part of the deal?" the fake vampire asked. "We get a show, too?"

"No!" Ravenwood yelled, then turning to Gilbert. "Did Delilah put you up to this? Get the hell out of here!"

"This is not a joke," Deanna insisted. "They're nearly here."

"No, they are not," Ravenwood spat, walking up the aisle and straight out the door. "There are no whatever-you-called-them."

Ravenwood exited the Temple to find a crowd of vagrants standing in front of the Temple. He audibly gagged at the smell.

"We don't do charity here," Ravenwood said. "I think the Fieldhands run a soup kitchen. Go bother them."

One of the men opened his jaw to reveal two huge canine teeth hanging out from the top of his mouth. Ravenwood froze. The monster lunged and nearly made Ravenwood a meal when Deanna raised her rifle and shot it in the chest. The monster's expression seemed to register surprise before its body exploded into dust. Ravenwood promptly pissed himself, and then ran back into the Temple, past Gilbert and Deanna. The teenage coven, now having abandoned their cheesy hokum, dove behind the pews and peeped out from the side.

Gilbert moved to the next familiar and aimed for the heart. He stalled for a moment, thinking of Simon, but then he pulled the trigger and hit the familiar in the shoulder. Other than a small jerk of the shoulder there was no effect. Gilbert fired again, and this time the shot found its way to the mark. Despite their losses, the zombies staggered towards the Temple. Deanna and Gilbert fired at will. One after another, the familiars disintegrated into the dust of the Earth. Behind them, Gilbert could hear the leader of the Goths bargain with the devil's minister.

"Hey, this doesn't cost extra, does it?" the leader asked Ravenwood.

Ravenwood didn't answer in any coherent words, but merely shrieked as the familiars approached and ran to the janitorial closet.

Gilbert and Deanna surveyed the battlefield as one familiar after another staggered toward the front doors.

"No time to board the windows now," Gilbert said. "Theo was right, they aren't too tough, but there are a lot of them. It's a good thing we've got a bottleneck."

"I've hit five so far," Deanna crowed. "How many do you think you can get?"

Gilbert flinched at the comment. He surveyed at the approaching wights, who looked like the kind of unfortunate souls his father taught them to help. If he were here, MacDonald would probably be telling them to mow down the lot, but it still gave Gilbert the willies to do it.

"Deanna, these all represent people who died," Gilbert said. "I don't think we should make a game of this."

Deanna fired again, evaporating another familiar, leading to another round of cheers from the pews behind them.

"Six."

St. Michael's Church, 10 p.m.
Gabe

Gabe sat in the pew, praying the rosary. It had been three hours since Theo had called and told him Scratch was after him. He hadn't seen hide or hair of either vampire since then. Supposedly, Scratch couldn't come into the church. Gabe was obviously anxious, but that was exacerbated by the sound of pure silence that surrounded him for the past few hours. It would have almost been better to have seen Scratch's red eyes staring through a window at him.

Just as Gabe finished his Hail Holy Queen, a loud, heavy knock sounded out from the door. The young priest dropped his rosary, and then picked it up again. Holy objects were supposed to keep the demon at bay, which is why he should probably get that host Theo told him to prepare. Gabe retrieved the thin disc of unleavened bread from the altar and walked to the door. Perhaps he shouldn't answer, but supposedly he was safe as long as he stayed in the church.

Gabe approached the door and there, standing right outside the window of the church was a tall, thin man who had the look of a corpse save for the fact that his fingernails and canines were longer than knives. Scratch wasn't hiding. Instead, he was tempting. The old screw kicked something at the foot of the door. The young priest looked down and found Theo, broken and bleeding on the ground, his face turning purple with bruises with one eye sliced open. Gabe's mouth hung open. He didn't think a vampire could get the snot beaten out of him.

Scratch tapped on the window twice to get Gabe's attention, which he obtained. The Bloody Puritan then took the nail on his right pointer finger and extended it downward, right into Theo's chest. The Irishman grunted in pain, and Scratch took his other pointer finger and elongated that nail into a blade which he placed across Theo's neck.

"So, you'll behead him," Gabe guessed.

Scratch nodded. The Irishman shook his head. No, don't you come out here. Yes, that was the smart move, Gabe thought. Theo has been in this position before. No doubt he has a plan. Like I could ever rescue him, thought Gabe. Then, Scratch raised his blade, and the young priest made an incredibly stupid decision: he opened the door.

As soon as the way was open, Scratch thrust his hand through and grabbed Gabe. The hand exploded into flames, but Scratch apparently thought little of it, as he had no problem throwing Gabe overhead to the concrete in front of the church like a rag doll. Gabe's body skidded across the paving into the asphalt driveway, tearing through his clothes and bruising Gabe's torso. Then, half a second later, the priest felt Scratch's entire weight fall upon him as the Bloody Puritan pounced like a snake after recoil. Scratch's claws dug into his left arm as Gabe turned to find the vampire's mouth open and cocking back for the final strike. The young priest considered praying to God before he died, but then he remembered the host in his pocket.

Gabe pulled out the eucharist and waved it in Scratch's face. Halfway expecting the demon to laugh at him, instead, the thin man emitted an unholy scream that shattered the quiet of the dark night. The Bloody Puritan leapt off the priest, ten feet in the air, and then turned into a falcon, flying away.

Gabe, still recovering from the effects of his stupid decision, slowly got up from the asphalt. Halfway up, he felt a hand pull him up. It was Theo, who had apparently recovered despite looking like ground beef.

"Wow, it worked," Gabe breathed.

"I wouldn't try that more than once," Theo warned. "Get back in the church."

Gabe didn't argue. He scrambled to his feet and got inside the threshold of the sanctuary. Theo joined him inside and closed the door.

"I guess you are now going to tell me that was stupid," the young priest ventured.

"I think you've surmised that by now, father," Theo replied. "Would you like to know why it was stupid?"

Gabe nodded his head dolefully.

"He couldn't really kill me. To kill me, you have to stake me in the heart, cut my head off, *and* fill my mouth with garlic. He can't touch garlic any more than I can. Garlic snaps people out of that hypnosis, so he can't make one of his puppets do that for him. He needs a willing servant. He might have one of those in Simon's little twerp, but I doubt he's around."

They stood in the church entrance and caught their breath. Theo took out a flask and took a swig. As he did, Gabe noticed his scars began to heal. Theo's eye fused back together.

"I'd offer you a drink, but it's cow's blood," Theo explained, as the bruises on his face deflated. "Regeneration with blood. Comes in handy."

"Where have you been?"

"Fighting Scratch for the last three hours. We've been fighting as birds for most of it. After a while, he whipped me in the dogfight and threw me to the ground. Thought I could take him one on one, but the old devil's learned a few tricks since the last time I fought him."

"How did you know he'd be attacking me?"

"Scratch has a hierarchy of hate. You're higher on his list than Ravenwood. You should consider it a compliment. I need to check in on Gilbert and Deanna."

Theo pulled out his phone and made a call while Gabe nervously scanned the windows, suddenly not wanting to see those eyes anymore.

"Gilbert, how are things? You're alive. How are the tourists? They love it. Ravenwood should pay you a kickback. How's Ravenwood? Hiding in a closet in a pool of his own urine and feces? Better than I expected then. Making any progress on thinning the herd? Deanna's made an inappropriate game of it? Well, if that's your attitude, it doesn't look like you'll win. Put $50 on Deanna for me."

Theo hung up the phone.

"Sometimes young men need motivation," Theo said. "Deanna and Gilbert are holding up pretty well over there. How are you doing?"

"That depends," Gabe asked warily. "I'm new to Pandemonium. Is that a common occurrence?"

Gabe pointed out the window, and Theo could see what he was alluding to. The orange glow of fire shone through the windows of the church. A chant could be heard from outside. "Destroy the Anti-Christ!" "Destroy the Anti-Christ!" Scratch's new cult had arrived.

"No, those are out of towners," Theo explained. "I suggest we make for the basement as neither vampires nor priests have a good history with angry mobs."

A brick flew through one of the windows, covering the floor with broken glass. It was followed by a flaming torch that lit the carpet up. Gabe and Theo ran for the hatch leading down to the basement as Scratch's mob busted windows and set the church ablaze. Gabe pulled the hatch up and proceeded to climb down to the basement level, followed by Theo, who locked the hatch behind them.

Up above, the fire raged. Heat radiated from the ceiling above, and it only seemed to grow. Then, explosions thundered across the building, and the fire grew even hotter. The young priest wiped his brow.

"They're pouring gasoline on the fire," he said. "Or something."

A few minutes later, fire engines could be heard arriving in the background, followed by gunshots. Scratch was serious, he really wanted this church gone, and it looked like he was getting his wish. Gabe could hear the support beams beginning to buckle.

"My first parish and it was burnt to the ground on my watch," Gabe sobbed, sitting in the dark. "What if we can't get out of here?"

"I can get out of here," Theo answered. "I can turn to mist and get help. Eventually, they'll move on, if for no other reason than that Scratch can't direct them so easily in the day."

The ground above them shook. The support beams started coming down. One by one, prefaced by the cracking sound of the church's structure coming apart, the roof caved in, followed by the walls. The lights went out in the basement, as the wiring in the building had been destroyed. After sixty years of serving tourists, St. Michael's was coming to the ground. The final collapse landed with a boom that nearly cracked the concrete. The church had been demolished.

Gabe and Theo sat in the dark under the ruins of the church. Gradually, the chanting faded.

"Sounds like they've moved on," Gabe whispered.

The Seventh Day of Christmas, Thursday, Second Satanic Temple, 7 a.m.
Deanna

Deanna fired another shot straight into a familiar's heart. Another old man, living rough laid to rest as he returned to the dust of the Earth, literally. Deanna leaned on her assault rifle, steadying it against the barricade she and Gilbert had set up at the entrance to the temple. Gilbert fired a shot next to her, hitting another familiar in the heart. Deanna's eyes grew heavy with fatigue. They had been fighting all night. Thank God they loaded up on ammunition before leaving Theo's apartment the day before. Wave after wave of vampiric zombies washed against the barrier she and Gilbert had made to protect the tourist trap. Ravenwood hid in the closet. His teenage guests, at first enraptured by the action scene, now laid in the pews, whining that they were bored. Granted, Deanna and Gilbert had just been doing the same thing, over and over, for the past 11 hours, even if it was killing zombies. That would be pretty dull.

"When do we get to leave? Our chaperones are going to be waking up at the hotel any minute."

Deanna rolled her eyes. Her father told her that bored tourists were always Ravenwood's true congregation, and now he had abandoned them. Still, they had more pressing things to worry about. The zombies were beginning to close in on the barricade, and they were running low on ammunition.

"How long until sunrise?" Deanna asked, throwing Gilbert another round.

"What?" Gilbert yelled, unable to hear her through his earmuffs and the constant banging of gunfire.

"How long until sunrise?"

Bang! Bang! Bang!

"If you have a surprise, you should use it now!" Gilbert yelled back.

One familiar got close enough to lunge at Gilbert, who took the bayonet mounted on his rifle and punched it directly into the monster's chest.

"No, how long until sunrise?!" Deanna repeated.

At that moment, a beam of light crested over the horizon. As the golden rays reached the steps of the Temple, the legions of the undead stopped, cracked, and collapsed into piles of dust in front of the Cartoon Devil in the window. Exhausted, Gilbert and Deanna lowered their assault rifles and took the earmuffs off their ears. They caught their breaths for just a moment before Gilbert spoke.

"Deanna, what were you saying?"

"Never mind."

Behind her, Deanna could hear the tourists coming up behind them. The leader, carrying his fake blood stained mirror, offered his hand to Gilbert.

"Great show at first, but a little repetitive as it went on. Have you thought about adding explosives?"

St. Michael's Church, 9 a.m.
Theo

Theo woke up with sunlight hitting his face, which he would normally find to be quite inconsiderate had it not meant that someone had dug them out from under the rubble. Sure enough, the city had cleared away the rubble of the church and uncovered the hatch to the basement.

"Thank God," Theo breathed. "I can't remember the last time I said that."

Theo woke up Gabe, who had similar sentiments. The emergency responders pulled them out of the basement to find Gilbert and Deanna waiting for them up top, looking like they had a long night.

"You're alive!" Theo and Deanna shouted simultaneously.

Theo ran to Gilbert and Deanna and threw his arms around them.

"Deanna beat me by three familiars," Gilbert confessed. "We took out about half of them, and sunlight took care of the rest."

"Well, you owe me $50 then," Theo said.

"What happened to the church?" Deanna asked.

"Scratch can use those eyes to whip up an angry mob rather quick," Theo explained.

"Is he going to be, okay?" Gilbert asked, pointing to Gabe.

Gabe kneeled in the ruins of his church and sobbed. Theo walked slowly over to him and put his hands on his shoulder.

"I'm sorry, Father," Theo said.

Gabe nodded his head and got off the ground. The Irishman carried him back to the ambulance. Gabe's first assignment as pastor had gone down in flames.

CHAPTER TWENTY-ONE

The Seventh Day of Christmas, Thursday, Davis Guest House, Noon
Beth

Gilbert and Deanna were fast asleep. They had collapsed on the beds in the guest rooms. Bryce went through the binder Gilbert found in Simon's desk, while Delilah and Hecate did the crossword in the *Daily Lament*. Beth flipped through the news stories on page one while her aunts contemplated what could be a ten-word synonym for the Book of Revelations beginning with A. Armies of undead attacking the Temple. Random people turning up missing. An angry mob occupying the town meeting hall. St. Michael's burnt to the ground. People afraid to leave their homes. The mayor announced the town's quadricentennial celebration had been canceled for reasons of 'zombie invasion.' Happy New Year, Pandemonium.

Alistair walked through the front door with an official announcement for the Satanic Temple.

"Fr. Ravenwood says the Satanic Rites are canceled this week," Alistair announced. "He ran to a hotel in Charleston. Hey, I guess I'm now the highest-ranking Satanic clergyman in town."

"Abandoning his post in a time of need," Delilah tsked. "Add another demerit to that man's record."

"Hardly the greatest sin he's committed, Delilah," Hecate countered. "He was attacked last night."

"The whole town is being attacked," Delilah protested. "I always knew that Simon man was no good. What the Elders of that church were thinking to have sold to him is beyond me."

Around this time, Beth would normally expect Bryce to chime in with some wisecrack about religion, but Bryce kept silent. He was studying one particular document he had found in Simon's research intensely. Hecate looked at the document over his shoulder, as did Beth. It appeared to be a set of technical specifications.

"Find that interesting, Bryce?" Hecate asked. "Any clue as to what it is for?"

"It's for a device to broadcast the image of a vampire across television waves," Bryce answered.

"You know just by looking at it?" Delilah asked.

"It's intended to make visible something invisible, like dark matter," Bryce explained, "that's why it's channeling this unfamiliar energy. There are lots of things holding the universe together we can't see, so we just call them dark. I don't think Scratch would build something like this to teach a science lesson about quantum physics though. I assume he wants to use television to broadcast his vampiric gaze."

"Hmmm…can it be built?" Alistair asked.

"It can be, but I don't know how long it would take," Bryce responded.

"I'd say Scratch plans for it to be done by Sunday morning," Beth ventured.

"How do you know that?" Bryce asked.

Beth took out her iPad and put on a YouTube video from the Ministries posted earlier that morning. Calvin appeared, wearing a cassock and visibly struggling with physical pain. He didn't have the same faraway look of Scratch's other servants, but he wasn't really all there either. His eyes were wide open like the other puppets, but they were concentrated on the camera broadcasting him.

"My spiritual mentor, Pastor Atticus MacDonald, would like to address true Christians across the country and the world this Sunday," Calvin announced. "This is a special message about the sacrifices necessary to return this country to its Christian foundations!"

"I found this a few minutes ago," Beth explained. "Looks like Scratch expects to be able to appear on camera within three days."

"We should tell Theo," Delilah said. "Where is he?"

Charleston, South Carolina, Charleston International Airport, 3 p.m.
Theo

"A broadcast?" Theo repeated back to Hecate over the phone. "Yeah, that was part of Simon's original plan. He wanted me to show up on camera and hypnotize people into giving him their money. Figures the old Devil would find a way to pull it off."

"What do we do?" Hecate asked.

"I don't know, but a better field general than me is walking off the plane, right now," Theo answered, hanging up.

Theo waited by the luggage carousel, looking at the escalator for his savior. And there he came, the silver-haired Fr. Eric Burton wearing a long black coat, his roman collar barely visible underneath. Fr. Eric spotted Theo and waved. When he arrived, they shook hands.

"Good to see you, old friend," Fr. Eric greeted, in his characteristic Etonesque tone. "I wish it were under better circumstances. I'm sorry to hear about MacDonald."

"When you're as old as I am, you learn to deal with friends dying," Theo responded. "I hope that doesn't bother you too much. It's not all hopeless. We've fended off his attacks on the general public so far. The town square has looked better, and the Ze'ev had to bury a wee lass today. On the positive side, we've discovered his evil plan."

"What's that?"

"He's found a way to broadcast himself. What will they think of next?"

Davis Guest House, 9 p.m.
Gilbert

"He can use television?" Gilbert asked.

"Apparently," Hecate answered.

"This is very bad," Gilbert said.

"What's very bad?" Deanna asked, coming downstairs. "Sorry, I overslept."

"What's very bad is that Scratch is figuring out how to broadcast his vampiric gaze to the entire country, the world even," Gilbert explained. "Other than that, it's been a quiet night. You didn't miss much."

"Other than my nephew going outside half-naked in the dead of winter, yes," Hecate said, pointing out the front window.

Deanna and Gilbert walked over to the window and found Alistair, wearing little more than boxers and an undershirt in late December. He had that same faraway look on his face. Gilbert then noticed the excessive mist in the area. The mist gathered and formed into the shape of a pale, thin man, who raised a claw behind Alistair's head. Gilbert ran outside and tried to stop the slash, but he was too far away.

Right before the claw came down, a white blinding light hit Scratch in the back of the head. Scratch's skull exploded into flame, with blood spurting out of the back of his cranium. Still, it didn't faze the immortal long. The thin man, evidently surprised, pulled a piece of metal out the back of his head, and turned his neck to the source of the fire. As he did, Gilbert could see the inside of the vampire's skull, where his brain and skull were both regrowing like a fungus, filling in the spot that had been shot out. Alistair snapped out of Scratch's control, saw him clearly for the first time, and ran to the guest house. Gilbert looked in the direction of the shot. There, on the front porch of the plantation house, stood Bryce, firing at the Bloody Puritan with his rail gun. Scratch screamed in annoyance and dove at Bryce, busting through the railing of the porch and colliding into Bryce, knocking the rail gun out of his arms. Bryce lay on the deck, the air knocked out of him, unable to breathe or move.

Scratch opened his jaw to obliterate the fly in his grasp, when suddenly, a vial of holy water busted on his shoulders. The thin man screamed in agony as hot, white steam formed off of his shoulder blades. Bryce rolled away from his grip. Below the deck, a man in a dark coat walked up to the Scratch with a piece of unleavened bread in his hands. The Bloody Puritan raged at the hated host and ran to the other end of the porch, transformed into a falcon, and flew away. The man ascended the steps to the porch and lifted Bryce off the deck.

"Aristotle taught that there is a line between courage and recklessness," the man said. "What you just did straddles that line fairly nicely, but the next time you want to assault Scratch, you might want to use something likely to do more than get his attention. By the way, I'm Fr. Eric Burton."

The Eighth Day of Christmas, Friday, Pandemonium, Davis Plantation House, Midnight
Theo

Fr. Eric led them all into the living room of the Plantation House except Alistair, who was passed out in his room after his encounter with Scratch. Delilah offered to get them all something to drink. They all turned her down save Fr. Eric himself.

"A brandy sounds wonderful right now," he responded.

"Well, if he's drinking," Theo relented. "I'll take a brandy too."

Delilah poured them both a snifter and after they satiated their need to indulge, Fr. Eric began.

"Theo has informed me of the situation in full. First of all, Deanna and Gilbert, I knew your father well, and I considered him a friend.

308

I'm sorry to hear he has died, but we have a job to do now. The Orangeman would agree."

"Next, it appears the big issue here is this device that will broadcast Scratch's vampiric gaze to the world," Fr. Eric continued. "As I understand it, someone here figured out how the device works. Who was that?"

Bryce raised his hand.

"Ahh, the man who assaulted a vampire with that ramshackle device," Fr. Eric said, pointing to Bryce. "Seems like you are a better inventor than you are a shot. Could you create a device that scrambles that signal?"

"Hmmm...yes, yes, I could," Bryce mused.

"You're mentioning this now?" Hecate asked.

"I hadn't thought of it before," Bryce responded, "but given that I understand how the machine works and the signal it will emit, I could develop a countermeasure to interfere with the broadcast. I just need to sketch out my plan, obtain the parts and build it. This will require some height and the device will be large. I may need to use the entire plantation house."

"If it stops those maniacs from rioting downtown, please do," Hecate said.

"Well, young man, let's get to it," Fr. Eric commanded. "Also, if you have the time, there's another device I'd like you to build."

"I'll take a look at the plans," Bryce promised.

"Next problem," Fr. Eric continued. "Those maniacs Ms. Davis was referring to. I assume they are under Scratch's influence. That can be dispelled by using holy objects. Holy water, consecrated Eucharists, crucifixes. Theo, I believe that this town has a priest?"

"Yes, he's living in an old hotel now, hiding from an angry mob," Theo explained.

"Because Scratch had his church burned to the ground," Fr. Eric ended the sentence. "He likely did that in the vain hope that he could get rid of the supply of consecrated Eucharist and holy water that would snap those crowds out of the gaze he has them under."

"That hadn't occurred to me," Theo admitted. "I assumed that he just hated priests that much."

"Probably true as well," Fr. Eric replied.

"What about the vampiric familiars?" Deanna asked. "He might be making more of them."

"Yes, he might be," Fr. Eric said. "But if we kill Scratch, they fall apart."

"What if he sends another army out?" Gilbert asked.

"Where was he keeping them the last time?" Fr. Eric asked.

"In a basketball court in the New Stranger Church," Gilbert answered.

"Collapse the roof using C4," Fr. Eric concluded. "I find it difficult to believe the Orangeman didn't have any grenades or explosives leftover from his time running around with Theo and me in Ulster. You and Gilbert should make an ammunition run at the rectory tomorrow."

"Yeah, he kept a cache around," Theo interjected, "that's why he insisted on getting to America by boat. That and we had Scratch's remains with us, and you should have seen the custom agent when we explained we were moving human remains."

With that, the meeting ended. They walked outside to find fireworks being set off, illegally, as the local government had banned any New Years celebration as too dangerous in the current environment. Some adventurous Pandemonians apparently didn't care. Theo smiled. A good sign. This town wouldn't let the Bloody Puritan keep them down.

Stranger Rectory, 9 a.m.
Gilbert

Gilbert and Deanna arrived at the Rectory early that morning, figuring it was better to do what they needed to do before there was any risk of getting caught out at night. Given his last encounter with Scratch, Gilbert expected to walk in on him in the form of his father. Thankfully, they were spared that indignity, as the Bloody Puritan was not present.

"He's stopped appearing as Dad," Gilbert remarked. "To Strangers at least."

"I think that might have to do with the emails we sent out to everyone," Deanna said. "Most of the Strangers know that he isn't Dad, so they won't be fooled."

"I wish we could have saved all of them. Theo says Strangers are still among the mob. I'd like to think he couldn't do such a thing, but look at what he's done so far."

Scratch had not seen fit to touch the rectory in any meaningful way. Deanna half expected the place to be torn to shreds, but then again, trashing one building would seem rather small time to Scratch after trashing all of downtown. They found their father's old travel chest. Deanna picked the lock. Inside they found Fr. Eric was not mistaken, their father did indeed have C4, and grenades, and any number of other explosives.

"I'm pretty sure this stuff is illegal," Gilbert guessed.

"I'm not complaining."

They heard a knock on the door, and both of them jumped. Who would be knocking on this door? They had told everyone in the church directory to stay away. Gilbert looked down from the window and saw Aaron Parker at the front entrance. Gilbert assumed he didn't want to talk about coming out to his parents.

"It's Aaron," Gilbert said.

They came down and answered the door.

"Hey, Aaron," Gilbert warned. "It's still not safe to be here."

"I know, but I saw your car parked and I wanted to speak with you," Aaron explained. "I've emailed, but I suspect you haven't had the time to answer."

"What did you want to tell me?" Gilbert asked.

"We've received some threats to the church," he replied. "The old church."

Aaron pointed to the old church a stone's throw from the rectory.

"A few people who drove by saw some of those protestors throwing stones at it, and one man interviewed on the news said they were going to burn it to the ground. At first, I didn't think anything of it. Then, I saw what happened to St. Michael's downtown, and it seems like things are different. When I was with Scratch, he really seemed to hate that church."

"Thank you for telling us that," Gilbert replied. "I'll have to ask Fr. Eric about how we plan to deal with this."

"Fr. Eric?"

"He's a friend of my Dad. Right now, he's supposed to be preparing the new priest in town."

McCloskey Hotel, Noon
Gabe

Theo put Gabe up in the McCloskey after St. Michael's burnt to the ground. He made it sound very nice. Told Gabe that in the past, Presidents and movie stars had stayed there. That all wore off the first time the heating went out. The walls bore water stains and the air conditioning units dated to the 1970s. The parking deck connected to the building had signs asking people not to grill in the lower floors. The electric sockets didn't even work. Gabe took one look at the ramshackle elevator, and instead decided to take the stairs. By the time Fr. Eric came to visit his room, the young priest was in a depressed state.

"I'm cursed," Gabe moaned. "My first parish and it was burnt to the ground within a month. What did I do such that God to let this happen to me?"

"You know, Father, Theo told me that you took his confession," Fr. Eric said. "That's a privilege I've never had."

"Really? So, you're saying that I should think of my mission as a priest in terms of the way I carry out the central vocation of priesthood?"

"I guess you could take that lesson. I'm also telling you that you sound like Theo with all this nonsense about how God could let this happen to you, and if you took his confession, you should know that. Best to get your mind on the task at hand."

Fr. Eric took out a few vials which he intended to fill with holy water. Then Gabe's phone beeped. A message indicated he had a message from Gilbert. He turned on speaker phone for Fr. Eric's benefit.

"Fr. Gabe, if you could tell Fr. Eric that we believe Scratch is about to attack the old Stranger Church tonight. We could use some help."

Gabe looked to Fr. Eric.

"What do we do?" the young priest asked.

"Hmmm…" Fr. Eric mused. "This is an excellent development."

"Excellent development?! I just told you they burned down a church two days ago! Now they are going to burn down another one! How can this be an excellent development?"

"Because now I can show you what you should have done with St. Michael's. We'll be at the church tonight as soon as the sun goes down. In the meantime, we fill these bottles with holy water. You can never be too prepared."

Junk Yard, 2 p.m.
Bryce

Bryce picked up Gary after having finished the plans for the signal interference generator and they drove to the junkyard. They both knew the owner by his first name. (It was Marvin) Marvin told them he wouldn't stay after dark, so they should get out before 5 p.m.

"How many people are going to tell me that?" Bryce asked. "I get the idea. There's a fanatical bloodsucker with magic powers out at night. I'll take precautions."

314

"Dude, when that thing attacked us on Tuesday, you wanted to piss yourself," Gary said.

"Yeah, and I don't want that to happen again. That's why I want to build this thing."

Gary shook his head at Bryce. He could tell his friend didn't think this was a good idea. Gary sometimes needed a little push, and Bryce was always happy to provide it.

Bryce and Gary sifted through the junkyard for the necessary parts. They'd have to be efficient, as chances are they would only get one chance to gather parts before Friday. One by one, they found the necessary pieces and tossed them into the back of the truck. When it came time to pay Marvin, he had already left with instructions to leave the money on the counter. Bryce put down the necessary amounts he earned from working in his aunts' funeral home business.

"Dude, it's getting late, and we're on the Stranger part of town," Gary warned. "Maybe we should take shelter. I heard he can't enter a church."

"Whatever," Bryce said.

Bryce and Gary got into the cab of Bryce's truck and took off. After a minute of driving in silence, Gary spoke.

"Hey, we're heading in the wrong direction," Gary objected.

"No, I'm taking the long way around," Bryce answered. "Going the direct route takes us through those religious nutjobs in the town square."

"Yeah," Gary muttered, nervously eying the New Stranger Church, which they were quickly approaching. "But it takes us closer to that church he's supposed to be hanging out at."

"Gary, when have I ever led you into trouble?"

"Well, there was that one time when we set the neighbor's dog on fire with that laser you made."

"How could I have predicted that? Lasers are normally harmless. So, I modified it a bit. I didn't know how well it would work."

Bryce paid no heed to Gary's objections and continued to approach the New Stranger Church, while Gary nervously tapped his fingers on the dashboard. The truck stopped at a stoplight right in front of the church, and Gary let out an audible squeak. After what seemed like an hour, but was really two minutes, the light turned green and Bryce moved forward, driving slowly toward the south side of the Line.

"See," Bryce insisted. "Nothing to worry about."

Then, the truck bounced as a very large object landed on the top of the cab with a dull thud. Both of them jumped in their seats.

"Could be a squirrel," Bryce said.

His sentence was punctuated by a set of long, thin claws slamming against the windshield of the truck and carving a set of white lines into the glass. Bryce and Gary both screamed as Bryce put his foot to the gas pedal. The truck's wheels screeched and the vehicle pushed forward, but the hand wouldn't relinquish its hold on the windshield. Instead, the nails dug in, piercing the glass at the top. A second claw clamped on the passenger's side window. Bryce turned to find Scratch's emaciated face looking right at him with an open jaw filled with teeth like knives, dripping with blood.

"Aaaaahhhhh!!!!"

Bryce swerved the truck to the left suddenly. Scratch turned his face forward toward the stop sign they were hurtling toward at 50 miles per hour. Unable to move in time, Scratch slammed into the stop sign face first, pulling his claws out of the cab of the truck.

"See, Gary, I always have a plan," Bryce said.

"What's Plan B?" Gary asked. "Look in the rearview mirror!"

Bryce checked his six to find that Scratch now bounded down the road toward them, unfazed from being thrown off a moving vehicle. Bryce took a sharp right turn down a side road. Scratch jumped on the side of a brick building and started running sideways to follow him. Bryce turned left to lose him again, and the Bloody Puritan found the top of a small building, and then the top of a larger one, jumping from one rooftop to the other, gaining on the truck. Bryce blew past a stoplight, and Scratch leaped over a four-lane street to keep up with them. Bryce scanned the road ahead, and he saw the old Stranger Church, where the lights were on. Bryce initially didn't recognize it, but Gary pointed out the obvious.

"Bryce, the church, get to the damned church!" Gary yelled.

"Errrrr, okay, fine, you win," Bryce said, turning into the church driveway.

The church driveway cut through a well-cut lawn, forcing Scratch to come down and pursue the truck on ground level. The vehicle's tires screeched and squealed as he sped down the asphalt. Scratch gained on them with every bound. They blew through the flowers planted out front and hit the brakes, stopping just in front of the church steps. Bryce and Gary got out of the truck and ran towards the front door. Bryce nearly got over the threshold when he felt a claw go through his heel. Bryce turned and found Scratch hanging onto him by his flesh.

Then, Fr. Eric stepped out of the church and pressed a crucifix on Scratch's head. The vampire screamed in pain and let go, retreating. Fr. Eric pulled Bryce into the church.

"Now Bryce, that's the second time I've saved your life," Fr. Eric pointed out. "You don't get too many more of those. If you kept holy water on you or a crucifix, you might not need them."

"He's an atheist," Gary explained.

"Oh, so you have principles against staying alive," Fr. Eric cracked. "Reminds me of the Orangeman. No Roman superstitions for me, thank you. Bryce, at least carry some garlic on your person."

Bryce, holding his bleeding heel and struggling with the sharp pain of having his Achilles tendon sliced in two, looked around and found himself surrounded by people. Deanna, Gilbert, and Theo, but also Gabe and a host of Strangers, were sitting in the church.

"What's everyone doing here?" Bryce asked.

"We heard that Scratch was attacking the church," Gilbert answered, "so, we put in some calls and they all came to man the barricades. We expected him to send the mob, not to show up personally."

Suddenly, they heard chants in the distance. The young priest audibly groaned. "Destroy the Anti-Christ," the mob repeated. Over and over again. That old chestnut.

"We've just cost these people their church," Gabe groaned.

"Would you like to make a bet on that?" Fr. Eric asked.

Outside, the mob marched towards the church with lit torches. The Strangers moved to barricade the windows, but Fr. Eric stopped them.

"Father, we have to stop them from getting into the church," Deanna said.

"No, we're going to let them inside the church actually," Fr. Eric insisted.

"Wait, we're going to do what?" Gilbert asked.

Fr. Eric walked to the front door and swung the doors wide open, much to the horror of the Strangers behind him.

"Come in! Come in! We welcome you!" Fr. Eric beckoned.

The mob, upon seeing an opening, ran towards the entrance to the church in a full battle cry. Gilbert and Deanna tried to close the doors again, but Fr. Eric waved them off.

"Trust him, people!" Theo yelled. "He knows what he's doing!"

The whole room hoped that Theo was right, as the mob was nearly through the front door. The first of Scratch's fanatics ran through the threshold and then stopped. The rest of the mob got through the door, and they ceased their charge as well. A few seemed to notice they were holding torches and put them out in the baptismal font. Annie Ferguson, and the rest of the Strangers in the crowd, went into the church and took their seats, a little confused as to how they got here.

"The spell's broken," Deanna remarked.

"Hello, ladies and gentlemen," Fr. Eric began, "it appears that you have realized that you aren't where you remember being. You came here to protest a vampire."

Fr. Eric motioned towards Theo, who raised his hand and nodded.

"You have fallen under the spell of a vampire, but not Theo," Fr. Eric explained. "You'll find that Simon has made a deal with a far lower power. You may want to inquire as to what you have been doing for the past few days and call an attorney. You may have claims against you, as well as claims against the ministries. As for tonight, I think Theo would like to speak with you.

"Thank you, Father," Theo took over, stepping up to the pulpit. "Hello, I am Theo, the man you came to kill. Yes, I think you came to kill me. I assume you know roses repel vampires. Simon did his homework on that one."

"I would tell you that Simon misrepresented me in that video, but I won't pretend to be an angel. I've made some mistakes in life. It's a very long story, maybe sometime I'll recount it in detail."

"But I can tell you that I've got people here who will vouch for me. The Strangers here will tell you that I'm no monster. I mean, I'm a monster in the Dracula sense, but not in the Charles Manson sense."

The crowd, still wondering how they had got here, found themselves unable to gin up much anger in this situation. The Strangers gathered around Theo in a show of support. The mob fell silent. A few of them left. After it was clear nothing would happen, Fr. Eric spoke.

"I can't guarantee that Scratch won't seek to reclaim you. I would leave town if I were you."

"You aren't the only one taking that option," Bryce said. "Has anyone heard from Fr. Ravenwood?"

CHAPTER TWENTY-TWO

The Eighth Day of Christmas, Friday, Charleston, South Carolina, Holliday Inn Express, 9 p.m.
Ravenwood

"Yes, I understand people are upset," Fr. Ravenwood told Tiberius Blackthorn, one of the trustees of the Temple, over the phone, "but I don't know what they expect me to do. That maniac is still out there."

"People expect you to do the one thing you're paid to do," Blackthorn responded. "You have one job, Ravenwood. We don't expect you to come back to Pandemonium. We've reserved a room at that Holiday Inn you're at in Charleston. We're calling it a special historical exhibit. All you have to do is come downstairs."

"But those monsters threatened me. I was traumatized. I'm getting so old. This travel has killed me I feel so tired."

"You're 63, same age as I am. And I ran a marathon back in April for Race for the Cure. It's two days away, Ravenwood."

"I'm just not doing it. I guess you'll just have to buy out my contract and force me to retire."

"Not if you don't bother to show up. Then we can just fire you."

Unbelievable, Ravenwood thought. How could they expect him to work under these conditions? Sure, he was safe, but he was so tired. No, he just couldn't do it. Tradition be damned. These were exceptional circumstances. The nerve of some people. What do they expect me to do? Go out there with a wooden stake and fight him off?

The Ninth Day of Christmas, Saturday, Southwest Sector, 3 a.m.
Scratch

Humiliated by his defeat at the Old Stranger Church, Scratch decided to drink his troubles away. He set his sights on an old woman, digging through some rubbish in an alley. She was alone, an easy target. Scratch dropped from the roof. He approached the woman, treading lightly in the filthy crevice. When she was within his grasp, he grabbed at her and then retracted his hand, which burned with holy fire. Scratch looked up and found that the woman was wearing a necklace of garlic.

"Buffet's closed unless you like garlic."

Scratch turned around at the sound of the voice. He saw a large Moor standing at the entrance of the alleyway. He held up a crucifix and moved slowly towards Scratch. Scratch crawled up the wall, and then when he was far enough away, transformed into a falcon and took flight.

New Stranger Church, 9 a.m.
Gilbert

"That was a great idea to stick garlic around their necks," Pastor Overstreet said, over the phone. "Granted, some of the people tried to eat them, but overall, it afforded more protection than food."

"That's good," Gilbert replied. "It was Fr. Eric's idea. He's a friend of my father."

"Hey, my condolences about Atticus. He was a good egg."

"Thank you," Gilbert responded. "If you excuse me, I'm afraid there's another matter I have to attend to."

Overstreet gave his goodbye and Gilbert hung up. Gilbert and Deanna looked to Fr. Eric, who was dressed as a vagrant. He wore a dirty old jacket and tattered slacks. His feet were wrapped with bread bags, and his normally coiffed hair was a matted mess which went every which way, matching his grizzled chin, soaked with cheap liquor from the night before. His body bore the clear scent of urine and sweat. Fr. Eric explained that the smell was the product of his own bodily fluids which he collected and left to stew for a time in a vial.

"How do I look?" Fr. Eric asked.

"Better than we did when pretending to be vagrants," Gilbert responded.

"That's a very low bar," Fr. Eric cracked, "but thank you."

Satisfied with his disguise, Fr. Eric approached the service entrance of the church. Gilbert and Deanna walked around to the back of the church with rock-climbing equipment. MacDonald took them rock climbing along with the Davis family in the Smokies, but Gilbert didn't think he'd ever felt quite so nervous before scaling a sheer wall. Of course, he'd never climbed a rock well carrying explosives. Sure, Fr. Eric gave them a crash course in the use of C4 as you generally don't even learn that in Bible camp, but that didn't stop Gilbert's heart from exploding with every step he took around the building. After breaking in twice, they had to worry about being spotted by guards who knew what they looked like. Gilbert looked over to the guards in front of the basketball court, who had apparently not spotted them. Gilbert breathed a sigh of relief. Then Deanna tapped him on the shoulder and pointed to the spot where they were to hook up.

They both very quietly made their way to the spot. When they arrived, Gilbert and Deanna tossed anchors on the top of the roof and hooked up, preparing to scale the wall. Just as they got into position, they heard Fr. Eric start his distraction.

"I'm here fer me support," Fr. Eric said, imitating an old southern accent. "My bones is weak, and it's cold out hur!

"Sir, please leave."

They began their ascent, walking up the outer wall of what should have been the basketball court, where Scratch would be keeping any remaining familiars. Down below, Fr. Eric appeared to be wrapping up.

"Ain't dis a church?" Fr. Eric asked. "I thought dis wuz a church. Yer supposed to help the needy!"

"Yes, there are missions set up for that, sir."

"Oh, I'll git!"

Gilbert and Deanna reached the top of the roof. They ran to the middle where there was a blacked-out skylight, obviously covered by Scratch to keep sunlight out. Gilbert took out a hammer while Deanna prepared the C4 she found in their father's chest. Deanna ran to the far-right corner of the roof to set the first charge. Gilbert smashed the skylight. He looked in and found that Scratch had indeed added to his collection, as the court was now filled with familiars. One of the vampiric zombies even cracked and dissolved when hit with sunlight. Gilbert also saw several living security guards, feeding the vampiric horde by pouring blood into the pit. Gilbert had asked Fr. Eric about the possibility of hurting those people below, and Fr. Eric said something about double effect.

"Look young man, Theo told me about that fellow you had to put in the ground," Fr. Eric groused. "People make their choices in life. Simon did, and so have his employees."

Gilbert grimaced and then made the call. He gave the signal to Deanna, who set the first charge at the far-right corner. Gilbert ran to the point opposite her to set the next charge while she went to the third point. After activating the charges, they would have less than three minutes to get off the roof. Fr. Eric didn't think the guards could get to the explosives within three minutes and Scratch wasn't going out in sunlight. Gilbert reached into his bag as he hit the appointed spot and retrieved three white blocks of plastic explosives with chargers attached. He set the package to blow and then went to the last blast point. Out of the corner of his eye, he could see Deanna going to the rappel point at the back. Gilbert set the final C4 charge, activated the timers, and then ran to Deanna at the repel point. She already had the ropes ready to go down.

"Hook up," she said, handing Gilbert a tether cord.

He did just that. Both of them took positions on the edge of the building and then hopped down the side until they reached the ground behind the building. As soon as their feet touched concrete, both Gilbert and Deanna unhooked themselves and turned and ran. After 100 yards, they stopped and turned around.

The roof exploded, sending bits of tile and concrete into the sky. The guards around the church hit the dirt. Gilbert and Deanna were thrown off their feet by their own work. Not perfect, but it was the first time they had used explosives, Gilbert thought. As the fire died down and the smoke cleared, sunlight poured through the now destroyed ceiling of the athletic court. Scratch's entire army of familiars evaporated in the morning sun.

Davis Guest House, Noon
Beth

"Did you see that device they're building?" Beth asked Gilbert and Deanna.

"That is inside," Fr. Eric answered, shaking his head. "The device is a television camera. We wait until Sunday so we know where it will be, and where Scratch will be. On stage in the main arena of the New Stranger Church. Theo will be in the building to confirm the location, but I always fingered Scratch for an egomaniac. He'll want to be on the main stage."

"How's our own egomaniac doing?" Deanna asked.

She looked out the window to see Bryce and Gary installing an antenna on the top of the plantation house. Theo had been carrying Bryce around the plantation house all day, as Bryce

connected the antenna above to the control in his lab
through a messy mosaic of wires. Now, Theo
supervised them, though the term could be used
loosely.

"The boy does appear to know what
he's doing when it comes to building things," Fr. Eric
said. "I should go out there to speak with Theo."

"I'll join you," Gilbert said.

They both walked outside, leaving
Deanna and Beth alone for the first time in days.

"So…you can speak with dead
people?" Deanna ventured.

"I don't like talking about it," Beth
explained. "It made my aunts think I was crazy."

"I don't think you're crazy. Thank you
for helping us save my brother."

"You're welcome. Yes, I've seen your
Dad. I am guessing that is what you are asking about.
He told me that Scratch was disguised as him."

"Really?"

"He's been following us all along.
He's in the room right now."

MacDonald was indeed in the room,
floating over the couch. Delilah had left an open
newspaper on the side table and he was trying to read
the funnies.

"Dad, I miss you," Deanna called.
"We're going to have a really great funeral for you.
Once we find your…."

Deanna broke down and started to
sob. Beth hugged her while shooting a pleading look
at MacDonald. MacDonald floated over to Deanna,
and he emitted a golden light. Deanna's tears began to
dry up and she caught her breath.

"Is it common for dead people to
follow the living around like that?" Deanna asked.

"No, your father says he's breaking the rules actually," Beth answered.

"Typical. Are there angelic cops looking for him?"

"Nothing so crude, Deanna," MacDonald remarked. "They're more like hall monitors."

"Yes, he's on the run," Beth relayed to Deanna. "I'm sorry, but as long as we're being honest, your father is being a little naughty being down here."

"That's alright," Deanna said. "You know whenever I pray at night, the voice I hear back always sounds like it grew up in Belfast. I wonder if that's what God is like when you see him in Heaven: he looks just like the perfect father."

"Beth, would you listen to her? A perfect father," MacDonald mused. "Hardly. I think I remember a month ago she was complaining about my limits on how much of the internet time she could have."

Beth shot MacDonald a dirty look.

"I just miss him so much," Deanna sobbed, "but I can't show it."

"You seem to be doing just fine now," MacDonald cracked, earning even more disapproval from Beth.

"It's a comfort to know he's right here," Deanna said, holding her hand out.

"I'm on the other side of you, Deanna," MacDonald said, floating by the other hand.

"Would you stop that? We're having a tender moment!" Beth yelled.

Deanna stopped crying. Beth covered her mouth.

"I apologize," Beth said.

"No, I'm sure he deserved that," Deanna said.

Davis Plantation House, 5 p.m.
Bryce

Bryce fine-tuned the antenna sticking out of the top of the plantation house. He looked at the horizon and found the setting sun. He worked a little faster. Theo, Gilbert, Gary, and Fr. Eric were sitting on the roof, watching him put the final touches on the device.

"Alright," Bryce concluded, "we need to go down to my lab and I can fire this thing up."

They all climbed down from the roof via a trap door into the attic with Theo carrying Bryce and made their way through the plantation house down to Bryce's lab/room. Once they got into the plantation house proper, Hecate brought them a wheelchair for Bryce. After Theo lowered him into it, Hecate apologized in advance for the mess in his room. Bryce burned a little at this, but his lab/room didn't disappoint, as they could barely move amongst all the wires and spare computer parts on the floor. As they entered the room, Bryce heard a soft chuckle behind him. He looked behind to find Fr. Eric surveying his room while shaking his head and laughing.

"Find something funny?" Bryce asked.

"Oh, nothing much, Mr. Davis," Fr. Eric answered. "I was looking at the…let's call them 'garlands' you've decorated your room with. Perhaps in an outburst of Christmas spirit?"

The old priest pointed to the cloves of garlic Bryce had hung from his walls. Outside the room, Theo stood in the doorway and eyed the same cloves warily. Bryce grimaced and swallowed his pride.

"Yes, I did take some of your advice," Bryce said. "I may disagree with your religious beliefs, but you seem to know what you are doing when it comes to vampires."

"Ahhh, did everyone here that? The boy can learn," Fr. Eric bragged. "You're less stubborn than the Orangeman. There's hope for you yet. Now show us what you can do.'"

Bryce booted up his desktop, which roared like a hot rod coming to life. He hit a few keys, ran a program, and the signal scrambler, which Bryce had installed throughout the building, hummed with energy. Bryce clicked a few more times.

"It's on," Bryce announced.

"Does it work?" Fr. Eric asked.

"Check your phone," Bryce replied.

Theo did and found he had lost his signal.

"So, it blocks all communications?" Theo asked.

"Yes, for all devices within a 50-mile radius, which should cover the entire island," Bryce answered. "The entire point is to block all communications. That's relatively easy to do compared to blocking just the vampire image. I assume you don't have a problem with that?"

"As a way to stop Scratch tomorrow at 9 a.m., no," Fr. Eric responded. "Right now, however, if you are blocking all communications across the island, that means that everyone at the New Stranger Church, right up to Scratch himself, provided he has bothered to get a cell phone at this point, has just lost their signal as well. We may have just tipped our hand."

Bryce turned the device off.

"There, it's off," Bryce said. "There still shouldn't be a problem. It was a momentary lapse in cell service to most people. Furthermore, how would they know we did it?"

330

"Scratch would suspect me and Theo," Fr. Eric said, "and he knows this is our base or one of them. I'm not disappointed, Bryce, this is very good, but we should prepare for an attack. Scratch will try to destroy this device tonight. Theo, I'll need you to talk to some of the locals."

Theo

Theo and Fr. Eric waited outside the plantation house on the deck while Gilbert and Deanna stood on the roof in the darkness of the night, and then he came. Scratch walked right down the path bisecting the graveyard in front of the plantation house as if he were just taking a stroll. Predictable, Theo thought, so very predictable.

Scratch smiled widely, his sharp teeth gleaming in the pale moonlight of the evening. He puckered his pale lips and whistled. The thin man looked around as if he expected an army to arrive. He whistled again. His smile faltered. And now Theo smiled.

"You were expecting your furry and feathery friends to come running?" the Irishman asked. "Won't happen. I had a word with the animals in the forest. Seems they weren't too happy with how many of them died the last time you called for help. I informed them that your previous promises to return the animals to their glory days when there were no humans on the island were garbage."

Scratch, realizing that his reinforcements weren't coming, growled at Theo, who smirked back at him. The thin man gathered himself like a cat and lunged at the Irishman head-on. Theo cocked his fist back, and then just as the thin man reached him, brought the fist forward onto Scratch's forehead. The Bloody Puritan's body flew back into a tree.

"I always had him on strength," Theo said. "He's a fast little bastard though."

Scratch was indeed a fast little bastard, as he got up, ran around the back of the house, and then crawled up the side. His goal was to knock out the antenna, but it was well guarded. As soon as Scratch came over the side, Gilbert shot him square in the head. The bullet lodged itself in his skull but didn't stop him long. Then Deanna shot him in the chest, and that stopped him in a moment. Theo told them that a bullet to the heart is like a stake, except it doesn't last long. By this time, Theo had flown up to the roof and now stood over the Bloody Puritan. Gilbert threw him a wooden stake. Theo caught it and raised it above Scratch's chest. Before he could bring it down, the thin man turned to mist.

"Turn it on!" Fr. Eric shouted.

Inside the house, Bryce switched on the very same bottle capture device the Brits and Calvin had used to capture Theo. A vacuum pulled air throughout the house, all the way up to the roof. Scratch found himself being sucked through an air vent on the roof. Fr. Eric asked Bryce to put the bottle device together if he had time, and lo and behold, he could multitask. Scratch, realizing what was happening, turned back into 'human' form. Theo gave him a swift right hook, knocking him off the roof.

Scratch fell to the swampy ground below and turned to mist before taking the impact. He regathered himself again. Fr. Eric took the consecrated Eucharist he prepared earlier and approached the Bloody Puritan. The thin man took one look at the host, screamed, and ran in the opposite direction. Perhaps realizing that his assault had failed, Scratch turned back into bird form and flew away.

"He's taken off!" Fr. Eric yelled.

Theo did a short salute to Deanna and Gilbert, transformed into a bird, and flew away in the direction of the New Stranger Church, seemingly in pursuit of Scratch, but really with another goal in mind: infiltration.

Deanna

"Alright, we've repulsed the threat," Fr. Eric said. "Group meeting!"

Everyone came into the yard in front of the plantation house for a recap. They formed a semi-circle around Fr. Eric.

"Theo has gone to take his place inside the New Stranger Church," Fr. Eric said. "Deanna, Gilbert, and I will meet him tomorrow morning. Bryce, we will leave you here to keep the device running and the signal blocked. Scratch will likely do something to enhance the signal, so we will be in touch if anything like that happens."

"Can we stop that if it occurs?" Gilbert asked.

"I can respond to a boost with a boost," Bryce answered

"You are positive that Scratch cannot come here during the day?" Hecate asked.

"He can't travel in sunlight, no," Fr. Eric replied. "Why do you ask?"

"We're the fifth wheel to a coach," Delilah answered. "Fr. Ravenwood is holding a service in Charleston, tomorrow. Alistair is still technically Fr. Ravenwood's assistant. We would like to attend. Bryce can stay if you need him."

"That's fine," Fr. Eric said.

"It might be good to have Beth around," Deanna suggested. "I think that we might bring her along to the New Stranger Church. I promise we won't take her inside."

Beth looked shocked by this proposal.

"Why would you need Beth?" Hecate asked.

"Beth is very observant," Deanna replied, winking at her friend. "She might see something when we scope the building out."

"Deanna, can I speak to you privately?" Beth asked.

Deanna expected this, so she agreed. Beth and Deanna walked behind the plantation house.

"What are you doing?" Beth asked.

"I am using the assets we have to gain an advantage," Deanna explained. "I have a friend who can see dead people, and supposedly, I have a dead father who can scout ahead and overhear conversations. Those are assets I have that I need to use."

"Isn't Theo supposed to scope the place out?" Beth asked.

"Theo is hiding under the stage to get a drop on Scratch when the time is right," Deanna said. "He's only becoming mist to get into the building and under the stage. The last time we tried to use him for reconnaissance they captured him using that suction device. They've still got it. A ghost would be better at scoping the place out than Theo would be. If my Dad is floating around, he could tell us exactly what Scratch is doing and if they've made any changes."

"She's right, Beth," MacDonald concluded. "They'd be fools not to use us."

"Okay," Beth relented, "but you have to promise me, I'm staying outside."

"We promise," Deanna and MacDonald said, simultaneously.

CHAPTER TWENTY-THREE

The Tenth Day of Christmas, Sunday, New Stranger Church, 2 a.m.
Theo

Theo watched the falcon land on the balcony to Simon's office, really Scratch's office now, and he didn't see it leave. In for the night, or at least he was sucking on Simon's intern pool rather than any locals. Looks like he learned not to mess with this town. The Church had quickly replaced the broken window and put a construction fence around the collapsed roof of the basketball court. After all, this place had been built less than two weeks ago, and this allowed Scratch to mask the wounds of war as a mere construction mishap.

Theo flew around the building and found a sewer drain. Seeing as it was unlikely the suction machine was connected to the sewage pipes (now that would be a nasty bottle to be trapped in), Theo turned to mist and wafted into the pipes of the church. Theo traveled up the P-trap in the form of bubbles. He had done this once in Belfast, so he knew it worked, but it was a little unpleasant. Traveling as bubbles broke him into pieces, making it difficult to concentrate. That, and he came out of a toilet, always an undignified entrance. Moving along the floor, Theo made his way under the main stage. He texted from his phone that he was in place.

New Stranger Church, 9:30 am
Gabe

"Repeat the plan back to me," Fr. Eric insisted.

Gabe closed his eyes and bit his tongue in an effort to remember Fr. Eric's entire scheme from start to finish. They were in the back of a church van from St. Michael's, now finally being put to some use, in an alley way across the street from the church. The sound of water droplets pounding the side of the van interrupted Gabe's thought. A freak storm had blown in on the very day they decided to take Scratch down. Perhaps the Devil had come to take his soul. Piece by piece, Gabe reassembled the sequence of events they needed to pull off. Then he opened his mouth and somehow got it running.

"We go in the back and splash holy water on the guards, freeing them from Scratch's power and gaining entrance to the backstage," he began. "We then position ourselves directly behind the mainstage and confirm both Scratch's position and the position of the camera."

Fr. Eric didn't seem disappointed. He didn't seem like anything. Instead, he just twirled his hands around as if to say continue. Deanna and Gilbert, also sitting in the van, simply loaded their tactical vests with crossbow bolts and wooden stakes while pouring holy water into the super soakers they had bought the day before. They were using cross bows instead of rifles, as they would be fighting Scratch in a populated area. It all seemed rather irreverent to Gabe, but there was a murderous undead monster on the loose and certain niceties had to be dispatched with.

"I will walk to the main auditorium down the sides of the stage so as to stay out of Scratch's line of sight and spread liquified host around the rim of the stage, creating a 'kill box' to trap Scratch in while Theo and the rest of you attack Scratch."

Gabe flinched a bit when he used the words 'kill box.' He didn't approve of using the eucharist to box in an enemy, even one as awful as Scratch. Fr. Eric apparently noticed the disapproval in the young buck's eyes.

"I have a dispensation," the old priest responded. "When you are finished?"

"I will then walk out of the auditorium, with my back turned to Scratch so he doesn't see my face, and get out of the way," Gabe repeated. "Then, I text Bryce to turn on the signal."

"Very good, father," Fr. Eric congratulated him. "Everyone, get a rosary on."

Gilbert and Deanna retrieved their rosaries from their pockets, while Gabe fumbled trying to reach his. Fr. Eric instructed them that keeping holy objects on them would make them immune to Scratch's hypnotism, a fact which he knew from experience. Gabe wondered why neither he nor Theo had thought to do this before, particularly after seeing how Scratch reacted to the host. He really was a good field general. After finally getting his beads out, Fr. Eric nodded. They were prepared.

Two loud knocks sounded on the back of the van. Deanna opened the door to reveal Beth, standing outside in the cold wearing a nice, floral dress and sunflower hat. Her lips quivered as the rain poured down around them.

"Our special helper tells me that Scratch is on the main stage and the device is suspended above them," Beth reported. "They have boosted the signal."

"Bless you, child," Fr. Eric replied. "Please text Bryce and tell him to increase our disruptor signal."

Beth did just that. Everyone else got out of the van, including Gabe who brought up the rear. They were all dressed in maintenance uniforms so as to blend in once they got inside the building.

"Are you sure the guards won't see through this?" Gilbert asked.

"As long as we don't get too close," Fr. Eric answered. "The guards are under Scratch's control. What he gains in loyalty, he loses in intelligence. Hypnotized puppets aren't as adept as true servants."

They walked out of the alleyway towards the rear of the church. Gabe spotted Gilbert's and Deanna's handiwork at the basketball court for the first time, seeing the collapsed roof obscured by construction fences.

"You two do good work," Fr. Eric said, beaming. "The Orangeman would have been proud."

They approached the back of the church, fully guarded by men in black uniforms. They noticed the four people coming towards them and forming a line to block their entrance. Gabe and the others in the group took out the super soakers and proceeded to douse the guards. Scratch's hypnotized servants didn't react at first. Fr. Eric explained that the reaction time of these brainwashed puppets would be down, as Scratch's influence over them had a deleterious effect on their reflexes.

As the holy water splashed on the already wet guards, they did not "come to their senses." It was more that their senses collapsed. Before the holy water, they all seemed very serious and sober. After being sprayed, the guards fell to the ground. Fr. Eric kept walking past them without making a sound. Gabe and the others followed his example. The old priest opened the back door and they all strolled in.

The backstage of the New Stranger Church buzzed with energy. Wires covered the floors, and curtains and backdrops segmented the bright room, lit up from above by stage lights. Maintenance men, security, production assistants, and any number of random men in suits zoomed around, plugging in monitors, mist machines, and laser light emitters. Whether any of these people were hypnotized, Gabe couldn't tell. They appeared merely very motivated, to the point that no one noticed the four of them. Gabe felt Deanna pull his arm to the left. The young priest looked to see Fr. Eric and Gilbert making their way to the area directly behind the stage, and he realized he was falling behind.

Gabe followed Deanna through the mess of wires, curtains, and backgrounds looking around him for fear that a set of red, glowing eyes would pop out of nowhere. The young priest did his best to suppress the terror that was creeping up his throat, but he still jumped with every odd sound coming from the backstage. As Gabe caught up in his own thoughts, he bumped into Deanna, who had stopped with the rest of the group. They were in position, directly behind the main stage, separated from Scratch by a curtain. Gabe surveyed the surroundings and found a shocking image: Atticus MacDonald (Scratch) on a monitor.

"So, it does work," Gabe said. "He appears on camera."

"I noticed," Deanna spat, gritting her teeth as she looked at Scratch in the visage of her father, once again.

"Gabe, I believe you are on," Fr. Eric ordered.

Gabe took his cue and found the stairs on the left side of the stage. He unbottled the liquified host, leaned down and began spreading a long, thin line of the body of Christ along the very edge of the stage. Looking back, he could see Fr. Eric doing the same, drawing a line across the back of the curtain. Gabe continued to hug the wall of the stage, spreading the host, until he walked into the main auditorium.

In contrast to the backstage, the arena was a large, dim room, lit up by purple lights and filled with rows and rows of seats on three levels which seemed to stretch into the heavens up to the cavernous ceiling. Unlike Gilbert, he'd never been inside Scratch's lair. Far from a dark, decrepit crypt, this place shone with an unnatural artificial light from the stage lights above. As his eyes drifted upwards, Gabe could see the structure of the ceiling, like a spiderweb made from metal railings, and it struck him. Of course, Scratch wouldn't want a drab, dark place like Theo's crypt. Some place like that might cause you to remember death, and you would want to avoid it. Scratch was trying to draw people in, so he needed a web to catch the flies.

Gabe was located in the pit next to the elevated stage. He looked above him to see Scratch in the guise of MacDonald. He wasn't hiding how he felt about Simon's flock, his face contorted in a deep rage. As they flooded into the arena, the congregation filled the bleachers, often carrying trays of food. The praise and worship band tuned their instruments on a separate stage on the left side of the pit. Mist wafted from the backstage and lasers blinked in and out.

Gabe pressed his body against the stage while spreading the Eucharist along the very outer boundary of Scratch's dais. He moved slowly, as he would very quickly be dead if he were spotted. The entire time, he sweated bullets, a fact noticed by Fr. Eric when the two priests met at the right sided stairs when Gabe finished his part.

"Why Fr. Gabe? If I didn't know better, I'd think you were frightened," the older cleric teased.

"Well, yeah, he's right there," Gabe whispered, pointing at Scratch. "He could kill me in a minute."

"Actually, now he can't," Fr. Eric replied. "You've just seen to that. He's trapped in this little box. Thank you for doing the difficult part, father. You may now take your rest."

Gabe nodded, wondering whether Fr. Eric actually meant this was the 'difficult part' and turned towards one of the large gates on the ground floor of the church. It occurred to Gabe that the very term 'gate' made this building more like a sports arena, and sure enough, it felt like he was leaving a basketball game, wading through attendees going the other direction. He kept his eyes forward, not looking back so as to alert Scratch to his presence. From the audio above he could hear Scratch's show begin. Better text Bryce, Gabe thought, so he dodged into a book shop and sent Bryce a message: turn on the disruptor. Triumphant horns blared from the sound system.

"Let's hope this works," Gabe muttered to himself, as he looked up at the monitor, focusing on the false MacDonald. A voiceover sounded.

"Ladies and Gentlemen of America and the World, Pastor Atticus MacDonald, the new spiritual leader of Miles Simon Ministries has a special message for you. We ask you to bring your entire family into the living room to hear his divine word, straight from the mouth of God."

For a split second, Gabe wondered if Scratch would give a sermon before brainwashing anyone. Then, in a flash, the demon discarded his disguise and reverted to his original form, and the thin, skeletal figure of a vile wraith appeared on national television, and his eyes burned red with anger and hate. Gabe could feel a power taking hold of him through the monitor. He reached for his rosary, but even then, thoughts flooded his mind. *I have come to bring you back to God. I am the new Shepherd and you are my sheep. Follow and obey!* Gabe gripped the beads tighter and prayed to his Lord for deliverance.

Then, the image cut out. Static filled the screen. The demonic visage of Scratch got fuzzy, like an old UHF channel during a thunderstorm. One of the workers at the book nook slapped the television.

"I was really getting into that!"

"Probably better that you don't," Gabe warned.

He checked his phone. No signal. His prayer had been answered by an eighteen-year-old Atheist. Whatever God Bryce didn't believe in, Gabe thanked Him for creating the nonbeliever. He looked back up at the monitor, and fuzzy though it was, he could see Deanna rush the stage with a stake. Should he get a better look?

Before he could answer that question, Gabe heard a stampede coming from the auditorium. Surprise forced him to run out of the book store and up the stairs to a balcony on the second level. Inside, he saw a mass of attendees rushing the stage. Scratch's eyes continued to burn red, and they were pointed at the congregation. Behind him, Deanna held her arm, bleeding from a slash she received as Gilbert and Fr. Eric came from behind. Apparently, Scratch had fended her off and then hypnotized the audience into attacking the stage and trying to disrupt things. However, the strategy wasn't working for him, as the crowd would reach the edge of the stage, and then halt as they came within range of the Eucharist.

"So, it does work," Gabe said.

Fr. Eric and Gilbert approached Scratch from behind with stakes. He turned to meet them. As they fought, mist wafted up from the stage. Sure enough, Theo reformed right behind Scratch and got an arm around his neck. Fr. Eric raised his stake, but Scratch turned to mist and slipped out. Then he became a falcon in mid-air. Theo then followed and flew after the target, who attempted to escape but turned whenever he tried to leave the area of the stage. The Bloody Puritan truly had been 'boxed in' by the host. A crossbow bolt flew by the falcon. Gabe looked down and saw Deanna recovering and loading up for another shot from the bow. Fr. Eric was apparently shouting some kind of instructions, but Gabe couldn't hear it over the chaos below. The crowd was beginning to come to, and many were arguing with others as to how they got there and why they were seemingly piled on top of each other. Then, Gabe heard a familiar voice behind him.

"Hello, father," Beth greeted him, weakly.

"Beth, you came in?" Gabe asked. "But why?"

"I've been told they could use some help," Beth answered. "The device is still operating, apparently."

Gabe looked up at the camera above.

"Well, sure but what do you plan to do about it?" he asked.

Beth didn't answer but just closed her eyes and seemed to concentrate. Gabe just shook his head. He looked down to find the group holding their fire as Scratch and Theo pecked and scratched at each other as birds, rotating around in the air while security tried desperately to get to the stage. Scratch unlocked from Theo and flew upwards...and then the device fell from the ceiling onto Scratch's avian body, which plummeted to the floor with a crash. The device, now destroyed by its fall, pinned Scratch's bird form to the floor long enough for Fr. Eric to wave the host above his head, keeping him down for the count.

"How did that happen?" Gabe asked out loud.

"Ouch," Beth said, holding her head. "That hurt. Need an aspirin."

Gilbert

Gilbert and Deanna approached Scratch's broken avian body with their weapons pointed straight at him. Fr. Eric hung over the bird, holding the Eucharist, as Theo came back to Earth and transformed back to human form. As they all surrounded their prey, Fr. Eric pushed the device off of Scratch with his foot. The form, still shaking in pain and draining blood, looked warily at his foes who had him trapped. Gilbert raised his stake and aimed for the heart. Then the bird transformed in a flash of light. Gilbert blinked, and before him appeared the image of his father. Scratch raised MacDonald's eyes up at Gilbert in a gesture clearly meant to elicit pity.

"Don't do it, lad," Scratch spoke through MacDonald's mouth.

For a second, Gilbert's grasp of the stake faltered. Then, recognizing that this thing was not his father but had *killed* his father, Gilbert strengthened his resolve. Gilbert brought down the stake quickly. Not quick enough though, as Deanna beat him to it. She drove the stake into Scratch's heart a split second before her brother could make contact. Gilbert, a tad miffed, dropped his own stake.

"What? You were stalling," Deanna said, looking at Gilbert's nonplussed face.

Scratch returned to his own form and fell limp. His mouth let out an ear-piercing scream that echoed throughout the cavernous auditorium.

"Pick him up," Fr. Eric said. "We need to get him backstage."

Theo

Fifteen minutes later, they were backstage, and Theo was sawing through Scratch's neck. The Bloody Puritan, while immobile, remained alive until they removed the head and filled the mouth with garlic. Blood gushed out of Scratch's neck like oil sprouting out of a newly drilled well. Theo remembered his adversary screaming bloody murder through the night when they killed him last back in Ulster, and he didn't disappoint. Half the town could hear him moan in agony until Theo finally got through his vocal cords. Scratch's screams did attract of a few of Simon's employees, who did complain, and even threatened to send them to the police.

"Please do," Fr. Eric responded. "Then the police can investigate everything that's been going on here. They might even get to whatever your involvement in it was."

The guards left without saying another word. Most of the ministry employees didn't bother to check where the screaming was coming from, but instead just stumbled for the exits, disoriented after being in Scratch's power for a week and a half. Theo finally cut through the vocal cords, silencing Scratch, and began to saw through the neck. The sound of this turned Gabe a pale shade of green. He left the room, returning a few minutes later with Beth.

"Beth, you came into the building?" Deanna asked. "Why?"

"I got a message you might need some help," Beth answered. "I called Bryce. No more signal. He's turned off the device, so your cell phone works now."

They all turned on their phones. Theo finished sawing through Scratch's neck. Gabe ran out of the room again. He held up Scratch's disconnected head, his features still moving wildly.

"Alright, the garlic," Theo said.

Gilbert took the garlic out of his bag and then, with Theo prying his jaw open, stuffed the garlic into Scratch's vicious maw. Scratch's head exploded into bright light before being engulfed in a blue flame. The same blue flame burst forth from the body lying on the floor. The fire burned bright until the flesh was burned away, leaving only the bones.

"Gather them up," Fr. Eric reminded them. "You don't want to leave those lying around."

"You don't have to tell me twice," Gilbert responded, collecting the bones.

"Beth, I hope you didn't feel too frightened," Fr. Eric said.

"Oh, it's okay," Beth replied. "I appreciated getting to do something today. Normally Sundays are pretty boring for me. Apparently, it was pretty boring for my aunts. Fr. Ravenwood didn't do the satanic ritual in Charleston."

"He didn't?" Deanna asked.

"Nope, he's locked up in his hotel room and won't come out," Beth explained. "Gosh, Aunt Delilah's mad at him. Says she'll have his job."

"Oh, no," Theo cracked. "What will this town do without him?"

This was met by a chorus of chuckles from everyone but the two priests in the room.

"I'll assume that was funny," Gabe said.

CHAPTER TWENTY-FOUR

The Eleventh Day of Christmas, Monday,
Pandemonium, New Stranger Church, 9 a.m.
Calvin

Calvin woke up that morning with a pounding headache. After several days of being under Scratch's power, he came to the prior afternoon, finding his body covered in shallow wounds and burns. Apparently, while under hypnosis, the Bloody Puritan made Calvin scourge himself. To deal with the pain, Calvin spent yesterday at a local distillery, trying to cope. Now, he was dealing with another set of self-inflicted wounds that not even legal moonshine could save him from.

"Wondering how you got here?"

Calvin turned to the source of the voice. It was the cassette tape player, which still had Scratch's tape loaded into it.

"What the Hell did you do to me?" Calvin asked.

"I gave you exactly what you wanted," Scratch replied. "If you check your current finances, you will find that you own Simon's ministries and his entire fortune. You've received your inheritance, prodigal son. The elder brothers back in Texas may try to sue you over this, but provided you don't confess to our little subterfuge, you should be free and clear."

Then he remembered. The ministries. The name. The fortune. Everything Simon owned was now his.

"And I got exactly what I wanted," Scratch said. "Through the intercession of that blasted Irishman, I have finally found the congregation I was destined to lead. The Strangers will be my flock, and I will be their shepherd. Now and forever. You can join us, Calvin. Your parents already have."

"It's true, Calvin," a familiar voice intoned. "Your father and I are finally together like we should be."

"Yes, son," Simon's voice came through the cassette. "I can't run off now. No denying you're my son here. Not with Scratch in charge. I don't even mind about you taking the ministries and disinheriting my other family. You know, I never really cared for them much anyway."

"See, Calvin, just follow the plan," the Bloody Puritan promised. "This is a temporary setback. I actually consider our business relationship to be a complete success. With the ministries you have an online streaming service that reaches the entire world, revenue that totals in the hundreds of millions, and facilities in every state in the country and beyond. People will line up to be the next sacrifice. I just need you to be my prophet, like St. John the Baptist, preparing the way for my next coming."

"No, no," Calvin mumbled, running his hands over the scars on his body as he began to remember the things he had done and been a part of. "No, I have to get away from this."

"No, Calvin, don't leave," his mother's voice begged. "We can all be together for eternity. We get to watch Scratch punish the sinners forever."

Calvin reached out to the cassette and turned it off. He had to find better business partners.

Stranger Church, 11 a.m.
MacDonald

MacDonald's first introduction to America was when his mother gave him a book called *Tom Sawyer* when he was eight. One scene that struck him was when Tom attended his own funeral. A young Atticus wondered what that experience would be like. Now that he had that opportunity, MacDonald did find it to be interesting. All things equal, he would have preferred to an open casket, but Beth was only able to lead Gilbert and the others to his body after it had been rotting for 10 days. Hecate, who was running the services, informed Gilbert and Deanna quite authoritatively that only a closed casket service would be appropriate.

MacDonald's children and Theo arrived in black, followed by the Davis family, which he expected. Next came his old congregation, always good to see they remembered. Then came his colleagues, the priest, the rabbis, Pastor Overstreet. MacDonald was glad to see Fr. Eric could be present, though ideally he would visit under better circumstances. The young priest sat down next to him. Maybe Fr. Eric would knock some sense into him. Mayor Mayfield and the council appeared. Expected. Strangers vote. What surprised MacDonald

351

was seeing the Sorcerer show up, though it made more sense once Delilah announced there would be a reception afterwards.

Deanna sang *Danny Boy*, per his funeral instructions. He always thought she had a beautiful voice, but Deanna felt embarrassed to sing. It's the reason why she never joined the choir. He would think that she got it from his mother, but then MacDonald had to remind himself Deanna was adopted. Presumably, there was some rational explanation for it. Deanna did fine, though her voice shook a little. How he raised a daughter who could face down Scratch without blinking but was afraid to sing in public, he didn't know. He barely knew how he raised two children without any help on a Pastor's salary anyway. After she finished, Gilbert gave a eulogy.

"We're going to have a collection for the Varnertown Mission in honor of my father. Please give," Gilbert began. "The Varnertown mission is important to me because that's where I first met my father. My mother was dirt poor. I remember living in that house when I was six. We didn't have working air conditioning and I thought the heat would kill me half the time. The other half, we had nothing to eat. One day, after having Deanna, Mom decided she just couldn't take care of us, so she took us to that mission and left us there. The first person I met was Dad, and the first thing he did was cook me breakfast. It was odd, because he made me this dish called black pudding that we don't have in America, and he had brought it for himself. What possesses a man to give the food off his own plate to a stranger I don't know. Then we went through the adoption process, and I remember no one wanting us, but then Dad said he would take us. What possesses a man to adopt two children that aren't his and put a roof over their heads, I don't know."

"Of course, I learned that what possesses a man to do that is the Christian faith, or at least that is how it was with my father. His God commanded him to care for the weak and the dispossessed, and he took that commandment seriously. Would that we would all take it so seriously. Some of us don't. That's a problem. If people don't believe the Christian faith can transform society for the better, we have no one but ourselves to blame for that."

Impressive, MacDonald thought, particularly given the circumstances. Gilbert would be a good pastor, once someone took the rough edges off. Then Theo rose from his pew and walked to the pulpit. Wow, the Orangeman thought, another surprise.

"I am not much for public speaking, so this will be short," Theo began. "Atticus was my best friend for over 40 years. He and I were inseparable. We had our share of fights. But I had to admit, he was right about a few things. Particularly, something I had to do recently. Given my unique condition, I've been tempted to try to make a go of it alone in life. Life reminds me I can't do that, but I keep trying because I'm afraid people will get hurt. I initially didn't want to share my life with him, or with Deanna and Gilbert, because I didn't want them to get hurt. Atticus shook me out of that scared complacency. All men die, or at least most men do, but few men truly live. He gave me two people who, much like Atticus himself, won't let me try to go it alone, as much as I may want to."

MacDonald tried to applaud Theo, but alas, divine hands cannot clap. They began to move the body. The pallbearers: Theo, Gilbert, and two other Strangers from the congregation rose and approached the coffin. Theo would lift one side while Gilbert and the other two Strangers would carry the other. As the coffin left the building, the mourners followed, gradually leaving the pews where MacDonald had ministered to them for years. Two other pallbearers joined Theo's side as he entered sunlight and his abnormal strength left him.

A burial site had been prepared outside. Bryce had used the backhoe the prior day to dig a hole, and the tombstone, selected by Deanna, had been placed at the head of the grave. A larger stone tomb had been fitted within the hole, where the coffin would soon be placed. Eventually, the procession stopped at the tomb, and the pallbearers laid down the coffin. Gilbert then stood back to do the readings. *We were buried therefore with him by baptism into death so that as Christ was raised from the dead by the glory of the Father, we too might walk in newness of life.*

After MacDonald was laid to rest in that home that lasts until doomsday, the procession headed in the direction of Delilah's best cooking. The Orangeman felt jealous, for though he was saved and destined to eternal bliss, Delilah did make a mean beef wellington. MacDonald flew over to Gilbert and Deanna to say his last good-byes.

"These are my children in whom I am well pleased," the old pastor blessed. "Gilbert, you'll make a fine clergyman. Deanna, you have a beautiful voice. It's a tragedy you haven't joined the choir."

"I've always thought so, too."

MacDonald turned around and saw Beth winking at him.

"Beth, thank you for helping me and my family through this difficult time," MacDonald said. "I think it is time for me to go now. Maybe see me off?"

"Sure."

While the rest of the crowd moved on, MacDonald floated back into the church with Beth in tow. As they entered the main chamber, Beth visibly squinted.

"Beth, what's the problem?" MacDonald asked.

"Ohh, just that," Beth answered, pointing above.

MacDonald looked above to the radiant divine light emanating from the top of the church's main chamber. From their perspective below, the Orangeman could make out a few other spiritual figures floating in its orbit. Presumably, those were the hall monitors ready to take him away.

"Oh, you mean the Source?" MacDonald asked.

"Yes, it's very bright," Beth said, "and the sound!"

"Yes, I suppose the choirs of angels are very loud," MacDonald said, just now noticing them again. "I think they're trying to get people on Earth to hear them."

"This is why I prefer services at the Second Satanic Temple," Beth said. "No spirits, no loud noises, no bright lights. Just Fr. Ravenwood and Alistair."

"Ohh, Beth," MacDonald sighed, "try to speak with you relatives, will you? I must now depart."

MacDonald then began to ascend up one of the beams of light into the Source, waving goodbye to Beth as he left Earth. The Orangeman turned around to find the hall monitors were indeed escorting him upwards and onwards to the New Pandemonium. He'd look up the Drunkard when he got there. They might have a lot to talk about.

The Twelfth Day of Christmas, Tuesday, Davis Plantation House, 7 a.m.
Beth

Hecate and Delilah were pleased to find Beth coming into the plantation house for breakfast that morning, though Hecate remarked that she looked nervous. Delilah cooked omelets, which Beth enjoyed immensely. After breakfast was over, Beth walked into the parlor.

There floating before her was the Bloody Bride, her white dress and long blonde hair drenched in crimson blood, and the Colonel, who bore a remarkable resemblance to Bryce, wearing a uniform shot to pieces, and the old Madam, whom Beth could see, up close, had a complexion that her elders would call "high yellar," and Beth's grandparents, along with a host of other spirits. They were all floating around in various states of injury and age, conversing about the latest goings on in the house, the main subject being Bryce's conversion of the plantation house into a signal disrupter. Beth cleared her throat, gaining their attention, and waved.

"Hi," she greeted.

The spirits all waved back. Beth's grandparents seemed very pleased to see her. The Colonel made a little gun with his fingers and shot at her. The old Madam rolled her eyes at the Colonel. Then the Bloody Bride approached Beth. Beth had the urge to run, but she resisted.

"Hello, Beth," the Bride introduced herself, "I'm your Aunt Hepzibah. I don't suppose we were ever formally introduced."

"It's nice to meet you," Beth reciprocated, her voice wavering.

"No one here wishes you any ill," the Bride assured her. "It's understandable you were afraid of us. You were six."

"Well, thank you."

"We wanted you to know that you aren't the only person who can see dead people."

"There are others? Like who?"

"Well, there are people here," the Bride answered. "Or rather, people who could see the dead when they were alive."

A few of the spirits behind the Bride raised their hands, followed by the Bride herself.

"Are there any people alive who can speak with the dead?" Beth asked.

"Yes, but none in this house since your mother died," the Madam responded. "You might want to go down to the Fieldhand church sometime."

"In the short term," the Colonel interrupted. "How do you plan to deal with those bullies at school?"

"I guess I can't go to the principal, can I?" Beth asked. "Particularly not this one."

"No, but let me tell you something you might not know," the Madam replied. "You can use your telekinetic powers to attack spirits. You can affect more than just physical objects, you know."

"Just focus your mind and push," the Bride told her.

Beth could hear her Aunt Hecate calling that it was time for school. She waved to the spirits again and repeated to herself "focus your mind and push."

Bothwell School, 9 a.m.
Beth

Beth arrived at school expecting a confrontation with Hannah White. Hannah didn't disappoint, waiting with the rest of the 1994 cheerleading squad at the front of the school, ready to welcome Beth back with their best shade of rotting skin.

"Hey, loser," Hannah called, approaching Beth from the front. "Ready for more punishment?"

Beth closed her eyes, concentrated, and then mentally pushed Hannah away. She felt her mind make contact with Hannah's spiritual body. She opened her eyes. Hannah was gone. The rest of the spectral cheering squad stared at Beth in disbelief. Beth had sent Hannah flying with one blow.

"Yeah," Beth managed. "And there's more where that came from!"

The squad, much to Beth's chagrin, took her up on that offer, charging her all at once with their eyes and teeth falling out. Beth closed her eyes again, concentrated, and put all her power behind one big push.

Then she heard glass shattering. Beth opened her eyes to find the cheer squad gone, and that her psychic wave had broken the front doors to the school, sending one of the metal doors flying.

"Wow, did I do that?" Beth asked.

"Apparently."

Beth turned around and found Jarvis floating behind her, looking rather impressed.

"Oh, hi, Jarvis," Beth greeted. "I spoke to my ancestors."

"I can see that," Jarvis said, nodding his translucent head.

358

Beth paused for a moment and then a thought came to her.

"Jarvis, do you spend much time at the Church of the Tobacco Fields?" Beth asked.

"When I'm not here, I practically live there," Jarvis answered. "Well, I don't 'live' there, but yeah, I spend most of my time with the congregation."

"Are there other people like me there who can see ghosts? The Madam said something like that to me."

"Oh, so she told you that? Yeah, there are other seers, and maybe you come down to meet them sometime, but for now, let's check and see what happened to that door you just blew off the hinges."

Beth and Jarvis walked down the hall to find the door, discovering that it had landed right across the back of Principal Jorek's skull. Jorek had been prowling the halls looking for a new victim, only to be caught in the crossfire of Beth's psychic energy. Now, the angry fat man lay on the floor, blood seeping out of his ear. Teachers and students, including Bryce, flooded the hallways finding their principal in an unconscious and injured state.

"Good God!" cried a teacher. "Someone, call an ambulance! This man could be dead!"

The crowd cheered.

"No, really I'm serious!" the teacher insisted. "This man could die!"

"It's a Christmas miracle!" Bryce exclaimed.

The faculty struggled to find a phone and call 911 before Jorek bled out. The school wouldn't be seeing him for a while. Later, the security cameras would show the front doors shattering on their own, leading the school board to file suit against the manufacturer. Beth didn't see Hannah or her squad the rest of the day, or the rest of the week. Bullies tend to be cowards, whether dead or alive.

CHAPTER TWENTY-FIVE

Feast of the Epiphany, Charleston, South Carolina,
Charleston International Airport. 8 a.m.
Theo

When Fr. Eric checked his bags, the woman at the desk gave him a raised eye when he declared 'human remains,' but he had the paperwork. Scratch's bones were headed to Rome, to be stored in a secure vault. Theo initially suggested just throwing the bones into the sea or burying them under 10 feet of concrete, but Fr. Eric protested.

"Scratch would just find some other poor soul like Calvin and direct that person to the bones. Hiding them does nothing. That being said, I'm glad you're finally giving them to me. It took you three resurrections to believe he should be kept somewhere more secure than under your ottoman," Fr. Eric teased.

"I typically trust myself more than I trust the church," Theo explained.

"Oh, you're trusting the church?" Fr. Eric asked, coyly. "Well, I've had the pleasure of seeing the Vatican Bank's books, and if that's who we're trusting, I'd better hand them back to you."

"Who are we trusting?" Theo asked.

"God, of course," Fr. Eric answered.

"Okay," Theo said, reaching for the bag.

"Theo, you're never short on blasphemy. Who are you trusting?"

"You. I know you pretty well, Father. I don't know God outside his works, and I'm not a fan of them."

"I am a work of God, and so are you."

"Well, that's one out of two I trust."

Fr. Eric laughed and slapped Theo's shoulder.

"You should go to mass and keep that priest in town company," Fr. Eric said. "Try to stay in touch with us mere mortals, Theo."

"Oh, I'll go to mass occasionally," Theo promised, half-heartedly. "You know the last priest in town killed himself. I guess that's another thing I have to feel guilty about."

"Theo, the only thing you should ever feel guilty about is what you have done to yourself. Everyone you have ever known is either in heaven or hell or headed there, and they have only themselves to blame for that. Any pain or suffering you may have caused on the way is incidental. Ask yourself, how do you want to spend eternity: with Gilbert and Deanna or with Scratch? Don't do it for Fr. Gabe. Do it for yourself."

Tom's Tavern, Noon
Gabe

Theo called Gabe that day and told him that he had a very deep and sincere spiritual problem, other than selling his soul to the Devil, which he had already done. However, the Irishman made the priest meet him at Tom's Tavern, rather than the church. Gabe arrived dutifully, ready to provide succor to a wounded soul. He saw Theo on the patio, doing shots at noon. It was then that Gabe learned of Theo's true motive.

"Father, get drunk with me," Theo commanded.

"It's lunchtime," Gabe objected.

"I know, I can only get drunk in sunlight. Any other time won't work."

"This is the spiritual malady you asked me to come cure?"

"Yeah, also I feel guilty about your church burning down."

"Insurance is paying for that. The church is supposed to be rebuilt later this year."

"Well, do you have a place to celebrate mass in the meantime?"

"No. I asked the diocese for a transfer, but they want a priest here to look like they are doing something about the whole Satanism thing."

"How about my apartment? I mean, you can celebrate mass anywhere, technically, right?"

"Well, that's very generous."

"So, get drunk with me. This will be a post-mass ritual of ours."

"Not my way of celebrating, but okay."

Theo bought Gabe a shot. They toasted and Gabe swallowed. Then he threw up.

"I've never had tequila before," he confessed.

Town Meeting Hall, 3 p.m.
Ravenwood

Ravenwood had been called to the Town Hall by the trustees for some reason he could not fathom. The Witch trustees held their meetings in a conference room on the third floor. The conference room was a long room with white tile and a long wooden table at one end where the trustees sat in leather reclining chairs with microphones in front of them. At the other end of the room, there were rows of metal and fabric chairs that stretched to the back, currently filled by prominent members of the community, and the new priest, who looked rather impaired alongside Theo. Calvin Lucas appeared as well, now the current pastor of the Stranger Church, flanked by the ministry's attorneys. Aides had cleaned Calvin up, but he still appeared rather shellshocked from his recent experiences. Ravenwood sat down.

"We are here to inform you," began Tiberius Blackthorn, "that you are being fired."

"Fired, what for?" Ravenwood asked. "What standards of performance do you hold the cleric of a religion no one believes in anymore?"

"The standard of tourist revenue," Blackthorn continued, "which has declined steadily during your tenure."

And with that an assistant set up a PowerPoint presentation, which indisputably showed that once Ravenwood's job was defined by bringing in money, i.e., actually achieving the earthly success his "faith" valued, Ravenwood sucked. Line graphs

364

indicated that the amount of money he had taken in as the operator of a tourist trap had decreased every year since his appointment once adjusted for inflation. His previous reports to the trustees did not include this calculation. The same presentation then segued into a segment entitled "Ravenwood's Greatest Flops," a ten-slide tour of his worst services: the time he performed the ritual in his fishing vest to get on the lake as soon as possible after it ended, his attempt to rap the satanic rituals to connect to today's youth, his recent performance as Col. Davis, the time he started taking shots during the ritual (held at 10 a.m. normally), and of course, the fact that he had lost the urn.

"That's your biggest innovation to the liturgy," Blackthorn said, "losing the urn, which we have had for nearly 400 years. The 400th anniversary of Pandemonium happened last year, and we had to use a replica. Jackson may have said that this temple was a museum, but at least he was good at being a curator. For an amateur historian, you suck at preserving history."

"Well, let me ask you," Ravenwood replied. "In a community where everyone wants their child to grow up to be a brain surgeon or a corporate lawyer, who the hell do you expect to take this dead-end job?"

At this moment, Alistair entered stage right. Delilah, who sat in the third row back, yelled "You're damned right." Alistair waved to the crowd and then presented his plan to reform the Satanic ritual.

"Thank you, Fr. Ravenwood for your service," Alistair said. He took control of the PowerPoint.

"In 1969, Satanic High Priest Blaise Jackson met with Anton LaVey, as part of a prearranged meeting of two Satanic traditions, one old, and one young," Alistair began. "LaVey offered to succeed Jackson, who was in failing health. Jackson refused the offer, saying that his church was a museum while LaVey's was a sideshow, and one did not belong in the other. I say, why choose?"

Alistair clicked the control. An image of a heavy metal band appeared on the screen with a fake demon floating above them. The drummer had a goat's head on the bass drum. The crowd made devil horns.

"These people think that worshipping Satan is cool, but they don't show up on Sunday," Alistair said. "Imagine if every person in South Carolina who listens to heavy metal bothered to show up here and bought a five-dollar ticket. How much money would that bring in?"

"For some reason, we don't think of it that way, but I think that's because we still see this as a religion and not a 'performance' but that's what we've become essentially: performers. Everyone here who is a Witch, stand up."

Half the room stood up.

"Of those standing, sit down if you don't actually believe in Satan."

The entire room sat down, including Ravenwood, who cursed himself when he realized he was helping his replacement make a point.

"We need to see the temple less as a temple and more like a playhouse or a movie theater. And we need to see this Satanic cult as entertainment, not faith. In light of that, here is my plan."

Alistair clicked the remote again. The screen now displayed an outline with three major bullet points: "historical reenactment," "entertainment multiplex," and "cultural center." Alistair clicked again, and the screen turned to a wood carving of Cramner's infamous sacrifice on the *Charon*.

"First, the current building will be used to hold a historical reenactment of Cramner's human sacrifice. The event, occurring once daily and twice on Saturday and Sunday, will be just that: a reenactment on a stage. The participants will be actors and the sacrificial victim will only appear to be slaughtered through special effects," Alistair continued. "Guests will be handed a card that informs them that no actual satanic worship will occur, but only a reenactment of a historical event."

Alistair clicked. The screen then showed a rough, architectural drawing of a dark castle covered in frightening figures of demons and monsters labeled "Third Satanic Temple." The drawing included a large sound stage, movie theaters, and a track labeled "dark ride."

"Second, a new building will be constructed to hold rock concerts and other cultural events. This building will also have built-in theaters for horror films, haunted houses, and even a dark ride."

Alistair clicked again, and the screen then flipped to a modern-looking cylindrical building with a first floor surrounded by glass and a top floor covered with marble. The building was labeled "Pandemonium Cultural Center."

"Finally, there are other churches of Satan in America today, and they see Satan as a symbol of creativity and rebellion. To cater to this demographic, we will start a creative arts center. This building will feature the talents of Pandemonium's great artists from painting, to sculptures, to classical and contemporary music. This project is in association with Cramner University."

Alistair clicked a final time, changing to a screen showing increased revenue by 500% within the next five years.

"Are there any questions?" Alistair asked.

"How do you plan to get the money for this?" asked Fr. Ravenwood.

"Good question," Alistair replied. "The current trust fund for the temple far exceeds the cost of building the Third Satanic Temple and the Cultural Center. Furthermore, amateur actors from Cramner and Winthrop Universities will be used to put on the historical reenactments. Next."

"So, no actual Satanic rituals will be performed?" Gabe asked. "Just heavy metal music and actors on a stage?"

"That's the plan," Alistair affirmed.

"The revenue projections are astounding," Blackthorn proclaimed. "Did you do this all by yourself?"

"Not by myself," Alistair explained. "I had help from accountants, architects in town, and my Mom, of course."

Delilah stood up and started applauding her son, and so did the entire crowd except for Ravenwood and the representatives of the New Stranger Church. Blackthorn pounded his gavel to bring order to the proceeding.

"Order, order," he commanded. "Well, I've heard enough. Our history is a gold mine and we've been just sitting on it for no reason. I am ready to take a vote to approve this plan."

"I protest!"

The voice came from the back. James Warrenton, the attorney for the New Stranger Church, stood up with his hand in protest. The room turned to him, somewhat surprised at this opposition.

"I would think the Strangers would be ecstatic," Delilah said. "After 400 years you've won, there are no Witches. Not in any meaningful sense of the term."

"Ms. Davis, I am elated with Alistair's proposal, and I think my father would be, too," Gilbert said.

"How do you think the Green Bay Packers would feel if the Chicago Bears closed up shop?" Warrenton asked. "They would say 'well there goes half our season tickets.' The Church of the McCoys needs the Church of the Hatfields around. My client would not have paid nearly as much for this Church if they knew that this would happen less than two weeks in. The Satanic Temple and the New Stranger Church have a mutual business relationship. If you do this, we will bring suit to vindicate our reasonable business expectations."

The room fell silent for a minute, and then Gilbert walked up to Calvin, passing right by Warrenton without a word.

"Do you really want to be the pastor of the Stranger Church?" Gilbert asked. "After everything that has gone on. Your father is dead. With what you've done, you're fortunate not to be in prison. Wouldn't it be better to walk away?"

"Do not speak to my client directly!" Warrenton shouted. "I represent the New Stranger Church—"

Calvin held up his hand to stop his raging attorney, who ceased his zealous defense of the ministry's interests.

"No," he answered, "I want to get out of this town and leave. Go away somewhere. Have some money so I don't have to work again. Just not be around this business anymore, but I don't want the things I've done here to follow me."

"That might be difficult," Gilbert said. "There will be investigations…"

Annie Ferguson stood up.

"We will buy it back from you," she offered. "All the money we have in the trust. We'll transfer it back to you if you just give us back the church."

"Ah, ah, ah, no you won't," Theo insisted. "That man just said this church isn't worth that much with the Witches changing their church into a show. I say you pay half of what you took it for."

"Half?" Warrenton muttered.

"Theo's got a point, Mr. Warrenton," Gilbert responded. "You just admitted this church isn't worth what it was when you bought it."

"I'll take it," Calvin said, before Warrenton could interrupt. "Just let me get out of this town without any criminal charges or lawsuits."

"We'll call it a settlement," Warrenton offered.

"Guilty as hell, free as a bird," Theo agreed, nodding his head. "What a country."

"That's great," Alistair said. "What's the vote on the Temple, by the way?"

The trustees unanimously voted to accept Alistair's plan, completing a 400-year-old process by which human sacrifice became a meaningless performance. The audience got to their feet and cheered. Warrenton said his legal team would draw up a contract and complete the sale. Ravenwood begrudgingly clapped his hands, having been robbed of his part-time job. The whole scene was then interrupted by the sound of a phone ringing. Ravenwood turned his head to see Theo, looking somewhat annoyed, pull his phone out of his jacket and answer.

"Yes," Theo responded. "Hello, Mr. Burns, I've been expecting this call.

THE END

CHARACTER LIST (Key)

In Order of Appearance

Fr. Gabe Strobel—Young catholic priest assigned to Pandemonium. A little sheltered in life and

disappointed that he's been assigned here with no flock to lead, as Pandemonium has no Catholics to speak of.

Gary Aaronson—Ze'ev teenager who works as a tour guide part-time. Friend of Bryce Davis. Generally responsible, able to keep Bryce in line.

Fr. Thomas Cramner—Satanic High Priest and one of the founders of Pandemonium in 1620. Made the Bargain with John Miller.

John Miller—Captain of the Strangers and the other founder of Pandemonium in 1620. Made the Bargain with Fr. Thomas Cramner.

Acton Ravenwood—Current Satanic High Priest at the Second Satanic Temple. Makes a deal with Miles Simon. A bit of a fool.

Miles Simon—Famed televangelist. Sees the Christian religion as a means to an end, to make money. Buys the Stranger Church as a way to expand his business.

Atticus MacDonald—Pastor of the Stranger Church. Opposes the buyout of the church by Miles Simon. Friend to Theo and adoptive father of Gilbert and Deanna.

Gilbert MacDonald—Adoptive son of Atticus MacDonald and youth pastor of the Stanger Church. Brother of Deanna.

Deanna MacDonald—Adoptive daughter of Atticus MacDonald and sister to Gilbert. Friend of Beth Davis.

Calvin Lucas—Illegitimate son of Miles Simon and employee of Miles Simon Industries. Works hard for his father's approval and receives nothing but abuse in return.

Theophilus—Pandemonium's resident vampire. A friend of Atticus and his adoptive children. Man about town. Lover of good drink and a good time.

Kimberly Smith—Adopted Stranger teenager who discovers she is a Ze'ev and transforms on a date.

Hecate Davis—Witch and member of the Davis family. Sister of Delilah and practical mother of Beth and Bryce Davis.

Delilah Davis—Witch and member of the Davis family. Sister of Hecate and mother of Alistair.

Darrell Overstreet—Pastor of the Church of the Tobacco Fields, the historic black church in town. Pastor MacDonald considers him a colleague.

Rabbi Barry Flom—Junior rabbi at the Temple Ze'ev. MacDonald and Overstreet consider him a colleague.

Beth Davis—Witch and member of the Davis family. Friend of Deanna and twin sister of Bryce. Very polite and meek. Overly concerned with evil spirits.

Bryce Davis—Rabid atheist, young scientist and inventor, and member of the Davis family. Twin brother of Beth and friend of Gary.

Alistair Davis—Son of Delilah and cousin of Beth and Bryce Davis. Assistant to Ravenwood during the Satanic Rituals. Has Down Syndrome, so he lives at home but is functional.

Aaron Parker—Stranger teenager who discovers he is gay.

Rabbi Maharam—Senior Rabbi at the Temple Ze'ev. Very elderly. Needs help getting around.

Steve Jorek—Principal of Bothwell School, a Witch educational institution. Jerk with emotional control issues.

Hannah White—A Dead cheerleader who bullies Beth.

Scratch—Theocratic vampire and rival to Theo. Murders men, women, and children. Genuinely believes that God wants him to do this.

Fr. Eric Burton—Head vampire hunter of the Vatican. Friend of Theo and MacDonald.

BIOGRAPHIES

AUTHOR

John "Jack" Willems is a published author and practicing attorney living in West Virginia with his wife, Rachel, and their two sons, Francis and Tony. Originally from Arkansas, Jack enjoys reading, writing, playing with his kids, and ranting about pop culture oddities on his blog, jaxbooknook.com. He also yells into the digital void on Twitter—find him there at @JackWillems1986.

In addition to Christmas in Pandemonium, Jack's work has appeared in Synthetic Reality Magazine and The Quagmire Magazine. He also released his novella Beer Run through Solstice Publishing. With any luck—and a little time—he'll have more fantastical mischief to unleash on the world soon.

EDITORS

Marie Moldovan is a Saskatchewan native and Ontario immigrant. Some would call them a reverse snowbird, who feels most comfortable surrounded by snowcapped mountains.

Nomadic by nature, Marie is multifaceted and has mastered many skills. They dub themselves a jack of many trades and master of some. However, because Marie has acquired a plethora of diplomas spanning the educational spectrum, Marie's mother on the contrary would call them a professional student.

Marie would accredit their adaptability to the training they received as a Canadian Forces medic, and their artistic ability to their family. Both attributes have aided her along their journey from the points of homelessness and despair to the place of stability and optimism Marie has arrived at today.

In 2018, Marie was diagnosed with service-related PTSD, and within the same breath of time became a widow.

Unresolved trauma, and the loss of their husband caused Marie to skirt the edges of insanity. Faced with losing complete touch with reality, they returned to writing and art.

In a sense writing and art saved Marie's life, at least that's their claim. Fortunately, for the world, Marie's choice to embrace creation has led them to captain a new life as a publisher, illustrator, writer and artist.

Marie is the author of *20 years of Winter, Miss Sally Anne* and has currently opened the doors of her own publication organization, aptly named, I Ain't Your Marionette Press.

20 Years of Winter is an autobiographical collection of poetry and art. She published it in hopes to make a way for others who have suffered similar traumas to feel safe knowing that they are not alone nor are they to blame for their experiences. *20 Years of Winter* is Marie's source of empowerment offered to those victims to stand up to their perpetrators and to speak out against victim shaming.

Joseph Mykut is a multidisciplinary creative from Alabama. They are an author, artist, illustrator, editor, photographer, and literary agent. Their artwork and photography have been exhibited internationally in Ontario, Canada, and featured in the anthologies 3 Amigos Ink, Splatter: Lonely Soul in the Darkness, The Way of the Crow, and Shattered Psyche, all published by I Ain't Your Marionette Press in Canada. They are also the author and illustrator of the children's books Beautiful Boy and There's a Me Under My Bed, both released by the same publisher. Joseph's artistic and photographic work centers on the often-overlooked, seemingly mundane aspects of daily life. Their intention is to draw attention to the subtle magic and quiet beauty found in ordinary moments. As a member of the LGBTQ2+ community and a practitioner of Shamanism, Joseph creates with the goal of forming a bridge between the physical world and the unseen, inviting others to connect with both through creative expression. Born and raised in the deep South of the United States, within the heart of the Bible Belt, Joseph's spiritual path has grown beyond traditional religion. Their perspective is now rooted in a broader sense of universal and personal spirituality. As an ordained minister with the Universal Life Church, they honor the idea that all religious traditions hold truths that are part of a greater whole. Joseph identifies as a two-spirited, and often multi-spirited, being. They resonate with the full spectrum of gender identity and believe in the balance between light and dark, positive and negative. To them, the truth of who we are is found in that sacred balance.

PUBLISHER

I Ain't Your Marionette Press distinguishes itself as a stronghold of artistic liberation. At its helm, Marie Moldovan, once a marionette of circumstance, now orchestrates a symphony of narrative freedom. The company's sanctuary breathes life into marionette authors, whose tales of resilience and aspiration paint a vivid tableau of human spirit.

The press's hallmark anthologies, *Shattered Psyche* and *The Way of The Crow*, are more than mere collections; they are immersive experiences that beckon readers to venture beyond the mundane. Each story or visual masterpiece is a declaration of independence, a narrative that defies the norm and invites a reimagining of the world.

MORE "GOOD READS"

Beer Run by John "Jack" Willems

In the year 2538, Bill Stiltson runs a microbrewery on the Moon, staffed by aliens, insufferable interns, and a business manager he briefly dated. He also happens to be one of the richest men on Earth, thanks to his late father, Professor Williams Stiltson—the brilliant mind behind the invention of the positronic brain. Bill's life is comfortably uneventful until, on the very day a bankruptcy trustee sells him a suspiciously illegal android from a junkyard, his former commander flies a starship straight into the Sun, taking the entire crew with him. Enter Isaac, Bill's newly acquired android brother, whose arrival sparks a chain of events that lands Bill in the crosshairs of a full-blown Luddite conspiracy.

Beer Run 2: The Great Reckoning by John "Jack" Willems

Bill returns from his last adventure only to discover that an irate customer has burned his brewery to the ground. To make matters worse, a cunning con man has turned his taproom into the epicenter of an online conspiracy swirling with claims of cannibalism, protectionism, and misplaced nostalgia. With the help of an eccentric insectoid plaintiff's attorney, Bill enlists his intern, Jimmy, to expose the con. But Jimmy dives so deep into the chaos that he begins believing he's the leader of a political movement determined to terrorize modern society. Can Bill pull Jimmy back from his delusions before he lands himself in prison?

A Banquet of Panacea by **Rick Powell**

The loss of a child is a wound that never heals. But what if there was a way to move forward, a method so unthinkable it's only whispered about in the shadows? The Richards are living every parent's worst nightmare, their child's life stolen by a remorseless killer. In their darkest hour, they encounter Zhang, a billionaire with a chilling solution: when the justice system fails, he invites the families to a dinner shrouded in mystery and darkness.

Winston by **Rick Powell**

Julie lives with her mother in a rundown part of town, struggling to adjust to her mom's new boyfriend, a man she distrusts for many reasons. During a fateful walk home, she encounters Winston, an enigmatic old man whose presence is as captivating as it is mysterious. As their bond deepens, Julie's life begins to change in unimaginable ways. Who is Winston, and what secrets does he hold that could lift Julie out of her adversity? Is he a savior, or a messenger of doom?

Two Lost Souls by **Rick Powell**

Love, like life, is one of the oldest mysteries. But what happens when love turns into an obsession? When the boundaries between passion and madness blur, and the veil between the supernatural and natural world is cast aside? David believed his bond with his wife Helen was unbreakable, forged in the fires of life's trials. Yet even the strongest love can be tested by the shadows that lurk in the corners of our hearts—and the darkness of a graveyard.

Thank you for your support.